STAR WARS®
THE
OLD REPUBLIC™
FATAL ALLIANCE

D0089178

BY SEAN WILLIAMS

The Unknown Soldier
(with Shane Dix)
Metal Fatigue
The Resurrected Man

EVERGENCE
(with Shane Dix)
The Prodigal Sun
The Dying Light
The Dark Imbalance

THE BOOKS OF THE CHANGE
The Stone Mage & the Sea
The Sky Warden & the Sun
The Storm Weaver & the Sand

ORPHANS (with Shane Dix)
Echoes of Earth
Orphans of Earth
Heirs of Earth

THE BOOKS OF THE CATACLYSM
The Crooked Letter
The Blood Debt
The Hanging Mountains
The Devoured Earth

GEODESICA (with Shane Dix)
Ascent
Descent

THE BROKEN LAND
The Changeling
The Dust Devils
The Scarecrow

ASTROPOLIS
Saturn Returns
Earth Ascendant
Remaining in Light

COLLECTIONS
Doorways to Eternity
A View Before Dying
New Adventures in Sci-Fi
Light Bodies Falling
Magic Dirt: The Best of Sean Williams

Star Wars: Force Heretic I: Remnant (with Shane Dix)
Star Wars: Force Heretic II: Refugee (with Shane Dix)
Star Wars: Force Heretic III: Reunion (with Shane Dix)
Star Wars: The Force Unleashed
Star Wars: The Force Unleashed II

THE FIXERS
Castle of Zombies
Planet of Cyborgs
Curse of the Vampire
Invasion of the Freaks

FATAL ALLIANCE

SEAN WILLIAMS

DEL REY • NEW YORK

Star Wars: The Old Repubic: Fatal Alliance is a work of fiction. Names, places, and incidents either are products of the author's imagination or are used fictitiously.

2014 Del Rey Mass Market Edition

Published in the United States by Del Rey, an imprint Random House, a division of Penguin Random House LLC, New York.

Del Rey and the House colophon are registered trademarks of Penguin Random House LLC.

Originally published in hardcover in the United States by Del Rey, an imprint of Random House, a division of Penguin Random House LLC, in 2010.

This book contains an excerpt from *Star Wars: Fate of the Jedi: Vortex* by Troy Denning. This excerpt has been set for this edition only and may not reflect the final content of the forthcoming editon.

ISBN 978-0-345-51133-1
eBook ISBN 978-0-307-79604-2

Printed in the United States of America

www.starwars.com
www.fateofthejedi.com
www.delreybooks.com

10 9 8 7 6

Del Rey mass market edition: June 2011

For Kevin and Rebecca:
friends, teachers, fellow
explorers.

With thanks to Shelly, Frank,
Daniel, Orion, and both Robs
for showing me the way.

The STAR WARS Legends Novels Timeline

BEFORE THE REPUBLIC
37,000–25,000 YEARS BEFORE *STAR WARS: A New Hope*

c. 25,793 *YEARS BEFORE STAR WARS: A New Hope*

Dawn of the Jedi: Into the Void

OLD REPUBLIC
5000–67 YEARS BEFORE *STAR WARS: A New Hope*

Lost Tribe of the Sith: The Collected Stories

3954 *YEARS BEFORE STAR WARS: A New Hope*

The Old Republic: Revan

3650 *YEARS BEFORE STAR WARS: A New Hope*

The Old Republic: Deceived
Red Harvest
The Old Republic: Fatal Alliance
The Old Republic: Annihilation

1032 *YEARS BEFORE STAR WARS: A New Hope*

Knight Errant
Darth Bane: Path of Destruction
Darth Bane: Rule of Two
Darth Bane: Dynasty of Evil

RISE OF THE EMPIRE
67–0 YEARS BEFORE *STAR WARS: A New Hope*

67 *YEARS BEFORE STAR WARS: A New Hope*

Darth Plagueis

33 *YEARS BEFORE STAR WARS: A New Hope*

Cloak of Deception
Darth Maul: Shadow Hunter
Maul: Lockdown

32 *YEARS BEFORE STAR WARS: A New Hope*

***STAR WARS:* EPISODE I**
THE PHANTOM MENACE

Rogue Planet
Outbound Flight
The Approaching Storm

22 *YEARS BEFORE STAR WARS: A New Hope*

***STAR WARS:* EPISODE II**
ATTACK OF THE CLONES

22–19 *YEARS BEFORE STAR WARS: A New Hope*

***STAR WARS:* THE CLONE WARS**

The Clone Wars: Wild Space
The Clone Wars: No Prisoners

Clone Wars Gambit
- Stealth
- Siege

Republic Commando
- Hard Contact
- Triple Zero
- True Colors
- Order 66

Shatterpoint
The Cestus Deception
MedStar I: Battle Surgeons
MedStar II: Jedi Healer
Jedi Trial
Yoda: Dark Rendezvous
Labyrinth of Evil

19 *YEARS BEFORE STAR WARS: A New Hope*

***STAR WARS:* EPISODE III**
REVENGE OF THE SITH

Kenobi
Dark Lord: The Rise of Darth Vader
Imperial Commando 501st

Coruscant Nights
- Jedi Twilight
- Street of Shadows
- Patterns of Force

The Last Jedi

10 *YEARS BEFORE STAR WARS: A New Hope*

The Han Solo Trilogy
- The Paradise Snare
- The Hutt Gambit
- Rebel Dawn

The Adventures of Lando Calrissian
The Force Unleashed
The Han Solo Adventures
Death Troopers
The Force Unleashed II

REBELLION
0–5 YEARS AFTER
STAR WARS: A New Hope

Death Star
Shadow Games

0

STAR WARS: EPISODE IV
A NEW HOPE

Tales from the Mos Eisley Cantina
Tales from the Empire
Tales from the New Republic
Scoundrels
Allegiance
Choices of One
Honor Among Thieves
Galaxies: The Ruins of Dantooine
Splinter of the Mind's Eye
Razor's Edge

3 *YEARS AFTER STAR WARS: A New Hope*

STAR WARS: EPISODE V
THE EMPIRE STRIKES BACK

Tales of the Bounty Hunters
Shadows of the Empire

4 *YEARS AFTER STAR WARS: A New Hope*

STAR WARS: EPISODE VI
THE RETURN OF THE JEDI

Tales from Jabba's Palace

The Bounty Hunter Wars
The Mandalorian Armor
Slave Ship
Hard Merchandise

The Truce at Bakura
Luke Skywalker and the Shadows of Mindor

NEW REPUBLIC
5–25 YEARS AFTER
STAR WARS: A New Hope

X-Wing
Rogue Squadron
Wedge's Gamble
The Krytos Trap
The Bacta War
Wraith Squadron
Iron Fist
Solo Command

The Courtship of Princess Leia
Tatooine Ghost

The Thrawn Trilogy
Heir to the Empire
Dark Force Rising
The Last Command

X-Wing: Isard's Revenge

The Jedi Academy Trilogy
Jedi Search
Dark Apprentice
Champions of the Force

I, Jedi
Children of the Jedi
Darksaber
Planet of Twilight
X-Wing: Starfighters of Adumar
The Crystal Star

The Black Fleet Crisis Trilogy
Before the Storm
Shield of Lies
Tyrant's Test

The New Rebellion

The Corellian Trilogy
Ambush at Corellia
Assault at Selonia
Showdown at Centerpoint

The Hand of Thrawn Duology
Specter of the Past
Vision of the Future

Scourge
Survivor's Quest

The STAR WARS Legends Novels Timeline

NEW JEDI ORDER
25–40 YEARS AFTER
STAR WARS: A New Hope

The New Jedi Order
- Vector Prime
- Dark Tide I: Onslaught
- Dark Tide II: Ruin
- Agents of Chaos I: Hero's Trial
- Agents of Chaos II: Jedi Eclipse
- Balance Point
- Edge of Victory I: Conquest
- Edge of Victory II: Rebirth
- Star by Star
- Dark Journey
- Enemy Lines I: Rebel Dream
- Enemy Lines II: Rebel Stand
- Traitor
- Destiny's Way
- Force Heretic I: Remnant
- Force Heretic II: Refugee
- Force Heretic III: Reunion
- The Final Prophecy
- The Unifying Force

35 *YEARS AFTER STAR WARS: A New Hope*

The Dark Nest Trilogy
- The Joiner King
- The Unseen Queen
- The Swarm War

LEGACY
40+ YEARS AFTER
STAR WARS: A New Hope

Legacy of the Force
- Betrayal
- Bloodlines
- Tempest
- Exile
- Sacrifice
- Inferno
- Fury
- Revelation
- Invincible

Crosscurrent
Riptide
Millennium Falcon

43 *YEARS AFTER STAR WARS: A New Hope*

Fate of the Jedi
- Outcast
- Omen
- Abyss
- Backlash
- Allies
- Vortex
- Conviction
- Ascension
- Apocalypse

X-Wing: Mercy Kill

45 *YEARS AFTER STAR WARS: A New Hope*

Crucible

DRAMATIS PERSONAE

Dao Stryver; bounty hunter (Mandalorian male)
Darth Chratis; Sith Lord (human male)
Eldon Ax; Sith apprentice (human female)
Jet Nebula; captain, *Auriga Fire* (human male)
Larin Moxla; former Republic trooper (Kiffar female)
Satele Shan; Jedi Grand Master (human female)
Shigar Konshi; Jedi Padawan (Kiffar male)
Ula Vii; Imperial agent (Epicanthix male)

A long time ago in a galaxy far, far away. . . .

PROLOGUE: WILD SPACE

THE LIGHT STAR cruiser looked deceptively insignificant against the backdrop of the galaxy. To the keen eye of a pirate, however, it displayed several desirable qualities: no Imperial or Republic markings; only moderate weaponry and shielding; a crew compartment barely large enough to hold a dozen people; no escort or accompanying vessels.

"It's your choice, Captain," hissed a guttural voice into Jet Nebula's ear. "But don't take too long about it. Our friend here isn't going to sit still forever."

The smuggler calling himself "Jet Nebula" enjoyed keeping his first mate on tenterhooks. He harbored no ill feelings about the mutiny in and of itself. The moment the *Auriga Fire* stumbled across something really valuable, a takeover attempt had been inevitable. He had hired Shinqo knowing exactly that and lost barely a minute's sleep since. Dealing with scum was part of the job.

He didn't like needless violence, though. The snub nose of a blaster digging into Jet's side was pure overkill.

"Well?" Shinqo prompted him in Rodese as he pretended to dither.

"Keep your shirt on," Jet said in mock-protest. "We only interdicted them a minute ago. It's way too soon to plot another jump."

"Just don't take any chances," Shinqo said, emphasizing

his point with another jab of the blaster. "And be glad we don't want your ship, as well."

Something heavy creaked to Jet's right. The boxy shape of Clunker swayed into view, dented and dusty, photoreceptors glowing bright. Jet shook his head minutely, and the droid backed out of sight again.

"Don't make me ask twice," Shinqo said.

"All right, then." Jet took the captain's seat and punched the comm active. "Since you put it so nicely, let's see who these guys are before we steal the hide off their backs."

The star cruiser's running lights blinked and flickered against the black. Its systems were still settling after their sudden wrench from hyperspace, but Jet felt sure the comm was working by now. All ears aboard would be straining to hear what the rugged ship hanging off their bows had to say.

He resorted to short, simple phrases that had served him well enough in the past: "You're nicked, my beauty. Stand by for boarding."

"Negative" came the immediate reply. Male, brusque, and human, most likely. "We do not recognize your authority."

That was a new one. "Who in their right mind would invest any authority in the likes of us?"

"You're a privateer. You work for the Republic."

"Now, that simply isn't true." *Not anymore, anyway,* Jet thought. "We're humble grifters of an independent set, and you happen to have stumbled across our patch. Submit easily, and I'll see that my bloodthirsty first mate doesn't blast you all on sight."

"That won't happen. We're on a diplomatic mission."

"To whom? From where? If I had a credit for every time someone tried that line, you wouldn't be talking to me now."

There was a long pause. "All right, then. What will it cost for you to let us go?"

Jet looked at Shinqo, who was calling the shots. Shinqo's true employers were the Hutts, and sometimes a bribe was worth as much as booty, after the cartels took their cut.

The Rodian shook his head.

"You're clear out of luck, mate," Jet told the person on the other end of the comm. "Best vent those air locks, smartish. We're coming in and don't want to scuff the merchandise any more than we have to."

The star cruiser had nothing to say to that.

Shinqo barked into a communicator as Jet brought the sublights into play. "Fekk, Gelss, get ready for action."

The two Sullustans were part of Shinqo's treacherous lot, and Jet wouldn't mind if they paid the price for the mutineers' haste. Jet had a strong feeling the cruiser wasn't going to give up lightly. Its lines were too lean, its hull too polished. The name on its starboard side—the only ID it was sporting—said CINZIA in bold black letters, recently affixed. That showed pride.

No, the owners of this ship might not be above offering a bribe to continue on their way, but they wouldn't roll over easily. Few did, these days. With the Empire and the Republic still at each other's throats, lacking but a declaration to call their squabbling an honest war, people were taking the law into their own hands. There was so much to lose and so little to gain on every front.

So much for the Treaty of Coruscant. And so much for avoiding unnecessary bloodshed, he thought, reminded of Fekk and Gelss. Be it red or green, blood was all the same. The less spilled around him, the smaller the chance it would be his, one day.

"What are we going to tell our former bosses when we haul in empty?"

"That's not my problem," gloated Shinqo. "On flimsi, you're still captain of the *Auriga Fire*. It's your job to come up with an excuse the Republic will believe. I'll be long gone before then, with the credits."

True to form, then, the Rodian was planning to stiff Jet at both ends of the deal. That changed everything. Jet glanced at Clunker, who was standing innocently in front of the entrance to the cockpit. No one would get in past him, if push came to shove. More important, no one would get out . . .

Barely had the *Auriga Fire* closed half the distance between the two ships when Jet's misgivings about the cruiser were violently justified. A scattering of red lights danced across the instrument panels; a buzzer harshly sounded. Jet studied the display for a split second, making absolutely certain of what he was seeing, before raising every shield to full and punching the sublights to maximum.

The *Auriga Fire* rolled edge-on to the cruiser and Shinqo staggered backward. Clunker caught him, deftly twisting the blaster out of the Rodian's grasp as he did so. At that moment the star cruiser that should have been their prize exploded, sending a blast of pure white light through every viewport, screen, and shield.

Jet had done more than just back the ship away. He had covered his eyes, and now he peered warily through his fingers at instruments gone completely haywire. There was barely anything left where the *Cinzia* had been. Thuds and clangs registered on the hull as bits of the star cruiser rocketed by.

Shinqo was barking into his communicator again, quick on the uptake, but not quick enough by half. "Who fired? Who ordered you to fire?"

"No one did," Jet said. "The ship blew *itself* up—and if I hadn't caught the neutrino spike from the drives before they went, we'd have been toasted, too."

Shinqo rounded on him as though he'd planned this all along. "I should shoot you right here."

"With what, mate?" Jet nodded at Clunker, who

pointed the Rodian's own blaster into his chest. Jet enjoyed the confusion nakedly displayed on his mate's green, leathery face. "Let's start this again, shall we? We work for the Hutts now. I get that. One master's as good as any other, provided the cut's the same. But we all get equal shares in that cut, right? Or I tell the crew, who will be spoiling for the fight they just missed. They won't be happy that you were about to rob some of them. And I tell Clunker here, who badly needs another oil bath, to tighten his grip on that trigger and send you after the crew of that ship, whatever dim part of creation they inhabit now. Get it?"

Acceptance replaced anxiety on Shinqo's face. His hands came up.

"Here, now, Captain, there's been some kind of misunderstanding."

"Perhaps you'd like to clarify, then."

"Sure, sure. You'll get your share. We all will. I never intended it otherwise."

"And the Republic?"

"We'll sort them out—together, like. It wouldn't be fair to leave it all up to you."

"I'm relieved to hear that, lad." Jet nodded at Clunker, who flipped the blaster over and handed it back to its owner. "While I'm captain of this ship, as written on flimsiplast, Barabel hide, or whatever, I expect a certain degree of civility and common purpose. So long as I have that, we're all going to get along fine."

He swiveled around to face the instruments, confident that Clunker would stop anything untoward happening behind him. And confident also that the Rodian was smart enough to recognize a compromise when he saw one. Jet didn't mind who paid him, just like the Hutts didn't care who handed them their treasure, so long as it was theirs. It all came out in the wash, for those left standing.

"Let's see what remains of our sorry friend out there . . ."

The debris field was expanding fast. Sensors tracked the largest chunks, many of which were human-sized or even bigger. That surprised him. A drive blowout usually left only slag and dust.

"That looks like part of the forward section," said Shinqo, leaning over Jet to point at a screen.

"No life signs."

"No witnesses," said the Rodian with satisfaction.

"That's normally our job," said Jet, although he had never killed a single person he'd robbed in all his years of pirating—not *after* he'd robbed them, anyway. Broken a few hearts, sure, and busted a few heads, but nothing worse. "Don't think they were doing it for us."

"Why did they do it, then?"

Jet shrugged. "That's the billion-credit question."

Shinqo rubbed his chin, making a dry rasping sound with his fingertips. Now that the situation between them was resolved, he had returned to being a proper mate. He had the makings of a good one, when greed didn't get in the way, otherwise Jet would never have taken him on in the first place. "They had something aboard, something they didn't want us to get ahold of."

"Something worth more than their own lives?" Jet turned to meet Shinqo's slitted eyes. "That sounds pretty valuable to me."

"Even in pieces, maybe."

"Exactly what I was thinking." Jet indicated the copilot's seat. "Strap yourself in and take control of the tractor beam. Let's see what we can find."

The *Auriga Fire* came about and began scouring the remains of the ship whose journey they had intercepted. A niggling feeling troubled Jet Nebula as he did so. It felt like guilt, and he told himself not to give in to it. *He* hadn't killed the crew of the *Cinzia*. They had pulled that trigger all by themselves. It was just hard luck that their path had crossed his, and his good fortune to be breathing afterward. If his fortune continued to hold, he might yet make a profit from this deep-space run, and then, finally, he could hire a slightly more reputable brand of scum and get back into smuggling again.

Some days were better than others. Maybe this was one of them. He told himself that with all the conviction he could muster, which was plenty for a man in his trade.

What could possibly go wrong?

PART ONE

VESTED INTERESTS

CHAPTER 1

SHIGAR KONSHI FOLLOWED the sound of blasterfire through Coruscant's old districts. He never stumbled, never slipped, never lost his way, even through lanes that were narrow and crowded with years of detritus that had settled slowly from the levels above. Cables and signs swayed overhead, hanging so low in places that Shigar was forced to duck beneath them. Tall and slender, with one blue chevron on each cheek, the Jedi apprentice moved with grace and surety surprising for his eighteen years.

At the core of his being, however, he seethed. Master Nikil Nobil's decision had cut no less deeply for being delivered by hologram from the other side of the galaxy.

"The High Council finds Shigar Konshi unready for Jedi trials."

The decision had shocked him, but Shigar knew better than to speak. The last thing he wanted to do was convey the shame and resentment he felt in front of the Council.

"Tell him why," said Grand Master Satele Shan, standing at his side with hands folded firmly before her. She was a full head shorter than Shigar but radiated an indomitable sense of self. Even via holoprojector, she made Master Nobil, an immense Thisspiasian with full ceremonial beard, shift uncomfortably on his tail.

"We—that is, the Council—regard your Padawan's training as incomplete."

Shigar flushed. "In what way, Master Nobil?"

His Master silenced him with a gentle but irresistible telepathic nudge. "He is close to attaining full mastery," she assured the Council. "I am certain that it is only a matter of time."

"A Jedi Knight is a Jedi Knight in all respects," said the distant Master. "There are no exceptions, even for you."

Master Satele nodded her acceptance of the decision. Shigar bit his tongue. She said she believed in him, so why did she not overrule the decision? She didn't have to submit to the Council. If he weren't her Padawan, would she have spoken up for him then?

His unsettled feelings were not hidden as well as he would have liked.

"Your lack of self-control reveals itself in many ways," said Master Nobil to him in a stern tone. "Take your recent comments to Senator Vuub regarding the policies of the Resource Management Council. We may all agree that the Republic's handling of the current crisis is less than perfect, but anything short of the utmost political discipline is unforgivable at this time. Do you understand?"

Shigar bowed his head. He should've known that the slippery Neimoidian was after more than just his opinion when she'd sidled up to him and flattered him with praise. When the Empire had invaded Coruscant, it had only handed the world back to the Republic in exchange for a large number of territorial concessions elsewhere. Ever since then, supply lines had been strained. That Shigar was right, and the RMC a hopelessly corrupt mess, putting the lives of billions at risk from something much worse than war—starvation, disease, disillusionment—simply didn't count in some circles.

Master Nobil's forbidding visage softened. "You are naturally disappointed. I understand. Know that the

Grand Master has spoken strongly in favor of you for a long time. In all respects but this one do we defer to her judgment. She cannot sway our combined decision, but she has drawn our attention. We will be watching your progress closely, with high expectations."

The holoconference had ended there, and Shigar felt the same conflicted emptiness in the depths of Coruscant as he had then. *Unready? High expectations?* The Council was playing a game with him—or so it felt—batting him backward and forward like a felinx in a cage. Would he ever be free to follow his own path?

Master Satele understood his feelings better than he did. "Go for a walk," she had told him, putting a hand on each shoulder and holding his gaze long enough to make sure he understood her intentions. She was giving him an opportunity to cool down, not dismissing him. "I need to talk to Supreme Commander Stantorrs anyway. Let's meet later in Union Cloisters."

"Yes, Master."

And so he was walking and stewing. Somewhere inside him, he knew, had to be the strength to rise above this temporary setback, the discipline to bring the last threads of his talent into a unified design. But on this occasion, his instincts were leading him away from stillness, not toward it.

The sound of blasterfire grew louder ahead of him.

Shigar stopped in an alley that stank like a woodoo's leavings. A swinging light flashed fitfully on and off in the level above, casting rubbish and rot in unwanted relief. An ancient droid watched with blinking red eyes from a filthy niche, rusted fingers protectively gathering wires and servos back into its gaping chest plate. The cold war with the Empire was being conducted far away from this alley and its unhappy resident, but its effects were keenly felt. If he wanted to be angry at the state of the Republic, he couldn't have chosen a better place for it.

The shooting intensified. His hand reached for the grip of his lightsaber.

There is no emotion, he told himself. *There is only peace.*

But how could there be peace without justice? What did the Jedi Council, sitting comfortably in their new Temple on Tython, know about *that*?

The sound of screams broke him out of his contemplative trance. Between one heartbeat and the next he was gone, the emerald fire of his lightsaber lingering a split instant behind him, brilliant in the gloom.

LARIN MOXLA PAUSED to tighten the belly strap on her armor. The wretched thing kept coming loose, and she didn't want to take any chances. Until the justicars got there, she was the only thing standing between the Black Sun gangsters and the relatively innocent residents of Gnawer's Roost. It sounded like half of it had been shot to pieces already.

Satisfied that nothing too vulnerable was exposed, she peered out from cover and hefted her modified snub rifle. Illegal on Coruscant except for elite Special Forces commandos, it featured a powerful sniper sight, which she trained on the Black Sun safehouse. The main entrance was deserted, and there was no sign of the roof guard. That was unexpected. Still the blasterfire came from within the fortified building. Could it be a trap of some kind?

Wishing as always that she had backup, she lowered the rifle and lifted her helmeted head into full view. No one took a potshot at her. No one even noticed her. The only people she could see were locals running for cover. But for the commotion coming from within, the street could have been completely deserted.

Trap or no trap, she decided to get closer. Rattling slightly, and ignoring the places where her secondhand armor chafed, Larin hustled low and fast from cover to cover until she was just meters from the front entrance. The weapons-fire was deafening now, and screaming came with it. She tried to identify the weapons. Blaster pistols and rifles of several different makes; at least one floor-mounted cannon; two or three vibrosaws; and beneath all that, a different sound. A roaring, as of superheated gases jetting violently through a nozzle.

A flamethrower.

No gang she'd heard of used fire. The risk of a blaze spreading everywhere was too high. Only someone from outside would employ a weapon like that. Only someone who didn't care what damage he left in his wake.

Something exploded in an upper room, sending a shower of bricks and dust into the street. Larin ducked instinctively, but the wall held. If it had collapsed, she would have been buried under meters of rubble.

Her left hand wanted to count down, and she let it. It felt wrong otherwise. Moving in—in *three . . . two . . . one . . .*

Silence fell.

She froze. It was as though someone had pulled a switch. One minute, nine kinds of chaos had been unfolding inside the building. Now there was nothing.

She pulled her hand in, countdown forgotten. She wasn't going *anywhere* until she knew what had just happened and who was involved.

Something collapsed inside the building. Larin gripped her rifle more tightly. Footsteps crunched toward the entrance. One set of feet: that was all.

She stood up in full view of the entrance, placed herself side-on to reduce the target she made, and trained her rifle on the darkened doorway.

The footsteps came closer—unhurried, confident, heavy. Very heavy.

The moment she saw movement in the doorway, she cried out in a firm voice, "Hold it right there."

Booted feet assumed a standing position. Armored shins in metallic gray and green.

"Move slowly forward, into the light."

The owner of the legs took one step, then two, revealing a Mandalorian so tall his helmeted head brushed the top of the doorway.

"That's far enough."

"For what?"

Larin maintained her cool in the face of that harsh, inhuman voice, although it was difficult. She'd seen Mandalorians in action before, and she knew how woefully equipped she was to deal with one now. "For you to tell me what you were doing in there."

The domed head inclined slightly. "I was seeking information."

"So you're a bounty hunter?"

"Does it matter what I am?"

"It does when you're messing up my people."

"You do not look like a member of the Black Sun syndicate."

"I never said I was."

"You haven't said you aren't, either." The massive figure shifted slightly, finding a new balance. "I'm seeking information concerning a woman called Lema Xandret."

"Never heard of her."

"Are you certain of that?"

"I thought I was the one asking questions here."

"You thought wrong."

The Mandalorian raised one arm to point at her. A hatch in his sleeve opened, revealing the flamethrower she'd heard in action earlier. She steadied her grip and tried desperately to remember where the weak points on Mandalorian armor were—if there were any . . .

"Don't," said a commanding voice to her left.

Larin glanced automatically and saw a young man in

robes standing with one hand raised in the universal *stop* signal.

The sight of him dropped her guard momentarily.

A sheet of powerful flame roared at her. She ducked, and it seared the air bare millimeters over her head.

She let off a round that ricocheted harmlessly from the Mandalorian's chest plate and rolled for cover. It was hard to say what surprised her more: a Jedi down deep in the bowels of Coruscant, or the fact that he had the facial tattoos of a Kiffu native, just like she did.

SHIGAR TOOK IN the confrontation with a glance. He'd never fought a Mandalorian before, but he had been carefully instructed in the art by his Master. They were dangerous, very dangerous, and he almost had second thoughts about taking this one on. Even together, he and a single battered-looking soldier would hardly be sufficient.

Then flame arced across the head of the soldier, and his instincts took over. The soldier ducked for cover with admirable speed. Shigar lunged forward, lightsaber raised to slash at the net that inevitably headed his way. The whine of the suit's jetpack drowned out the angry sizzling of Shigar's blade as he cut himself free. Before the Mandalorian had gained barely a meter of altitude, Shigar Force-pushed him sideways into the building beside him, thereby crushing off the jet's exhaust vent.

With a snarl, the Mandalorian landed heavily on both feet and fired two darts in quick succession, both aimed at Shigar's face. Shigar deflected them and moved closer, dancing lightly on his feet. From a distance, he was at a disadvantage. Mandalorians were masters of ranged weaponry, and would do anything to avoid hand-to-hand combat except in one of their infamous gladiatorial pits. If he could get near enough to strike—with the soldier maintaining a distracting cover fire—he might just get lucky . . .

A rocket exploded above his head, then another. They weren't aimed at him, but at the city's upper levels. Rubble rained down on him, forcing him to protect his head. The Mandalorian took advantage of that slight distraction to dive under his guard and grip him tight about the throat. Shigar's confusion was complete—but Mandalorians weren't *supposed* to fight at close quarters! Then he was literally flying through the air, hurled by his assailant's vast physical strength into a wall.

He landed on both feet, stunned but recovering quickly, and readied himself for another attack.

The Mandalorian ran three long steps to his right, leaping one-two-three onto piles of rubbish and from there onto a roof. More rockets arced upward, tearing through the ferrocrete columns of a monorail. Slender spears of metal warped and fell toward Shigar and the soldier. Only with the greatest exertion of the Force that Shigar could summon was he able to deflect them into the ground around them, where they stuck fast, quivering.

"He's getting away!"

The soldier's cry was followed by another explosion. A grenade hurled behind the escaping Mandalorian destroyed much of the roof in front of him and sent a huge black mushroom rising into the air. Shigar dived cautiously through it, expecting an ambush, but found the area clear on the far side. He turned in a full circle, banishing the smoke with one outthrust push.

The Mandalorian was gone. Up, down, sideways—there was no way to tell which direction he had chosen to flee. Shigar reached out through the Force. His heart still hammered, but his breathing was steady and shallow. He felt nothing.

The soldier became visible through the smoke just steps away, moving forward in a cautious crouch. She straightened and planted her feet wide apart. The snout of her rifle targeted him, and for a moment Shigar thought she might actually fire.

"I lost him," he said, unhappily acknowledging their failure.

"Not your fault," she said, lowering the rifle. "We did our best."

"Where did he come from?" he asked.

"I thought it was just the usual Black Sun bust-up," she said, indicating the destroyed building. "Then he walked out."

"Why did he attack you?"

"Beats me. Maybe he assumed I was a justicar."

"You're not one?"

"No. I don't like their methods. And they'll be here soon, so you should get out of here before they decide you're responsible for all this."

That was good advice, he acknowledged to himself. The bloodthirsty militia controlling the lower levels was a law unto itself, one that didn't take kindly to incursions on their territory.

"Let's see what happened here, first," he said, moving toward the smoke-blackened doorway with lightsaber at the ready.

"Why? It's not your problem."

Shigar didn't answer that. Whatever was going on here, neither of them could just walk away from it. He sensed that she would be relieved not to be heading into the building alone.

Together they explored the smoking, shattered ruins. Weapons and bodies lay next to one another in equal proportions. Clearly, the inhabitants had taken up arms against the interloper, and in turn every one of them had died. That was grisly, but not surprising. Mandalorians didn't disapprove of illegals per se, but they did take poorly to being shot at.

On the upper floor, Shigar stopped, sensing something living among the carnage. He raised a hand, cautioning the soldier to proceed more slowly, just in case someone thought they were coming to finish the job. She glided smoothly ahead of him, heedless of danger and with her weapon at the ready. He followed soundlessly in her wake, senses tingling.

They found a single survivor huddled behind a shattered crate, a Nautolan with blaster burns down much of one side and a dart wound to his neck, lying in a pool of his own blood. The blood was spreading fast. He looked up as Shigar bent over him to check his wounds. What Shigar couldn't tourniquet he could cauterize, but he would have to move fast to have any chance at all.

"Dao Stryver." The Nautolan's voice was a guttural growl, not helped by the damage to his throat. "Came out of nowhere."

"The Mandalorian?" said the soldier. "Is that who you're talking about?"

The Nautolan nodded. "Dao Stryver. Wanted what we had. Wouldn't give it to him."

The soldier took off her helmet. She was surprisingly young, with short dark hair, a strong jaw, and eyes as green as Shigar's lightsaber. Most startling were the distinctive black markings of Clan Moxla tattooed across her dirty cheeks.

"What did you have, exactly?" she pressed the Nautolan.

The Nautolan's eyes rolled up into his head. "*Cinzia,*" he coughed, spraying dark blood across the front of her armor. "*Cinzia.*"

"And that is . . . ?" she asked, leaning close as his breathing failed. "Hold on—help's coming—just hold on!"

Shigar leaned back. There was nothing he could do, not

without a proper medpac. The Nautolan had said his last.

"I'm sorry," he said.

"You've no reason to be," she said, staring down at her hands. "He was a member of the Black Sun, probably a murderer himself."

"Does that make him evil? Lack of food might have done that, or medicine for his family, or a thousand other things."

"Bad choices don't make bad people. Right. But what else do we have to go on down here? Sometimes you have to make a stand, even if you can't tell who the bad guys are anymore."

A desperately fatigued look crossed her face then, and Shigar thought that he understood her a little better. Justice was important, and so was the way people defended it, even if that meant fighting alone sometimes.

"My name is Shigar," he said in a calming voice.

"Nice to meet you, Shigar," she said, brightening. "And thanks. You probably saved my life back there."

"I can't take any credit for that. I'm sure he didn't consider either of us worthy opponents."

"Or maybe he worked out that we didn't know anything about what he was looking for in the safehouse. Lema Xandret: that was the name he used on me. Ever heard of it?"

"No. Not *Cinzia*, either."

She rose to her feet in one movement and cocked her rifle onto her back. "Larin, by the way."

Her grip was surprisingly strong. "Our clans were enemies, once," Shigar said.

"Ancient history is the least of our troubles. We'd better move out before the justicars get here."

He looked around him, at the Nautolan, the other bodies, and the wrecked building. Dao Stryver. Lema Xandret. *Cinzia.*

"I'm going to talk to my Master," he said. "She should know there's a Mandalorian making trouble on Coruscant."

"All right," she said, hefting her helmet. "Lead the way."

"You're coming with me?"

"Never trust a Konshi. That's what my mother always said. And if we're going to stop a war between Dao Stryver and the Black Sun, we have to do it right. Right?"

He barely caught her smile before it disappeared behind her helmet.

"Right," he said.

CHAPTER 2

ELDON AX LICKED her wounds all the way to Dromund Kaas.

The damage to her body was most easily treated. Many of the cuts and gashes she left to scar naturally, believing as her Master had taught her that a lesson quickly forgotten is a lesson poorly learned. The rest she treated with the help of the medkit built into her interceptor's cockpit, avoiding painkillers and anesthetics completely. It wasn't pain that worried her. That was good for her, too.

The damage done to her confidence would take much longer to heal—not to mention her prospects of advancement. Darth Chratis would see to that. It didn't matter that her record on solo missions had been perfect up to this one. It didn't matter how highly she had been awarded by the Sith Academy. All that mattered was success.

The interceptor burst back into realspace and the Empire's grim-faced capital, Kaas City, hove into view.

"I will kill you, Dao Stryver," Eldon Ax swore, "or die trying."

THE DEBRIEF WENT as badly as she feared.

"Tell me about your mission," her Master instructed in clipped tones from his meditation chamber. Ax had been admitted into his presence before his morning rituals were complete, and she knew well how that annoyed him.

She bowed and did as she was instructed. Her Master doled out orders with an unbendable desire to test her willingness to obey. She knew better than to outright defy him, even when she was doing her best to keep her failure from him.

It was during her mission that the Mandalorian had found her. And it was this encounter she did her best to conceal from her Master, inasmuch as that was possible.

"Tell me more," said Darth Chratis, rising slowly out of his sarcophagus. In order to focus most effectively, he occupied at least one hour a day in a coffin-like shell that allowed no light or air, forcing him to rely solely on his own energies to survive. "You have not sufficiently explained the reasons for your failure."

She couldn't read his mood. His face was a mess of deep wrinkles and fissures from which two blood-red eyes peered out at the world. His knife-thin lips were twisted in a perpetual sneer. Occasionally, a tongue so pale it was almost transparent appeared to taste the air.

"I will not lie to you, Master," she said, kneeling before him. "While infiltrating an enemy cell, my identity was revealed and I was forced to defend myself."

"Revealed?" The bloodless lips twitched. "I do not sense the foul stink of the Jedi about you."

"No, Master. I was exposed by another—one whose people were once allies in our war against the Republic."

That was the gambit she had settled upon, to turn the blame for the incident back on the person who had caused it.

"So." Darth Chratis stepped free from the confines of his sarcophagus. The soles of his feet made a sound like dry leaves being crushed. "A Mandalorian."

"Yes, Master."

"You fought him?"

"Yes, Master."

"And he defeated you."

This wasn't a question, but it demanded a response. "That is true, Master."

"Yet you are still here. Why is this?"

Darth Chratis stood directly before her now. One withered claw reached down to touch her chin. His fingernails were like ancient crystals, cold and sharp against her skin. He smelled of death.

She looked up into his forbidding visage and saw nothing there but the implacable demand for the truth. "He did not come to fight me," she said. "This I believe, although it makes no sense. He asked for me by name. He knew what I am. He asked me questions to which I knew no answer."

"He interrogated you?" That prompted a frown. "The Emperor will be displeased if you revealed any of his secrets."

"I would rather die a lingering death at your hands, Master." Her reply was utterly sincere. She had been a Sith in training all her life. The Empire was as much a part of her as her lightsaber. She would not betray it to a pack of prideful mercenaries who worked with the Empire when it suited them.

But how to convey the truth of this to her Master when it was here, on this critical point, that her story fell apart?

"He asked me nothing about the Empire," Ax told her Master, remembering the scene with grueling clarity. Her assailant had disarmed her and pinned her with a net resistant to all her efforts to escape. A dart had paralyzed her, leaving only the ability to speak. "He did not torture me. I was wounded solely in self-defense."

She held out her arms to show Darth Chratis the injuries she had sustained.

He regarded them with no sign of approval.

"You are lying," he said with ready contempt. "You

expect me to believe that a Mandalorian hunted down a Sith apprentice, interrogated her, asked her nothing about the Empire, and then left her alive afterward?"

"Were I lying, Master, I would be sure to do so more plausibly."

"Then you have become unhinged. How else can I explain it?"

Ax lowered her head. There was nothing more she could say.

Darth Chratis paced across the angular narthex in which he conducted his audiences. Displayed on the walls around him were relics of his many victories, including bisected lightsaber hilts and shattered Jedi relics. Absent were the tributes to his many Sith enemies. Although Darth Chratis hadn't earned the fear and respect of his peers simply by outperforming them, he didn't boast about those he had forcibly removed from his path. His reputation was enough.

Only one in three apprentices serving under him survived their training. Eldon Ax wondered breathlessly whether the time had come for her to join those who had failed. Her life had been too short—just seventeen years!—but she wouldn't raise a hand to defend herself, if her Master chose to end it now. There would be no point. He could strike her down as easily as swatting a fly.

Darth Chratis stopped, turned to face her again.

"If this Mandalorian of yours didn't ask about the Emperor's plans, what *did* he ask you?"

At the time, the questions had puzzled her. They still puzzled her now.

"He was looking for a woman," she said. "He mentioned a ship. The names meant nothing to me."

"What names, exactly?"

"Lema Xandret. The *Cinzia*."

Suddenly her Master was standing over her again. She gasped. He had made no sound at all. The cold, strong grip of the Force was back at her throat, pulling her irresistibly upright until she was standing on tiptoes.

"Say those names again," he hissed.

She couldn't wrench her gaze away from his. "L-Lema Xandret. The *Cinzia*. Do you know what they mean, Master?"

He let her go and turned away. With two swift gestures, the ruin of his body was wrapped from head to feet in a long, winding cape, as black as his soul, and his right hand gripped a long, sharp-pointed staff.

"No more questions," he said. "Come."

With long strides, he left the room.

Eldon Ax took a long, shuddering breath, and hurried in the wake of her Master.

THE SORTING AND storing of Imperial data was a growth industry on Dromund Kaas, albeit one kept carefully hidden from view. Vast inverted skytowers drilled deep into the jungle's fertile soil, entombing centuries of multiply redundant records tended by tens of thousands of slaves. Extensive compounds spread out around the entrances, maintaining the highest possible security. To one of these compounds Darth Chratis led Eldon Ax.

He offered not a word of explanation throughout the long shuttle flight from Kaas City, and she endured his silence with something like relief. At least he wasn't berating her. Her mission had become a complete failure. She'd had to practically hack her way to the spaceport and off the planet—but not before running a search through landing records in recent days. There she found a reference to the Mandalorian. He had the temerity to travel under what appeared to be his real name: Dao Stryver.

Once again she renewed the vow to see him humbled as she had been, no matter how long it took. Perhaps death was too good for him. A quick one, anyway.

Darth Chratis commandeered a private data access

chamber seventy floors beneath the surface of the world, one equipped with a giant holoprojector, and ordered that the two of them not be interrupted. Ax trailed obediently behind him, increasingly mystified. Not once in her years of training had he shown any interest in this aspect of Imperial rule. *Interstellar bookkeepers* was his derogatory term for those who preferred service in the data mines to a more direct pursuit of power. She went to sit in the data requisitioner's place, but he waved her aside.

"Stand there," he said, pointing at a position directly in front of the screen and taking the seat himself.

With brisk, angular movements, he began inputting the requests. This as much as anything convinced her that events were taking a very strange turn indeed.

Menus and diagrams came and went in the giant screen. Ax found it difficult to follow, but she sensed that her Master was leading her through the vast and convoluted structure that was Imperial records to one location in particular.

"This," he said, tapping the keyboard with finality, "is the recruitment database."

A long list of names appeared on the screen, scrolling by too fast to read.

"Every person to enter the Sith Academy is listed here," he went on. "Their names, origins, bloodlines—and their fates, too, where applicable. The Dark Council uses this data to arrange matches and to anticipate the potential of offspring. The fortunes of numerous families rest on the nature of this data. It is therefore protected, Ax. It is very secure."

She indicated her understanding, thus far. "I'm in there," she said.

"Indeed you are, and so am I. Watch what happens when I input *Lema Xandret.*"

A new window appeared, showing a woman's face.

Round-featured, blond, keen eyes. It meant nothing to Ax. The space below the picture was filled with words highlighted in urgent red. At the bottom of a long list of entries were two bold lines:

Termination ordered.
File incomplete: target absconded.

Ax frowned. "So . . . she was a traitor? A Republic spy?"

"Worse than that. We keep fewer records on the Jedi than we do on people like this." Darth Chratis swiveled in the seat to face her. "Tell me, my apprentice, what happens when a Sith is recruited."

"The child is removed from its family and placed in the Academy. There its life begins anew, in the service of the Emperor and the Dark Council—as mine did."

"Exactly. It is a great honor for a family when a child is selected, particularly if their bloodline has not been so honored before. Most parents are pleased, as they should be."

"And those who are not are executed," she said. "Was Lema Xandret one of them?"

A cadaverous smile briefly enlivened the withered landscape of Darth Chratis's face. "Exactly. She was something unremarkable—a droid maker, I think. Yes, exactly that. From a long line of unremarkable droid makers, with no trace of Force sensitivity. She produced a child with the potential to be Sith, and so the child had to go."

Ax's Master didn't show amusement often. It disturbed her more than his rage.

"The file says 'target absconded,'" she said.

"First she tried to hide the child—a late bloomer, who she feared would not survive training on Korriban. When that failed and the child was taken anyway, she ran with the rest of the child's family—uncles, aunts, cousins, anyone at risk from reprisals—and has never been heard of since."

"Until now."

"From the mouth of a Mandalorian," Darth Chratis said, "to your ears."

"Why me?" she said, sensing that her Master was studying her closely. "Because my family attempted to hide me, too?"

"Perhaps."

"What I was before I met you is unimportant," she assured him. "I am untroubled regarding my family's fate."

"Indeed. I trained you well." Again that desiccated smile. "Perhaps too well." He leaned closer.

"Look here, Ax. Into my eyes."

She did so, and the red horror of his gaze filled her.

"The block is strong," he said, and it was as though the words came from inside her head. "It's standing between you and the truth. I release it. I release you, Ax. You are free to know the truth about your past."

She staggered back as though struck, but no physical force had touched her. A silent detonation had gone off in her mind, a depth charge deep below her conscious self. Something stirred there. Something strange and unsuspected.

Ax looked up at the picture in the holoprojector.

Lema Xandret stared back at her with empty eyes.

"She was your mother, Ax," her Master said. "Does that answer your question?"

Numbly, Ax supposed it did. But at the same time it posed many more.

DARTH CHRATIS USED the chamber's holoprojector to conduct a secure audience with the Minister of Intelligence. Ax had never met the minister before, nor seen him in any kind of communication, but the immense trust her Master showed by allowing her to remain in the room was utterly lost on her. Her head still rang from the liberation from her Master's conditioning. Not because of what it revealed, but because of what little difference it made to her.

Her family's lack of Force sensitivity had been the one thing of which she was certain about her life before becoming a Sith. She had assumed that her family had been killed, but that had never bothered her. She had certainly never worried about it, and it wouldn't have bothered her now but for one thing.

The block was removed. Memories should have come flooding back about Lema Xandret and her early life.

But there was nothing. Block or no block, there was nothing left. Lema Xandret remained a complete stranger.

With half a mind, she attended to the conversation her Master was having with the minister.

"That's why the Mandalorian sought to interrogate the girl. She's a potential lead."

"A lead to Xandret?"

"What other conclusion can we come to? She must be alive—in the same bolt-hole she fled down in order to evade execution, I presume."

"What would the Mandalorians want with her?"

"I don't know, and the fact that we don't know makes it vital that we find her first."

"As a matter of principle, Darth Chratis, or Imperial security?"

"The two are often inseparable, Minister, I think you'll find."

The man on the screen looked uncomfortable. His was the highest rank any mundane person could attain in the Empire's intelligence arm, yet to a Sith Lord he was considered fundamentally inferior. Disinclined he might be to acknowledge that a single missing droid maker warranted his attention, even one who tried to hide a Force-sensitive child from the Sith, but to disobey was inconceivable.

Then a thought struck him, and the conflicted look on his face eased.

"I wonder," he mused, tapping his chin with one long digit. "Just yesterday, a report arrived from our informer in the Republic Senate. The Hutts claim to have gotten their hands on something valuable, and they think the Senate would like to bid for it. Against us. I searched diplomatic dispatches and learned that we've received exactly the same offer, but couched in the opposite terms, of course. Ordinarily I would dismiss such an approach as unworthy of attention, but the fact that it came from two widely different sources does lend it some credence. And now this."

"I fail to see how the Hutts are connected. They are compulsive liars."

"Undoubtedly. But you see, Darth Chratis, this is where it gets interesting. The ship from which the Hutts claim to have retrieved this mysterious, ah, artifact, data, what have you—that ship is called the *Cinzia*. And I note in the file you accessed that this is the girl's birth name."

Darth Chratis nodded. "There must be a connection."

"That the ship was named after Lema Xandret's daughter and a Mandalorian is asking after both of them? I think so."

"But it helps us very little without knowing *what* the Hutts are auctioning."

That took some of the triumph out of the minister's expression. "I will pursue that information immediately, Darth Chratis."

"I trust you will, Minister, as a matter of principle."

The long-distance audience ended with a shower of static.

It took Eldon Ax almost a minute to realize. Disconnected phrases filled her head like birds, looking for somewhere to roost.

. . . *a potential lead* . . .

. . . *named after Lema Xandret's daughter* . . .

. . . *the girl's birth name* . . .

It occurred to her only then that the name she thought of as hers was nothing but a version of her mother's initials.

What have you been doing these last fifteen years, Mother?

"Tell me what you remember, Ax."

"I don't want to remember, Master."

"Why not?"

"Because it's nothing to do with who I am now. So what if Lema Xandret was my mother? If I met her tomorrow, I probably wouldn't recognize her. I've never known her, never needed her."

"Well, you need her now, Ax—or at least, you need her memories." Her Master came so close, she could feel the deathly cold of his breath. "It appears that knowledge of Lema Xandret and her missing droid makers is important to the Mandalorians. That means it's important to the Empire, too, for what strengthens another weakens us. Anything you can remember about your mother's whereabouts might be crucial. I therefore suggest you try harder. To reward you, I will put the block back in place afterward, so the memories will disappear again, like they never existed."

"All right, Master," she said, although her head hurt at the thought. What if nothing came? What if something did? "I'll try."

"You'll do better than try," Darth Chratis told her with chilling finality. "In ten standard hours I expect to be standing before the Dark Council with you beside me. If you let me down, both of us will suffer."

CHAPTER 3

ON A GOOD DAY, Ula Vii didn't talk to anyone. He just listened. That was what he was good at. In his time off, he would sit in his quarters and replay the week's recordings, scanning whole conversations for anything important. Important things were happening all the time on Coruscant, of course, but isolating items of greatest significance was a critical part of his job, and he liked to think that he was very good at it. Ula was an Imperial informer in the Republic Senate. He bore that responsibility with pride.

On a bad day, he was thrust out of the shadows and into the light: the trouble with playing a part was that sometimes Ula had to actually *play* it. As a senior assistant to Supreme Commander Stantorrs, Ula was often called upon to take notes, conduct research, and offer advice. All of this placed him in a unique position to assist the Empire in its mission to retake the galaxy, but at the same time he was forced to perform two demanding jobs at once. On bad days, his head ached so much that it felt like it would crack open, spilling all his secrets out onto the floor.

The day he heard about the *Cinzia* was a very bad day indeed.

The Supreme Commander had had a busy morning: countless visitors, endless supplicants, the eternal buzzing of his comlink. Ula didn't know how he stood it. Then came the request from Grand Master Satele Shan for an audience, throwing the Supreme Commander's schedule completely out of whack.

"Can't you put her off?" Stantorrs asked his secretary, with a look that signaled annoyance. The longer Ula occupied his role, the better he was getting at understanding the expressions of aliens, even noseless, moon-faced Duros like this one. "She was here only an hour ago."

"She says it's important."

"All right, all right. Send her in."

Ula had never formally met the Jedi Grand Master before. He regarded the Jedi with suspicion and dislike, and not just because they were the Emperor's enemy.

She strode into the palatial office and offered the Supreme Commander a bow of respect. With a finely boned face and gray-streaked hair, she was not a tall woman, but the position she occupied in the Republic hierarchy was considerable.

Stantorrs stood and offered a nod that seemed much slighter in comparison with hers. Like Ula, he didn't approve of Jedi, but his reasons had nothing to do with philosophy. Many in the Republic placed the blame for the Empire's ascendance firmly on the Jedi Council's collective shoulders. The Treaty of Coruscant had wrenched the galactic capital out of the Emperor's control once more, but only at great cost to the Republic and its allies, and at terrible loss of face. The Council's retreat to Tython hadn't helped.

"How can I help you, Master Shan?" he asked in gruff Basic.

"I've received a report from my Padawan of a possible bounty hunter loose in the old district," she said in measured tones. "Running riot among the criminal classes, apparently."

"That's a minor issue. Why bring it to me?"

"Your brief is restoring security on Coruscant. Furthermore, the bounty hunter is a Mandalorian."

Ula didn't need to read minds to know what Stantorrs was thinking now. A Mandalorian blockade of the Hydian Way trade route in the last decades of the Great War had crippled the Republic and very nearly led to its ruin. Since his defeat, Mandalore had lost many of his raiders to the gladiatorial pit fights on Geonosis, but Ula wasn't the only person on Coruscant who knew that Imperial operatives had been behind the anti-Republic action, and that he was still looking for a fight. If he was considering making a move on Coruscant itself, it had to be addressed immediately.

"What can you tell me about him?"

"His name is Dao Stryver. He's looking for information regarding a woman, Lema Xandret, and something called *Cinzia*."

Ula's ears pricked up at the latter name. He had heard that recently. Where, exactly?

The Supreme Commander was performing the same mental search. "A report," he mused, drumming his long fingers on the desk. "Something from SIS, I'm sure. Perhaps you should ask them about it."

A hint of Grand Master Satele Shan's true authority appeared in her voice. "I am to contact Tython immediately regarding our earlier discussions. General Garza impressed upon me the urgency and secrecy of the matter. I cannot afford to be delayed any further."

Stantorrs's waxy skin turned a deep purple. He didn't like the Republic's own policies being used against him. Ula hoped for a momentary loss of control, that something might slip about the nature of those earlier meetings. Try as he might, he could learn nothing about them, although he was certain they were of grave importance to his Masters on Dromund Kaas.

Unfortunately Stantorrs's self-control was a match for his temper.

"I haven't got time to investigate every minor disruption," the Supreme Commander fumed. "Ula! Look into it, will you?"

Ula jumped at the mention of his name. "Sir?"

"Follow up this incident for Master Shan. Report to both of us when you find something. *If* you find something."

The last was directed at the Grand Master with a generous amount of ill feeling.

"Of course, sir," said Ula, hoping that the concession was simply a ruse to get the Grand Master off Stantorrs's back.

"Thank you, Ula, Supreme Commander. I'm most grateful."

With that, Satele Shan swept from the room, watched resentfully by Stantorrs and his staff. Every department in the Republic was overstretched and understaffed. The last thing anyone wanted was the Jedi sticking their noses in, finding fault, and handing over *more* work.

Ula's job wasn't to sow dissent, but sometimes he wished it was. Dissent practically sowed itself on cursed Coruscant, where the sky was the same heavy gray as its pedwalks and the pockmarks of war still scarred its artificial face.

The Supreme Commander resumed his seat with a heavy sigh. "All right, Ula. You'd better get started."

"But sir," Ula said, "surely you don't—I mean, I thought—"

"No, we'd better do exactly as I said, just in case it does turn out to be important. No sweeping anything aside when Mandalorians are involved. If that rabble of troublemakers is helping the Empire make another move on Coruscant, we need to know about it. But don't spend too much time on it, eh? The rest of the galaxy won't wait."

Ula inclined his head in frustrated obedience. He was dismayed that the Grand Master's minor request was removing him from the Supreme Commander's presence. How was he going to gather the intelligence he needed now? This pointless quest could cost him valuable data.

There was no use arguing, and perhaps some benefit to complying, too. Mandalorians weren't any kind of rabble: their vast numbers of individual clans, each available for hire to the highest bidder, added up to a potent fighting force capable of shifting the balance of power in a major battle, as the Republic had already learned to its cost. The Empire had given the Mandalorians the means of returning to the galaxy and gaining revenge on their enemies, but there was no loyalty lingering between the two sides. With the signing of the Treaty of Coruscant, Emperor and Mandalore had gone their separate ways.

It was worth pursuing this lead, he told himself, even if an hour or two's research proved that someone had been chasing at shadows and business returned to usual afterward.

It would be out of character, too, to do otherwise. Ula Vii, the amenable functionary, always did as he was told. That was how he had gained such intimate access to the Supreme Commander's affairs. With a brisk bow, he smoothed the already impeccable front of his uniform as he left the office and headed for the headquarters of his opposite number in the Republic.

STRATEGIC INFORMATION SYSTEMS didn't advertise its offices in the Heorem Complex, but anyone with any seniority in the administration knew where they were. Ula had had reason to visit only once before, while covering for a Cipher Agent, and he'd made a point of avoiding it ever since. The company of other intelligence operatives bothered him, no matter whose side they were on. They were all of the same breed, more or less: observant, quick thinking, used to seeing—or imagining—deception all around them. Creatures of few words, they gave little away, and their eyes were as pointed as the needles of an interrogator droid.

Ula masked his nervousness behind a façade of calm as he entered the spacious, cultured atrium. The secretary smiled warmly at him.

"Can I help you, sir?"

"Ula Vii, adviser to Supreme Commander Stantorrs."

His voiceprint was checked, naturally, but unobtrusively. The secretary waved him through. He was met in a conference room by an unreadable Ithorian, possibly female, dressed in simple, black robes bearing no name tags or insignia.

"You're an Epicanthix," she said bluntly, from both of her mouths.

As conversation starters, it was a disconcerting one. Most people failed to notice that he wasn't fully human. He refused to give her the advantage.

"Supreme Commander Stantorrs requests information," he said.

"Why doesn't he follow the usual channels?"

"We need an answer quickly," he said, thinking: *So I can get back to my real job. Both of them.*

"Ask," she said.

He gave her the Mandalorian's name, and the other names associated with the case.

The Ithorian produced a datapad from beneath her robes and tapped at it with one long, slender finger. Apart from that digit, no part of her body moved. Ula waited with no outward sign of impatience, wondering how the creature breathed.

"A ship registered to a Dao Stryver landed on Coruscant two standard days ago," she finally said. "It left an hour ago."

"What was the name and class of the ship?"

"*First Blood,* a modified Kuat D-Seven."

"Destination?"

"Unknown."

"Tell me about Lema Xandret."

"We have no record of that name."

"Nothing at all?"

"Once," she said, "information flowed freely across the galaxy, ebbing and flowing as readily as light itself. We prided ourselves on the ease with which we knew all things. Then the Empire came, casting a shadow across the Republic, and the constant shine of knowledge was shattered. Much we would know now comes sluggishly, and in incomplete forms. Our task is as much to reconstruct as to gather."

"That's a no, then," said Ula testily. He was very aware of the state of information in the galaxy, and he didn't like the Empire being blamed for it. From his point of view, the Republic had never gotten it right, and only the establishment of Imperial rule would enable the right and correct flow of data to everyone.

He wasn't getting very far with the alien, but he had one question left.

"What about the third name: *Cinzia*?"

"We have three appearances: two from the Senate and one from an allied spy network. Both point to the same source."

More *spies,* Ula thought with distaste. He hated that word. "Who are the Senators?"

"Bimmisaari in the Halla sector and Sneeve in the Kastolar sector."

"Can you tell me their source?"

"Readily. There are no security warnings attached to this subject." The Ithorian tapped again. "Both Senators and the spy network report on an unusual auction in Hutt space. Tenders have been called for."

"Where does the name *Cinzia* fit in?"

"It appears to be a vessel of some kind."

"Anything else?"

"Speculation varies among the three parties. I can offer you no hard facts."

Ula thought quickly to himself. So Dao Stryver was real, and the *Cinzia,* too. But what was one doing on Coruscant while the other was in Hutt space? How did the greed of a species of malignant criminals connect them?

"Thank you," he said. "You've been some help to us."

The Ithorian walked him back to the atrium and left him there. The secretary waved cheerfully as he left. A film of sweat covered Ula from head to foot. It could have gone much worse, he told himself, if they had only known what he really was . . .

Ula had a contact in the office of the Senator from Bimmisaarian. He made an appointment by comlink as he walked. With luck, he hoped, this whole thing could be wrapped up before day's end and life would return to normal.

"OH, I KNOW exactly what you're talking about," breezed Hunet L'Beck over a pot of traditional ale. He had insisted on meeting for lunch, and Ula had found it impossible to talk him out of it. Ula didn't like eating in public. It was one of the things he preferred to keep to himself, without worrying about what other people thought.

"Go on, then," he said, moving scraps of yot bean fry-up around his plate. "Tell me everything."

L'Beck had finished eating long ago and was on to his second pot. That made him even more loquacious than normal, which wasn't a bad thing. Ula needed him to talk.

"The Senator's offices on Bimmisaari received a communiqué from Tassaa Bareesh seven days ago. Do you know who she is?"

"A member of the Bareesh Cartel, I presume."

"Only the head, the matriarch. She has close ties to the Empire, so we keep an eye on her as best we can. There's nothing we can do about the smuggling, but open slavery is something we try to crack down on."

Ula nodded. Bimmisaari's home sector butted directly on Hutt space, so the behavior of the cartels could have a hugely destabilizing effect on the local economy. "Go on."

"The communiqué was a pitch, really, and a fairly unsubtle one at that. Bareesh was attempting to interest us in something one of her pirates had found in the Outer Rim. Information, apparently, and an unspecified artifact. She didn't say where they had come from, exactly; way out past Rinn was the only hint she dropped. We didn't pay it much heed at first, naturally."

"Why 'naturally'?"

"Well, we receive dozens of offers from the Hutts every day. Most are scams. Some are traps. All are full of lies. Not so different from what we receive from the Resource Management Council, but at least that's supposed to be on our side." L'Beck toasted his own cynical witticism and ordered another drink.

"So you ignored the communiqué," Ula prompted.

"And that normally would have been the end of it. Except another one arrived, and then another, each adding a little to the story until eventually we had to pay attention. It was quite a clever campaign, actually. We wouldn't have accepted it if it had arrived all at once, but doled out bit by bit, letting each piece of the puzzle fall into place before offering us the next one, eventually it was enough to get even the Senator himself interested."

"In what, exactly?"

"The Hutts found a ship. The *Cinzia*. There was something inside it, apparently, an artifact they're trying to sell, but that's not the most important thing. What really makes this interesting is where the ship came from."

Ula was getting tired of playing games. "Just tell me, will you?"

"I can't. That information is what the Hutts are selling." L'Beck leaned forward. "We've been trying to generate interest in the Senate. Support is sprcading for an official response, but not fast enough. The auction is in a few days' time, and I'm afraid we'll miss out." L'Beck's voice lowered until it was barely audible over the background noise. "How would you like to be the one to hand the Republic a previously unknown, resource-rich world, ripe for the picking?"

Ula kept his expression neutral. So *that* was what the fuss was about. New worlds weren't especially hard to come by, but anything steeped in minerals or biosphere was fiercely contested between the Empire and the Republic. If the Hutts had stumbled across the location of one such world, there was indeed a real chance to profit from the knowledge.

"Are you sure it's real, not another scam?" he asked L'Beck.

"As sure as we can be," L'Beck said lightly, taking his third pot from the waiter and knocking back a hefty swallow. "Supreme Chancellor Janarus would authorize a bidding party from Bimmisaari, I'm sure, if we could only get word to him. Do you think you can help?"

And there it was, the appeal for assistance in shoring up local politics. Halla sector wanted not only to be the ones who brought a new world to the Republic's attention, but access to the Chancellor's coffers as well. A small percentage would be skimmed off the top to cover administration expenses, no doubt—providing more ale for the likes of Hunet L'Beck and his ilk. Thus the Republic doomed itself, and all it purported to represent.

Ula suppressed his ideological revulsion. "I'll bring it to Supreme Commander Stantorrs's attention," he said. And that was the truth. He had no choice now. If he returned with nothing, and two days later the information did reach the Supreme Chancellor's ears from another source—well, it wouldn't pay to be diminished in Stantorrs's eyes. Maintaining that contact was paramount.

But that wouldn't stop him from spreading the information elsewhere first.

"I owe you," said L'Beck as Ula paid the bill and took his leave. That was the best way to leave an informant: in one's debt. Ula's coffers, like the Republic's, weren't limitless, but they contained enough credits to grease the path to Imperial domination, just a little.

MANY MEANS EXISTED of getting secret transmissions off Coruscant. One could stash an antenna on a little-used building and broadcast when official satellites were out of range. One could pay a lowlife to take a recording to orbit, there to send the message farther by more ordinary means. One could employ a code of such baroque complexity that the transmission resembled layers of noise upon noise, with no significant features.

Ula believed that the best way to arouse suspicion was to go too far out of his way to avoid it. So his preferred method of contacting his superiors was to place a call to Panatha, the planet of his birth, leave a message for his mother, and wait for the reply to come to him. That way, the burden of guilt was shifted elsewhere. It was much easier to brush off receiving an illicit communication, one possibly misplaced, than the accusation of making one.

After notifying the Supreme Commander that he was hot on the case, he went immediately to his austere quarters and sent two signals. Ula lived in Manarai Heights, near his work in the Senate District while at the same time close enough to the Eastport Docking Facility to make a quick getaway if he needed to. He had stashes of documents, credits, and weapons in several locations between home and the spaceport. He also had a secondary apartment, little more than a closet, really, in case he needed somewhere to hide for a while. He wasn't one for taking chances. The illusion of innocence he had wrapped around himself could be all too easily dispelled. He had seen it happen before. One mistake was all it took . . .

The bleep of his comlink broke him out of the nervous reverie in which he had spent the last hour. The call was on its way, in response to the first of his signals. He readied himself by straightening his uniform for the dozenth time and taking position in front of his holoprojector. This was the part of his job he liked the least.

A ghostly image appeared before him, flickering blue with static. There was little more than a hint of a face, and the voice was both genderless and species-less. Ula had no idea whom he spoke to on distant Dromund Kaas.

"Report," said Watcher Three.

Ula summed up everything he had learned in as few words as possible: A ship from an unaffiliated resource-rich world in the Outer Rim had been captured by the Hutts, who were offering information about it to the highest bidder. That same ship was the object of a search by a Mandalorian, Dao Stryver. Another name, Lema Xandret, was implicated. The origins of the ship were unknown, as was its cargo, the mysterious object L'Beck had alluded to. Both were up for auction.

When he finished, the noisy line crackled and fizzed for almost half a minute before Watcher Three responded.

"Very good. This is a matter of concern to the minister. Maintain a close watch and report all developments."

"Yes, sir."

"Dismissed."

The transmission ended, and Ula sagged with relief. For all he knew, Watcher Three was a perfectly ordinary person, just another functionary like him, but there was something about that hollow voice that made him feel utterly unworthy. Bad enough that he wasn't fully human, but worse even than that. He felt dirty, unclean, vile, for no reason at all.

Watcher Three made him feel like he did when he talked to a Sith.

His comlink buzzed again. He prepared himself again, with very different reasons to feel nervous. Whereas the last call had come through perfectly official channels from the Ministry of Intelligence, this one had a very different purpose, and bore risks of its own.

This time, when the holoprojector stirred, it revealed a perfectly clear image of a woman who still struck Ula as looking entirely too young for the role she played in Imperial administration.

"Hello, Ula. How nice to hear from you again. To what do I owe the pleasure?"

Ula swallowed. Shullis Khamarr's smile seemed perfectly sincere, and Ula had no reason to believe it otherwise. The current Minister of Logistics was the same age as he and shared his passionate belief that the Empire was a civilizing force to be reckoned with. They had discussed this subject at length during a shuttle flight from Dromund Kaas, the one time he had visited the Imperial capital world. He had been attending a briefing for members who hadn't qualified to be Cipher Agents but were still considered useful to the intelligence arm; she was on her way to be promoted to lieutenant. Since then, her rise had been meteoric, while he remained essentially nowhere.

"I have something for you," he told her. "A world ripe for annexation, discovered by the Hutts."

"I've heard something about this already," she said. "No one knows where it is, and we won't until we pay up. Do you have anything to add, Ula?"

He deflated slightly. So he wasn't the first to make a report. "Not yet, Minister. But I'm well placed to follow it up and hope to learn more soon."

"That would be to the benefit of us all, Ula," she said with another smile. "Why did you call me about it?"

"Because it's the opportunity we've been waiting for," he said, feeling his pulse thudding in his neck. This was as dangerous a territory now as it had ever been. "We don't need fanatics to rule a galaxy. We just need proper governance and administration. Rules, laws, discipline. When you see those lunatics wreaking havoc on the worlds out here—Jedi and Sith alike—I have to ask what *benefit* they bring." He used her own word deliberately. "There wouldn't be a war at all without them stirring things up."

"I remember this, Ula," she said with patience that cut through him like a lightsaber. "I understand your views, but there's nothing I can do—"

"All we need is just one world, a strong world capable of defending itself, on which the Imperial citizens could thrive without fear or oppression."

"The world you've heard of belongs rightfully to the Emperor. I cannot claim it for myself."

"But you're the Minister of Logistics now! The entire Imperial bureaucracy is yours."

She rebuffed him gently, as she always did. "It is the Emperor's, as it should be. I am his instrument, and I would not betray his trust."

"I would never ask you to do that."

"I know, Ula. You are as loyal as I am, and you mean well, but I fear that what you ask is impossible."

He took pains never to push their friendship too far, but he was unable to hide his disappointment. "What will it take to change your mind, Minister?"

"When you have the location of the world, talk to me again."

He knew all too well that betraying the Republic while at the same time trying to convince a senior minister to increase the influence of ordinary people in their relations with the Sith ruling class could bring his entire world to ruin.

"Thank you, Minister," he said. "You are kind to indulge me."

"It's neither kindness, Ula, nor an indulgence. You may call me anytime."

She ended the transmission, and this time Ula didn't sag. He already felt fully deflated, insignificant—even if Watcher Three did describe his mission of being *one of significance* to the Emperor himself. He felt like a grain of sand buffeted by powerful ocean currents. No matter which shore he landed upon, the waves pounded him harder than ever.

Maintain a close watch and report all developments.

That he could do. Exhausted from his day of talking, he filed a written report for Supreme Commander Stantorrs. Then he undressed and lay on his hard bed and waited for dawn.

CHAPTER 4

LARIN MOXLA STOOD in the Senate Gardens, on a busy thoroughfare lined with benches. It was early evening, and the sky was full of lights. She felt uncomfortably exposed, and was struck by how used she'd become to the old districts. Only a few months had passed since she'd been drummed out of Blackstar Squad, and already the hazy sky of the upper levels looked too large, the people too refined, the droids too clean, and the buildings too new. Give her a year, she thought, and she'd be completely at one with the dregs of society.

Her feeling of alienation was only confirmed when a quartet of Senate Security officers strode by, three men—Twi'lek, Zabrak, and human—and a stocky Nikto woman. The SSOs caught sight of her and approached.

"Are you lost?" rumbled the Twi'lek. "You look like you've been pulled backward through a Sarlacc."

"Twice," the Nikto woman chittered, not unkindly.

Larin wanted to walk away. They were speaking to her soldier-to-soldier, using familiar, bantering tones, but her heart wasn't in it.

"Thanks, guys," she said. "I'm okay, and I won't be here long." She was waiting for Shigar to return from talking to Satele Shan, and this was where she had said they should meet.

"No worries," said the human with a wink. "Just try not to frighten anyone."

"Wait," said the Zabrak, peering at her. "Do I know you?"

"I don't think so," she said.

"Yeah, I do," he said. "You're Toxic Moxla, the Kiffar who snitched on Sergeant Donbar."

Larin felt the blood rising to her head. "That's none of your business."

"Oh, yeah? I've got a cousin in Special Forces who'd disagree," said the Zabrak, right into her face.

She held his stare, fighting the urge to retreat, or to head-butt him—one swift, solid lunge that might cut her forehead to the bone on his horns, but would certainly lay him out cold.

But then she'd have a probable affray charge to wear afterward. The gardens were full of witnesses, fine, upstanding witnesses who didn't sleep in an abandoned warehouse and hand-weld their clothes from castoff scrap.

"Easy, Ses," said the Twi'lek to the Zabrak. "You've had one too many fizzbrews over lunch again."

"When did you hear from your cousin, anyway?" added the Nikto woman, taking his arm and guiding him firmly away. "Last I heard, he owed you money."

The human cast Larin an apologetic look as the trio led their drunk friend away, but not before he could call over his shoulder, "Crawl back into your hole, Toxic Moxla. We don't want your kind up here!"

Larin watched the Zabrak go with her face burning hot. How did such a lout ever get into the SSO, let alone know someone in Special Forces? It didn't seem possible.

But mixed with her outrage was a feeling of deep shame. Yes, she had snitched on her commanding officer. Yes, she was playacting at being a soldier in a poorly made costume. But neither came lightly to her. She had her reasons.

Larin turned to face the distant Jedi Temple. Abandoned in ruins and sealed off ever since the sacking of Coruscant, it was an ominous, shadowy presence against the lights of the skylanes and skyscrapers. Like fate, ever-present.

SHIGAR WAITED FOR five minutes before his Master appeared as though out of nowhere, right by his side. He never heard her coming, but had learned at least not to be as startled as in the early days of his apprenticeship. That, he assumed, was the heart of this particular lesson: some things could never be anticipated, but he could control the way he reacted to them.

They stood together for a moment in the empty cloisters, staring up at the looming, silver cylinder that was the Galactic Justice Center. Its lights burned brightly, and never flickered once.

"You've put something in motion, Shigar," she said.

"Do you see this in the future, Master?" The foresight of Grand Master Satele Shan was legendary, and never wrong.

She shook her head. "Not this time. I received this a moment ago from Supreme Commander Stantorrs."

She passed Shigar a datapad, and he read the packet of information displayed there twice. It contained everything uncovered about Dao Stryver, Lema Xandret, and the *Cinzia* in the previous hours. Someone had been busy, he thought.

"The Hutts certainly recognize an opportunity when they see one," he said, wrapping the new data around everything he had already gleaned about the Mandalorian, the Black Sun, and the attack on Larin Moxla.

"The *Cinzia* gives Tassaa Bareesh two plays for the price of one," his Master said. "To the administrations of the Republic and the Empire, the primary concern is the ship's origin. Where it came from matters much more than its purpose or what it contained. We all know that the Republic is desperate for resources, and any new world will aid its cause. It goes without saying that Supreme Commander Stantorrs will pursue this matter further, on that ground alone.

"From the point of view of the Jedi Council, however, the situation is precisely reversed. The Hutts are auctioning more than just information: there's the cargo of the ship to consider, too. The object they're selling presumably has some recognizable value, but as yet we do not know what it is. It could be anything. We can't ignore the possibility that they have stumbled upon something critical to the Jedi Order—an artifact, perhaps, or a weapon. Many are spoken of in ancient records but are yet unaccounted for; just one might make a difference in the war against the Emperor."

"It could be a Sith artifact," he said, knowing full well that the forces of the enemy had their own arsenals, as ancient as the Jedi Order's.

"That's also a possibility. We must, therefore, do everything in our power to ensure that this thing the Hutts have—whatever it is—does not fall into the wrong hands."

"It's already in the wrong hands," he said.

"That's true, but Tassaa Bareesh only recognizes one side: her own. I have no fears of her using this find directly against us. Still, we need to know more about it, and soon. That's where you come in, Shigar."

Shigar studied his Master's face. He had felt that the conversation was more than idle chat, but he hadn't expected an active role in the situation.

"I will do anything you wish, Master."

"You will go to the court of Tassaa Bareesh and uncover everything you can about the *Cinzia* and its contents. You're to travel incognito in order to minimize our apparent interest in the sale. You will report what you find to me directly, and I will decide what to do with that information. You will leave this evening."

Her voice was brisk and matter-of-fact, belying the significance of her words. This was a major assignment, cutting through the thick of a complex political knot. Were he to fail, it would reflect badly on the Jedi Order, and perhaps hinder the entire war effort. The responsibility was considerable.

Coming so soon after his disappointment of that morning, however, it was impossible to silence a nagging, doubtful voice.

"Are you sure I'm the right choice?" he asked, dragging the words out as though they were made of lead. "After all, the Council believes me unfit for the trials. There must be someone else better qualified who can do this for you."

"Are you telling me you don't want to go, Shigar? That you're not ready?"

He bowed his head to hide his mingled pride and uncertainty. "I trust your judgment, Master, better than my own."

"Good, because I believe my reasoning is sound. Your face is unknown on Hutta; you will therefore find it easier to pass unnoticed. And I have faith in you. Remember that. I am certain that this is the path laid down for you."

"So you have seen something!"

He tried to read her expression in the flickering lights of the city. She could have been amused, concerned, or completely blank. It was hard to tell. Perhaps all three.

He swore to himself that he would make her proud. "What about the situation here—the gangs, the poverty?"

"That's the responsibility of the local authorities," she said, fixing him with a firm stare. "They are doing their best."

He heard the warning in her voice. The Jedi's role in the galaxy led them outward, to Tython; he had been told many times before that the Republic's many social problems should not be his, even if this time Mandalorians were involved. Until Mandalore declared himself a particular enemy of *someone,* he could be considered more or less neutral. "Yes, Master."

"Go now. There's a shuttle waiting for you."

Shigar bowed and went to walk away.

"Be kind, Shigar," his Master added. "Some roads are harder than yours have been."

When he turned back, Satele Shan was gone, vanished into the night as though she had never been there at all.

WITH RELIEF, LARIN saw Shigar striding along the thoroughfare toward her. He had been gone less than half an hour, but it felt much longer than that. After the encounter with the Senate Security Officers, she had spoken to no one and avoided catching anyone's eyes, feeling more out of place than ever. When he returned, she promised herself, and when he had finished assuring her that he *had* spoken to his Master about the situation down below and she *would* do something about it, Larin could vanish back down her hole again, just as the Zabrak had advised her to.

It wasn't that she thought the Zabrak was right. On the contrary. She just didn't know where to fit in anymore, up here. At least she had something to do in the old districts. Ever since her discharge, she had committed herself to protecting the weak and disenfranchised, those whom even the justicars ignored, to the extent her meager resources allowed. Unlike the justicars, she was interested in something more important than territory, and if that meant working alone, so be it.

"How did it go?" she asked Shigar when he reached her.

"Well. I think."

"Are you sure about that?"

She didn't know him well enough to be able to tell what troubled him, but he didn't seem remotely content. His brow was knuckled, and the blue chevrons on his cheeks were twisted out of shape by the clenched muscles beneath. Perhaps the reassurance she'd been hoping for wasn't coming after all.

"I have to go somewhere," he said. "Will you walk with me, part of the way?"

"Sure. Where are we going?"

"Eastport."

"I thought you only just got to Coruscant."

"That's right." He glanced at her, as though surprised that she had remembered. "I've been traveling all my life—since Master Satele took me on, anyway."

They walked at an easy pace through the temperate night. A light breeze ran its fingers through her short hair, and she was reminded of one good thing about life topside: weather. The last time anything had rained on her was when a sewage line had burst two levels up.

"I haven't seen another Kiffar for years," she said to break the silence. "Were you on Kiffu during the Annexation?"

"No. Master Tengrove, the Jedi Watchman of that sector, found me the year before. I was on Dantooine when it happened, helping my Master dig through some ruins."

"Find anything interesting?"

"I don't remember." He glanced at her again. "What about you? The Annexation, I mean."

"I was there, although I don't remember it clearly. I was too young. My parents slipped me into a shuttle and got me offworld before the worst of it hit. The shuttle took me to Abregado-rae, where a host family adopted me. They had taken on a lot of kids after the Treaty of Coruscant, but there was always space for another. It was a madhouse."

"What happened to your parents?"

"They died in prison on Kiffex."

"I'm sorry," he said.

"Don't be. It's just more ancient history. What about yours?"

"Dead, too—from a vacuum seal accident on a Fresian shuttle, though, nothing to do with the Annexation."

They walked in silence for a while again, he looking fixedly ahead and she down at her booted feet. She felt the usual mixture of relief and sorrow whenever the matter of her parents' sacrifice came up. She hadn't known it at the time, but she had worked out later how much her narrow escape had cost them. With Imperial warships crowding their home planet, they must have bribed an Imperial gunner to overlook an escaping shuttle, plus the shuttle pilot and who knew how many spaceport guards? They had given up everything, just to save her.

And how had she repaid them?

"I have to go to Hutta," he finally said.

"Why?"

"One of the cartels has discovered something. I need to find out what it is."

"Is this connected to that Mandalorian?"

"Seems so. But he's off Coruscant now and won't be bothering you again."

"Are you sure he won't come back?"

"As sure as I can be."

"Well, that's something," she said with more satisfaction than she actually felt. Now that she had accomplished everything she'd set out to do that day, she could reasonably retreat to her sanctuary in the old districts and go back to doing what she did best. The trouble was, she wasn't quite ready to cast free of Shigar Konshi. He reminded her of what it was like to be given a new mission: objectives, resources, constraints, deadlines. She missed the days when everything was sharply defined and unambiguous.

"Ever been to Hutta before?" she asked him.

"No. Not the surface."

"It's vile and dangerous. I was there on a covert op two years ago. Very nearly didn't get out again."

"You've done covert work?"

"More than I care to think about." She hadn't told him about Special Forces and the Blackstars. As far as Shigar knew, she was just an ordinary trooper, taking a temporary break from duty.

"What about slicing?" he asked her, visibly picking up. "Do they teach you that kind of thing, too?"

"The basics. I learned a whole lot more from a girl called Kixi when I arrived here. Now I could do it in my sleep."

"And you're familiar with some of the rougher gangs that run around the underworld. You'd even pass for one of them, with a bit of a wash."

"Hey, watch it." She threw a punch at his shoulder, which he dodged with surprising ease.

He stopped walking, not joking around at all, and they stood facing each other.

"You could come with me," he said, as though the idea had just occurred to him. "To Hutta, I mean."

"I thought you'd never ask," she said.

He didn't laugh. "I'm serious. You just implied I'd need a guide there, and I could certainly use the help. It's a big job."

"Will you tell me what we'd be looking for? I don't like being left in the dark, ever."

"I don't know what it is myself. Not yet. I know as little about it as you do."

"Well . . ." She pretended to think about it, although she'd worked out her answer while he had been asking about her covert ops qualifications, just like he had been wanting to ask her ever since he finished talking with his Master. That was what he'd had trouble spitting out this whole time. She could see it perfectly now. He didn't want to ask her outright for fear of putting her on the defensive. And maybe he imagined that she didn't want to ask him for fear of looking desperate. This way, it looked like they were coming up with the idea together. No one needed to be rescued. They were a team.

His transparency both amused her and warmed her to him. She had no choice but to go to Hutta, if only to save him from what was waiting for him there. Sure, the Sith were hard work, but the Hutts would eat him alive if they captured him in this state.

"All right," she said, "but one condition."

"What's that?"

"You stop thinking that you're doing me a favor."

He flushed. "All right."

"And you buy me a proper meal. I've been living on concentrates for weeks."

"That's two favors."

"Think of that last one as good troop management. You don't want me losing my concentration on the job, do you?"

"I guess not." He smiled in a way that made him look even younger than he was. "Come on, Moxla. We're not getting any closer just standing here."

She sloppily saluted.

They strode off into the night, and within three paces their steps had unconsciously fallen into time.

CHAPTER 5

BLACK ON BLACK, and a hint of bright steel.

The twelve Lords of the Emperor's Dark Council stared at Eldon Ax and her Master with the combined force of a glacial avalanche.

". . . and so you see, my lords," Darth Chratis concluded, "how this situation can be advanced by the application of swift and appropriate action: the right people in the right place at the right time. My apprentice and I are the people. The place is Hutta. The time to strike is right now."

They were standing in a recessed section of the floor, surrounded by the Dark Council. Twelve monstrous visages gazed down at them—some exposed and scarred, others hidden by masks—all radiating cool and constant hate. These were the Emperor's confidants, his most prized servants. They alone saw his face, and now they were seeing Ax's.

She felt her Master's fear for the first time, and it thrilled her.

"Spare us the rhetoric, Darth Chratis," said one of the Dark Lords, a being that might once have been a woman but whose face now was little more than a sexless skeleton. "We will not be moved by speeches."

"What is it, exactly, that you want?" added another, his voice a high-pitched stiletto issuing from a featureless iron mask. "Tell us your plans."

"My apprentice will infiltrate the court of Tassaa Bareesh," Darth Chratis said, "in order to steal the information from the Hutts. I will wait offworld. When she has succeeded, I will proceed to the location of the colony and begin its annexation, to the continued glory of the Empire."

He bowed low, and Ax was filled with contempt.

"A simple plan," said another of the Dark Lords. Darth Howl had teeth sharpened to points, and his face was slashed by random patterns of straight lines. "I admire its directness. We do not negotiate with criminals."

"Tassaa Bareesh has been of use to us," said another. "It would not be wise to anger her."

"My apprentice will be circumspect," Darth Chratis assured them. "She is unknown to them. They will not detect her."

"And the annexation itself. How will you facilitate this? You cannot have sufficient resources of your own to capture an entire world."

"No, my lords. I will require at least a division to quash any resistance."

"An entire division?" Dry mutterings circulated around the ring of Dark Lords. "You ask too much."

"Do you expect significant resistance?"

"Yes, Darth Howl." Here Ax's Master hesitated. The one point he had downplayed during his summary was at last being dragged into view. "The colony was founded by fugitives from the Empire."

"What kind of fugitives?"

He outlined everything they had uncovered about Lema Xandret while the Council listened in chilly silence. When he described the connection between Xandret and Ax, all eyes turned to her. She did her best to stare right back, although it caused her physical pain at the back of her eye sockets. It was like meeting the gaze of a black hole.

"The Mandalorian let the daughter of the fugitives live," said Darth Howl when the account was finished. "Can you be sure there is no connection between them?"

"I have examined her thoroughly. She feels no sympathy for the ones we seek."

"What say you, girl? Tell me what you remember of your mother."

Ax forced her tongue to unfreeze. She had been spoken to, so she must reply. That was how it worked.

"I remember nothing, my lord. That is both a curse and a blessing."

"Explain."

"My lack of memory means that I can offer no clue as to the whereabouts of the fugitives. That is a curse, because it would be simplest to avoid dealing with the Hutts altogether. But if I *did* remember, my feelings might indeed be clouded, and you would be right to mistrust me. I offer you my assurance that I am loyal, and that the Hutts can be dealt with."

She felt a pressure on her mind, as though a mountain were leaning on it.

"You are confident," said Darth Howl. "Perhaps overconfident. But you are not lying."

"Thank you, my lord." She bowed deeply.

"That doesn't mean, however, that we can trust you."

She straightened. "If I may address the Council once more, there is something I wish to say."

"Speak," Darth Howl instructed her.

Darth Chratis shot her a warning glance, but she ignored him.

"This mission is paramount, and not just because of the world we stand to gain. There is something my Master has not raised with you, and it concerns the actions of the Mandalorian, Dao Stryver. His master was once an ally of the Empire, but in recent years Mandalore has been distant, threatening, even. Yet this one knew my history, knew of my biological connection to Lema Xandret, knew where to find me. He knew all these things—how? I believe that finding him and obtaining an answer to this question is critical to the security of the Empire."

That provoked another round of whispering. A Mandalorian spy in the Imperial administration? Unthinkable—yet potentially disastrous if it was true. It could signal the turning of hostile Mandalorian eyes onto the Empire. Whole chains of command would need to be scrutinized. Purges would be required. Heads would roll, perhaps even the Minister of Intelligence's. The turmoil could be tremendous.

Darth Chratis stared at her with lips pressed so tightly together he might have been making diamonds out of his teeth.

Then, unexpectedly, Darth Howl began to laugh. It was an awful sound, full of bile and rot and cruelty, and it punctured the tension like a dagger. It echoed through the Council chamber like the sound of breaking glass, bringing all else to silence.

"Eldon Ax," he said, when his malignant mirth subsided, "you do not fool me."

The blood in Ax's veins turned to ice. "I swear, my lord—"

"Do not interrupt." The whip-crack of command was backed up by the full power of the Force. "I know a liar when I meet one."

Ax could not move. She could only stare in horror, wondering what had gone wrong.

"You speak of infiltrators in the Empire, of Mandalorian infiltration," her accuser went on. "But I see you clearly, Eldon Ax. I know what stirs in you, which you would hide from all of us. I feel your hatred for the Mandalorian and the desire for revenge. I know that this mission has nothing to do with the Empire. It is all about proving that Dao Stryver was wrong to dismiss you by not killing you. You yearn to turn the tables on him, to defeat him in turn, and then to kill him. That is all you desire. That is what fills your heart."

An icy smile spread across Darth Howl's face.

She braced herself to receive the punishment she deserved.

Instead he said, "I approve."

The invisible hand gripping Ax from head to foot relaxed. "My lord?"

"You have demonstrated to me that you are a true servant of the dark side, Eldon Ax. I endorse your plans, and I advise my colleagues on the Council to do the same."

Relief swept through Ax. Coming so soon after her certainty that she was about to die, it made her feel lightheaded. "Thank you, my lord."

Darth Howl raised a hand for silence. "I have just one clarification to make."

Ax's Master looked up at him. "Yes, my lord?"

"The issue at hand is not the security of the Empire. There are a dozen sources from which Dao Stryver could have learned the girl's heritage, including, and not to be forgotten, the girl's mother herself. The issue is not even the world you hope to bring us, although naturally that would be a significant boon to our preparations for war. No, Darth Chratis, the issue is *defiance*. Fifteen years ago, Lema Xandret made a stand against the Sith and escaped the punishment that was rightly hers. Now comes this opportunity to correct that oversight. We must take it in order to demonstrate to all that our strength has only increased, and that we never forgive."

The Council greeted his pronouncement with a murmur of approval. Some eyes glanced at the holoprojector in the center of the room, as though even the absence of the Emperor's image was enough to inspire respect and fear.

Darth Chratis bowed low. "You have my word, my

lords, that an example will be made of the girl's rebellious kin. Their names will be expunged from history, except as an example to those who would defy us."

Darth Howl didn't look at Darth Chratis. His gaze remained firmly fixed on Ax.

"I understand," Ax told him. And she did. This was a test of loyalty as much as it was a mission to punish forgotten traitors. Being a Sith was not just about feeling hatred and anger; it was finding a way to focus those feelings toward the attainment of mastery. Ax said she had forgotten her mother and held her no affection, but when Lema Xandret stood before her and the time came to deliver her rightful punishment, could Ax be the one to administer it?

She swore that she would. There was no affection in her bones for anyone. Not even her Master.

She stood in silent obedience as Darth Chratis confirmed the details of his plan. The Empire would provide him with half a division to command as he saw fit. They would await word from Ax on Hutta before moving on to their final destination. An Imperial envoy would be sent to provide cover for Ax, but that person would play no significant role in the affair. He or she would simply assure Tassaa Bareesh that the Emperor wasn't suspiciously disinterested in the auction of her prize.

"Your ambitions are plain to us, Darth Chratis," Darth Howl told him. "Deliver us this world, and you will be rewarded."

With one last, overlong bow, Darth Chratis took his leave of the Council, and his apprentice followed respectfully two paces behind.

Only when they were in the shuttle did he turn on her. His slender staff clicked open lengthways at one end and the other retracted, forming the crosspieces and handle of his bloodred lightsaber. It stabbed at her face, stopping just short of her skin, and she froze.

"You surprised me in there," he said in a deceptively quiet voice. "Don't ever surprise me again."

She didn't say: *You're a fool. You mishandled the whole thing. If you'd let me talk to you beforehand, instead of raging about my inability to remember anything, I could have told you in advance. Instead of betraying you, I saved you, and our plan, from being dismissed out of hand.*

"I will not, Master" was all she said.

Satisfied with her compliance, Darth Chratis deactivated his lightsaber and stepped away. *Truce,* she thought, *for now.* With a grunt, he settled back to ride out the trip from Korriban back to Dromund Kaas—and from there to Hutta, and the attainment of all their dreams.

CHAPTER 6

"THE HUTTS HAVE created quite a stir," said Supreme Commander Stantorrs, leaning back in his chair and tapping one finger on his desk. "I've received four Senatorial inquiries overnight, and I expect more during the day. Whether this auction is a scam or not, we'll have to do something about it now."

Ula said, "We can't be seen to be sitting on our hands, sir." Obedience and assurance: that was all the Supreme Commander wanted from his aides. A true meritocracy, however, would have demanded much more from its citizens.

"Indeed not!" Stantorrs exclaimed. "When every world in the Republic, from the outlying settlements to the Core itself, is crying poverty, to let a possible source of resources slip through our fingers would be a public relations disaster, not to mention a setback for galactic security."

"When the Mandalorians are involved," said another aide, "it's often a security issue."

"Indeed. And that's why I've decided to pursue this, publicly and politically, to ensure that it can't come back on us later."

The martial rhythm of the Supreme Commander's tapping put Ula on edge. *Give it a rest,* he wanted to yell at them. *It's a smokescreen, a distraction from the real issue—the cold war you're losing! The Hutts are exploiting and feeding your paranoia at the very same time. Don't you see how gullible this makes you all look?*

So wound up was he in his internal dialogue that he almost didn't hear the Supreme Commander's next words.

"That's why I've decided to send you, Ula, to Hutta as an official envoy of the Republic."

Ula's thoughts hit the roadblock of that pronouncement and formed a five-skylane pileup.

"You—what, sir?"

"I need someone to investigate and, if necessary, negotiate on our behalf. Not someone senior—we don't want the Hutts thinking we're *too* interested—and not someone from the military, either, since this is a political matter. We need someone informed and dedicated, and the reports you filed last night indicate that you are nothing if not both. Ula, I want you on the first available shuttle."

The other aides stared at him with undisguised envy as Ula tried to find a way out of the situation.

"I'm flattered, sir, but—"

"Your portfolios are already full, I know, but there's nothing you can't delegate. And if it's security you're worried about, I've requisitioned a full detail. We can't afford to lose someone of your abilities, Ula."

Ula swallowed. Stantorrs had shot down his two major objections in little more than one breath. While it was indeed pleasing that the Supreme Commander afforded him such trust, what use was he as an informer in the wrong sector of the galaxy? He needed to be here, in the office, not mucking around with filthy Hutts and potentially coming under fire.

The gang war that had led to Stantorrs hearing about the *Cinzia* would be just a minor skirmish if the ship's home was as valuable as the Hutts said it was. Of that Ula was certain, and he was an informer, not a soldier, for a *reason*. He liked fighting as little as he liked being in the spotlight. He simply wasn't trained for that kind of thing.

There seemed no way to escape it, though, so he accepted with all the grace he could muster.

"Excellent. I know I can rely on you, Ula. Off the record, I'll expect you to keep a sharp eye out for Jedi, of course. Satele Shan says she'll take no official action, but I don't trust her. You know the major players, don't you? You see one of them, you let me know."

Ula nodded. "I will, sir."

"And if there's any substance to the Hutts' claims, report immediately. I'll have a fleet on standing orders to offer the world protection from the Empire."

"Yes, sir." Like anyone with any political savvy, Ula knew that "protection" was something many worlds simply did not want, for fear of the so-called protectors pillaging natural resources and talent. Also, the mere presence of a Republic cruiser, let alone a Jedi, was likely to draw the wrath of the Sith, who could be even worse. "What if it's nothing?"

"Then we've lost nothing, and you get to keep your promotion." Stantorrs stood and held out his hand. "I'm elevating you to senior aide, effective immediately, and appointing you as acting envoy to the Bareesh Cartel. Congratulations, Ula."

Ula shook the Supreme Commander's hand but barely registered the soldierly crush of the strong Duros fingers. Numb from head to foot, he could barely accept what had just happened. The best he could manage was to find ways to profit from it.

As his former colleagues pressed in to offer their congratulations, he realized that this put him in an ideal position to make sure that the Republic *didn't* gain from the Hutts' offer. He could downplay the importance of any information he discovered—even actively interfere with the auction, if it came to that. Whatever the Hutts had, the Republic wouldn't get access to it.

And then there was the Republic fleet that awaited the outcome of his investigation. If he could send them on a fruitless quest to an empty sector of the galaxy, that could help the Empire in a dozen tangible ways. That the Supreme Commander of the Republic's military forces and parts of the Senate were absorbed in this unfolding drama was also useful. What had started as a minor curiosity could end up playing a deciding role in the conflict, if he was careful.

"When do you want me to leave, sir?"

"Immediately. Your security detail is waiting."

"Thank you, sir."

Ula swallowed his nervousness, made his farewells, and exited the room.

HE DIDN'T GET very far. In the hallway outside the Supreme Commander's suite of offices, a squad of six soldiers awaited him. They wore smart service dress uniforms and saluted on sight of him.

"Sergeant Robann Potannin," the lead soldier introduced himself. "We are your escort, Envoy Vii."

Potannin was swarthy and muscular, and though he was as tall as Ula, he loomed as though from a great height.

"Thank you, Sergeant Potannin. I'll be grateful for your protection on Hutta. What's the arrangement? Shall we rendezvous at the appropriate spaceport when the shuttle is ready?"

"Shuttle departs in one hour, sir."

"Then I'd better get moving, hadn't I?"

He moved off along the corridor, and the squad fell into formation around him. He stopped, and they stopped, too.

"Where are you going?" he asked Potannin.

"Escorting you to Diplomatic Supplies, sir."

"That's not where I'm going. I need to swing by my apartment to pack my bag, and I'm sure I can manage that on my own."

"Negative, sir. All offworld necessities are provided by Diplomatic Supplies."

"But my clothes—"

"Not required, sir. Ceremonial attire is being tailored to your measurements as we speak."

Ula had never seen this side of the Republic administration at work. It was surprisingly, and irritatingly, efficient.

"I have a pet voorpak," he said, improvising wildly. "If I leave it alone, it'll die."

"Not to worry, sir. Provide us with your key and I'll have it cared for."

"No, no. That's not necessary." Ula ran a hand through his hair. Both packing a bag and his imaginary pet were covers for his real intention. He wanted to send a message from his apartment to his Imperial masters, informing them of this sudden development. Otherwise they might worry at his silence.

Luckily, he had prepared for every contingency.

Pulling his comlink out of his pocket, he said, "I'll call a neighbor. She'll look after it. Give me a moment."

He walked a short distance from Potannin and placed a quick call. The neighbor was imaginary, too, but the number was real. It led to an automated message service that was regularly checked by Watcher Three's network of agents on Coruscant. After the tone, he recorded his name and ordered two innocuous dishes from a nonexistent menu. The name of the first dish contained nine syllables, the second thirteen, and those numbers allowed Ula's real message to be decoded from stock phrases every Imperial operative knew by heart: he had experienced an unplanned interruption and would reestablish contact as soon as possible.

At least via the voice-drop his abbreviated message would get through. Who knew when he would find an opportunity to send another?

That thought triggered a whole new wave of trepidation. Bad enough to be in the spotlight, but to be completely cut off from his chain of command was even worse. He could feel his hands beginning to tremble, and to hide that he stuffed them with his comlink into his pockets.

"All right," he said, turning back to the attentive Sergeant Potannin and beaming the brightest smile he could manage. "I'm all yours."

Smoothly falling into formation around him, they marched him off to be outfitted for his new role.

PART TWO

HUTTA

CHAPTER 7

THE GLORIOUS JEWEL of the Y'Toub system rose like a bloated corpse from the bottomless sea of space. Shigar squinted out at it, glad for the first time that they hadn't found more opulent transport. The passenger lounge of the *Red Silk Chances* was filthy, and its viewports barely counted as translucent, but the squalor matched the view. Hutta looked every bit as foul as its reputation suggested, moldy green and brown like a fruit left to ripen too long, bursting with rot from within.

Larin sat next to him, and their shoulders jostled together every time the freighter rattled beneath them. Her face was hidden by the helmet of her increasingly nonregulation armor, but he could tell from the straightness of her spine that she was paying close attention to everyone around them. The droids and lowlifes taking the trip with them warranted it. Thus far there had been two knife fights, several games of rigged dejarik, numerous arguments over the outcome of the latest Great Hunt, and a vigorous sing-along—in a dialect Shigar had never heard before—that had felt as though it might last forever.

Seeking to calm his nerves, he closed his eyes and concentrated on an oddly shaped shard of plastoid in his right hand that he had picked up in the streets of Coruscant as they had waited to board their shuttle. Nothing about it was familiar, so there was no way his conscious mind could guess its origins or purpose. Determining either or both of those was where his psychometric ability was supposed to come in.

About one in a hundred Kiffar were born with this particular Force talent, deciphering the origin and history of objects by touch alone. Shigar's came and went despite his every effort, and it was this lack of control that had at least partly put off the Jedi Council when it came to allowing his trials. Plenty of Jedi Knights had no psychometric ability whatsoever, but all were supposed to intimately know their own strengths and weaknesses. A wild talent of any kind was not acceptable.

Shigar focused on his breathing and let the Force flow strongly through him. The shaking of the freighter and the chattering of its passengers receded. He felt only the complex shape of the object in his palm, and examined the way it sat in the universe without recourse to his usual senses. Was it old or new? Did it come from nearby or far away? Was it precious or disposable? Had it been dropped deliberately or without care? Was it manufactured or handmade? Were there thousands of such things in the galaxy, or was this the only one that had ever existed?

Half-felt impressions came and went. He saw a woman's face—a human woman, with wide-set brown eyes and a distinctive scar across her chin. He pursued that mental scent as far as it went, but nothing more came to him. He let it go, and realized then that he had seen this woman in the old districts, while walking off his anger at the Council's decision. She had been selling roasted spider-roaches to an Abyssin with one eye. His mind had thrown up her face in desperation. She had nothing at all to do with the scrap of plastoid.

A Jedi Knight is a Jedi Knight in all respects, Master Nobil had said. Until he controlled this talent, he could hardly be said to have control over himself. On that point he had no defense.

Frustrated, he opened his eyes and put the scrap back into his pocket. He had a few pockets now, mainly down his chest and the front of his thighs. They added several kilograms to his body mass and jingled when he walked. The unfamiliar textures and cut of his disguise came courtesy of a market on Klatooine, where he and Larin had boarded the *Red Silk Chances* for Hutta. He was still getting used to it.

Through the grimy viewport, the foul world's fifth moon, Nar Shaddaa, was slinking by.

Almost there, Shigar told himself.

"You're a little small for a bounty hunter, aren't you?" a six-fingered smuggler asked Larin.

She turned her head the tiniest fraction. "So what? You're a little too ugly to bc human." Her voice was artificially harshened by the vocoder added to enhance her disguise.

The smuggler only laughed. "You don't intimidate me, girl. I lost my ship playing pazaak in a den owned by Fa'athra. I'm going to ask him for it back, out of the goodness of his heart. What do you think of that?"

The Hutt called Fa'athra was widely known as the cruelest, most sadistic of all.

"I think that makes you stupid as well as ugly."

The smuggler laughed again, his face opening like a wound to expose a bewildering variety of snaggled teeth. Shigar was ready to intervene if the exchange became violent, but the smuggler seemed satisfied by Larin's response.

"Tell your friend here," the smuggler said, leaning close, "that if he really wants to pass himself off as a rancor racer, he'll have to roughen his hide up some. Those guys have a life expectancy of less than five minutes.

You don't last longer than that without some kind of damage."

He turned away to butt heads with someone else, leaving Shigar and Larin to exchange a quick glance.

"I'll put on the mask when we land," Shigar whispered to her. He hadn't wanted to on Klatooine, disliking the grotesque appearance it lent him and the stench of poorly cured leather. "You can say *I told you so* then."

She just nodded. He was glad he couldn't see her expression.

BILBOUSA SPACEPORT WAS crowded with every kind of sentient species and droid model that Larin had ever heard of. The air was thick with spices and a dense mélange of language. As the *Red Silk Chances* disgorged its passengers with nary a pretense of courtesy, they blended into the muddy stream of life as character befit: pushing, shoving, appealing for passage, or simply standing still and waiting for an opening.

Shigar, now clad in the snarling visage of a rancor racer, blended in perfectly.

They negotiated the press as gracefully as possible and chartered a hopper to take them to Gebroila, the city closest to Tassaa Bareesh's palace. There was no need to pass through security or to change currencies. All forms of credits were accepted on Hutta. After checking that Shigar's chip wasn't counterfeit, the Evocii driver swept them recklessly into the never-ending stream of traffic, provoking a dozen potentially fatal near-misses. Larin kept her eyes and attention on the interior of the cab. Their mission was dangerous enough without worrying about everyday threats.

The journey to Gebroila was a long one, and it felt even longer. Hutta's damp biosphere was poisoned by millennia of industrial abuse, making it hazardous even to breathe there. Those few species to survive the Hutts' takeover of the world had mutated beyond recognition. Some, like the hardy chemilizard, had evolved the ability to take sustenance from compounds that might kill an ordinary animal. Others perfected elaborate and expensive chemical defenses, or occupied those few niches that weren't sodden with pollutants. Such niches were vigorously contested, making their inhabitants some of the most vicious in the galaxy.

The Hutts themselves were a prime example of evolution in action. Corpulent and slug-like, their ancestors must have made easy prey on their original homeworld. But environmental catastrophe had forced them to become hardier in several ways at once, developing surprisingly powerful muscles beneath all their flab, and minds to match. They were the original niche dwellers and now formed the summit of the food chain.

Larin rode in silence, very familiar from her time in Special Forces with long periods during which nothing happened. She would have liked to make plans for their arrival in Gebroila, but Shigar was silent, caught up in his own thoughts. She let him be and pondered the matter herself. Security around the palace was bound to be tight, and they had been unable to purchase the right IDs to get in. In a culture of fakes and lies, demonstrating appropriate authenticity was going to be difficult—unless they found a back entrance that wasn't watched from a dozen angles at once. Somehow, she didn't think it was going to be that easy.

THE PALACE WAS as large as the neighboring city. Shigar was both intimidated and reassured by its sprawling vastness. It would be easier to hide behind those ornate walls, among the thousands of servants, penitents, and other enemies that converged wherever money concentrated. At the same time, there would be eyes everywhere. They couldn't afford to slip up once.

Shigar paid their hopper driver and added a substantial tip. The driver was a slave, bound by chains to the vehicle he commanded. Evocii had once been the owners of Hutta, but they were now on the very lowest rung of its opportunistic society. Countless generations of inbreeding had reduced them to a pallid, sickly species. Only outside the cities did their fighting spirit remain, in the form of rebel tribes whose vigor caused the Hutts no end of trouble.

The driver's permanently pained but placid expression didn't change as he pulled the hopper away from the palace forecourt and sped off.

"Now what?" asked Larin.

"We go in."

"Just like that?"

"Just like that."

He led the way up a long flight of steps—their first taste of Tassaa Bareesh's imposition on her guests. She would never climb such an obstacle herself. No doubt she had teams of litter-bearers or repulsorsleds to take her wherever she willed. By forcing visitors to do what she would not, before they even entered her domain, and to suffer for it, she automatically placed them at a lower social level.

Larin was fit. She didn't break stride as they climbed briskly to the guard level, overtaking several other parties along the way. There were three entrances with weapons emplacements mounted over each. Shigar picked the leftmost at random. Four armored Gamorrean guards awaited them, two outside and two inside. Their deep-set eyes regarded every being who approached with equal amounts of suspicion. Behind them, one of the parties they'd overtaken was forcibly pushed back down the stairs, screaming plaintively.

"Are you sure you want to do it this way?" she asked him.

"This is the easy part," he told her. "Watch."

The guards crossed vibro-axes as they approached. Shigar stopped obediently and addressed them in a calm voice.

"You don't need to see our documents. We have the required authorization."

The axes parted, allowing them through.

"Two down," Larin's vocoder crackled.

Shigar repeated the mind trick on the other side of the entrance. Again the axes parted and they walked through. One door up, a loud party of Ortolans did the same, but with official IDs.

"Don't look so smug," Larin said to him. "I can see it even through your mask."

A silver protocol droid stepped out in front of them, backed up by a pair of bug-eyed TT-2G guard droids. "This way, please. Purser Droog will assign you quarters sufficient to your needs."

"That's okay," said Larin. "We know our way around."

"If you'll only allow us to verify your IDs," said the droid more insistently, "Purser Droog will ensure that you are accommodated appropriately."

"Really, you don't need to worry."

"No worry at all, honored guests. You must allow us to show you the proper hospitality."

Heavy emphasis on the word *must* prompted Shigar to look up. Weapons emplacements on the interior side of the wall had tracked to target them. The Gamorreans clearly weren't the only barriers to entry to Tassaa Bareesh's castle.

"Of course," Shigar told the droid, suppressing the slightest sign of concern in his voice. "We don't want to make a fuss."

The droid bowed and led them to a desk, behind which sat an ill-looking Hutt with deep pouches under his eyes. He was busy with the noisy Ortolans, who appeared to have mislaid one of their passports. This was another setback. Hutts were immune to all forms of Jedi persuasion, so that wasn't going to work this time. Shigar thought frantically. Fighting his way in wasn't an option, given the emplacements and the need for secrecy. Neither was fighting his way out, since there were just as many weapons that way. If he didn't think of something else fast, they would be trapped.

Finally, the purser waved the Peripleens on and gestured for Shigar and Larin to approach.

"Kimwil Kinz and Mer Corrucle," he said, giving the Hutt the fake names they had settled on during the journey to Hutta. Cupping his hand over his credit chip, he slid it across the desk as though it were some kind of official documentation. Indicating the backs of the Ortolans, disappearing in a huddle into the palace proper, he added, "We're with them."

The jaded eyes of the Hutt regarded him with a mixture of hostility and disdain. There was no way of telling which way he would fall. Was he automatically loyal to Tassaa Bareesh, who had placed him in this position of responsibility, or was he bored or drunk enough on his own small power to take up the opportunity Shigar presented? The contents of the credit chip were considerable; they represented everything he had been given to fulfill his mission. If he took it, that would be money well spent.

The purser swept up the chip and tucked it into the folds of his body.

"You'd better hurry," he rumbled in Huttese. "They're leaving without you."

Shigar led Larin away, feeling exposed under the emplacements and full of loathing for the Hutts and the corruption they embraced so readily. Most likely, the purser would betray them within minutes of letting them through, but if he could just get out of his direct line of sight, he and Larin could disappear into the palace's throng, never to be seen again.

They walked twenty-five paces without interference. At the first available doorway, he turned left, then immediately left again. When no sound of pursuit rang out behind them, he let the breath he'd been holding escape through his teeth.

Larin heard it. "That went as planned, did it?"

"Precisely," he said with fake cheeriness. "You weren't worried, were you?"

"Not for a second." She shook her head. "Let's find somewhere quiet and out of the way. We need to change the way we look."

They squeezed into a niche and Shigar gratefully rid himself of the mask and a large amount of his leather rancor-riding gear, leaving him wearing just pants, boots, and a tight black vest on his upper body. He felt 50 percent lighter and was grateful to regain free use of his arms. Larin unsealed her helmet and hitched it securely to her belt, then surrendered the cloak she had been wearing and gave it to him to cover his exposed shoulders. Rubbing dust into their cheeks and foreheads, she did her best to make them look as filthy as everyone else they had seen so far.

Shigar felt dirty enough as it was, and not just because of the close, stinking air of Hutta. They were in, and the first real hurdle of the mission was behind them. Now they could get on with uncovering what Tassaa Bareesh had found on the *Cinzia*.

Leaving the rest of his disguise tucked well out of sight, they moved off into the halls of the palace, keeping their ears and eyes wide open for surprises.

CHAPTER 8

AT THE REAR of the palace, where a heavily fortified cliff provided a natural shield against snipers and missile attacks, was a private spaceport large enough for a dozen suborbital transports. Six of the berths were already full when the Imperial envoy approached to land. None was registered to the Republic. One looked like a privateer, bulbous and battered, and extensively blackened across one side as though by a powerful blast.

"Good," said Darth Chratis when Ax communicated that intelligence to him. "We have the jump on the Republic, at least. Any sign of Stryver?"

"None as yet, Master."

"Keep your senses alert for his presence, but remember your place. Your desire for revenge comes second to the orders of the Dark Council. Fulfill them first, then you may act freely. We need to know what was inside the *Cinzia*."

"Yes, Master," she said with all apparent obedience. In her heart she swore to take whatever opportunities arose, whether Darth Chratis approved or not.

The shuttle came down with a gentle thud. Ax would much rather have come under her own direction, in her own interceptor, but her new role forced her to accept some compromises. She unstrapped herself and moved forward to meet the envoy: Ia Nirvin, a dour, capable man who understood all too well that his role in coming events was ceremonial. His credentials were genuine, and the line of credit he had access to came straight out of the Imperial treasury. He was, however, under express orders to make no deals unless Eldon Ax failed in her mission.

"This way, Envoy," she said, ushering him to the rear egress ramp. A welcoming committee had already gathered outside. Nirvin adjusted his uniform, waited until his escort had assembled around him, then exited the shuttle.

Ax came last, striding confidently down the ramp. The security detail surrounding the welcoming party noticed her instantly. She was dressed entirely in black, as befit an emissary of the Sith, and her lightsaber hilt dangled openly at her side. The security detail's uncertainty pleased her. Envoy Nirvin came with the full authority of the Imperial bureaucracy, but who held the real power? Was she bodyguard or puppet master?

A massive Houk approached her. "Your weapon, please."

Ax unhitched her lightsaber, ignited it, and without saying a word removed the Houk's head.

Four more Houks moved forward to force the issue.

"There's no need for such baseless hostility," said Envoy Nirvin, pressing fearlessly between her and the guards. "She comes in peace as my adviser on esoteric matters. Let the matter drop, or I fear we might as well turn back right now."

His words were addressed to the welcoming committee, not to her, and she was glad for that. She didn't care how many Houks she had to kill to make the point to the servants of the Hutts that she wasn't relinquishing her lightsaber under any circumstances.

The welcoming party conferred in hurried whispers, then nodded their acceptance of the situation. Ax waited until the Houks had retreated, though, before deactivating her blade and relaxing her defensive stance.

"Nice to do business with you, gents," she said, following the envoy and his retinue into the palace.

"**TASSAA BAREESH OFFERS** her distinguished guests a most cordial welcome and wishes them a profitable stay in her humble abode."

Hardly humble, thought Ax, eyeing the garish décor of the throne room. What hadn't been gilded was encrusted with jewels or draped in silk. No less then one hundred court functionaries had gathered to welcome the modest Imperial contingent, and she had no doubt that the crowd was a deliberate attempt to impress.

The droid translator, a lanky A-1DO "conehead," did its best to keep up with its mistress's rumbling speech.

"Tassaa Bareesh invites her distinguished guest to take full advantage of the palace's amenities before proceeding to the official program. We have a fine array of baths, restaurants, dance halls, fight pits—"

"We'd prefer to press on," interrupted Envoy Nirvin in a restrained but firm voice. "With all appropriate thanks and gratitude, of course."

Instead of looking offended, Tassaa Bareesh beamed a wide, lascivious smile. The Hutt matriarch was impressively large, sprawling slug-like with short-fingered hands resting on her bulging belly. Jewels gleamed from numerous necklaces and rings, and silk draped across her sloping shoulders, but nothing could hide the repulsiveness of her skin, which was as green and oily as a swamp reptile's back. The matriarch rumbled briefly, then reached for a snack. It wriggled and squirmed uselessly before dropping into the cavernous maw and dying with a crunch.

"Tassaa Bareesh understands your urgent desire to proceed to business," said the translator. "Would you like to view the merchandise?"

"Please."

The Hutt matriarch barked a command. From the crowd of onlookers stepped a tall, bejeweled Twi'lek, who bowed and said, "My name is Yeama. I will be your guide."

Nirvin bowed in return. "If the merchandise meets our needs, we may wish to offer a price immediately."

"Of course," Yeama said, "but I'm afraid we have another party due to arrive shortly. We could not possibly come to any arrangements until they have had an opportunity to see what you have seen."

"When is this other party due?"

"Today, I believe."

"From the Republic?"

"I cannot reveal their identity."

"Can you tell me how many other interested parties there are?"

Yeama smiled with his lips only. "This way, please."

Envoy Nirvin's expression was sour, but he did as he was told. The Twi'lek led him and his retinue from the throne room. They formed a gaudy procession, with Yeama and Nirvin at the lead, accompanied by one Bareesh soldier for every Imperial bodyguard. Ax brought up the rear, glad to be moving again. She tolerated diplomacy rather than enjoying it.

Balancing Ax was the biggest Houk she had ever seen. He matched her stride pace for pace, his expression impassive.

As she left the room, Ax glimpsed an unassuming figure at the back. A human of average height, he wore practical clothes that had seen better days. His salt-and-pepper hair looked as though he had been hauled from bed just moments before. On a street anywhere else in the galaxy, Ax would have ignored him as a matter of course, but in Bareesh's palace he was the only being not dripping with finery. Standing directly behind him was a boxy old combat droid that looked even more battered than he was.

He saw Ax looking at him and glanced away, as though bored.

She turned her eyes forward and followed the envoy.

YEAMA LED THEM through a maze of corridors, each more opulent than the last. Had Ax any interest in paintings, sculptures, and tapestries—or even just the value of such things—she was sure she would have been impressed. Instead, while carefully memorizing the route, she kept her eyes open for tactical information: how many guards stood at each intersection, which areas were covered by security cams, where blast doors were located, concealed or not.

Unsurprisingly, she quickly concluded that the palace was a fortress wrapped up in tinfoil. The Hutts loved their luxury, but they loved their lives more. Tassaa Bareesh hadn't elevated herself to head of a Hutt cartel simply by throwing the biggest parties. She knew how to watch her back, too.

There were weaknesses to every security detail, though. Ax was sure she could get to the matriarch if she needed to. Luckily for Tassaa Bareesh, her mission was simply to steal.

Yeama brought the commingled retinues to a halt in a large circular room under a domed roof distinguished by a chandelier made from thousands of pieces of baroquely curved glass. There were only two entrances to this room: the one they had just come through, with thick armored doors currently standing open under a massive stone statue of Tassaa Bareesh herself, and the other ahead of them, with a pair of doors to match, thus forming a security air lock. Yeama clapped his hands, and the doors behind them slammed shut. Ax kept her hand on the pommel of her lightsaber, even though she knew Tassaa Bareesh couldn't possibly be stupid enough to plan an ambush, and she noted with approval that the envoy's bodyguards had moved in closer around him.

A thud and a clunk came from the doorways on the opposite side of the room. They swung open, revealing an antechamber that was pleasingly devoid of decoration. Walls, floor, and ceiling were a uniform, spotless white. There was easily enough room for everyone as they filed in after Yeama. The antechamber could have held more than fifty humans.

Four circular vault doors opened onto the antechamber, each more than four meters across. Small but very thick transparisteel portals in the center allowed visual access to the contents. Only one of those portals appeared to be unshuttered. It was to that vault door that Yeama led them.

"Here at last, Envoy Nirvin, is the prize you have been promised. But allow me first to describe how it came to be in our hands."

Nirvin glanced through the portal, frowned, and turned back to Yeama. "Do so," he barked.

Ax was too far away to see. She itched to push past them and look for herself, but for the moment she would have to be satisfied with words alone.

"Some of what I am about to tell is known outside this room," Yeama said. "The rest is not. Two weeks ago, one of our affiliates stopped a ship in the depths of Wild Space."

Affiliates, Ax assumed, was a diplomatic term for "pirate." And *stopped* surely meant "interdicted and boarded under arms."

"It was a routine encounter, but it soon took a surprising turn."

"Surprising how?" asked Nirvin.

"Here is the conversation that took place between our affiliate and the vessel."

An audio recording filled the antechamber, rich with breathing, static, and comm crackle. A couple of clicks suggested that it had been edited, but the ambience sounded authentic.

"Stand by for boarding."

That was the affiliate, Ax guessed: experienced, pragmatic, with an edge of tension that belied the Twi'lek's description of the encounter as "routine."

"Negative. We do not recognize your authority."

That was the *Cinzia,* Ax assumed—and here a strange feeling ran down her spine. The speaker was male and sounded impossibly distant. Had he known her mother? Was he related to *her*?

She forced herself to concentrate on the rest of the conversation.

"You're a privateer. You work for the Republic."

"Now, that simply isn't true."

"We're on a diplomatic mission."

"To whom? From where?"

There was a long, static-filled pause.

"All right, then. What will it cost for you to let us go?"

"You're clear out of luck, mate. Best vent those air locks, smartish. We're coming in."

The recording ended with a blast of white noise that made the envoy jump.

"What was that?" he asked.

"An explosion," said Yeama. "The ship our affiliate approached possessed an ion drive of unfamiliar design. It was this that blew, taking the ship and all hands with it."

As though the Twi'lek were reading Ax's thoughts, he added, "We believe that the drive's power cells were deliberately ignited."

"They blew themselves up?"

"Yes, Envoy Nirvin. Rather than be boarded, they chose to destroy their ship and all its contents. Unfortunately for them, the destruction was not complete.

Significant fragments survived. What you see before you are two items retrieved from the detritus. The first is the *Cinzia*'s navicomp, which contains the coordinates of its origin. The second is more mysterious. What do you make of it?"

The envoy peered through the thick transparisteel portal a second time. He frowned once more.

"I've never seen anything like it."

"Our sentiments exactly," Yeama said.

Again, Ax resisted the impulse to push past and see for herself.

"This much we can tell you." Yeama folded his hands across his midriff. "We have detected signs of machining on the outer shell, which is made from an alloy of two extremely rare metals, lutetium and promethium. So it is a construct of some kind, and one of considerable material value alone. On the other hand, there is also a biological component, the nature of which we have been unable to fathom. It is undoubtedly present, we know it's in there, but we cannot examine the source of the reading more closely without physically penetrating the casing. Doing so would, of course, reduce the object's value, so we will leave that up to the ultimate purchaser."

"Can we get any closer?"

"The combination to the vault is what you will be bidding for, Envoy Nirvin. Until you have purchased it, the door remains shut."

The envoy nodded his understanding, but his frown remained intact. Stepping away from the window, he finally waved Ax forward.

"Take a look," he said. "See what you make of it."

Although it rankled to take the administrative puppet's orders, Ax did as she was told, peering with intense curiosity at what lay inside the vault. Finally, she could see what all the fuss was about.

The navicomp was easily identifiable, although it had

been twisted and partially melted by the blast that had destroyed the ship around it. It was a handheld model, unexpectedly small, more resembling a chunky satellite comlink than the heart of a starship's navigation system. Presumably it was voiceprinted, but such security provisions could easily be circumvented by a talented slicer. Ax could only take Yeama's word for whether it still worked or not. It rested in a transparisteel box on a glass plinth to the left of the room's center, and was closely observed by numerous sensors mounted in the vault's durasteel walls, floor, and ceiling.

Sitting on the floor to its right was the second object. Nirvin was correct: it didn't match any design aesthetic she'd ever encountered. It was squat, like a T3 utility droid, but without any legs or visible environmental interfaces. Its body was tubular and rested flush to the floor of the vault. There were no markings apart from a series of almost gill-like ripples around its middle. Its head was slightly convex, as though it had been pushed down from above, and part of it was scorched black. The natural color of its casing appeared to be silver. No writing, no symbols, no identifying markers at all.

Ax didn't know what it was, either, but she didn't say so immediately. Taking the opportunity to inspect the interior of the vault in more detail, she memorized sensor emplacements, estimated the strength of the walls, and measured the distance of each object from the door, just in case she had to perform in the dark. It would be much better, of course, to take the prize once it was out of the vault and away from all these impediments, but she would be prepared for anything.

"It could be a bioreactor," she said to the envoy, returning control of the window to him.

"Plague agents, perhaps?"

"Hard to say without opening it."

"Indeed." Nirvin turned back to Yeama. "Is that all you have to show us?"

"All?" The Twi'lek showed his teeth. They were as pointed as the tips of his lekku. "I will escort you to a waiting room, where you may examine data relating to our find in perfect comfort."

"Very well." Nirvin indicated that Yeama should lead the way.

Ax fell in behind them, with her huge Houk shadow at her side. The objects in the vault didn't speak to her either as a Sith apprentice or as the biological offspring of Lema Xandret. The plague bioreactor, if such it was, provoked no memories at all.

The sparse information they had been given told her only a little more. That the object was made from an alloy of extremely rare metals boded well for her Master's dreams of giving the Emperor a rich new world, but it meant nothing in itself. With the crew of the *Cinzia* dead, there were no leads to follow there, either, unless she could uncover something that had been hidden by the Hutts—like a survivor, perhaps, or another clue as to the ship's origins. She didn't put it past Tassaa Bareesh to auction only half of what they'd found while keeping something extra in reserve, to sell to the auction's losing party.

Yeama took them out of the antechamber and back into the circular security air lock, where the heavy doors cycled again. From there, Yeama led them along a new set of luscious corridors in the direction of the no doubt equally luscious waiting room.

Ax made it her business to be elsewhere. Confusing her Houk escort with a well-placed mind trick, she slipped away from the group and vanished into the shadows.

CHAPTER 9

ULA ENDURED TASSAA Bareesh's welcoming spiel with ill-disguised contempt. Cordiality and profitability made untrustworthy bed partners, particularly when honesty and ethics weren't invited, too. When his host promised him an array of amenities including chemical enhancements and even more dubious forms of entertainment, it was all he could do not to spit to get the bad taste out of his mouth.

"I think we can dispense with all that," he said. "Why don't we just get down to business?"

Tassaa Bareesh's slit-like grin widened even farther, if that were possible.

Her pointy-headed protocol droid assured Ula that Tassaa Bareesh understood completely.

She waved forward an underling, a salacious-looking Twi'lek, who took over negotiations from that point. The Twi'lek promised that they would soon see the legacy of the *Cinzia*. As Ula was led from the throne room, he glimpsed a scruffy-looking man leaning up against the rear wall with a blank look on his face and a battered orange droid close at his shoulder. The man's ennui had a manufactured air, and it was this that caught Ula's eye.

"Who was that fellow back there?" he asked his guide.

"Which fellow?" Yeama didn't even glance over his shoulder.

Ula described him, not yet willing to give the matter up. Being a good informer meant taking nothing for granted and noticing all the details.

"Grayish hair, prominent nose, brown eyes—with an old droid."

"Oh, no one in particular," the Twi'lek assured him. "A pilot whose ship is currently berthed here. He has the favor of my mistress, and therefore the run of the palace."

"What's his name?"

"Jet Nebula, Envoy Vii. You won't have heard of him."

That was true. It didn't even sound like a real name. But he wasn't fool enough to take Yeama at his word. The Hutts and their servants were natural liars. Like him.

He filed the name away in his memory.

YEAMA TOOK HIM through several ridiculous security measures in order to introduce him to the cause of all this fuss. A navicomp and a battered bit of space junk—it all seemed an utter beat-up as far as he could tell, although that in itself was something of a relief. If the charade amounted to nothing, it would soon therefore be over. Nonetheless, he attended carefully to the details and asked the questions expected of him.

"No survivors, you say?" he asked after hearing the last transmissions from the *Cinzia*. "How can I be sure your *affiliate* didn't murder them and concoct this mad story to cover the deed?"

"The fate of the passengers is irrelevant to us," Yeama answered. "We would not lie to spare your sensibilities."

That Ula believed completely, and it revived the moral outrage he had felt at being in the court of a Hutt. Tassaa Bareesh's venal tactics only confirmed his low opinion of her kind and his hopes that they would be undone, somehow. The Hutts were walking a very fine line. The more valuable the items they were auctioning, the more they could obviously charge—but how long until one or another party simply walked in and took them?

He wondered if either side had just such contingencies in place. Supreme Commander Stantorrs obviously suspected so, with respect to the Jedi, and there had been no chance to ask Watcher Three if the Emperor had sent someone other than an official envoy. A Cipher Agent, perhaps, capable of far greater feats than a mere informer such as himself. Ula had glimpsed an Imperial shuttle in the dock at the rear of the palace, so he knew he wasn't the only envoy Bareesh had entertained that day.

It had occurred to him on the way that the Imperial envoy wouldn't know that the Republic envoy was actually a traitor with no intention of winning the auction for his so-called masters. If he could only find some way to communicate that message, it might save the Emperor a great deal of trouble and expense . . .

Yeama was speaking again. "The auction will be held tomorrow, with all parties present. You will be bidding for the combination to this vault. The safety of all parties is our primary concern, so the process will be anonymous. I will take you to your secure accommodation now, and you may examine the data there overnight."

"If the bidders are anonymous," said Ula, seeing his chance of getting a message to the Imperial envoy slipping away from him, "how will we know that the bids are genuine?"

"How indeed?" said Yeama, with a knowing smile. "I advise you to bid fairly, so you can be sure that the winning bid reflects the prize's true worth."

Thieves and liars and economic rationalists, thought Ula as Yeama led him to the embarrassingly lush hospitality center. *To chaos with the lot of them.*

ANALYZING THE DATA took the better part of an hour. The *Cinzia* shown in recordings taken by Bareesh's pirate had been a light star cruiser of unfamiliar design, but Ula's sharp eye detected hints of an Imperial chassis under a refurbished hull. It could have been an old S-class model, stripped down and rebuilt from the inside out. The drives had a similar signature, although their emissions had been baffled somehow. Fragments of the hull collected after the explosion showed high proportions of rare metals—similar to those of the object sitting in Tassaa Bareesh's vault. Nothing about the ship gave any hint as to its origins.

A world rich in exotic metals would be a prize indeed, Ula thought as he scoured the data for clues. Perhaps his trip hadn't been for nothing after all. Such rare substances were the backbone of many industries, from communications to war. Shortages had delayed many projects crucial to the Empire's expansion already, including some so secret that he heard of them only through reports issued to Supreme Commander Stantorrs by Republic spies. His own side didn't trust him to know.

"It's all a game," he muttered to himself, pushing the holovid away from him in frustration.

"Is anything the matter, Envoy?" asked Potannin, standing to attention by the entrance to their suite.

"Oh, nothing, Sergeant," he said. "I'm just tired."

"Would you like to retire? You have a choice of beds—"

"I don't think I'll sleep tonight."

"You have received several invitations from other parties in the palace, sir. If any interest you, I could make arrangements."

"Would that be safe?"

Potannin's angular face displayed confident assurance. "I would hazard a guess, sir, that so long as the Hutts propose to profit from us, we're in the safest place in the galaxy."

"True." Ula thought for a moment. "All right, then. Let me see the list."

He scanned it quickly, glossing over minor ambassadors, ambitious crime bosses, and several beings whose intentions were even less honorable. One name caught his attention.

"Jet Nebula, that pilot with the ridiculous name who has free run of the palace. What does he want from me?"

"I couldn't say, sir. But he's invited you for a drink in a cantina called the Poison Pit."

"Sounds unpleasant."

"Shall I turn them all down, sir?"

"Yes. No, wait." There had been something odd in Jet Nebula's disaffected stance, and in his placement in the welcoming hall. If he was truly so bored, why had he put himself in a position from which he could study everyone in the room?

"Tell Nebula I'll meet him in half an hour."

"Yes, sir."

Ula picked a refresher at random and changed his robes for something more sensible. The ones Diplomatic Supplies had provided him with made him feel like a clown. And besides, he didn't want to stand out. If he was going to discover who this Jet Nebula really was—or at the very least, what he knew—he would do it dressed properly.

Before he left the refresher, he took the compact holdout blaster he'd packed and slipped it into his breast pocket. Just in case.

THE CANTINA WAS as bad as he had anticipated, with alien and human lowlifes clustered in twos and threes over pots of dense-looking brown beverages. A complex roar of ever-changing frequencies blasted the space, performed by a quintet of Bith; Ula could only assume they considered the noise they made to be music.

He exchanged a glance with Potannin, who stationed watches at both entrances and put the three remaining soldiers at strategic points around the cantina. Their presence alone caused some patrons to pick up their drinks and stagger elsewhere.

Jet Nebula occupied a dark corner, sprawled across a low padded lounge with his head tipped back and his battered droid standing protectively at his feet. The glass in front of him was empty. As Ula approached, Jet's head came up and fixed him with the same stare he had been using earlier that day.

"Nice duds," he said.

Ula felt his face turning red. Diplomatic Supplies' idea of "sensible" amounted to a mock-military uniform in purple, with meaningless epaulets and insignias on every available surface. He had taken off the baubles, but there was nothing he could do about the color except drape a gray cloak across his shoulders and hope for the best.

"You wanted to talk with me," he said, cutting right to the chase.

"That depends, mate. Are you buying?"

"Is that all you're after—a free drink?"

"So what if I am? A man's got to take it where he finds it, in my line of work."

"Which is?"

"Can't you guess? It takes a faker to know a faker."

A cold chill ran down Ula's spine. What was Jet saying? That he knew Ula was an informer? Was he going to blackmail him for money—or worse?

Jet smiled and scratched lazily at his chin. "All these questions are making me thirsty. How about you send your man to buy us a round of Reactor Cores and we'll talk like proper gentlemen."

Ula had no choice but to agree. On the off-chance Jet did know something, he didn't want it revealed in front of his security detail.

Ula gave the orders, and the droid tottered off after Potannin. He sat down, ignoring the sudden weakness in his knees. "What do you want?"

"I've already told you, and you're already providing."

"I'm not talking about alcohol. Be more explicit."

"If you can't figure it out, then you're no use to me."

"What do you mean?" Ula felt his indignation rising, but before he could lash out in return, something occurred to him. "Wait a minute. Yeama said you had the favor of Tassaa Bareesh. What are you doing down here cadging drinks off me?"

Jet said nothing.

Ula examined everything he knew about Jet, and found a clutch of previously disconnected facts taking a surprising new configuration in his mind.

"That's your ship in the dock," he said, "the one with the blast damage. You ordered a smuggler's drink. You said *faker* because of what *you* do, not me."

" 'All politicians are liars,' " he said, "to quote Chancellor Janarus."

Ula didn't laugh at the paradox. "You're the pirate who found the *Cinzia.*"

"I prefer *freight captain,*" said Jet, "but I am that fellow." He executed a mock-bow from his slouched position on the lounge. "The Hutts don't forget who their friends are."

"You don't look like you're enjoying yourself."

"What's not to like? My ship's impounded, and I can't leave the palace. I'm in paradise."

Ula leaned in closer and whispered over the table, "Is that what you want to talk to me about? If so, I don't have the authority to—"

Jet waved him silent. Potannin had returned with the drinks. They were large, murky, and dangerous looking. Jet raised his, blew off the scintillating foam, and toasted the Republic.

Ula echoed the toast and took a sip. Electric fire burned a skylane down his throat and caused a slow detonation in his stomach.

"Are you all right, sir?" asked Potannin.

"Yes, Sergeant," he managed. "Leave us for the moment. But stay close." *In case I need a medic . . .*

"Yes, sir."

The security detail moved respectfully out of earshot.

"Not your usual?" said Jet with a sly smile.

Ula normally didn't drink at all, but he wasn't about to admit that. "I can get word to my superior, if you want to arrange an extraction, but—"

"That's not why I invited you here. I just think someone should know what really happened to the *Cinzia* in Wild Space that day."

Ula's curiosity was roused by that. "I've already heard the recording and seen the data. Are you telling me there's more?"

"Much more. Drink up and listen."

So began a long and rambling tale about rivalry and betrayals among smugglers. Ula paid close attention at first. Jet had been worse than a smuggler: he had been a privateer hired by the Republic to scour the fringes of the inner galaxy for theft-worthy matériel to assist the Republic cause. That was interesting for two reasons. It confirmed reports suggesting that the Republic did indeed engage in this inglorious tactic. It also showed how easily the objects up for auction could have fallen right into the Republic's possession. The intervention of the Hutts had, for once, worked to the Empire's advantage.

Ula felt a little discomfited by that. He believed that civilized society should never allow such decadence and corruption to thrive. That the Republic traded with the likes of Tassaa Bareesh was evidence, if he needed it, of his enemy's invalidity to rule—but what did it say about the Empire if he allowed it to profit by similar means?

As Jet talked on, Ula's attention began to drift. Who cared about the invidious Shinqo and whether he had been allowed to leave the palace or not? What did it matter if Jet Nebula felt poorly used by his new masters, who had no intention of sharing the massive profit they were bound to make from the auction with anyone else? Why was he wasting his time on such a self-absorbed, self-pitying display?

Sip by sip, Ula worked his way through the drink. Jet didn't appear to be touching his much, and that puzzled him, distantly. By the time the smuggler finished describing the sad end of the *Cinzia,* Ula's eyesight was beginning to get a little fuzzy.

"Say that again," he said, finding it strangely hard to keep his elbow planted on the table. "Something about diplomomo—ah, diplomats."

"They were on a diplomatic mission. I asked them who to, and they didn't answer. Doesn't it make you wonder? Both the Republic and the Empire are bidding for information on where these people came from and what they were carrying. If the crew of the *Cinzia* weren't coming to talk to either of you, who were they coming to talk to?"

That was an interesting point. Ula filed it away to think about later, when the floor stopped wobbling.

"Then there's the explosion."

"What about the explosion?"

"Well, it was a bit overdramatic, wasn't it? But at the same time, it wasn't very effective. You'd think if they really wanted to make the point, if they'd cared enough to kill themselves, they'd have gone out of their way to do it right."

"You would think so. You would," Ula agreed. "But what if they argued? What if not everyone wanted to be blown up? I wouldn't want to be."

"That's a good point, Envoy Vii," Jet said. "I hadn't thought of that."

Ula was developing a strong liking for Jet Nebula, despite the fact that he appeared to have grown an extra head. "Another round?"

"Wait," said the smuggler, sitting up straight all of a sudden. "Something's not right."

Ula looked around. It had become very quiet without him noticing. The Zelosian band was making no noise anymore. The cantina's patrons had all slumped over their tables. Some of them were actually snoring into their drinks. Even the bartender was sprawled across the counter, twitching slightly.

As he watched, Sergeant Potannin sagged forward and fell bonelessly to the floor.

That couldn't be right, Ula thought. Since when did anyone in a security detail get drunk?

"Obah gas!" Jet was on his feet with a blaster in his hand. "Clunker!"

The battered droid came instantly to the smuggler's side, its photoreceptors glowing bright.

"Good. Keep an eye on the door. I'm going to—"

A sharp crack came from behind them. The droid tottered, enveloped in bright blue bolts of energy. A whining noise came from its innards. It froze, a restraining bolt projecting from the side of its head.

"Don't move, Nebula," called a vocoder-enhanced voice from Ula's right.

Ula turned in time to see a section of the ceiling fall away. The head and shoulders of a Mandalorian projected from the hole. The rifle he held was aimed squarely at Jet's chest.

"Stay where you are, Envoy Vii. This doesn't involve you. Put the blaster down, Nebula—now."

The smuggler obeyed. "If you wanted to cut in, all you had to do was ask."

With an elegantly muscular flip, the Mandalorian landed feetfirst on the floor below him. "Your droid will recover. So will the bystanders. I used enough gas to knock them out, no more."

"Lucky we were drinking Reactor Cores," Jet said.

"Why do you think smugglers order them so much? They taste awful, but they grant immunity to all sorts—"

"Enough talk," said the Mandalorian, indicating with the rifle's business end that Jet should step out from behind the table.

"Are you at least going to tell us who you are?" asked the smuggler.

"I know," said Ula, although he was still struggling to think through the narcotic drink. "You're Dao Stryver. What is it you want with Lema Xandret, exactly?"

The Mandalorian's attention turned squarely to him, and suddenly Ula felt completely sober.

"You, too," said Stryver, swinging the rifle. "You're both coming with me."

"Or what?" Jet asked.

"You don't want to know 'or what.' Get moving."

Too late Ula remembered the hold-out weapon in his pocket. He staggered to his feet and was propelled at blasterpoint from the cantina, Jet Nebula gray-faced at his side.

CHAPTER 10

THE SIGHT OF a distinctively rounded, low-chinned helmet brought Larin to an abrupt halt. With an urgent wave of her hand to signal to Shigar to stay under cover, she backpedaled into a crowded corridor and stayed there until the Mandalorian went safely by.

A second glance told her that it wasn't Dao Stryver. This one's armor was silver and blue, not gray and green, and Stryver was both taller and more massive. People moved out of the way.

She grabbed a passerby at random. "Who was that?" she asked, indicating the receding helmet.

"Only Akshae Shanka," said the mousy Evocii, as though she were an idiot. "Stay away from him, if you know what's good for you. He's come second in two separate Great Hunts."

"And I bet that hasn't improved his mood," Larin muttered as the slave hurried away. While the Mandalorians waited for the next big war to break out, they amused themselves by ritual fighting among themselves, drawing in anyone foolish enough to show an interest in their violent ascendancy games. They were dangerous and unpredictable in all things except one: having returned to the galaxy during the Great War, they weren't going to slink away again anytime soon.

Larin waited a full minute to make sure Shanka didn't

come back, then she moved back out into the flow of the main branch and waved for Shigar to follow.

They were following information gleaned from one of the palace's chefs. Two high-security visitors—the Republic and Imperial envoys, Larin and Shigar assumed—were being housed in one of the luxury wings deep in the heart of the rambling structure. It was difficult to get into those parts of the palace, but they'd learned of a shaft connecting the underlying service routes—like the one they were following at the moment—and the high-security basements. Getting from one to the other was taking time, but thus far it wasn't proving to be especially difficult.

Larin led the way, following the map she had memorized and keeping her eyes firmly forward. Shigar was hard on her heels, somewhere; she was sure of that, although she couldn't see him. He walked as lightly as an Alderaanian swan and vanished into a crowd like a puff of smoke. When she stopped at the next junction to check her bearings, he simply appeared beside her, as if from nowhere.

"Almost there," he said. "I'll take point for the next leg."

"All right," she said. "But I've been thinking: why are we going this way in the first place? Shouldn't our priority be the vault?"

"It would be, if we knew where it is. When we reach one of the envoys, then we'll have our guide. We know they've both seen it. Asking the right people is always better than asking at random."

She heartily agreed with that. They'd learned a lot by mingling with the palace's downtrodden staff, but every important piece of information they had gathered came with a wealth of worthless trivia. Sorting the one out from the other had taken more time than either of them would have liked.

"After you," she said, waving him ahead of her. It was her turn to trail after now. A pair of people walking side by side always drew more attention than individuals in a crowd. Surrounded by unknown serfs and servants, they blended in, passed by, and were instantly forgotten. That was something Akshae Shanka would never manage.

THEY REACHED THE entrance to the subterranean shaft without incident. There, Larin tripped a passing Gamorrean into a heavily laden Evocii, and during the resulting distraction Shigar activated his lightsaber and cut through the door's massive security bolt. Rusty hinges groaned as he swung the door open; no one noticed over the shouts and recriminations. The argument was barely reaching its peak when Larin crept in after him. Together they pulled the massive door closed.

It was much quieter on the other side, and darker, too. Shigar took a deep breath, glad to be out of the multispecies press and the poverty they endured. He had glimpsed the luxuries lavished on those at the top of the social pyramid on Hutta. He knew what privileges they enjoyed. All around him was the cost, in filth and sentient misery.

That the underbelly of Coruscant was exactly the same gave him some pause in blaming the Hutts. Perhaps it was simply the nature of things. Perhaps Master Nobil's rebuke was well earned. How could the Jedi Order change something that had endured for millennia? It wasn't the Council's brief, not when the Emperor's wolves were snapping at the galaxy's throat.

A faint yellow light flared into life. "Straight ahead, then left, wasn't it?"

Larin's voice echoed sibilantly in the miles of metal pipe ahead of them. By the light of her blaster rifle's utility torch, he raised one finger to his lips and nodded. She rolled her eyes and said, "There's no one down here. That's what we were told."

He shook his head and indicated that it was her turn to lead. *Better not to take any chances,* he thought.

Larin moved off at a cautious lope through the tunnel. The pipe was dry and empty, and easily large enough for them to stand upright. They could have run side by side if they'd wanted to. Occasionally the ceiling was interrupted by pipes and clusters of cables, forcing them to duck, and on two occasions they had to jump across a shaft, but apart from that there were no interruptions.

They reached the junction in fifteen minutes. As Larin approached, Shigar reached out for her shoulder. With a firm grip, he pulled her to a halt.

She looked at him inquiringly. He put one hand over the rifle's lamp, extinguishing the light.

All was black for a moment; then a dull glow appeared. The sound of faint movement echoed around them. Someone was in the tunnel, just around the corner.

Shigar moved forward, hardly daring to breathe. Through the Force, he sensed three organisms in a cluster, but not clearly enough to identify their intentions. If they were lying in wait, why the light? If it wasn't a trap, why the silence?

He eased his head around the corner. Three large, horned figures stood in a cluster around a lamp, looking up at the ceiling and scratching their heads. They were clearly Hortek, which explained why they weren't talking: they were telepathic. Furthermore, the thick work uniforms they wore and the tools scattered at their feet explained what they were doing in the tunnels. They were a maintenance team, and therefore perfectly innocent.

Shigar took a moment to reassure Larin, then closed his eyes. His telepathic powers were modest at best, but they had been enhanced under the Grand Master to the point that she could convey simple concepts to him without speaking. The Hortek were receptive to outside thoughts and vulnerable to Force persuasion. If Shigar could combine the two, he could easily get rid of them.

He found the focus required with surprising ease. The practice on the way to Hutta had done him good. Within moments, the Hortek picked up their tools and moved off.

"Nice one," whispered Larin when the sound of heavy footsteps faded away. She eased around the corner and flicked the light to its lowest setting.

"It gets tougher from here on," Shigar said, unhitching his lightsaber hilt. "Let's not get complacent."

"Hey, look at this." Larin had the light aimed up at the ceiling, where the Hortek had been working. Something had burst through the shaft's metal wall, melting it. Several silver threads dangled down like strands of web. Larin blew gently on one of them. It swayed stiffly from side to side. "That looks like wire."

"It can't be," said Shigar. "It's getting longer."

Larin pointed the light at the bottom of the thread. Its terminus was visibly extending lower.

"Growing," she said, "or extruding?"

"Doesn't matter, either way," he said. "What's going on up there is none of our business."

"In a Hutt's palace," she said, "I'd call that a lifesaving philosophy."

THE FIRST SECURITY drone they encountered was a metal sphere that dropped whirring out of a chimney, sprouting weapons as it came. Larin downed it with one shot, beating Shigar by a bare millisecond.

She blew imaginary smoke from her blaster. "You'll have to do better than that to beat, uh, me."

She'd almost said *to beat the Blackstars,* but caught it in time. She didn't want him to wonder what one of the

Republic's elite commandos was doing skulking about with him in the bowels of Tassaa Bareesh's stronghold. Just thinking about telling that story punctured her confidence. Still, what they were doing felt like old times, and the mental state was surprisingly easy to fall into. The brashness, the boasting, and the belligerence—alongside the running around dark places and shooting things.

"Stay alert," said Shigar. "There'll be more of those."

"I was born alert," she said, not ready to abandon the old-time feeling just yet.

The second security drone whizzed out of a side tunnel, flashing its lights and issuing a warning to stand still. Shigar caught this one, spearing it through the middle with the blade of his lightsaber.

"Not so fast that time, were you?"

She smiled.

They moved cautiously. Drones were a danger, but their presence meant that they were nearing their objective. The luxury wings were almost as heavily protected as Tassaa Bareesh's sleeping chamber.

The shaft began branching and doubling back on itself. Shigar navigated them unerringly—she hoped—as drones converged on them like millflies. Their reaction times improved with practice until the drones barely had time to appear before being destroyed.

Then a drone three times as large as the others hummed down the shaft toward them, shooting rapidly. Shigar spun his lightsaber like a shield, reflecting its own fire back at it. Gesturing with his hand, he brought down part of the ceiling and crushed the drone under rubble.

"We don't want to do that very often," he said when the dust cleared.

"People are bound to notice when the floor caves in under them."

They picked their way over the pile of fallen masonry.

"Up here," said Shigar, spying something ahead.

She followed close behind him. There was a ladder mounted firmly in the wall, leading up into a vertical shaft.

"You're sure this is the one?" she asked.

"As sure as I can be." He tested his weight on the rungs. They held without complaint. "I'll go first."

"Don't kill anything until I get there," she said.

THE SHAFT LED to a basement filled with barrels of oil buried under two centimeters of insect shells and dust. It looked as though they hadn't been touched for decades. Shigar moved lightly through them, leaving barely a footprint. Larin was nearly as stealthy, and she was a sharp shot with that snub rifle of hers. Several times he had been tempted to ask why she had been wasting her time in Coruscant's old districts, but he didn't want to pry. Behind the banter, she was tight-lipped. If there was something he needed to know, she would tell him eventually, he was sure.

Be kind, Master Satele had said. He had thought very carefully about that instruction. It had to apply to Larin, the young woman he had already rescued once, from the Mandalorian. Was it a kindness, though, to be ripped out of your home and plunged into the middle of someone else's war? Some would have thought not. But he sensed in Larin a corrosive rootlessness that could poison her if it wasn't counteracted. On Coruscant she was just another disenfranchised person caught up in food riots, separatist uprisings, and corruption. What she needed was direction, a purpose. He could give her that much, temporarily, if she wanted it.

The basement of barrels delivered them to a door that had been welded shut. His lightsaber soon disposed of that obstacle. They entered a narrow, musty stairwell that led them up, level by level, to a cellar that was currently in use. A team of Evocii was busy unloading crates of delicate foodstuffs into an expansive cool room. They were far too busy to notice the fleeting figures that ran past them, into the kitchens.

Larin found a closet, and Shigar lured a relatively well-dressed slave in after them.

"We are guests of your mistress," Shigar told her, encouraging her acceptance of the lie by means of a gentle nudge through the Force. "Obviously, we've lost our way."

"You're a long way from the throne room, sir."

"Do you know where the two envoys are quartered?"

"Yes, sir. I work in the laundry detail and am frequently called upon to attend those areas."

"You'll be happy to remind us how to get there."

The Evocii provided a detailed description of the two suites. They were practically side by side, with entrances facing in opposite directions. The suite belonging to Envoy Vii of the Republic was closer.

"Ever heard of this Vii fellow?" Larin asked him in an aside.

Shigar had to confess that he hadn't. "Politics is my Master's business."

"It should be everyone's business."

"Between you and me, I agree completely."

Shigar interrupted the slave, who had descended to ridiculous detail in her efforts to help. "You'll give us access codes to the secure areas, too, in case we've forgotten them."

"Yes, sir, but not to the suites themselves. I don't know what they are. The guards can help you with that when you get there, I expect. They will know you, of course . . . ?"

"Of course," Shigar reassured her. "You don't need to worry about that."

"No, sir. I don't need to worry about that."

The Evocii obediently gave them all she knew, and Shigar committed it to memory.

"Before you go," he said to her, "I want you to know that it's unsafe down here today. Find somewhere to hide, and stay there until the fuss dies down. You don't want to get hurt."

"I don't want to get hurt."

"That's right."

The slave left the closet and hurried off to obey his command.

"Ready?" he asked Larin.

"I was born ready."

"You've already done that one."

"I have? Well, you'd better tell me where to shoot before I embarrass myself further."

They eased out of the closet and hurried through the well-appointed corridors. It made a pleasant change not to be kicking up dust and running through cobwebs. Instead, fragile vases and statues lined the corridors, and Shigar took great care not to damage anything unnecessarily. Someone had made these things. The preservation of culture was among a Jedi's many missions.

They came to the checkpoint the Evocii slave had described. Five Houk sentries guarded the entrance to the Republic guest quarters. That was more than expected. Larin took in the situation at a glance, and communicated her strategy to Shigar with a series of brisk, concise hand gestures. He nodded, happy to take her lead.

She rolled out from cover and came up on her knees, firing into the shoulders of two of the Houks. They toppled backward. Shigar leapt past her, using his blade to defend both of them. A third Houk went down, struck by a bolt from his own weapon, deflected back at him from Shigar's lightsaber. That left two. Larin took a close burn from one of them and retaliated with two shots to the chest. Shigar sliced the remaining one's arm off.

He stood still in a defensive pose in the curling smoke, ready to strike again if any of the fallen so much as twitched. Larin moved lightly to his side, unhurt by the near-miss, although her shoulder now boasted a new charcoal patch.

"No alarm," she said with satisfaction. "We got them all in time."

"The door will be locked. See if you can get through without triggering anything."

She knelt down by the lock and took off her helmet while he kept an eye out for passersby. A stream of precision tools came out of the left thigh hatch of her armor. She applied them one by one to the lock mechanism, humming softly as she worked. Shigar was about to ask how much longer she would be when she pocketed the tools, stood up, and touched the access panel.

The door slid open, surprising two Houks on the other side. Shigar deflected their blasterfire while Larin neatly dealt with them. Then they hurried into the suite and closed the door behind them.

The scene awaiting them was utterly unexpected.

A gaudily dressed Twi'lek was standing over the bodies of a Republic security detail. He reached for a communicator, but Shigar whisked it out of his grasp with a quick Force pull.

"What's going on here?" Larin asked in crisp, commanding tones. "What have you done with the envoy?"

"I?" The Twi'lek looked mortally affronted. "These creatures came to harm through no action of my own. They were found this way, drugged, in a cantina. The envoy is missing."

Larin pressed the barrel of her rifle under the Twi'lek's chin. "You're lying."

"The envoy is an honored guest, invited here solely to do business! We bear him no ill will!"

"He's got a point," Shigar said.

"That doesn't mean I have to like it." She reversed the rifle and clubbed the Twi'lek across the head. He dropped like a stone. "You stay there while I double-check your story."

Shigar closed the door behind them and locked it again. Larin pulled one of the fallen bodyguards up to a couch and lightly slapped his face. "He's got a pulse. That's a start."

Before she could do the man any serious damage, Shigar came to help, lowering the bodyguard's head onto a cushion before trying to wake him up.

One hand stayed on the cushion. The other cupped the bodyguard's forehead. Concentrating, Shigar nudged the flow of the Force through his body, encouraging wakefulness.

The bodyguard twitched and opened his eyes in alarm. There was a tearing sound as all the spines on his scalp shot out. The cushion absorbed them all.

"I'm sorry to startle you," Shigar said in calm voice. "You've been drugged. My name is Shigar Konshi. This is Larin Moxla. Grand Master Satele Shan sent us to aid you." That wasn't entirely true, but as an explanation it would do.

The man pushed him away and sat up. He ran his hand across his scalp and cleared his throat.

"My apologies for attacking you. I am Sergeant Potannin. Where is Envoy Vii?"

"We don't know," said Larin. "We were hoping you could tell us."

Potannin shook his head. "We must have been ambushed. Envoy Vii was talking to a man who works for the Hutts. His name is Jet Nebula. And there was someone else—a Mandalorian."

"What Mandalorian?" Larin asked, leaning close. "Do you have a name?"

"I don't remember." He looked at Larin and Shigar in appeal. "We have to find the envoy."

Shigar nodded. An active Dao Stryver on Hutta would

be an unexpected complication, but it wasn't necessarily a disaster. The primary mission could still continue.

"All right," he said. "You and Larin look for the envoy. If the Twi'lek is telling the truth, the Hutts will help you."

"And you?" asked Larin.

"I'm going to check out that vault. What you can't learn from the envoy, I'll find out there. Sergeant Potannin, will you give me directions?"

Potannin provided a comprehensive description of the route from the luxury suite to the vault, via a security air lock. Shigar committed it to memory.

"Did you see what was in there?"

"There's the *Cinzia*'s navicomp and an artifact Envoy Vii couldn't identify. Made of some weird metal." Potannin looked apologetic. "I'm sorry, but that's all I know."

"No matter." Shigar wished Potannin had learned more. Ancient Sith and Jedi relics could sometimes be identified by their markings. "I'll take a look myself and see if I can figure it out."

"Are you sure you want to do this alone?" asked Larin before he set out.

"I have my comlink," he said. "I'll call you if I get into trouble."

"You'd better." She touched his arm briefly, and then pulled away. "See you later, either way."

Shigar left her and Sergeant Potannin to wake the others. With lightsaber at the ready, he eased back into the ebbs and flows of Tassaa Bareesh's palace and counted off the intersections, one at a time.

CHAPTER 11

DARTH CHRATIS'S VOICE carried faintly across the thousands of kilometers separating him from his apprentice.

"Did you see any Jedi in the Republic envoy's party?"

"None at all, Master." Ax could hear the disappointment in her own voice. She'd been looking forward to fighting something more challenging than the inept palace guards. "If they're here, they're maintaining a very low profile."

"It's clear, then, that they plan to steal the artifact before us. Otherwise they would be visible. Your orders are unchanged. You must move quickly to ensure you get there first."

"It will be difficult, Master. The doors are massive, and there are bound to be alarms—"

"That's for you to worry about. Fail me and you will report to the Council yourself."

The line clicked shut, and Ax smiled in the darkness. Darth Chratis was as transparent as glass. If she succeeded, he planned to take the credit; if she failed, the blame would be hers. But some of the tarnish would inevitably rub off on him if she *did* fail, halting his plans for advancement. It was amusing, therefore, to keep him nervous. That made him predictable.

Barely three minutes had passed since she had set the

charges. They were old, leftovers from a mining expedition that had abandoned its gear in one of the palace's three warehouses, but she had taken enough of them to knock a small chunk out of a hill. If the timers worked properly, Tassaa Bareesh's guards would soon have something to occupy their attention.

Meanwhile, she had crawling to do. Plans of the vaults sliced from the palace's mainframe showed that they were freestanding structures with their own power and air supplies. Surrounding all of the broad durasteel boxes was a meter of clear space, filled with laser trip wires. If anything got past the trip wires and simultaneously touched both box and wall, a circuit would trip, sounding an alarm loud enough to wake the Emperor himself on Dromund Kaas.

The plans also showed that the vault was held in place by a series of repulsors, powered by induction coils at the base of a ferrocrete cradle. Ferrocrete was relatively easy to cut through with a lightsaber. Ax wormed her way through tiny crawl spaces to a position directly under one corner of the vault containing the remains of the *Cinzia*. Wiring schematics showed no cables at that point. All she would have to do was wait for the distraction, cut her way upward, disable the trip wires, and leap across the gap. Within the hour, she hoped to be touching the outside of the vault with her bare fingertips. From there, she would play it by ear.

She slithered like a rat through spaces that were barely large enough for her to breathe, angling awkwardly around sharp corners and edging with her toes and fingertips. She held her lightsaber ahead of her, ready to cut through any serious obstacles. The air was thick with dust and smoke. She blinked frequently to clear her eyes.

A subsonic *boom* came through masonry surrounding her, followed quickly by another. She held her breath as the palace shook, and pressed outward with the Force, just in case something heavy shifted into her. A series of smaller booms reverberated when the charges triggered a chain reaction in the palace's primary reactor, as she'd hoped they might. She imagined the Hutts and their slaves scurrying to find out what had happened. Whether they did or not didn't matter to her. Neither did she care if the secondary reactor restored power immediately. The vault was self-contained. Keeping her hosts distracted was her primary objective.

Another minute's crawling brought her to the place she needed to be. The crawl space was broad enough for her to squat, and she did so, holding her lightsaber pommel before her. Closing her eyes, she ignited it and raised the blade slowly into the ceiling above her. Ferrocrete bubbled and hissed; stinging flecks struck her skin. When the hilt was flush with the ceiling itself, she stopped.

The power of the dark side flowed through her, raising the temperature of the ferrocrete to scalding. She breathed lightly through her nose, not caring if she was scalded. A red glow surrounded her, radiating from the surface above. She maintained her concentration, forming a self-protective bubble about her as the ferrocrete became molten and began to drip.

The bubble rose gently through the lava, delivering her without further effort to the space under the base of the vault. When the bubble broached the top of the molten ferrocrete, she lowered her lightsaber and opened her eyes. By the red glow she made out the durasteel vault through the top of the bubble and a tangle of cables that was part of the ferrocrete structure around her. They remained entangled as the lava cooled. Not one of the cables had been cut, so in theory no alarms should have sounded.

Almost there.

Only the trip wires remained. She raised her head carefully out of the cooling bubble, but didn't see any sign of lasers anywhere. They should have been clearly visible in all the smoke, but not one glowing line broke the view.

Intrigued, she placed her gloved hands on the still-warm lip of the bubble and raised herself bodily into view.

No alarms. None other than those caused by her explosions, anyway. Against all expectations, the vault's external security system appeared to be disabled.

Could the Jedi possibly have beaten her to the prize?

She crouched in the space under the vault, next to one of the repulsors holding the massive structure above her head, and reactivated her lightsaber. By its ruddy glow, she made out the lenses of the laser system staring blindly at her. They hadn't been physically interfered with, at least. She reached up and touched the base of the vault. No footsteps or other obvious movements from within. That was another positive sign.

An unexpected detail gave her further reason to be cautious. The midsection of the vault had been physically connected to the cradle beneath by a series of silver wires. She approached them, careful not to snap them. Their purpose was unknown, as was the way they had prevented the second alarm system from going off. As soon as the vault was penetrated, all of Tassaa Bareesh's palace should have known.

Something unexpected was going on, and she didn't like it.

Ax deactivated her lightsaber and sat cross-legged on the hot ferrocrete. If someone deactivated the repulsors, she would be squished like a bug. Quashing that thought as best she could, she cast her feelings out into the space around her, searching for signs of anything out of place.

The vault, first of all, was uninhabited, apart from the faintest glimmer of biological activity inside the anomalous artifact recovered from the *Cinzia*. She took the opportunity to examine it this way, and felt a rare shiver race down her spine. What was *in* there? The tiny life signs were clustered in four groups, but they didn't feel like minds, exactly. And something about them made her instincts recoil.

My mother made this, she couldn't help but think. *My mother, who should be dead.*

Putting all speculation on that front firmly from her mind, Ax examined the antechamber and the other three vaults, next. It was possible, albeit exceedingly unlikely, that an entirely independent thief had targeted something in one of the other vaults, shutting down hers in the process. A quick scan proved that theory false. There was no one out there at all.

She almost gave up there, chiding herself for overreacting. The distraction she had created wouldn't last forever. And she didn't want Master Chratis to worry *too* long. Part of the point of telling him that the mission would be difficult was to surprise him when she pulled it off quickly. The thought filled her with anticipatory satisfaction.

Before rising, she cast a quick mental look through the circular security air lock outside the antechamber.

Her face twisted into an immediate scowl. Jedi! She would recognize that humorless and inhibited mental stench anywhere. A single specimen had bypassed the alarms and burned through the locks on the outer door. That was impressive work, but he wasn't moving fast enough. She could cut her way under the vault and up into the antechamber long before he had the inner door open. And then, when he did, he would get a whole lot more than he bargained for.

Grinning, she moved from cross-legged to a crouch, and began melting her way through the last barrier standing between her and her enemy.

CHAPTER 12

DAO STRYVER USED a dense, adhesive web extruded from a nozzle on his left cuff to lash Ula and Jet into their seats. The dining room he had led them to was empty, containing nothing but chairs and a table, but as befit the palace of Tassaa Bareesh these were fine examples of precious materials and design, and therefore too sturdy for the prisoners to break.

Ula's head was pounding with the aftereffects of the Reactor Core, but he noticed the gleam of metal revealed when Stryver welded the door shut. Durasteel, most likely, also befitting the palace of a Hutt. All manner of safety-conscious criminal celebrities might have eaten in this room. And died here, possibly.

Ula tested the bonds and found them to be immovable. His fingers were already going numb.

"You know my name," said the Mandalorian, standing over him. "How?"

Trying and failing to suppress a stammer, Ula described the report received by Supreme Commander Stantorrs from Grand Master Satele Shan. That was where the Mandalorian had first been identified to him. He had no compunctions about revealing the extent of the Republic's knowledge, since it would assure Stryver that little else had been uncovered about him or Lema Xandret.

"Will you untie me now?" Ula asked him.

"The only reason you are still alive is because there is

no honor in killing you—and no advantage, either." The Mandalorian towered hugely over him. "That could easily change."

Ula fell back into his seat and closed his mouth.

Jet sat in the chair next to Ula, staring unflappably up at their captor.

"I assume you know me from somewhere," he said. "Did I ruin your sister's reputation? If so, I'm afraid she was quite forgettable."

Stryver didn't rise to the bait. "Captain Nebula, I'm told it was you who spoke to the crew of the *Cinzia.*"

"Who said that?"

"A former crewmate of yours called Shinqo."

"He'd say anything to get your blaster out of his face."

"My assessment precisely. Is what he told me true?"

"How do you know I'm any different from him?"

"I'll be the judge of that."

"Why you want to know? What's so important that you'll go halfway across the galaxy to find it out?"

"Just answer my questions, Nebula. What did they tell you?"

"Do you mean 'what' or 'how much'?"

Ula didn't understand why Jet was making things more difficult than they had to be. "I've heard the recording," Ula said. "They didn't say anything to him."

The Mandalorian turned back to him. "What were their exact words?"

"That they were on a diplomatic mission and didn't want to be boarded."

"Did they mention any names?"

"None."

"Could the recording have been edited?"

"I suppose it might have been, but—"

"Be silent." Stryver turned back to Jet. "Does the name Lema Xandret mean anything to you?"

"If that's your sister—"

The butt of Stryver's blaster dug into Jet's throat. "Do not play games with me. She was an Imperial droid maker who disappeared fifteen standard years ago. Was her name mentioned by anyone aboard that ship?"

"No," Jet said. "And there were no survivors, if you think she was aboard. Shinqo told you that, I'm sure."

"He told me there was wreckage and that you gave it to the Hutts."

"Why would I do something like that?"

The muffled boom of an explosion rocked the floor, making Ula jump. Dust rained from the ceiling. Stryver pointed his rifle at the door, ready to fire on anyone who burst through it, but the blast had come from much farther away. A second quickly followed the first, and the lights flickered. Distantly, alarms began to sound.

"The palace is under attack," said the Mandalorian. "There is no time now for prevarication. If you know what survived the explosion, you must tell me."

There was something in the Mandalorian's voice, a rising urgency that made Ula speak out of more than just self-preservation.

"I've seen it," he said. "It's in a vault not far from here."

"What is it?"

"There are two things, and they're both for sale. The *Cinzia*'s navicomp—"

"Intact?"

"So I was told."

"And the other item?"

"I don't know what it is."

"Describe it."

"Silver, tubular, about a meter high—made of rare metals and some kind of organic component. No insignia. Do you know what it is?"

The Mandalorian fiddled with his armor and projected

a tiny holovid of the palace grounds. "There are seven maximum-security vaults in Tassaa Bareesh's enclave. Tell me which one contains these two items."

"Why?" asked Jet. "It's just space junk."

"You did not believe so," said the Mandalorian.

"I'll sell anything, or try to."

"If you release my hand," said Ula, "I'll show you which vault it is."

"You're not after this mystery planet as well, are you?" asked Jet, rolling his eyes as Stryver loosened the web restraining Ula's left hand. "Unless—ah! Yes. Unless you want the navicomp for an entirely different reason."

Stryver ignored him. "Point," he said, holding the holovid out to Ula.

"Bring it a bit closer. That one there, I think."

As the Mandalorian studied the floor plan, Ula slipped his hand into his pocket and produced the hold-out blaster.

He listened to himself speak calmly and without fear, as though he were standing outside his own body, watching what was going on.

"Release my other hand," he said, pointing the blaster at Stryver's stomach. "I'd prefer to talk as equals."

Stryver pushed the holovid into Ula's eyes, blinding him. Ula squeezed the trigger, but Stryver was too fast. With one sweep of his other arm, he swatted the blaster away. The single shot discharged harmlessly into the ceiling.

"Nice try." Jet chuckled as Stryver reaffixed Ula's hand to the chair. "You've never dealt with his kind before, have you?"

Ula was having trouble seeing the funny side. The fear had come crashing back in. His eyes were still dazzled, and his hand felt like it was broken. "How can you tell?"

"Mandalorians don't believe they *have* any equals."

* * *

LARIN SLICED INTO another layer of the palace security program and conducted another search. Dao Stryver's name still appeared only once: his ship, *First Blood,* was docked in the palace's private spaceport. Mentally, she kicked herself for missing something as obvious as that, but she didn't lose any time over it. The architecture of the palace's security programs was even more baroque than the palace itself. Even if she had thought to search for the Mandalorian's name, chances were it wouldn't have appeared the first time.

"Anything?" asked Sergeant Potannin, who was peering worriedly over her shoulder.

She shook her head. Searches on Ula Vii's name had turned up nothing as well.

"You're blocking my light." Potannin was trying to be helpful, but he was no Shigar. "I'll holler when I've found something."

Pulling another decryption algorithm from her repertoire, Larin tried another route.

Behind them, the Twi'lek, Yeama, entered the missing envoy's suite and sketched a bow. The bump on his temple stood out in bright red against the green of his skin.

"My mistress offers her profound apologies. The hunt for the kidnappers and those who attacked your sentries will begin immediately."

Larin scrambled the holoprojector's view so Yeama wouldn't see what she was up to in his mistress's security infrastructure.

"You have a Mandalorian loose in the palace," she said, "and you didn't know about it?"

"He is one of many. They do not like to be watched too closely."

"Now you know why. Perhaps you'll think twice about the kind of scum you're dealing with."

Yeama stiffened. "And you are—?"

"Does it matter who I am? I'm helping you find the envoy. What are *you* doing?"

The Twi'lek turned an unhealthy color, even for his species. "Everything in our power, naturally—"

"Good, so hop to it. We're busy here."

Yeama retreated and Larin de-scrambled the view she'd been looking at.

"There's a whole other layer down here," she muttered, marveling at the intricacies of the system. Either it had evolved piece by piece, as each new development added an extra level to what was already there, or it had been designed by the galaxy's most paranoid software engineer.

Still no luck with *Dao Stryver,* however. And *Envoy Vii* didn't produce a hit. If either of the two men was moving about in the palace, none of the security system's pattern recognition systems was tracking them.

Larin was beginning to get desperate. This was the one job she had to do, while Shigar attended to the rest of the mission, and she was failing at it. Proving herself capable wasn't the issue—she knew she was, or had been, at least, otherwise she would never have been in Special Forces. Getting a score on the board was the main thing, after so long on the bench.

In desperation, she tried "Jet Nebula."

Instantly a hit appeared. Not just a location, but a coded tag she recognized as a smuggler's call for help.

"Got something." Potannin hurried over. "You said Envoy Vii was with that Nebula character, didn't you? Well, I've found him, at least."

Potannin clapped his hands together and grinned without humor. "Good work, Larin."

He turned to the escort squad and rattled off a series of orders. Half would stay; the other half would come with him. Larin had to fight the reflex to obey. Had she remained enlisted in the Blackstars, Potannin would have outranked her.

"I'm coming with you," she told him as his group assembled, checking weapons and light armor.

He nodded. "I was just about to ask you, Larin. Thank you."

"Don't mention it, Sarge."

"Take point, and lead the way."

Her face was burning as they hurried through the corridors, the echo of their booted feet preceding them, encouraging the throngs to part. This was too familiar, she told herself—dangerously familiar. She couldn't let herself think that she was back in the fold. If they found out who she was, they would turn on her, just as the goons on Coruscant had. Better to stand apart, for the future's sake.

They had almost reached the location on her holopad when an explosion shook the ground beneath them, followed by another a short time later. She called a halt, wondering if they were walking into a trap, but the blasts didn't come any closer. The lights dimmed for a second, then brightened. The palace's generators, she guessed—damaged either by sabotage or by accident.

The inhabitants of the palace hurried to find shelter. They didn't scream or panic. They simply gathered up their valuables and loved ones and went somewhere else. Such things were clearly not uncommon on Hutta, Larin gathered.

"Nearly there," she said, waving the squad forward again. She moved more cautiously as she approached the flagged location. Just because someone had blown up the power plant didn't mean there wasn't a trap ahead.

The map grid correlated with an industrial-sized but very empty kitchen. Larin fell back and let Potannin take the lead. His squad spread out silently to check every hiding space, communicating solely by gestures. They were well practiced and efficient, yet they turned up nothing but a battered old droid who had taken shelter from the fuss. After scanning it for munitions, they let it alone. It returned to the corner it had been lurking in, watching them silently.

"No sign of Envoy Vii," said Potannin, stating the obvious. "Are you sure this is the right location?"

"I'm positive. The flag said Nebula was here and in some kind of distress."

"He must've been here at some point, in order to leave that clue, but now he's been taken elsewhere."

"There's no evidence of a struggle . . ."

A disturbance distracted Larin from the search. The droid had stepped out of its corner and was gesticulating wildly.

"Someone quiet that thing down, will you?" barked Potannin.

"No, wait." Larin approached it, closely watching every move it made. "I recognize the signals it's giving. They're from the civil war. It's saying . . ." She searched her memory for the correct translation. It had been a long time since she'd taken The History and Use of Military Languages during her Special Forces training. "He's saying *he* left the flag for us to find. Not us specifically, but anyone who could help him. Reinforcements. He followed his Master—Nebula, I presume—via a transponder of some kind, probably hidden in Nebula's clothes or body. He's trying to mount a rescue, but . . . but he lacks the resources to complete his mission objective."

The droid nodded, and she addressed him directly. "Who has captured Nebula? A Mandalorian?"

The answer was yes.

No wonder, Larin thought, the droid had been looking for reinforcements. "Is Nebula the only prisoner?"

The answer was no.

"Do you know where they are?"

An emphatic yes. The droid took Larin around to the corner, where he'd scratched a detailed map into the metal wall. She recognized that location from her own data. It was a dining room not a dozen meters away.

"I think we can help each other," she told the droid, who nodded solemnly. "Weapons ready," she told the squad. "This Mandalorian is big and dangerous. If you get a shot, take it. But watch out for the prisoners. We can't afford to harm the envoy."

The droid tapped her firmly on the shoulder with one square, metal finger.

"Or Nebula," Larin added.

They took their safeties off and fell in around her. Only when they were moving, with the droid taking the lead, did she realize that she had given the orders, not Potannin, who had obeyed along with the rest of his squad. That made her feel both guilty and pleased, although technically, she supposed, she had no rank now, which meant she had no superiors to worry about. That was the thought she clung to as she ran to face Dao Stryver for the second time.

IT WAS ULA'S turn to have the Mandalorian's rifle wedged under his chin. He arched his back as far as it went, but the barrel followed him, digging deep into his throat. He was so close to Stryver now that he could hear the whir of his suit's many mechanisms, even the hiss of air through its respirator as the Mandalorian drew in a breath to speak.

"Answer this question very carefully, Envoy Vii," Stryver said.

Ula nodded. After his solitary act of defiance, he had no intention of doing anything other than exactly as he was told. His eyesight still sparkled from the dazzling effect of the holoprojector shoved into his face.

"I will."

"You pointed to a location on the map. Was the vault you indicated the correct one?"

"Yes."

"It contains the wreckage recovered from the *Cinzia*?"

"Yes." He nodded as vigorously as he could to convince Stryver of his sincerity.

The pressure of the rifle fell away. Ula rocked forward, chest heaving. He hadn't noticed that he'd stopped breathing.

"And you?" Stryver asked Jet. "Do you have any more questions?"

"What, me?" The smuggler watched the weapon closely. It was aimed right at his chest. "Just one. What now? I can't help commenting that you've welded yourself in here with us . . ."

Something thudded against the sealed door. Stryver and his two captives turned to look at it. The thud came again, and a faint voice calling:

"Open up!"

The Mandalorian turned away and busied himself with his suit, stowing his rifle and pushing buttons with swift, practiced movements.

"I can assure you," said Ula, "that I have very little value as a hostage."

Stryver said nothing. As a bright red line began creeping across the reinforced door, the Mandalorian stepped away from them and looked up. A rising whine came from his backpack.

"I suggest closing your eyes," said Jet, turning his head toward Ula and shielding it as best he could with his shoulder.

There was a flash of light. Smoke and debris filled the

air. The whine became a roar, and at that moment the door burst in.

Ula ground his eyelids shut on a cloud of stinging particles. He heard shouts and blasterfire, and felt bodies moving rapidly around him. Something crashed into him, and he felt gloved hands working at his bindings.

"It'll be all right, sir," said a familiar voice. "We've got you covered now."

Potannin! Ula could have wept.

When he opened his eyes, the smoke had cleared along with the sparkles from the holoprojector, and Dao Stryver was nowhere to be seen. Two members of Ula's escort stood guard over the door, while two more picked through the wreckage. The droid Stryver had disabled was pulling Jet free. A soldier in scruffy white armor was peering up into a giant hole in the ceiling, her rifle held at the ready.

Stryver had never had any intention of going out the door, Ula understood. His plan had always been to go up.

The scruffy soldier turned to him. "What did Stryver say to you? Did he tell you what he was looking for?"

"He's gone to get the navicomp," said Jet, wiping dust from his eyes.

"Why? Are the Mandalorians after the same thing as we are?"

"I don't think that's the only reason. The navicomp wouldn't just show the ship's origin, would it? It'd show the intended destination as well."

The soldier's helmet cocked slightly. "What difference does that make to anyone?"

"Not to anyone, I'm guessing. Just to him."

The soldier nodded. "Are you Nebula or the envoy?"

"Call me Jet."

Ula staggered to his feet, freed at last from the Mandalorian's sticky web. "Ula Vii, at your service. Thank you, all of you, for rescuing us. Both of us."

"It's our duty, sir," said Potannin with a brisk salute.

"Me," added the soldier, "I'm just here for the fun of it."

With that, she slipped her helmet off, revealing the most beautiful woman Ula Vii had ever seen.

CHAPTER 13

UNDER A MASSIVE statue of Tassaa Bareesh, Shigar sealed the outer door behind him, using the Force to assist the hydraulics he'd damaged on the way through. He recognized this type of room; the inner door wouldn't open until the outer door was closed. He crossed the circular expanse of the security air lock, noting but not being distracted by the gentle tinkling of the glass chandelier above. The air stank of smoke, which was odd. The mysterious explosions had been distant, and he assumed the air-conditioning system of the vault was completely independent.

His senses prickled. Moving slowly and silently, he approached the inner door.

It was unlocked.

There was one thing he would say about the Hutts: when it came to protecting their valuables, they didn't scrimp. The door was a marvelous piece of machinery, precision-tooled to very precise measurements. It might not withstand a Jedi and his lightsaber, but it would keep a horde of safecrackers busy for a month, and would easily withstand a small nuclear blast.

It certainly wouldn't open itself.

Shigar deactivated his lightsaber and stood still for a full minute. His slow, shallow breathing and steady heartbeat were all he could hear. If there *was* anyone on the other side of the door, they were being as quiet as he was.

Reaching out a hand, he tugged on the door's handle. So well balanced was it that it swung smoothly aside, revealing the antechamber he had been looking for. The four vault doors were exactly as Sergeant Potannin had described. None of them had been interfered with. Behind one of them was the mysterious wreckage that consumed so many people.

In the center of the room, a black pit had been burned into the floor, scarring its otherwise impeccable whiteness. That was where the smoke was coming from. He approached cautiously and looked down. Someone had burned into the room from below, presumably to steal the vault's contents. But how had they avoided triggering any alarms? And where were they now?

He looked around. The antechamber was empty. There was nowhere to hide. None of the vaults appeared to have been tampered with. All four doors were sealed. There was no other way out, except back through the hole, or—

The small of his back itched. He turned to face the door he had come through. Certainty filled him. Activating his lightsaber, he strode into the air lock room.

"You don't look like a Jedi, but you sure smell like one." With a tinkling smash, a skinny girl dressed all in black dropped out of the chandelier. Her hair flailed in thick red dreadlocks like the tentacles of a living thing. "You stink of *repression.* Let's see what we can do to change that!"

The girl activated a brilliant crimson lightsaber.

Shigar didn't return her bloodthirsty grin. He kept his heartbeat steady, raised his lightsaber in return, and adopted a stance of readiness.

She came at him in a storm of blows, feet moving lightly across the floor, almost dancing, blade swinging like a propeller. Their weapons clashed with a furious electric sound. He matched her move for move, but doing so sorely tested him. Every block jarred through him like a hammer blow. His opponent was small, but she was strong, and her eyes were full of hate. The dark side flowed through her in powerful waves.

She drove him back to the room's inner door and, with a telekinetic sweep, slammed it shut behind him.

"Nowhere to run now, Jedi," she gloated. "Why don't you stop fighting defensively and show me what you've got? I'm going to kill you either way, but let's at least make some sport of it."

Shigar ignored her. He knew that some Sith used verbal attacks alongside physical ones to dispirit their opponent, but he would not fall victim to such a ploy. Neither would he allow fear or anger to dictate the way he fought. His Master had trained him well. He knew how to fight a Sith—and that was the same way he would fight anyone. The key was to make fewer mistakes than your opponent, and to take every opportunity when it came. The element of surprise could make the difference between a drawn-out battle and a decisive early victory.

Smiling calmly, he faced the snarling girl and reached out his left hand.

AX HEARD THE sound of glass tinkling from behind her and ducked barely in time. Hundreds of tiny shards rushed at her, ripped out of the chandelier by the power of the Jedi's mind and hurled at the exact spot she had been standing. A second stream followed her as she rolled and flipped away, pushing off with her hands and landing on her feet halfway across the room. Recovering her poise, she wrapped a kinetic shield about her and flung the shards away. Only a handful got through, one cutting her arm and another putting a bloody gash over her left eye. She blinked blood away, relishing the sharpness of the pain.

The tall, skinny Jedi was coming for her, green blade foreshortened by a strong, stabbing blow aimed at her midriff. She swept it aside, only to find that the move was a feint. He aimed a kick at her right knee and brought the blade sweeping around for her head. With a grunt, she took the kick on her shin and saved herself from decapitation only by reducing the hold on her hilt to one hand. Their lightsabers met just centimeters from her skin.

They locked there for a moment, his blade pressing down toward her face, her left leg twisted behind her, in a difficult position to use her weight against him. He was physically stronger than she, and wasn't above taking advantage of that fact. One solid push and his blade would be burning more than air.

He was stronger, but she was more cunning. Whirling his cloak around his face and throat took barely more telekinetic energy than it did to think of it, and the move had the effect she needed. Taken by surprise, he reeled backward, clutching at the flapping fabric. She retreated only long enough to regain her footing and balance before moving in again, while he was blinded.

Even without the use of his eyes, he still matched her. He anticipated her moves and blocked them one-handed. His other hand tore at the cloak, fighting its strangling folds. When he finally threw it away, he faced her two-handed again, lips pursed and bare-shouldered, and she knew that the game was really on now.

They fought back and forth across the room, slashing and blocking and leaping and running, using walls, floor, and ceiling as launching pads for each new attack. Glass crunched beneath their feet and swirled around them in distracting, potentially blinding streamers. He was good—she had to grudgingly admit that—but she was good, too, and she fought to the very edge of her abilities. Her mission wasn't going to end here, skewered on a Jedi's lightsaber. If Darth Chratis was going to stand before the Dark Council and admit that he had failed, then she was going to be there to see it.

The end came unexpectedly for both of them. She had tuned out the sound of alarms and the distant aftershocks of her sabotage, but she remained alert for everything in her environment, just in case her sparring partner tried something new. When a noise came from the other side of the air lock room's inner door, she initially dismissed it as a ploy to distract her. She had sealed her ferrocrete tunnel behind her, so no one could be coming up that way, and there was no other entrance to the vault.

The sound came again—a muffled metallic thud—and this time she caught the Jedi's reaction to it. He was distracted, too. His eyes flicked to the sealed inner door.

In that instant she struck.

Her ability to produce Sith lightning wasn't fully developed yet, and she didn't dare hope that it could overwhelm anyone with Jedi training, but she used it anyway, blasting her opponent with everything she had. He caught it badly, as though he wasn't used to facing such attacks—and it occurred to her only then that he was an apprentice like herself. Like her, this could be the first time that he had faced his enemy alone. Unlike her, he wouldn't live to learn from the experience.

He staggered away, flesh tortured and smoking. She maintained the surge as long as she could, and followed it with two quick strikes to midriff and throat. He barely blocked them, swinging one-handed, holding his other arm across his eyes as though the light blinded him. Thrilled by his weakness, Ax lunged again and again, driving him backward until he hit the wall. He slid down it, blade raised ineffectually to block the killing blow.

His comlink squawked.

"Shigar, watch out. Stryver's on his way. He's after the navicomp!"

Triumph turned to all-consuming hatred. Dao Stryver—here!

It was her turn to be surprised.

With one swift kick, the Jedi, Shigar, knocked the lightsaber from her hand. It skittered away, blade flashing and deactivating automatically. She staggered backward, disarmed, and he came to his feet, eyes bloodshot and full of determination. Not hatred. Not anger. She didn't even have the satisfaction of that small victory.

She ran backward, Force-pulling her fallen hilt to her even though she knew it couldn't possibly arrive in time. The Jedi followed her, driving her toward the outer door.

When the door burst in behind her, she didn't need to look to see who was there. She felt his presence as keenly as a dagger in her back.

Dao Stryver.

Caught between a Jedi apprentice and a Mandalorian who had already beaten her once, all she could do was hit the activation stud and hope for a miracle.

CHAPTER 14

LARIN WAS HALFWAY to the vault when Yeama intercepted her. He was standing in the deserted passageway ahead with his hands upraised in the universal signal to halt. She would have pushed right past him had he not been backed up by five Weequay and a dozen ax-wielding Gamorreans.

"I see the missing envoy has returned," he said, taking in the group behind her with baleful red eyes. "The pirate, too. My mistress will be pleased."

Larin didn't have time to discuss the situation. The thought of Shigar facing Dao Stryver alone filled her with urgency. It might already be too late. Her attempts to hail him on the comlink had prompted nothing but silence in reply.

"Thank her for her concern," she said. "We're returning the envoy to his quarters now."

"Are you? Excellent. You may have heard the, ah, occasional disturbance in the last hour. There is nothing to worry about, I assure you of that, but it would be advisable for you to remain in the high-security wing until told otherwise."

"Sounds like you're under attack, mate," said Jet. "Has Fa'athra made his move at last?"

The Twi'lek smiled tightly. "We have many items of great value stored in the palace, so attacks are not uncommon."

"It's not coming from outside," said Larin, growing impatient. "It's the Mando I warned you about earlier. He's after the *Cinzia*'s navicomp."

"Impossible. No alarm has been raised in that sector of the palace."

"That's bound to change, and soon."

Hefting her rifle, she went to continue on her way.

"Not so fast." The Twi'lek sidestepped in order to block her path. The Weequay backed him up. "You are going in the wrong direction. The envoy's quarters are that way."

"Really? It's easy to get turned around in here."

"I don't believe you're turned around at all. I believe you know exactly where you're going." The Twi'lek wasn't smiling now. "You are not a registered visitor to this palace. The kidnap was a distraction, giving you time to go about your true business. We found the trail you left in our security systems. The sabotage is another distraction. What is your business now? Are you all in league, or just opportunistic collaborators?"

His cold gaze swept the group before him.

Larin didn't like where this was heading.

"Look," she said, "we're not planning to steal your precious things. But someone else is, and we're trying to stop them. I'm serious. Dao Stryver will be in and out before we get there if you don't step out of my way right now. Don't make me make you."

The Twi'lek didn't flinch from her ultimatum. "You admit that you are heading for the vault?"

"That's what I just told you."

"And yet you insist that your motives are pure?"

"As pure as they'll ever be."

"Then you won't mind if I advise the Imperial envoy to meet us there?"

"Whatever! Just get moving—that's all I ask."

Yeama signaled his entourage, who fell in around her

and her companions. Once the way was clear, she set a brisk pace while Yeama growled in his native Twi'leki into a comlink.

Behind them, the Republic envoy put up a sustained display of bluster.

"I resent the implication," he said, "that this is a conspiracy of any kind. If anything, it is I who should be suspicious. I'm the one who has been kidnapped and had my escort neutralized. I've been imprisoned and tortured—under the roof of a host whose servant now calls me a criminal! You'll be lucky if we stick around at all for this sham auction of yours."

Yeama ignored him, and so did Larin. Still nothing from Shigar.

"No alarms," she said to the Twi'lek. "And in the middle of all this fuss, too. Doesn't that strike you as odd?"

Yeama looked at her for a full three seconds. His only other response was to pick up the pace and begin barking orders into his comlink again.

ULA MAINTAINED HIS diatribe long enough to ensure that his point had been made. It wasn't even *his* point. He was playacting the loyal Republic envoy in a difficult situation. Wasn't that what one should do?

Ula didn't know. He was light-years out of his depth and heading farther out by the minute. He wished they really were going to his secure quarters rather than rushing headlong into danger. All that stopped him from asking to be exempted from the coming action was the thought of how Larin Moxla would regard his cowardice. She didn't seem the type to brook anything of the sort.

He couldn't take his eyes off her. Everything about her—from her beaten-up armor to the black tattoos across her cheeks—captivated him.

"Don't even think about it."

Ula glanced at Jet. He was also watching the remarkable woman who had come from nowhere to lead their mismatched ensemble.

"What do you mean?"

"She's no good for you, and vice versa."

Ula flushed. He'd had no idea his instant fascination with her was so obvious.

"What are you talking about?" he said, lowering his voice so no one could overhear. "You know as much about her as I do."

"I know she's faking it. And that's about the only thing you two have in common."

Again that sly hint that Jet thought Ula was more than he was saying. Or less, if his tone of voice was anything to go by.

"What exactly are you suggesting?"

"Me? Nothing. I'm just making conversation."

That rapidly became difficult. Their pace was increasing by the minute. Soon they were jogging alongside Potannin and the security detail, with Weequay loping long-legged beside them and Gamorreans struggling along behind. More palace security personnel joined them, Niktos and Houks mainly, forming an ever-growing caravan heading toward the vaults. It was hard to see what lay ahead past the Twi'lek and Larin, but it looked like there were further guards waiting for them. And more than that, besides.

At the entrance to the security air lock lay a scene of utter demolition. Walls had fallen in; the ceiling had collapsed. Tons of stone and reinforced ferrocrete lay between them and their objective. Evocii slaves and security guards picked at the rubble, getting in one another's way such was their haste to clear a path. Conflicting orders flashed back and forth. Yeama hurried into the mess, trying in vain to impose order.

"This is outrageous," announced a high-handed voice over the hubbub. It was a tall, long-nosed man in Imperial uniform, shouldering his way toward the Republic entourage. "If you've had a role to play in this fraudulent affair—"

"We've as much to lose as you," snapped Ula, wishing he could take his fellow Imperial aside and reveal to him the secret role he was playing. There was no need to argue, except for appearance's sake. "And are as much in the dark."

From the other side of the rubble came an explosion, crisp and floor shaking. Ula put his hands over his ears and backed away. Two enormous dirt-moving droids shouldered forward to plow through the mess.

"Stay here," Larin ordered him, and he was happy for the moment to obey. She joined Yeama in the wake of the heavy lifters, clearly determined to be among the first inside. The Twi'lek didn't disabuse her of that intention. Once again, Ula admired her confidence. What on Korriban did Jet Nebula mean that she was a faker as well?

A cry went up. The barrier was breached. A cloud of smoke and dust rolled over those assembled. The sound of combat came to them, fierce and pitched.

Larin yelled something over her shoulder.

"What did she say?" Ula asked Jet.

"Something about a Sith. I didn't catch all of it."

Ula glanced at the Imperial envoy, who studiously avoided everyone's gaze.

Yeama waved for reinforcements. A line of Weequay moved in, followed by Potannin and his opposite number on the Imperial side. There was more confusion as all three columns tried to squeeze through space for one. Ula lost sight of Larin, and craned for a better view.

"Why don't you go closer?" asked Jet.

"I, ah, don't think that would be safe. Do you?"

"I think it's all relative, right now."

Shamed, Ula headed toward the widening hole. Jet followed, leaving his droid to watch the entrance. Seeing Ula moving in, the Imperial envoy followed, not wanting to be left out. The tunnel through the rubble was crowded with people. What lay at the end of it was not clear through the smoke and dust. Blasterfire cast strange lights into the haze, and Ula distinctly heard the sound of the Mandalorian's jetpack. On top of that scraped the volatile hum of lightsabers.

They passed a twisted sheet of metal that might once have been the security air lock's outer door. The smell of ozone was overpowering.

"Down, sir!" cried Potannin on seeing him.

Ula let himself be dragged to a relatively sheltered position behind a wall of rubble. From there he still couldn't see the action, but he could see the back of Larin's helmet. She was crouched next to Yeama, sighting along her rifle. Her voice came clearly across the sound of battle.

"*Still* no alarms, eh?"

Ula didn't hear the Twi'lek's reply.

A massive explosion brought down most of the ceiling, deafeningly loud. Ula put his back to the stone shield and covered his ears with his hands. Ash and debris rained on him in thick waves. He closed his eyes tightly.

When he tentatively removed his hands, an uncanny silence had fallen. All he could see were people jostling for position, as pale as ghosts. Rubble continued to fall from the roof. Beside him, Jet slowly inched his head upward to view what was going on.

His expression changed to one of astonishment.

"What the brix is that?"

Before Ula could look for himself, a voice spoke, female and full of rage.

"We do not recognize your *authority.*"

A chill went through him. He had heard that phrase before.

CHAPTER 15

SHIGAR STOOD AT one corner of an equilateral triangle, with the young Sith and Dao Stryver occupying the others. The Mandalorian hesitated, clearly surprised to see them both.

"It's a small galaxy," reflected Shigar.

"You know him, too?" The Sith's hostile façade cracked just for an instant.

"You should both have let it be," said the Mandalorian. "This doesn't concern you."

"You were killing people on Coruscant," Shigar said. "Of course it was my concern."

"Stay out of this," the Sith snarled. "He's mine!"

"I've beaten you once already," Stryver said. "Being killed won't honor your mother's actions."

The young woman turned a shade of red brighter even than her hair.

The Mandalorian raised his left arm and blasted her with his flamethrower.

Shigar ducked and rolled, wondering about the scene that had just played out. Fate had delivered all three of them to the same place at the same time. They were all after the same thing—whatever it was inside the vault—and they had a narrow window before the Hutts realized what was going on and brought the entire weight of the palace's security forces to bear on them. Stryver would want to move quickly and decisively. Yet he had stopped to chat to the Sith girl. Why?

It was clear that all the talk of her mother had been a ploy to distract her. Her rage was fully enflamed now, which would make her stronger, if she survived the next few seconds. Shigar juggled several options. Retreating to the vault and leaving them to it was one, but there was only one exit from that position, meaning that he would have to face Stryver eventually. And the Mandalorian had bested him, too. Better to fight now, when there was at least a chance that the Sith might serve as a distraction.

Flames roared after the girl's cartwheeling silhouette. Shigar came at Stryver from the opposite side, swinging his lightsaber to deliver a crippling blow to the shoulder. Stryver raised his arm to block, and Shigar's blade skated along the powerful Mandalorian armor, leaving a bubbling welt but not penetrating. A hatch in Stryver's pack opened and a collapsible shockstave fired into his hand. Shigar came in for another strike, and the shockstave stabbed at his chest, blasting him from his feet.

On Stryver's other side, the Sith burst from the flames, lightsaber upraised and hatred blazing in her eyes. Her leap took her over the flamethrower's deadly jet and was timed to deliver a spearing thrust to the Mandalorian's domed helmet. He ducked with startling speed for one so big and thrust the shockstave up at her. She cut it in half, kicked him off-balance, and returned for another slash.

Shigar was back on his feet, circling to take Stryver when an opportunity arose. Again the flamethrower burned, but the element of surprise was lost. The Sith girl easily batted aside the flames. Instead Stryver cast a razor net at her. She ducked its piercing barbs and attempted to shock him with lightning. His insulated suit took the charge and grounded it into the floor, blackening and buckling it. Shigar took the chance to Force-push Stryver to his knees, but the Mandalorian was as solid as a mountain, and he had other weapons he hadn't revealed yet.

From a thigh hatch, Stryver produced a stubby pistol. He pointed it at Shigar and fired a single time. Shigar dodged but not so quickly that the fringes of the shot missed him completely. He was tossed like a leaf into the wall and slid to the ground, temporarily stunned.

STRYVER TURNED THE weapon on Ax, who dodged more effectively than the slow-witted Jedi had. She had recognized the weapon instantly and knew how dangerous it was. Disruptors were outlawed in every civilized part of the galaxy. She wasn't surprised to see one on Hutta, in a Mandalorian's gloved hand.

Ax also knew that handheld disruptors were effective at short range only and could manage a bare handful of shots. If Stryver kept firing and missing, the weapon would soon be useless. So she kept moving around her enemy, practically running on the walls of the battle-blackened security air lock, goading him on by hurling broken glass at his joint seals. Twice, he narrowly missed her, and even the fringes of the beam sent powerful shock waves through her flesh. Only her rage kept her going. She used the pain to fuel the dark side.

The third time he fired in their little dance—the fifth shot overall—she barely felt its aftereffects. The weapon's charge was dying. Grinning with triumph, she turned her circling run into a headlong launch. Time to bring the fight back to him.

He met her attack with a vibroblade aimed at the throat. She screamed, trying to drive her blade through his armor with all the strength of her muscles and willpower combined. His buzzing blade was so close it brushed her skin, raising a fine spray of blood, but still she didn't let up. The Mandalorian was reeling back on his feet from her attack. This was the best shot she'd ever had.

His jetpack activated with a whine. Suddenly they were moving, jerking upward as though lifted by a giant puppeteer. Taken by surprise, Ax lost her grip and fell away. Stryver rose above her on twin jets of fiery exhaust. She rolled to avoid their intense heat and covered her eyes from the glare.

Stryver stopped when he reached the domed recess that had once held the tinkling chandelier, and hovered there, punching commands into his weapons systems. Ax had just enough time to realize that he now had the advantage of height before a strong hand gripped her wrist and dragged her aside.

A stream of missiles struck the ground, exactly where she'd been lying. The Jedi had saved her, and she wrenched herself from him, even as she felt a twinge of gratitude. Surely he hadn't done it out of the vile goodness of his heart! No, she told herself. He knew he couldn't defeat Stryver on his own. It was either save her or be the next to die.

Concussion missiles blew her and the Jedi into the security air lock's inner door. They separated to avoid another round, which blasted the door back into the antechamber, exposing the four vault doors and the hole through which Ax had entered. She had a split instant to note that one of the vault doors was glowing bright red, then a rain of blasterfire came from an entirely different part of the room and she realized that someone else had joined the party. The Hutts, presumably, had noticed that their treasure was at risk.

Before she could take advantage of the shift in the battlefield, the Jedi launched himself at Stryver, deflecting missiles away from him as he came. The missiles exploded into the ceiling, bringing down huge swaths of masonry on all three of them. A large chunk struck the Mandalorian, dropping him from his superior vantage point. Ax dodged a slab large enough to crush a bantha and sought her bearings in air suddenly thick with dust. Shadowy figures danced around her—tasseled Weequay, officers in Imperial uniforms, Gamorreans, and more—but Stryver was nowhere to be seen among them. Either a stunned silence had fallen or her ears were overwhelmed by the most recent explosions.

Red light played across the battlefield, then died. Just light, no concussions. Ax blinked and turned to find the source, remembering as she did the glowing vault door. Not a random hit from the Mandalorian's weapons systems, as she'd initially assumed. It was clear now that the door had melted entirely away, releasing the vault's precious contents to all comers.

No one was breaking into the vault, however. That much was immediately apparent from the splatters of molten metal on the antechamber floor. It was, rather, the other way around.

SHIGAR MOVED CLOSER, weaving around the newcomers to the fight. They had provided an unexpected but very welcome distraction, yet he worried now about the danger they were putting themselves in. Stryver was down but not out, and the Mandalorian had wiped out an entire cell of the Black Sun syndicate on Coruscant single-handedly. Shigar—his head still ringing from the near-miss with the disruptor—knew that Dao Stryver would stop at nothing less to achieve his goals on Hutta, if he had to.

For the moment, though, all eyes were on the vault. The Hutts' security measures had failed. Someone had melted the door and gained access to the inside. Shigar wondered if they had come up through the floor of the vault, much as the Sith had attempted. But if so, why not leave that way? Why go to the trouble of melting another exit?

The pool of molten metal that had once been a door cast a bloody backlight on the figure that stepped out of the vault. It didn't look like any kind of being Shigar had seen before. It stood two meters high and seemed at first to be an ordinary biped, with skinny arms and legs of equal length. Then it unfolded another pair of arms attached to its midriff, spaced equally between shoulder and hip joints. It bore no resemblance, however, to insectile species like the Geonosians or the Killik. Its body was a perfect hexagon, stretched vertically. There was no head. Black sensory organs dotted the central body like the eyes of an arachnid, gleaming in the light. Apart from those organs, its skin was silver. He couldn't tell if it was a creature in an environment suit or some kind of construct.

With unerring steps it crossed the pool of molten metal on feet that were duplicates of its hands. It turned 180 degrees, revealing a back that was identical to the front. When it reached the wreckage of the inner door, it stopped there and swiveled slightly, taking in the ruined security air lock and the beings it contained: the Mandalorian, the Jedi Padawan, the palace guards, the Twi'lek, and the Sith.

"We do not submit to your *authority*!" it screamed, dropping smoothly into a new posture. The body became a regular hexagon instead of a stretched, almost rectangular torso, and its legs bent into a crouch. All four of its arms splayed out to target different parts of the room.

Shigar instinctively tightened his grip on his lightsaber. He lacked the foresight ability of Master Satele, but every cell in his body screamed in alarm. Whoever or whatever it was that had broken into the Hutts' vault, it wasn't going to walk away quietly.

The hands of the creature spat darts of blue fire that ricocheted off armor and lightsaber blades and exploded whenever they struck flesh or stone. The Sith girl stood at the focus of their initial attack, but when she went down the fire became more indiscriminate. Bodies dived in all directions, either hit or seeking cover. It wasn't easy to tell which. The room's tortured walls surrendered still more of their mass to dust and gravel.

Shigar stood his ground, reflecting the unfamiliar energy streams back at their source. The creature's silver skin re-reflected them in turn, setting up a resonant stream between him and it that only became more intense with each pulse it fired—then doubled in intensity as it added an extra arm to the attack.

Shigar braced his feet and held on, determined not to give in before it did. The air hummed and crackled with energy along the pulses' combined path. He had never seen anything like this before.

Finally something gave. The stream dissipated with a flash sufficiently violent to blow the creature backward into the antechamber. High-energy sparks ricocheted around the security air lock, making everyone duck again.

Shigar dropped his lightsaber, not his guard. His arms felt like they had been hit with hammers. The ringing in his ears was louder than ever. But until he was sure the thing was incapacitated, he wasn't going to relax one iota.

A second creature stepped from the vault's steaming interior. It didn't say anything. It just screamed and fired.

Shigar jumped as high as he could to evade the converging energy pulses. Staccato blue streams followed him, tearing a shallow, meter-wide furrow in the wall and ceiling. He glimpsed Larin's face below him. She was standing in full view, pumping shot after shot into the second creature's body. Its silver skin dissipated them like raindrops, and he began to worry that he wouldn't be able to outrun the creature's vengeance forever.

A trio of tightly spaced concussion missiles from Dao

Stryver saved Shigar from bisection. They turned the antechamber into a furnace, finally cutting off the deadly beams. Shigar landed on a section of collapsed roof, winded and singed but largely unharmed.

The creature backflipped, landing on six legs, and stood up again, this time on its hands. It looked exactly the same as it had before.

Behind it, the first one crawled out of the rubble in which it had landed.

A third creature stepped out of the vault.

Shigar's stomach hollowed.

"Get everyone out," he shouted to Larin through the comlink before the firing started again. "It's not safe in here."

"What about you?"

"I'll do my best to hold them back."

"Why not just let them go?"

He didn't have a short answer to that question. Because doing so would mean admitting failure. Because whatever these creatures were, he wasn't going to let them have what was inside the *Cinzia*. Because he wasn't going to let things this murderous rain fire upon the hapless denizens of the Hutt palace. "Just because."

"All right," she said, "but I'll be back with heavier munitions as soon as—"

Everything else she said went unheard. With an earsplitting screech, the three creatures fired in tandem, tearing the air apart.

CHAPTER 16

LARIN CAUGHT YEAMA by the lekku as he ran for dear life. "Assault cannon, sniper rifles, mass-drivers," she said. "Everything you've got—now!"

The Twi'lek dithered, torn between conflicting fears: of his mistress; of the things wreaking havoc in the demolished security air lock; and of Larin. Given a choice, he looked as though he would run for the nearest ship and head for the stars.

To help change his mind, Larin raised her rifle and aimed it between his eyes. "You won't get a single step unless you make the call."

Yeama brought his comlink to his mouth and began issuing orders.

She ran back to where Sergeant Potannin lay on his belly, watching the battle unfold through the standard-issue electromonocular scope she had loaned him. He handed it back to her and said, "I think they're droids. Look at the one on the left. It's been damaged."

She focused the scope on the spider-like creature Potannin had indicated. One of its forelimbs had been sliced away, revealing not flesh or exoskeleton but a mess of wires that flexed and twisted, showering golden sparks. She narrowed the field of view to see more closely. Wires, definitely, as thin as hairs and as lithe as quicksilver.

Her mind cast back to the Hortek maintenance crew

she and Shigar had stumbled across in the tunnels below the palace. There she'd seen silver threads as well.

Before she had time to follow the thought through, Yeama returned, pushing a long-barreled sniper rifle into her arms.

"More coming, I hope?"

He nodded unhappily and hurried away.

She lined up the rifle, resting its weight on a protruding chunk of stone.

"Go for the joints," Potannin advised her, but she ignored him. The hands were doing the damage. If she could take them out, that would reduce the threat to Shigar. At the moment, only he and Stryver were doing anything to stop the killer droids from getting out of the antechamber.

The droids moved fast, and they didn't move like anything Larin had fired at before. Any of the six limbs could act as a leg, meaning they didn't so much run as cartwheel from place to place like spindly, animated tumbleweeds, firing as they went. They could also crouch with anywhere from three to all six legs on the ground, giving them a more stable base to fire from. They could even curl into a ball to protect their hexagonal midriffs. Furthermore, the damaged one demonstrated a potent kind of shield when Shigar got too close. It crossed two limbs into an X and created a short-lived circular electromirror that bent his lightsaber back into a V, almost taking off his arm in the process. He retreated, and the droid went back to firing at him.

Larin took her first shot, and missed. Her second hit the forelimb and was deflected. Her third struck the wrist joint squarely, severing the fire-shooting hand with a reddish flash. Instantly the droid rotated to make that limb a foot, bringing another hand weapon into play. She moved her target reticule to aim at that one next.

Another sniper rifle arrived, and Potannin took up the

fight. He tried the joints, with little success, and moved on to the sense organs scattered across the chests of the things. The black circles reacted differently from the silver skin under fire. They absorbed everything that came at them, and radiated the energy as heat. Their reflective black surfaces soon turned to red, then ramped up to orange and yellow. Eventually one hit purple and exploded, making the droid spin around in circles for a moment before recovering.

Larin steadily picked off the hand weapons of her chosen target. When there were just two left, the droid transferred its weight to its four injured legs and hopped to where one of its fellows was trading fire with Dao Stryver. The injured droid jumped onto the back of its counterpart, and the two bodies locked together. The four injured legs retracted, creating a more massive droid with eight legs, all willing and able to fire.

"Oh, come *on,*" she said.

Larin and Sergeant Potannin's efforts didn't go unnoticed. The droid menacing Shigar sprayed a wave of blue pulses in their direction, forcing them both to take cover. When it was over, the barrels of both their rifles were blackened but still seemed capable of firing. Sergeant Potannin, however, had not been so lucky. A ricochet had caught him in the eye and killed him instantly.

Before she could get revenge, someone tapped her on the shoulder. She turned to see Yeama and three Houks pulling in a wheeled, turret-mounted laser cannon.

"About time," she growled, crawling over. "Here, let me. I've used this model before."

Yeama waved her away. His look said as clearly as words that if anyone was going to fire it in his mistress's palace, it would be him.

She backed down as another wave of blue pulses converged on them. A fourth six-legged droid had emerged from the vault.

"How many of these things are *in* there?" she asked no one in particular.

Then the cannon was firing, driving all higher thoughts of the situation from her mind. She was a soldier. It was her job to fight, not to analyze. Dropping onto her belly, she picked up the sniper rifle again, test-fired it, and began peppering the enemy with rounds.

"HOW MANY OF those things are *in* there?" Ula heard Jet say over the sound of blasterfire.

He craned his neck over the fallen beam and risked another look. Sure enough, another of the hexagonal droids had stepped into view.

"Are they in there," he asked, "or just coming *through* there?"

"I'm not sure it makes sense if they have another way into the vault. I mean, if they could just turn around and go back, why aren't they doing that? Why are they fighting to get out past everyone else?"

Ula had wondered why they didn't just blow a new hole out, but he had soon found an answer to that. Their blue pulses knocked fist-sized chunks of stone from the wall, and plenty of them. They were lethal against flesh, too, but they lacked the punch to get through reinforced ferrocrete. The security air lock was the only route open to them.

It was also the only escape route open to him and Jet, but they had been cut off from it by the reinforced beam they now took shelter behind. Between them and the exit was ten meters of open space, littered with broken glass, rubble, and the occasional body. One of them belonged to the young Sith girl, who had been the first targeted by the hexes, as Ula had come to abbreviate them. Jet's droid watched helplessly from the other side of the room, unable to get any closer to help his master.

"Watch Stryver," said Jet.

"Why?" Ula had seen enough of the Mandalorian in action for one lifetime.

"He's holding back, almost like he's testing them."

"Testing who?"

"The droids, of course. Why would he test Shigar? They've fought twice already."

"Why test the hexes?"

"I don't know. Curiosity, perhaps? Maybe the Mandalore is looking for a new species of pit fighters. Nice name, by the way: *hexes*."

They watched as Yeama and Larin positioned a laser cannon for optimal coverage. Larin's face was hidden by her helmet, but Ula was glad to see that she was still on her feet.

"Maybe that's what Stryver has been after the whole time," Jet said. "After all, it was him who talked about droids before. What was that woman's name? The droid maker?"

"Lema Xandret."

"Whoever she was, he knew of her, and you said he was asking questions about her all over the place. What if that thing in the *Cinzia* had something to do with her work? What if the hexes are here now to steal it back?"

"What if they were on the ship the whole time?"

"That can't be the case. The thing you saw was too small, judging by your description. No, they must've gotten in somehow. Maybe someone let them in."

Ula was watching Shigar, who had developed a new tactic against the hexes. When one of them fired up at Stryver, he hurried in low, under the blue-firing limbs. In close, they were more vulnerable, and he managed to get a couple of good stabs to the body of one of them. It was listing badly to one side, and two of its limbs no longer worked at all.

"That Sith girl is still alive," said Jet, nudging him with an elbow.

Ula glanced across the battlefield and found to his surprise that this was true. She was rising sluggishly to her hands and knees, shaking her head with a furious expression. Her hair danced like liquid flames. She looked to Ula as though she had been woken from a powerfully unhappy dream.

"They make them tough on Korriban," said Jet with grim admiration.

The girl was on her feet now. The moment her lightsaber activated, the hexes noticed her. Fourteen streams of energy pulses converged and Ula had time enough to feel sorry for her before she vanished into a glowing sphere of light.

With a boom the laser cannon fired, spearing the eight-legged hex through the midriff. It flailed on its back, screaming piercingly. The two remaining hexes directed their pulses at the cannon's shield, turning it bright red.

Ula was staring at the Sith girl. Amazingly, she hadn't died in the concentrated attack. Even more amazingly, she was still standing, and looking angrier than ever.

"Whose authority do you recognize?" she shouted, lurching headlong into the battle. "*Whose authority do you recognize?*"

The pitch of her fury was so high that part of Ula actually felt sorry for the hexes as she landed among them and started swinging.

CHAPTER 17

AX DREAMED OF a world much larger than normal, where everything seemed strange and mutable and full of threat. She was prone to getting confused, even though she tried very hard to keep up. When she made a mistake people shouted at her, giant people with terrifying voices. It hurt her to be yelled at. She covered her ears with her hands and tried to run. The voices followed her everywhere, shrieking her name.

Cinzia!

Cinzia!

She woke with a start in the middle of a firefight, and couldn't for a moment remember who or where she was. Every cell of her body hurt. Someone was screaming. Not her. It was the screaming that had woken her. Only on awakening did it become clear that the voice wasn't coming from a human throat.

She remembered.

Hutta.

The vault.

Lema Xandret.

Her muscles burned as she willed them into action. Raising her head was like lifting a mountain of pain. She felt a scream of her own boiling inside her, a scream of rage and despair and fear. Containing it hurt her, but at the same time it gave her strength. She needed every ounce of strength she could muster to survive the next few seconds.

Out of everyone in the security air lock, the six-legged droid-things had targeted her first of all.

We do not recognize your authority!

She, however, recognized their defiance. It was the same offered by the crew of the *Cinzia* when they had been confronted by the smuggler. But whose authority *did* they recognize? There had to be something—or someone—behind their murderous natures.

Ax raised herself to her knees, and from there, with a supreme effort of will, to her feet. The world swayed around her, but the scream was intact, and growing. The dark side swelled inside her.

The creatures from the vault saw her, and instantly turned their blue pulses onto her.

She set the scream free.

A Force barrier surrounded her, bare millimeters from her skin. It shimmered and flickered as wave after wave of energy crashed against it, but it held. It held as long as she screamed, as long as she didn't want to die.

The attack ceased, and she staggered back a step, breathing heavily. Her lungs were full of hot smoke and ozone. Her head rang with sound. One of the things attacking her had been blown back by some kind of weapon. The details eluded her. The important thing was that the droids were distracted. This was her chance to find out how tough they really were.

"Whose authority do you recognize?" she shouted, launching herself at the nearest. Its hand weapons were concentrated on the shield of a laser cannon and didn't turn in time. "*Whose authority do you recognize?*"

The droid-thing didn't answer.

Her rage spun instants out into hours.

First, she tried spearing the hexagonal body with her lightsaber.

Some kind of shield appeared between them, bending her blade back at her own arm, forcing her to retreat.

Next she tried blasting it with Sith lightning.

The thing's body caught the energy and discharged it from the tips of its limbs. Four sparkling arms lunged at her, forcing her to duck again.

She reached out a hand and tried to crush its insides telekinetically.

Its honeycomb skeleton resisted more powerfully than durasteel. The hex's deadly limbs flailed to impale or shoot her, no matter how hard she strained.

They screamed together, locked in a vicious stalemate. She couldn't kill it, and it couldn't kill her. It moved on lean, powerful servos that matched her own strength and agility. Its black sense organs tracked her every movement. But every blue pulse it fired at her was reflected by the Force barrier, and every wild slash of its razor-sharp limbs was deflected harmlessly.

Then suddenly it retreated. Its limbs worried at its metallic skin as though scratching itself for fleas. She followed it, puzzled and wary. Was this a trap, some strange new tactic to throw her off her guard? She lunged at it, and it backed rapidly away, firing a stream of blue to keep her at bay.

Then it stopped, stood its ground, and vanished.

For a second Ax doubted the evidence of her own eyes. How could a droid just disappear? It wasn't possible!

A blast of blue energy struck her from the side, out of thin air, and she realized: the droid had activated a camouflage system, reducing its appearance to little more than a blur. It was blending into the background, circling her, trying to shoot her in the back.

Ax narrowed her eyes. She didn't know what these

things could or couldn't do, exactly, but of one thing she was completely sure. One way or another, they were going to die. She was going to destroy them all.

SHIGAR BLINKED SWEAT out of his eyes and took the chance to catch his breath. Backup couldn't have come too soon, even if it was in the form of a Sith and a green-skinned Twi'lek at the controls of a laser cannon. He didn't have the energy to complain. With one of the droid-things down, speared by the Twi'lek right through the middle, and another occupied by the girl, that left just one for him and Stryver to finish off.

The Mandalorian hovered over it, peppering it with blasterfire and concussion missiles. Shigar waited for an opening.

His comlink buzzed.

"You should fall back," Larin told him. "We've got it covered now."

"I don't think it's that simple."

"But you're hurt. At least have someone look at that for you."

He looked down and noticed for the first time that his left arm was covered with blood. He had been completely oblivious to the pain.

The laser cannon fired again. This time the droid-things were ready. The one Shigar was watching dropped to a crouch and threw up its electromirror shield. The bolt from the cannon knocked it backward, but the bolt itself was reflected into the wall. There it exploded harmlessly, showering two crouching noncombatants with gravel.

Stryver swooped in on his jetpack and landed next to Shigar. Shigar raised his lightsaber, but the Mandalorian wasn't on the offensive.

"Tell them to aim for the vault," he said, indicating the comlink.

"Why, what's in there?"

"Just tell them."

Then he lifted off and went back to harrying the target. Again the laser cannon fired, and again the bolt exploded into the wall.

Shigar relayed the instruction. "The door's open," he said, "and it's a confined space. Anything left in there will be fried."

Larin passed the message on to the Twi'lek. From his position, Shigar could see his lekku swinging in an instant negative. A brief argument ensued before Larin came back to him.

"The navicomp might still be in there," she said over the comlink. "If you can get it out, *then* they'll fire into the vault."

Shigar didn't dismiss the plan out of hand. Far be it from him to aid the Hutts in their venal pursuits, but the Republic needed all the help it could get in the war against the Empire. It wasn't his primary mission, but it was still important.

"All right," he started to say.

Then two things happened that put all thought of the navicomp from his mind. First, the droid-thing attacking the Sith girl disappeared. Second, the laser cannon fired again, and the bolt was deflected a third time into the wall.

Into the *same section* of the wall, Shigar realized. The shots weren't ricocheting at random. They were being *aimed*.

"Stop firing!" he shouted into the comlink. "Tell him to stop firing!"

Larin tapped her helmet, obviously thinking she had misheard his order.

The Sith girl was moving, following a dimple in the air. It fired back at her, blue pulses appearing out of nowhere and bouncing off her Force barrier. The nearly invisible droid-thing was heading for the two noncombatants Shigar had seen earlier.

"I said stop firing!" He waved his arms to convey his urgency. "Now!"

The Twi'lek ignored him. Another bolt went into the wall, widening the crater that had already been bored into it. One more shot, Shigar thought in alarm. That was all it would take to ruin everything.

The hand weapons weren't strong enough that the droids could shoot their own way out, so they were using the Hutts' weaponry instead. Instead of killing them, the laser cannon was going to set them free.

Shigar ground his teeth together and sprinted forward. If Larin couldn't stop the Twi'lek from firing, he would have to throw himself at the camouflaged droid and hope to succeed where the Sith had failed.

Distantly he heard the roar of Stryver's jetpack pass overhead, but the significance of it eluded him. The shot he had feared came from the laser cannon and bounced off the electromirror shield, into the deepening pit in the wall. Long cracks spread out from it, and suddenly masonry was tumbling down from the wall. The two noncombatants lay directly in the path of the rubble.

Shigar had a choice. He could intercept the droid or save the two men. He couldn't do both. There was just a split second in which to decide.

Ignoring his pain and exhaustion, he let the Force flow through him and did the only thing he could.

YEAMA'S TEETH WERE bared in determination as he fired at the cowering hex. Larin yelled at him to stop—she had guessed the droid-thing's intentions, just like Shigar—but the Twi'lek was blindly resolute. He thought he was doing the right thing. He honestly believed that he was on the verge of overpowering his target. He wouldn't listen.

She braced herself to physically wrench Yeama from the laser cannon's controls, but the rising whine of a jetpack made her look up. Stryver was on his way. He must also have seen what the laser cannon was doing. But he wasn't flying to defend the breach, as Shigar was. He was coming right for her.

Barely in time, Larin realized his intentions. She hurled herself away from the cannon and dived for cover. Behind her, the cannon erupted into a ball of flame. Bits of metal whizzed past her, pinging off her armor. A wave of heat engulfed her. She felt like a rancor had gripped her in its jaws and was shaking her back and forth.

When it was over, she looked back at the laser cannon. It was a smoking ruin, destroyed by Stryver's missiles. Of Yeama, there was no sign at all.

Stryver dropped heavily next to her. His armor was as blackened and dented as hers. "Get into the vault. Destroy everything you find there."

"What are you going to do?"

"Finish things. I've seen enough."

As he spoke, more of the damaged wall fell away, revealing empty space on the other side. The hexes were already heading for the opening, followed by the Sith. Stryver grunted and took to the air, activating weapons systems he had not yet used against the droids. Larin watched him go, thinking hard.

There would be time for thinking later, she reminded herself again. The priority was to put an end to the current crisis. Stryver wasn't above taking drastic steps to do exactly that—killing Yeama to put the cannon out of action was just one example—and he seemed to know what he was talking about. Looking around her, she found two of poor Potannin's guards and called them to her.

Moving gingerly through the rubble, they headed for the battle-scarred antechamber, and the gaping mouth of the vault.

ULA STARED UP in horror at the descending mass of masonry. There was nothing he or Jet could do to avoid being crushed, and Jet's droid was too far away to intervene. There wasn't time for last regrets or second thoughts. The law of gravity was unbreakable, even on lawless Hutta.

He raised his arms in a futile attempt at self-preservation and closed his eyes.

He didn't die. His thoughts ground on with increasingly amazed vitality, until eventually it occurred to him that someone had intervened to help him live a little longer.

He opened his eyes. The avalanche had been deflected around them by an invisible force. By *the* Force, he realized as he looked around for the source of his salvation. It was the Jedi, standing with his left hand outstretched in a warding motion and his expression fierce. Ula himself could feel nothing at all arising from that gesture, but he was profoundly grateful that the stones seemed to do so perfectly well.

Another rumble came from above. The wall wasn't stable. The Jedi deflected another falling slab, which crashed next to them with a thunderous sound.

"Come on," said Jet, tugging at his arm. "I think it's time we found somewhere else to stand."

Ula wholeheartedly agreed. Conflicted but grateful, he nodded his thanks at the Jedi and scurried with Jet out of the danger zone. Jet was leading them toward what had once been the external exit to the security air lock but was now a path cleared through mountains of rubble. Jet's droid was waiting for him there, waving his arms. The stubby barrel of the laser cannon protruded from between two large slabs. Behind it, Ula could see Larin and Yeama fighting over the controls.

Then Stryver swooped in, firing at the cannon. Larin jumped or was thrown clear, and Ula's heart hammered in his chest. Was she hurt? Could he help? Jet pulled him down as the cannon exploded and shrapnel pinged around them. He belatedly covered his head with his hands, feeling as though he had spent the last hour in that position.

This wasn't becoming of an Imperial operative, he told himself, weary of his own cowardice. He had once had aspirations of being a Cipher Agent, whose job was to negotiate exactly such situations. Here he was, right in the thick of things, and what was he doing? When he wasn't being saved by Jedi, he was cowering and whimpering at the slightest noise. It simply wouldn't do.

The droids were busy with Stryver, Shigar, and the Sith. The way into the antechamber was wide open.

"I'm going to see what's in there," he said. "Coming?"

Jet looked at him as though he had gone stark, staring mad. "You can't be serious."

"Why wouldn't I be? This is my chance to get in before anyone else does."

"Isn't that cheating?"

"If it is, I'm not the only one. Look." He gripped Jet by the shoulder. "Larin's moving. I have to stop the Republic from getting there first."

Jet smiled tightly at that. "I think you mean 'the Imperials,' my friend."

Ula flushed. "Yes. Yes, of course. That's exactly what I meant."

"Envoy Nirvin is over there. I don't think he cares much, either way."

Jet pointed at a body so badly crushed that Ula couldn't identify it. Ula winced and averted his eyes.

"Regardless, I'm going. You can come if you want. I don't care."

"All right, all right—but keep your head down!"

Jet wiped his palms on his dusty trousers and took the lead, as if by doing so hc might increase the chances of either of them returning alive.

CHAPTER 18

THE WALL COLLAPSED despite the Jedi's best efforts to prop it up. Fresh air rolled in on a wave of dust and ash. Ax's nearly invisible droid hopped agilely from outcrop to outcrop toward the opening. In two leaps, it reached the hole and jumped into the light of the outside world.

The droid following in its wake fired at her. Its pulses had turned purple, somehow, and now packed a more powerful punch. She rolled, keeping her shield intact, and reflected the pulses back at it. More dust went up, and the droid vanished into the cloud. She didn't need to use the Force to know that it had followed in its sibling's footsteps.

Stryver was hot on their heels, jetpack blazing. Ax risked being burned in his afterwash, she was following so close behind him. The Jedi followed her, looking worn out and battered. She considered turning on him and striking him down, taking the chance to finish what they had started earlier, but more important concerns drove her now. She could hear the droids screeching as they burst into the unsuspecting populace of Tassaa Bareesh's palace. The sound of their voices fueled her desire to destroy them, to see them all very, very dead.

Evocii and other aliens were running everywhere, fleeing both the droids and the Mandalorian firing at them. His concussion missiles brought down ceilings and walls in the droids' path, stopping them from getting too far ahead. They fired back at him, causing still more collateral damage. If this kept up, Ax thought, it wouldn't be long before Tassaa Bareesh's entire place was destroyed. She couldn't find it in her heart to care.

When Stryver was within range, he used his net launcher to bring the semi-visible droid down. He hadn't tried this tactic before, she noted. Furthermore, the net was different from the one he had used on her. Why he had changed his tactics was, however, less important at the moment than the fact that they were working. The net's mesh was electrified, and delivered a powerful pulse of energy to the droid-thing's silver skin. The six-legged creature spasmed and twitched, shedding sparks into everything it touched. Its keening took on a new, desperate note as its camouflage failed.

Ax prepared to rush in and finish it off.

Then she stopped.

What am I doing?

The answer took surprisingly long to come. This wasn't her fight. Unless one of the droids was carrying the navicomp, she had nothing to gain by killing them. Revenge might seem sweet at that moment, but she would be full of regret later if attaining it meant failing in her mission. Darth Chratis would make sure of that.

The *Cinzia,* Lema Xandret. *They* were what mattered.

The Jedi rushed past her, lightsaber upraised. Let him finish off the fallen droid, Ax decided. To him could go that minor spoil. Then he and Stryver could surely finish off the one droid left to deal with on their own.

Unnoticed by either of them, she turned and headed back to the security air lock.

SHIGAR STABBED DOWN into the guts of the fallen droid, pressing hard to penetrate the surprisingly tough metal of its exoskeleton. Its legs strained against the net, failing either to fire at him or to form its electromirror defense. Sparks still discharged all around it, and Shigar was careful not to be either burned or shocked. As it was, the hairs of his arms were standing on end, electrified even along the shaft of his lightsaber.

The droid's gleaming sense organs turned matte black when it died. It slumped back with a metallic rattle, and its legs hung limp. Still Shigar worked through its body, making sure nothing survived. The case split open, spilling several white, shell-like hemispheres. Fearing they might create some kind of last-minute attack, Shigar speared them, too. They hissed and collapsed, oozing a dark red liquid.

When he was absolutely positive the droid had no life left, he stepped away and hurried after Stryver. The final droid was peppering the Mandalorian with its newly potent pulses, keeping well out of range of his net launcher. Stryver in turn had managed to maneuver it into a cul-de-sac and pinned it between him and a trio of Nikto security guards. Their blasters were ineffectual against the thing's armor, but they had a distracting effect.

Shigar came up behind the Mandalorian and considered how best he could help. The roof was low and much less sturdy than that of the security air lock. Reaching out through the Force, he loosened a key beam and brought a shower of bricks and ceiling tiles down onto the droid. The distraction was sufficient for Stryver to get close enough to cast the net.

The droid went down with a shriek of pain and anger. Stryver pumped three concussion grenades into its chest, not caring about the Nikto standing nearby. Shigar pushed past him to finish off the droid himself, before anyone else could get hurt.

Prior to delivering the killing blow, he tried talking to it.

"Why are you fighting?"

"We do not recognize—"

"You're a combat droid. You must have core protocols."

"*—not recognize your—*"

"Who is your commander? Your maker?"

"*—your authority! We—*"

Stryver leaned past him and plunged his collapsible shockstave into the thing's chest. Its legs flailed, and it squealed so piteously that Shigar almost felt sorry for it. Then its vocabulator function degraded and its voice became little more than piercing electronic tones. He was glad when it finally fell silent.

His comlink buzzed.

"Shigar, I'm in the vault," said Larin. "You need to see this."

"What is it?"

"I don't know. It—"

With a blast of static, the comlink went dead.

Shigar turned and ran back the way he had come, Stryver's massive form five long steps ahead of him.

LARIN STEPPED GINGERLY onto the pool of molten metal that had once been the vault's door. It was still hot. She could feel the heat even through her insulated boots. But it was solid, and her soles held. The body of the droid killed by the cannon lay nearby, its eight legs splayed out and its double body inert.

She quickly surveyed the antechamber and found it to be empty. What had once been white walls were now blackened and scarred, but the other three vaults remained tightly sealed. There was a depression in the center of the room that looked like a tunnel mouth. Re-solidified ferrocrete sealed it shut, however, followed by a layer of molten door metal.

Satisfied that nothing was going to jump her from behind, Larin approached the door itself. Her rifle was cocked and ready, and she had armed backup. Potannin's squad members were tight-lipped and efficient. Most important, they were following her orders.

The interior of the vault was lit by a single flickering globe. Via the flashes of light it provided, she at last saw with her own eyes the object Potannin had described: a low, domed cylinder made of gleaming silver. The image of a battle-scarred soldier standing low behind her weapon was reflected in its curved front. In the irregular light, she looked both menacing and hesitant.

Gesturing economically, she ordered Potannin's squad members in past her. They went in separate directions, coming around the object to cover it from every angle. One of them stepped on a long glass tube that shattered with an alarming sound. Nothing sinister, she noted with relief.

There was no sign of the navicomp.

"Destroy everything you find," Stryver had told her, and she had come armed with grenades to do just that. But she wasn't about to do anything rash. Who knew what valuable information might disappear forever if she acted precipitously? She may have been dumped from the Republic Special Forces, but that didn't mean she was about to take orders from a Mandalorian without question.

Larin came forward a step. The toe of her boot caught on something, and when she looked down she saw more of the shining silver threads running across her path.

It came to her in a flash what they might be, and she reached for her comlink to call Shigar.

With a crack, the top of the silver object snapped open. From it issued another droid. She dropped the comlink and fell to one knee, her rifle rising to fire. The droid was coming right for her, legs flailing and screeching like a mad thing. Its wild shape was frozen in a flash of light, silhouetted like a bug on a window. She registered five arms of varying length, and patches in its body that light shone right through. The shots from her rifle tore more holes in its hide and knocked it backward. It flailed and screamed.

She backed away, her heart pounding, pouring round after round into the droid and the object from which it had emerged. This droid wasn't entirely complete. That much was obvious, even from the brief glimpse she'd received. If it had been, she'd be dead now. It was new, made from scratch inside the object pulled from the *Cinzia*. As the others had been.

The droid stopped moving. She signaled for a cease-fire, and was grateful for the sudden silence. The air was thick with smoke and static discharges. The tick-ticking of cooling metal was the only sound.

She moved closer to the blaster-scarred droid and the object that had made it. Standing warily over the latter, she pointed her rifle into its gaping maw and peered inside. She saw a mass of silver threads and slender manipulators, still moving despite the damage inflicted upon it. She fired two shots into the maw, and the swirling mass grew frantic. Half a droid foreleg appeared, stunted and deformed. A black sense organ came and went.

Larin knew what it was now. It was a compact droid factory, and it had been busy ever since the Hutts placed it here, sending out tiny threads in search of metals and power, infiltrating security systems and taking everything it needed. Hence the threads she and Shigar had stumbled across under the vaults. Hence the lack of alarms.

She bet herself that if she took a knife to the metal walls of the safe, she would find them barely flimsi-thin—enough to fool a casual glance, but otherwise utterly plundered, dissolved, and removed, ion by ion, for use in the factory's secret work.

Building vicious, determined, reticent droids that wouldn't take orders.

Why?

That was a whole other mystery. But the thing was

still moving, still functioning. Given enough time, she bet it would repair itself and start all over again. No wonder Stryver wanted it destroyed.

She picked up the comlink.

"Shigar, I'm in the vault," she told him. "You need to see this."

"What is it?"

"I don't know. It—"

Something red flashed in front of her eyes. A searing pain struck the hand holding her comlink. She stared down in horror at the terrible cauterized wound where her fingers had once been.

Over the humming of her crimson lightsaber, the Sith said, "Give me the navicomp or it'll be your head you lose next."

•

ULA CRANED TO see what was going on inside the vault. He and Jet stood in the antechamber and had been just about to venture in after Larin when the sound of blasterfire brought them up short. Bright flashes of light lit up the cramped space. Larin and her two companions were shooting at something. But what? Not another droid, surely!

Ula and Jet dived for cover just in case, and kept their heads down until the rattle of weapons fire died away.

Ula looked up. He could just see Larin's silhouette leaning over the object Yeama had shown him. Its top was open, and she fired twice into it.

He was about to clamber to his feet when his eyes caught something out of place among the bits of stone and other rubble on the floor.

It was the navicomp.

One of the hexes must have knocked it out when they emerged to do battle. He scrambled for it before someone else saw and took it. Its transparisteel container was intact, and the device itself looked no worse than it had before.

A feeling of triumph filled him. If he could open the case and get the thing itself free, he could smuggle it under his cloak without anyone else seeing. But first he had to distract Jet. If the smuggler saw it, there was bound to be another fight over it. The whole extended disaster could start all over again.

Footsteps crunched behind him, and he turned, fearing that his find had already been discovered.

It was the red-haired Sith. She was heading for the vault, not him.

His relief was short-lived. The Sith's lightsaber flashed and Larin gasped with pain.

"Give me the navicomp or it'll be your head you lose next."

Ula froze in horror.

"I don't have it," Larin said, voice tight.

"I don't believe you."

One of Larin's companions fired at the Sith. She easily deflected the bolt back into his throat. He went down kicking then fell still.

"I'm telling the truth."

"I'll count to five. Then I'll start hacking up your friend here. And *then* it'll be your head, I promise."

The Sith approached the last surviving member of Ula's security detail. He backed nervously away.

"One."

The box containing the navicomp was in Ula's possession. All he had to do was surrender it to the Sith and Larin would be saved. *And* he would safely deliver the information to the Empire. It was a simple solution to all his problems.

"Two."

But Ula couldn't move. The Sith and the Empire weren't

the same thing. Oh, to trillions they were inseparable—the Emperor himself was the Sith to whom all others deferred!—but to him they were very different. On the one hand, the Empire offered a society of rules and clearly defined justice that could, if allowed to do so, bring peace and prosperity to every planet in the galaxy. On the other, oppression and constant conflict. Could he in good conscience give any advantage to the followers of the latter? Would Larin want him to?

"Three."

If only he could deliver the navicomp to the Minister of Logistics. With it in her hand, she could surely find a way to turn it to their advantage. The Empire was so huge it wouldn't miss this world's resources, for all the squabbling over them now. All Ula wanted was the chance to prove the rightness of his principles. He didn't mind the existence of the Sith, but they shouldn't be allowed to run roughshod over everyone else.

"Four."

Yet there was no point dreaming. The Minister of Logistics might have been in another universe entirely. He could no more give her this vital piece in the puzzle than he could stand up to the Sith himself and survive. He was just a pawn in a game much larger than he could imagine. He was insignificant and disposable. How foolish to think that he could ever have changed the way this would turn out! The navicomp had been earmarked for the Sith the very moment she arrived.

"Five." The Sith moved in to start slashing.

"Wait!" he called out.

All eyes turned to him. The Sith glared at him with hateful eyes. Jet looked as shocked as though Ula had sprouted wings and flown up to the ceiling. Larin's expression was hidden by her helmet, and that was the one he most wanted to see.

"Here," he told the Sith, holding up the navicomp. "Take it. Just leave her alone."

The girl's expression became hungry, triumphant. Ula didn't want to get any closer to that blade than he had to. He hefted the box and tossed it to her.

At the height of its arc, a gleaming web reached in and snatched the box clean out of the air.

"What—?" Ula spun around.

The Mandalorian caught the box neatly in one hand and tossed something back to Ula in return. He caught it automatically. It was a heavy metal sphere with a blinking red light.

"No!" screamed the Sith, robbed of her prize.

Stryver was already moving, rising up on his jetpack and heading for the exit.

"Chuck it!" yelled Jet to Ula. "That's a thermal detonator!"

Ula hurled the sphere away from him as hard as he could. It went up, and kept going up as Shigar, the Jedi, used the Force to sweep it away. The tactic wasn't entirely defensive. The detonator exploded high in the creaking scaffolding that had once been the security air lock's roof, directly above Stryver's escape route. The statue of Tassaa Bareesh toppled and fell. Yet another avalanche came crashing down after it, burying the Mandalorian and a herd of palace guards that had come to quell the disturbance.

The floor gave way, and kept giving way as Stryver fired downward, riding the tide of collapse into the palace's deeper levels.

Snarling, the Sith girl went after him, determined not to lose her prize. She vanished into the roil of stone and ferrocrete, and didn't reappear.

Ula took one step toward Larin, but Shigar beat him to it.

"Are you all right?" the Jedi asked her.

She was leaning against the outside of the vault with her crippled left hand compressed under her armpit. With her right hand, she tugged off her helmet. Her face was white and pinched.

"I'll live," she said. "Meanwhile, it's not over. Stryver will head for his ship first chance he gets. You have to cut him off and get the navicomp back, any way you can. Do you think you can do that without me?"

Shigar nodded, tight-lipped, and loped off across the shattered floor to the hole in the wall, leaping gracefully from girder to girder.

Larin held her grin until Shigar was out of sight. Then she slumped in pain.

Ula's pain was different but no less real. It was clear that Larin had a close connection with Shigar. The Jedi even had tattoos similar to hers. It was some kind of cultural thing, surely. Perhaps they were married. The thought made his chest ache.

He knew it was ridiculous to feel this way. He knew it was based on nothing at all. He knew he had built it all up in his own head, and that made him an idiot of the highest order. He had more important things to worry about than this.

The battle for the navicomp was over. Tassaa Bareesh's palace security forces would be converging on the site to clean up and make accusations. He didn't want to be there when that happened. His loyalties were so compromised, he wasn't sure he could convince anyone that he wasn't guilty of everything.

"Stryver will be going for his ship, like she said," he told Jet, "but he's going the wrong way around. I'll head him off and see if I can salvage something. Tell her—tell the others I'll meet them at the shuttle."

The smuggler studied him closely, and then simply said, "All right, mate. I might need a lift myself."

"Isn't your ship—?"

"Impounded and crewless." He shrugged. "And what's a freight captain without his ship? Guess I'd better start thinking about a normal job."

Ula patted him on the shoulder with what he hoped was appropriate bonhomie, because it was utterly genuine. *A normal job.* Those three words had struck him with the force of one of Stryver's thermal detonators.

He hurried off, following with infinitely greater clumsiness Shigar's route across the shattered floor. He ignored the shouts and screams coming from the levels below. He ignored the shaking of his hands. He kept his mind firmly on its goal.

There was an Imperial ship in the palace's dock. That was where he was headed. If he could get there before it left, he could reveal his true identity and claim amnesty. He could escape with the Sith and the navicomp when she returned from hunting Stryver, and he could finally report to his superior.

He could relax the disguise, and speak freely, without lies or deceptions.

He could be himself. And then . . .

A normal job?

Nothing at that moment appealed to him more.

PART THREE

THE CHASE

CHAPTER 19

AX FELT LIKE she was being swallowed whole by a space slug. Even through the Force barrier she threw around herself as protection from the tumbling surf of rock, every sharp edge and crushing pressure squeezed the breath utterly from her. Almost instantly she gave up trying to guide her descent.

She consoled herself with the knowledge that Stryver had to be faring just as badly. Escaping this way was the height of desperation. She admired his guts even while she despised him for capturing the navicomp out from everyone else.

It wasn't over yet, though. She would find him, no matter what it took. There was absolutely no way she was going to report to her Master empty-handed.

The rough-and-tumble finally eased off, and she was able to make her way through the debris, using the Force to help shove aside rocks and gravel, cutting through larger obstacles with her lightsaber if she had to. At every pocket of air she stopped to breathe, grateful for every single lungful of oxygen. It was almost completely dark, but very noisy. When the debris itself wasn't groaning and grinding around her, she could hear voices crying for help.

Finally one arm emerged into free air, then her head. A trio of dusty Evocii grabbed her armpits and began to pull. She shrugged them off and got herself out. At the sight of her lightsaber, they squealed and ran.

Ax dusted herself down.

Now, Stryver.

She had emerged in some kind of dormitory, with bunks lining two walls and the rest crushed under the avalanche. The true extent of the collapse was hard to measure. She could have fallen a dozen levels or just one. Judging by the relative poverty she saw around her, however, she guessed that she was a long way from the luxurious upper floors. These were the beds of slaves, not valets.

Stryver would be farther down, and he would want to go up. His ascent, no doubt, would not be a quiet one.

She closed her eyes and tuned out the screams, the settling debris, the occasional blaster shot. She was looking for one particular sound out of the multitude surrounding her. It would be faint, but it would definitely be there.

The whine of Stryver's jetpack.

There.

The moment she had it, she swung her lightsaber in a circle around her feet. The floor fell out from under her, and she arrived with perfect poise in the middle of an attempt to rescue a Hutt slave driver's tail from its squashed position under a fallen wall.

She ignored everyone involved, crossed to the nearest wall, and slashed an impromptu doorway through that in turn. This led to a torture hall, where indolent or disobedient slaves were publicly punished in order to serve as examples to others. Again, Ax didn't stop to admire the techniques of the Dug in charge. She noted only that many of the screams she had assumed to be caused by the collapse of the building actually emanated from here.

Through another wall, and Stryver's jetpack was definitely sounding louder. She could also distinguish the dull booming of his assault cannon from the welter of other sounds. Like Ax, he was using the weapons in his arsenal to blast a way through the palace. Where doorways or corridors didn't exist, he wasn't above making his own.

Ax skirted the edge of a deep rancor pit. The massive beasts snapped and roared at her, enraged by all the commotion. The handlers did their utmost to restrain them, using chains, hooks, and heavy weights, but the rancors' wild natures weren't so easily subdued. The truncated scream of one of the handlers followed Ax as she Force-leapt across the enclosure in pursuit of her quarry.

The jetpack was close enough now that she could smell its exhaust.

Through a junkyard, a cantina, and a Tibanna gas containment facility, at last Ax had reached Stryver's trail.

It was instantly recognizable. His assault cannon had blasted a tunnel diagonally upward through every structure in his way. The series of holes led through walls and floors in a perfectly straight line. At the end of it, Ax could see a glimmer of bright light: the jetpack's fiery wash.

Baring her teeth in anticipation, she set off after him. Each leap took her one step higher on the long ad-hoc staircase. The surfaces she landed on were unreliable. Sometimes they crumbled beneath her; sometimes they slipped, still molten from the heat of the cannon. Sometimes people fired at her, made trigger-happy by the Mandalorian's violent passage. Ax kept her footing and deflected every shot. She didn't stop for anything or anyone.

Closer and closer she came to Stryver. He didn't look behind him. His attention was focused solely on going upward. Past the glare of his jetpack she could see the transparisteel box clutched tightly in one massive hand. The navicomp was still inside. She almost reached for it through the Force, but held herself back. If she revealed her presence prematurely, Stryver would have time to react. Better to strike him in the back and take the prize from his dead hands.

Two more floors. Three. She threw up a barrier to prevent the heat of the jetpack from flaying away her skin. Four. Now she was so close she could almost have reached out and tripped him. The pounding of his cannon was deafening.

Now.

She lunged for the navicomp just as Stryver burst through the roof of the palace. A brown glare struck them, and Ax squinted as she struggled for possession of the box. Stryver showed no surprise, although he momentarily lost control of his jetpack. They spiraled and swooped across the roof, while guards peppered them with blasterfire.

Stryver's gloved hands let go of the box.

For a fleeting instant, she felt triumph. She braced herself to kick away from him.

Then his left hand lunged out to catch her around the throat while his right brought up the assault cannon and fired into her stomach.

At point-blank range, the shot was like being hit by an aircar in full flight. Had she not put a Force barrier in place, her entire midsection would have been instantly vaporized. As it was, she was blown backward out of his cruel grip and left sprawling, momentarily insensate, on the roof.

Stryver caught the box neatly, one-handed, and flew off into the sky.

Ax watched dazedly, too stunned to feel anything other than curiosity. Where was he going? His jetpack couldn't possibly have enough fuel to get him far. Tassaa Bareesh would have a price on his head within the hour—a price large enough to guarantee he would never leave Hutta.

Then a sleek black shape swooped into view. A ship. She recognized the angular foils of a Kuat scout but couldn't determine the model. It dipped low to intercept Stryver, and then roared up into the sky.

Her quarry was gone.

She felt nothing.

A blurry shape occluded her view of the muddy sky. She tightened her focus. It was a Nikto guard. She was nudged by a business-like boot, as though to ascertain whether she was alive or dead. Another Nikto joined it, then a third. She watched them as though from the bottom of a deep, dark well.

I will kill you, Dao Stryver, or die trying.

Her rage returned, like life itself. She had lost the navicomp, but that didn't have to be the end of the world. She would find another way to satisfy Darth Chratis and the Dark Council—and herself, too. It wasn't really about Stryver and the navicomp, anyway. It was about where they led. The mysterious rare-metal world. The fugitives from Imperial justice. Her mother.

It couldn't end here.

She wouldn't let it.

She was on her feet in a single eyeblink. The dozen or so guards converging on her across the roof weren't going to be a problem at all.

HER FIRST STEP was to devise a new plan. Stealing the navicomp and cracking its secrets obviously wasn't going to be possible now. Stryver had it, and she had no illusions at all regarding the likelihood of him sharing those secrets.

There had to be another way. All she had to do was find it.

The palace was in an uproar as she fought her way back to the site of the battle with the droids—the "hexes," as she had overheard someone calling them. It made sense to return to the scene, since only there lay any chance of learning anything about their origins. She wasn't sure exactly what she hoped to find, though. Maybe the smuggler hadn't told the Hutts everything he knew. Maybe she could torture him to extract every last piece of information.

As she wound through the palace's labyrinthine halls, she passed a clutch of Gamorreans bearing the unconscious Jedi captive over their heads. She smirked but didn't stop. It was good to see someone worse off than she was.

When she arrived at the ruins of the security air lock, she found it sealed behind a dense press of guards wielding laser cannons. The hole in the wall was protected by a bank of portable particle shields. Getting in wasn't going to be as easy as getting out—and she had no intention of crawling back up the avalanche of debris. Fighting was an option, of course, but fatigue was beginning to take its toll. Under better circumstances, she would never have let Stryver beat her like that.

She needed to be smarter, rather than stronger.

Retreating to a quiet place to think, she examined everything she knew about the hexes. It wasn't much. They were single-minded—but what did she know about the minds they possessed? They refused to acknowledge any authority beyond that of their maker. They killed everyone else with impunity. Was there anything else she could say about them?

She remembered the way they had tricked the Twi'lek into blowing an escape route for them through the wall. That displayed resourcefulness and cunning, qualities lacking in many droids, but not all. It wasn't a unique feature of their design.

Something niggled at the back of her brain. A thought stirred there, hesitantly pushing itself forward for consideration.

Escape.

The hexes had been trying to escape.

So where were they trying to escape *to*?

Home.

But how did they know where home was?

The answer to that question burst into her mind with crystalline clarity.

The navicomp isn't the only map.

Ax was moving, circling the ruin until she found the path that the two escaping droids had taken. No one stood in her way until she reached the first of the bodies. It was cordoned off by Gamorreans, and she let them be. The Jedi had made a real mess of that hex, spilling its guts out in a mess of silver and red. The second, she hoped, would be in better condition.

It, too, was cordoned off, but she could see through the guards that the body was intact, tangled up in a net like an animal caught in a trap.

Perfect, she thought, bringing her lightsaber into play.

WHEN SHE HAD the corpse safely slung over her shoulder, all she had to do was leave. That was accomplished as easily as walking through the palace to the spaceport, where the Imperial shuttle awaited her pleasure. Palace security had been tightened in an attempt to stop anyone from leaving. The attempt was doomed to failure.

Two armed Imperial guards stood at attention by the air lock's inner door. They saluted as she stepped through.

"Any problems?" she asked them.

"There was a guy sniffing around the Mandalorian's ship before it took off," said one.

"And some nonhuman scum trying to get in here," said the other. "We sent him packing."

"Very good."

She strode confidently up the ramp and into the cockpit, where the pilot sat waiting. He took in her dusty, battered appearance but didn't remark upon it.

"We're leaving," she said. "Advise Darth Chratis of our imminent rendezvous. I want a droid tech on hand the moment we dock."

"Yes, sir. But what about the envoy?"

"He's no longer with us."

The pilot nodded uncertainly, obviously comparing his standing orders with those he had just been given. A Sith always outranked a superior officer. That was the only conclusion available.

While the repulsors warmed up, Ax took the dead hex and stored it in the secure hold that had been set aside for the navicomp. This cargo was no less precious. The good thing about a droid was that, although dead was indisputably dead, memory took time to fade. With the right expertise, the location of the mystery world could be extracted from the data stored in the carcass, and her success would be assured.

A warm glow filled her, part relief, part pride, part exhaustion. She was looking forward to sitting down. But there was something she had to do first.

The shuttle was lifting off when she returned to the cockpit. She gazed through the viewports at the spaceport and its minuscule cluster of ships.

"Which ship did the Republic envoy arrive in?"

"That one," said the pilot, indicating a stubby, fat-nosed craft resting on four wide-spaced legs.

"Destroy it," she said.

"Yes, sir."

The shuttle's cannon fired, strafing the back of the defenseless ship. It burst into a ball of flame so bright it outshone the sun.

Ax smiled in satisfaction as the palace's scarred roof receded into the distance. With any luck, she thought, that was the last she'd ever see of Hutta.

CHAPTER 20

SHIGAR HAD SEEN the spaceport on plans of the palace, but hadn't been there before. He moved quickly and carefully through the corridors of the palace, counting corners and noting landmarks while avoiding guards and security cordons. Getting lost or pinned down was the last thing he needed. Stryver would have farther to go but he knew the layout better. If there was going to be another confrontation, Shigar wanted to have the advantage.

Also on his mind was Larin's well-being. Again he debated the wisdom of bringing her to Hutta. She had been a great help, and good company, too, but now she was hurt, possibly maimed, and that made her future prospects even grimmer. He swore to make sure her hand was properly tended, but was that enough? Had the kindness he had assumed he was doing for her turned into an intolerable cruelty?

He was afraid of what his Master would think when she saw where his judgment had led him.

All the more important, then, to succeed with Stryver. The entire palace was in an uproar, which was to be expected after explosions in the lower levels, a fight in the security air lock, rogue droids running wild through the corridors, and the multilevel collapse Stryver had engendered. Conflicting alarms overlapped wildly, creating a head-jangling row that Shigar did his best to ignore. He could only imagine how Tassaa Bareesh was taking it.

The spaceport guards were on high alert. Shigar plucked a sentry from his regular patrol and used the Force to persuade him into revealing the command structure of the emplacement. There had been enough killing already that day. Besides, any evidence of a struggle would alert Stryver to an ambush.

Encaasa Bareesh was a junior nephew of the palace's matriarch. He oversaw the security detail from an office two floors away, and was notorious for only occasionally glancing at the cam views. It was a simple matter to convince Encaasa that a completely unrelated crew member wanted to board their ship, but had misplaced their clearance code. Shigar imagined the indolent Hutt wearily slapping his fat fingers on the right controls and then settling back into his hammock. Not even a palace-wide security alert could ruffle him.

The main entranceway to the spaceport slid open. Shigar walked through, watching behind him for any sign of the Mandalorian. None, yet. The doors closed, leaving him alone in the circular disembarkation area.

Shigar had asked the guard which berth the *First Blood* had been assigned to, and he headed straight there. The spaceport's umbilical door was open, revealing the gray skin of Stryver's ship at the far end. Shigar wasn't so foolish as to go anywhere near that inviting portal. It would be booby-trapped for certain.

Instead he waited nearby, in full view of both the *First Blood* and the spaceport entrance, with his lightsaber inactivated but held tightly at the ready. Stryver had to come for his ship sometime, and Shigar would be prepared.

He emptied his mind of all concerns—every worry about Larin and his mission, every ache and pain—and stood poised and ready for action.

The sound of repulsors activating broke him out of his trance. One of the ships was warming up its engines for liftoff. He circled the disembarkation area to identify which one, but the sound wasn't coming from any of the closed air locks. It was coming from Stryver's berth.

That surprised him. He had assumed Stryver was traveling alone. There could, therefore, be no one inside his ship to warm it up for him. Either Shigar was wrong on that point, or Stryver had activated it by remote.

The repulsor whine continued to rise in volume. This wasn't just warming up. The ship was about to take off.

Cursing under his breath, Shigar abandoned subtlety. Approaching the ship's outer air lock, he quickly examined it for weak points and found just one. The door was keyed to Stryver's biometric signs—height, breadth, proportion of limbs, and so on—but it also featured an override, just in case Stryver was ever grievously injured in the course of a mission. If he lost a major limb, for instance. That override could be sliced into by someone clever enough.

Shigar wasn't as good a slicer as Larin, but he had seen this kind of trick before. Mandalorian ships had been Jedi targets ever since the Great War, and he had been taught over and over again the best way to disable them. Working quickly, he tapped a series of codes designed to reset the override function back to a commonly used default. When he typed in the default, the door slid open.

Not a moment too soon. The repulsors were at screaming-pitch and the ship was hovering lightly on the ground. In another second, it would've been high above the palace.

Shigar leapt lightly into the air lock and was swept upward with it. The moment his boots touched the floor, however, a secondary security system kicked in. Powerful electric shocks coursed through his body, sending his muscles into irresistible spasms. He fell onto his side, unable even to cry out. His jaw was locked open in a silent scream.

The autopilot raised the ship straight above the spaceport and adjusted its trim. Shigar felt himself rolling toward the open air lock, but couldn't move a finger to save himself.

The electric shocks ceased the moment he cleared the air lock. That was something to be grateful for as he fell like a stone to the roof below.

HOW LONG HE was unconscious he didn't know. Minutes, probably. Sufficient time for his helpless body to be gathered up by a roof security team, secured with binders at wrists and ankles, and gagged for good measure. When he woke, he was being transported through the palace on the shoulders of a squad of Gamorreans. Neither his lightsaber nor his comlink was within reach.

Instead of fighting, he concentrated on easing his body's many bruises and batterings. He didn't know how far he had fallen, but fortunately he had ended up with no broken bones. A ringing skull, yes, and a crushing blow to his dignity, but nothing worse. For the moment, he was grateful simply to be alive.

His captors whisked him at a brisk jog through the palace. He memorized the turns but without a starting point had no way of knowing exactly where he was going. His general impression, however, was of opulence increasing around him, not decreasing. When he arrived at a large space full of people whispering and talking, with one loud voice booming away in Huttese over the top of them, he guessed instantly where he was.

The Gamorreans came to a halt in the center of Tassaa Bareesh's throne room, and with a coordinated grunt dumped him onto the floor. Silence radiated around him as people noted his presence. He clambered awkwardly to his feet and looked about.

A large crowd of beings stared back at him, whispering and pointing. He saw no less than twenty different species in one quick glance, from trunked Kubaz to feline Cathars, with bipeds occupying a pronounced minority. Their exotic origins belied their unified purpose: to pander and preen before the one who controlled their fates.

"*Bona nai kachu,*" roared the matriarch of the palace, "*dopa meekie Seetha peedunky koochoo!*"

Shigar turned to face Tassaa Bareesh. She was sprawled heavily on a horrifically ornate throne-bed at one end of the hall, and decorated almost as ornately as it was. He didn't know enough about the Hutts to read her expression, but the quivering of her lipless mouth and the spittle she sprayed as she talked left little to the imagination.

An A-1DA protocol droid shuffled forward on spindly legs. "Tassaa Bareesh wishes you to fully comprehend the certainty that you will be punished, treacherous Sith."

Shigar considered his options. There were at least two dozen weapons trained on him. Behind the crowd, armed guards ran back and forth, responding to various emergencies unfolding in the palace.

He bowed as ceremonially as he was able, given his bindings. "I must correct your mistress. I am in fact a Jedi."

"Stoopa dopa maskey kung!"

He ignored the insult. "I can hardly have double-crossed you when we had no agreement between us. Beyond trespassing on your territory without permission, I mean no harm."

Tassaa Bareesh rumbled threateningly, shifting to a different dialect now that she realized he could understand at least some of her words.

"Tassaa Bareesh says: Your intention was to steal from her. For that, you must die."

"If you search me, you'll find I'm carrying nothing I didn't come here with."

"Tassaa Bareesh says: Your accomplices have made off with the prize."

"The navicomp? The last time I saw that it was in the grip of a Mandalorian, not a Jedi."

"Tassaa Bareesh says: Your treachery is surpassed only by your puniness. He stole it from you after you stole it from us."

"You are upset," Shigar said. "Your judgment is clouded. A moment ago you thought I was a Sith. Perhaps the lie you think I am telling is actually the truth."

The crowd muttered in consternation. Clearly few people were bold enough to question Tassaa Bareesh's judgment to her face.

The Hutt matriarch growled something long and involved that didn't really need translation. The droid rapidly blinked its round blue eyes and made a valiant effort anyway.

"Tassaa Bareesh is most displeased. She has, ah, devised numerous ways to use you for entertainment."

Shigar didn't argue the point. He had finished counting the guards and exits, and reached the conclusion he'd expected. There was no way to fight his way out of this one, and he couldn't rely on reinforcements. He would have to talk. He might even have to make a deal. That thought sickened him to the stomach.

"Your anger is perfectly justifiable," he said. "Your palace has been attacked, and the property and information you planned to sell have been stolen. You've been deprived of the profit you deserve. No one would deny that you have a right to seek revenge, to make an example out of those who have caused you embarrassment and significant harm." He bowed again. "All I beg is that you blame the right people."

Another explosion ripped through the palace, causing great upset in the throne room. Tassaa Bareesh's huge eyes showed white around the edges as she waved a

Twi'lek over to her. His comlink was squawking urgently. They hastily conversed, too quietly for Shigar to overhear. Then anger got the better of the matriarch. She backhanded the Twi'lek away from her and roared at the translator.

"Tassaa Bareesh wishes you to understand that the spaceport has been attacked," said the droid, its tapering head bobbing obsequiously.

"By whom?"

"By Imperials. The Republic shuttle has been destroyed."

Shigar considered saying nothing. On one level he didn't need to. The actions of the Imperials had won the argument for him, by their blatant violation of the Treaty of Coruscant. But on another level he was still in hot water. Tassaa Bareesh could have him executed just for being an irritation, and an inconvenient reminder of her loss. He had to give her a reason to spare him, not kill him.

He had to appeal to her business sense.

"We are both the victims here," he said, choosing his words with exquisite care. "Killing me won't get the navicomp back, and it will make an enemy of the Jedi Council. Either way, you end up worse off. Letting me live, however, offers you a way to cut your losses."

"Tassaa Bareesh asks: How?"

Shigar swallowed. A bad taste had crept into his mouth. "I intend to follow the Mandalorian wherever he goes. He has injured both my pride and my companion, and he will pay for these crimes. The information he has stolen might no longer be of value, in and of itself, but every new world offers opportunities for trade and exploitation. In return for releasing me, I will ensure that those opportunities come to you first, before anyone else."

The matriarch hummed a pitch almost too low for a

human ear to hear. Her eyes didn't leave Shigar's face, but they had an inward cast now.

"Tassaa Bareesh is considering your offer," said the droid, glancing back and forth between them.

"I worked that out."

She rumbled something, and the translator said, "Tassaa Bareesh wonders how you intend to follow the Mandalorian when you don't have a ship, let alone directions."

"I'm a Jedi." He tapped his forehead, hoping to hide the fact that he hadn't the faintest idea on either point. "We have our ways."

A new wave of whispering spread through the crowd.

"Tassaa Bareesh says that your ways are insufficient. The investment is too risky."

"But—"

The translator raised a metal hand. "She says that in order to protect her stake in this venture, she must be allowed to provide you with assistance."

" 'Must be'?" The choice of words gave him pause. What was being forced on him, exactly? "Tell me more."

The matriarch settled back on her throne. Her eyes narrowed to slits.

"Tassaa Bareesh will provide you with transport. Her nephew will make the necessary arrangements. If you accept the offer, you may leave immediately."

Shigar wondered what would happen if he rejected her offer. He mistrusted the matriarch's sudden satisfaction. Just moments ago she had been seething with rage at the way her plans had been ruined. Had that been an act, or was *this* the act?

"All right," he said, following his instincts. Living right now was better than dying. That was the bottom line. And if he got even luckier, he might be able to do something to help Larin as well, assuming she was still alive. "I accept the offer."

The matriarch broke out into an enormous and unsavory smile. One chubby finger pointed at him. *"U wamma wonka."*

"Tassaa Bareesh says—"

"I know what she said." He swallowed another foul taste.

She clicked her fingers and the guards dropped their weapons. A Gamorrean scurried forward to return his comlink and lightsaber. He fixed them to his belt and bowed. The crowd watched him, silently now.

"Thank you," he said. "It's been a pleasure doing business."

As the guards led him from the throne room—a guest now, rather than a prisoner—the sound of the Hutt's chuckling, low and lugubrious, echoed and re-echoed through the sybaritic halls behind him.

CHAPTER 21

"ARE YOU FEELING all right?"

Larin turned to look at the smuggler. She had left herself for a moment, left the ruins of the security air lock and the blasted droid factory, left the clamor of palace security digging through the rubble, even left the occasional potshot in their direction from an ambitious Houk, currently stationed in the hole that shortsighted Yeama had blown through the wall. Now she was back, and the view wasn't pretty.

The answer came to her at last.

Are you feeling all right?

"Yes."

They were hunkered down out of sight in the entrance of the vault. She was squatting on her knees, still applying pressure to her injured hand under her right armpit. The suit had sealed the wound as best it could, leaving her nothing else she could do about it now. She knew that well enough, having been injured in combat before. Once, she had been caught in an intense urban guerrilla exchange that Special Forces Blackstar Squad had been sent in to deal with. Intel had leaked, leading Larin and three squad members into a trap. She still dreamed sometimes of the way frag grenades had torn into the group, instantly reducing two of her friends to ribbons. She had been sheltered from the bulk of it, but even so the skin down her right leg and side had been flayed completely away, along with a fair chunk of muscle. It had taken an extended period in a bacta tank to regrow the tissue, and three months of rehabilitation to restore her to full flexibility.

This was different, though, and it wasn't just because fingers couldn't be regrown. In the Blackstars, she had had many clear-cut reasons to fight: among them strengthening the Republic cause, enforcing principles of liberty and equality among all beings in the galaxy, and furthering her own career. She had thought herself perfectly normal in that regard. Why else did one join Special Forces but to be a hero on the side of good?

She knew now that not everyone was like her. Every barrel contained a bad apple or two. She also knew just how important at least two of those principles were to her. More important, combined, than the last one. Sacrificing her career to uphold them had seemed the right thing to do, at the time.

Without her career, though, it was very hard to fight for any cause at all. And now her situation was totally muddied. Was invading a sovereign state—albeit one comprising criminals and murderers—the best way to go about enforcing freedom and equality? How did squabbling with Mandalorians and Sith over a battered navicomp help the Republic? To whom did she owe her allegiance now, if not herself or her former peers?

She didn't have good answers for any of these questions, yet she had lost the fingers of her left hand fighting for them. That made the pain worse, somehow.

"What happened to your droid?" she asked Jet in return.

"Clunker? He's somewhere under that lot," the smuggler said, indicating the pile of masonry left in the wake of the thermal detonation. He had armed himself with a blaster dropped by one of the dead soldiers outside. "Don't worry. He'll be back when he's ready."

"I recognize his model," she said, clutching at the fact as though it would explain everything. "J-Eight-O, soldier class. That's why he talks in combat signs. But they were phased out, weren't they?"

"Perhaps," he said. "I found him on a scrap heap two years ago. His vocoder was dead, and when I tried to fix it, he just broke it again. That proves how smart he is. He's worked out that if you don't respond to orders, no one can prove you heard them."

"That's a pretty good survival tactic," she said, "for anyone in the army."

They leaned out of the vault to see if anything had changed outside. The Houk kicked up some pebbles nearby, but missed by more than a meter. Potannin's last surviving escort returned fire from the other side of the antechamber. He missed, too. Larin could have aimed better, even with just one hand.

"What's your name, Private?" she called to him.

"Hetchkee, sir," he called back. He was a young Kel Dor, and his face was mostly hidden behind a face mask and goggles designed to protect him from a harsh oxygen atmosphere.

"Who told you to call me 'sir'?"

"No one, sir."

He obviously didn't know anything about her past. She wasn't going to be the one to fill him in.

The sound of digging grew louder.

"Larin," said Jet, leaning in closer, "do you think we've been left to hold the baby?"

"In what sense?"

"In the someone's-going-to-have-to-explain-this-mess-to-Tassaa-Bareesh-and-it-might-as-well-be-you sense."

"Don't worry," she said. "He'll be back."

"Who? Your Jedi friend or Envoy Vii?"

Larin looked around. She hadn't noticed that the envoy was gone—although now that she thought about it, she did remember Jet telling her something about Ula meeting them at the shuttle. It hadn't occurred to her to wonder when and how they would go about getting there. Ula had left before the security forces had sealed their only way out.

"I mean Shigar," she said. "Jedi Knights always keep their promises."

"And what exactly did he promise you?"

She suppressed a sharp reply. What was Jet getting at? Sure, Shigar may not actually have promised to come back for her, but she knew he would if he could. And while Tassaa Bareesh's security forces amassed outside, there was nothing else she could do but trust him. She had given up trying to hail him on the comlink long ago.

She stood up.

"I suggest—"

The sound of a distant explosion cut her off. The floor shook, and a rain of dust settled down on them from above.

There was no way to tell where this latest blast had come from, so she finished what she'd been about to say.

"I suggest we look at this thing while we still have the chance."

She crossed to the miniature droid factory and peered inside. The swirling silver cilia were still now, so she felt safe assuming it was dead. She tried tipping it over to see the base, but it was firmly affixed by the wire-like threads that had eaten down into the vault floor like tree roots.

A piece of the silvery alloy had melted off during the firefight in the vault. She picked it up and weighed it in her hand. It was surprisingly heavy.

"Let me get this straight," she said. "This thing was on the *Cinzia*. You found it in the wreckage and brought it to Hutta. Tassaa Bareesh locked it in here. It looked inert, but it wasn't. It sent out those thread things into the floor and began scavenging metal. It infiltrated the security system. It started building the droids."

"Ula called them hexes."

That was as good a name as any, for now. "Maybe just one or two hexes at first, to defend itself. It kept them hidden inside, like a nest or an egg. If you look into one of the hexes, you'll see they're not solid all the way through. They have a honeycomb structure. So two could easily fit in here, if they were collapsed down." She poked the cilia with the barrel of her rifle. "Two would be enough to take over a ship."

Jet looked at her, not the droid-nest. "You think it was waiting for someone to win the auction and take it away?"

"I do. The hexes would've emerged, overpowered the crew, and gone safely home."

He nodded slowly, thinking through her proposition.

"I think you're partly there," he said. "Given enough time, I reckon the hexes could've escaped from here on their own steam. Note how they emerged from the vault the moment everyone started fighting over it. The door melted like butter, probably thanks to wires like these. If everyone had waited just one more day, I think our nest here would have turned up empty."

"You might be right," she said.

"It's just a guess," he said self-deprecatingly.

"Here's another one," she said, edging back to the door. "If the homing instinct theory is right, then the hexes must know the way home."

Jet's face brightened. "So if we can get out of here with one of their brains, we won't need the navicomp after all!"

They peered out at the body of the double-hex lying on the floor of the vault. The laser cannon had blasted a hole right through both conjoined abdomens. The innards were blackened and melted, totally unsalvageable.

Jet's face fell. "Worth a thought, anyway."

Larin leaned back against the wall and closed her eyes. Shigar sure was taking his time. Her blood sugar was low, and the endless pain was making her dizzy.

The sliver of metal from the factory was still in her one good hand. She slipped it into one of her suit's many sealed compartments. At least they wouldn't return empty-handed.

A disturbance outside distracted her. "Someone's coming!" called Hetchkee.

Larin propped the barrel of her rifle on the back of her left hand and trained it through the door. The mound of rubble at the far end of the security air lock was moving. Someone was clearly coming up through it—but was it Stryver, the Sith, or Jet's loyal droid?

A scuffed orange hand, reaching out of the gravel to find purchase on a fallen beam, soon answered the question.

"Told you," said Jet with a satisfied expression. "Over here, mate!" he yelled to the droid.

Clunker extricated himself from the rubble and limped over to join them, utterly unmolested. The Houk had stopped firing. Instead of reassuring Larin, that worried her. There was no way to know what was going on outside their impromptu redoubt. She presumed the Hutts wouldn't leave them alone for long.

"Good work, Hetchkee," she said, returning to the safety of the vault's interior. "I think we'll have more company soon, so stay alert."

"Yes, sir." If the soldier was worried by that prospect, he didn't show it.

Clunker was communicating with Jet via a series of rapid signs.

"Bad news," the smuggler translated. "Stryver got away with the navicomp."

"That's the end of that, then," she said, unable to hide

her bitterness. The trail had gone cold. Any hopes she might have entertained about redeeming herself by means of a successful volunteer mission were now officially dead. "What does he want with this colony, anyway? Doesn't Mandalore have enough soldiers already?"

"Doesn't Tassaa Bareesh have enough money?" His cynical smile flashed again. "I think Stryver wanted the navicomp for two reasons. To find the *Cinzia*'s origins, and to hide its destination. That would make sense if Mandalore has been part of this right from the beginning."

She stared hard at him. "You could be right. Stryver knew about the *Cinzia* long before anyone else. It was him going around asking questions that tipped us off."

"And the *Cinzia* was on a diplomatic mission, but neither the Empire nor the Republic had ever heard of it. Can you name any other major players in the galaxy at the moment?"

She granted him the point. Even if the Mandalorians hadn't acted as a united body since the war, it wasn't inconceivable that they might do so again, for honor, or the right price, or just because they needed a good war. "Why did those things attack Stryver, then?"

"I don't know."

"And who saved the nest from destruction when the *Cinzia*'s crew blew themselves up?"

"I don't know that, either."

She shook her head. "Every way I look at this, it keeps on getting crazier."

"Tassaa Bareesh had no idea, did she?"

The sound of grinding rubble came from outside the vault. Larin hurried to the door before Hetchkee could call. The giant mass of stone blocking the far entrance was moving forward. Behind the crunching of rock and ferrocrete, she could hear a hissing and pounding that could only have come from dirt-moving droids.

"Okay," she said, "this is it. If you've got any other bright ideas, Jet, now would be the time."

"You've had your daily quota, I'm afraid."

"Well, then, you'd better join me in hoping that Shigar turns up soon. Otherwise, we'll see what Tassaa Bareesh's hospitality is really like, behind all the chintz."

"I suppose we could try to make a last-ditch break for it," he said.

"And go where?"

"Well, there's my ship."

"I thought it was impounded."

"Oh, that. A small technicality."

"Like getting out of here alive."

He winked. "A man can dream, can't he?"

Levity in the face of unspeakable odds always buoyed her spirits. It surprised her how much she had warmed to the smuggler in their short time together. Maybe their cells would be next to each other in Tassaa Bareesh's dungeon. Maybe they would be stretched on adjacent racks.

With a rumbling crash, the droids broke through the rubble. Once the way was clear, they retreated to allow the palace's security forces past. There were dozens of them, all heavily armored and armed, creeping forward across the exposed beams of the floor with sights trained on the vault.

Larin almost laughed. Tassaa Bareesh had sent an army to capture just four people! It would've been absurd if she hadn't been on the wrong end of the equation.

"What do you think, Hetchkee?" she called to the Kel Dor soldier. "We can try surrendering to them, if you like. We haven't done anything wrong, when you think about it. Your boss was actually invited."

"I don't reckon they're in the mood to care about that, sir."

That was true enough. The ranks of Weequay, Houks, Niktos, and Gamorreans looked as though they expected a whole army of Sith, Jedi, and Mandalorians to burst out of the vault and make off with their mistress's fortunes. If only they knew there were just three people and a droid. It hadn't even occurred to Larin to try unlocking the other three vaults.

"All right, then," she said. "Wait until you can see the red of their eyes."

Her opposite number among the security team was saying much the same thing, judging by the sudden tightening of their ranks. One enormous Weequay raised his right hand to give the signal to attack.

At that moment, Larin's comlink buzzed.

She froze, unable to fire and answer at the same time. What was more important: the last shots she might ever fire in her life, or the last communication she might ever receive?

The Weequay had frozen, too. A blue-skinned Twi'lek had appeared at the far end of the room, waving and shouting something in a language she couldn't understand.

"Can you follow that?" she asked Jet.

He shook his head. "Sounds important, though, whatever it is."

No one was coming for them at that moment, so she took the opportunity to put her rifle aside and reach for the comlink.

"Larin, it's me," said Shigar. "Where are you?"

"Right where you left me. Tell me you've got a flip card up your sleeve."

"I might just have. Has Tassaa Bareesh sent anyone to you yet?"

She peered out at the masses of security guards. "You could say that."

"Go wherever they take you. I know what she has in mind."

"You want me to surrender?"

"It won't be surrender. We, ah, reached an agreement, she and I."

Larin didn't like that moment of hesitation. What if he was under duress and walking her into a trap?

She asked him, "Do you remember lightning season on Kiffu, when the static trees take to the air?"

"What—? Yes, I do. Spark-dragons lure them into caves to steal their charge. I'm not setting you up, Larin. You can rest easy on that score."

"All right," she said, keeping a close eye on the leading Weequay. He was yelling at the Twi'lek and brandishing his massive fists. "You'll be where they take us?"

"Count on it."

She put down the comlink and turned to Jet. He had heard everything.

"I will admit," he said, "that I prefer resolutions that involve talking rather than shooting."

"So you think we should do this?"

"I do. And Clunker agrees."

The droid looked as though he was fully prepared to shoot his way out, but nodded stiffly.

"Hetchkee! Put down your rifle. When I say so, we're coming out."

"Uh, yes, sir."

"Wait for the signal. If we get the timing right, I think we've got a good chance of surviving this with a little class."

The Weequay shook his hands overhead one last time, then let them fall to his sides. The Twi'lek looked satisfied. The Weequay turned to his troops and grunted a series of commands.

The security detail rose to its feet one at a time, and lowered their weapons.

"Right," said Larin. "That's our cue. Put down your blasters, but keep your hands at your sides. We're not surrendering."

She stepped first out of the vault, and the Twi'lek came to meet her.

"I am Sagrillo," he said with a short bow. "By the order of Tassaa Bareesh, you are free to go."

Larin kept her relief completely hidden. "You better believe it."

"And me?" asked Jet hopefully.

"Alas, Captain Nebula, my mistress still has need of your services." The Twi'lek bowed again. "If you will accompany me, please, all of you, I will take you where you are required to be."

Larin fell in behind the Twi'lek, with Jet beside him. Clunker and Hetchkee brought up the rear. The only sound was a subterranean growling from the Weequay as the security detail parted before them. Larin considered tipping him a salute farewell, but thought better of it.

She glanced at Jet. Apart from the slow clenching and unclenching of his jaw muscles, he showed no emotion at all.

CHAPTER 22

ULA SAT IN Encaasa Bareesh's office and tried not to weep. He should never have come to Hutta. He should have argued with Supreme Commander Stantorrs and made him send someone else. It didn't matter how it would have looked. He would happily take a greatly diminished position of responsibility in the Republic's military administration rather than endure another minute in this slovenly disaster area.

From the moment he heard the name of the accursed *Cinzia,* everything had gone wrong. First he had been kidnapped and interrogated. Then he had been caught in the crossfire among a Sith, a Jedi, and a Mandalorian. Then the brutal hexes had almost killed him. And now . . .

He put his head in his hands, barely able to think of it.

From outside the office came the sound of constant commotion. The destruction of the Republic shuttle had damaged the palace's spaceport. Fire and repair crews ran backward and forward, shouting at one another and into comlinks, requesting reinforcements. Ula didn't offer to help. The palace could burn to the ground with everyone in it for all he cared.

The chances of Larin Moxla still being alive were slim indeed. Of that he was completely certain.

He wasn't proud of himself for running from the ruins of the security air lock, even though he had been sure at the time that his motives were pure. His performance as a Republic envoy had never been convincing; Jet had seen through him straightaway, even if he hadn't outright named him an Imperial spy. Better to let that life disappear and start a new one in the Empire, where he could spend less time worrying about who other people thought he was and more on actually doing the right thing.

Getting through the spaceport guards hadn't been hard, even after the unexpected departure of Dao Stryver's scout ship. They remembered him from his arrival and let him through. He had approached the Imperial dock without hesitation, confident that the guards would allow him admittance.

It hadn't gone that way at all.

The shame of it still burned. His fellow Imperials—of a junior rank, what's more—had turned him away, recognizing him as belonging to a near-human species rather than pure-blooded like themselves. *Epicanthix scum,* they had called him. *You belong in this hole,* they told him. *Go away before we shoot you dead.*

He had staggered out of the spaceport, stunned by the sudden reversal. If his own kind wouldn't take him in, who would? Barely able to think straight, he had wandered in circles around the neighborhood for what had felt like days, but couldn't have been any more than an hour. His choices were limited. He could either go back to the Republic and his old job under Supreme Commander Stantorrs—if he wasn't sacked for failing so miserably in his mission—or do as the Imperial guards had suggested and stay on Hutta. The latter he simply would not do.

When he returned to the spaceport, determined to take his leave of the planet forever, he learned that the Republic shuttle had been destroyed. Bad enough that his fellow Imperials had rejected him; now they had destroyed his only means of getting offworld! He had been so wrapped up in his misery he hadn't even heard the explosion, and he bore the news that things had gone from bad to worse with a distressing lack of grace.

Luckily, the situation wasn't without hope. The Imperials' blatant breaking of the Treaty of Coruscant might, on more civilized worlds, have resulted in all-out war, but on Hutta it was likely to be ignored along with the many other infringements perpetrated by the Sith and the Jedi that day. Furthermore, Ula's status as a Republic envoy still carried some weight. Tassaa Bareesh's nephew had installed Ula in his fetid office—a place of leathery drapes and entirely too much velvet, with living *things* crawling all over the desk—and left him there to sort himself out while the spaceport dealt with much more important emergencies. Ula couldn't blame him.

The only person Ula blamed was himself. If he hadn't run away like a coward, he might have been able to make a difference to the mission's outcome. Larin was very capable, but she was also wounded. And now with Stryver and the Sith gone, one of them presumably with the navicomp, and the guards outside babbling about the Jedi someone had captured, Tassaa Bareesh was unlikely to show anyone involved the slightest clemency. He himself expected a wrathful backlash. All of Hutt space would quiver until she found a way to mitigate her losses.

A swarthy Weequay burst into the office. He didn't knock. His face was melted into a permanent sneer.

"Up," he said, poking Ula with his force pike.

Ula's stomach sank. Here it came, the moment he had been dreading. How would Tassaa Bareesh deal with him? If he was lucky, it would be quick. If he got what he deserved, it would be exceedingly slow.

The Weequay poked him again, and he rose wearily to his feet. Several tiny lizards fell squeaking from his back and crawled off under the couch-bed. At least, he thought, he would be leaving this ghastly menagerie behind.

He was led out into the spaceport, where Encaasa

Bareesh and a clutch of Gamorreans were waiting, ceremonial axes at the ready. In their midst was a dirty, beaten man whom Ula didn't immediately recognize. A crude bandage stanched the flow of blood from a wound on his left arm. A dozen other small cuts and grazes had been left unattended.

"Envoy Vii, I don't believe we've been formally introduced," the young man formally said. "I'm Shigar Konshi, Jedi Padawan under Grand Master Satele Shan."

Ula was so surprised by the unexpected deference that it was difficult to respond in kind.

"I thought you'd been captured."

"I was."

"So what are you doing here?"

"I'm waiting for—" He glanced over Ula's shoulder. "Yes, here they come now."

Ula turned and took in the scene behind him. If he'd been surprised into rudeness before, he was utterly speechless now.

Larin Moxla led a procession of a Weequay, a Twi'lek, Jet Nebula and his droid, and one of Potannin's surviving guards. They weren't being shoved along; they weren't in binders. Like Shigar, they were being treated more like guests than prisoners.

"Nice to see you again, mate," said Jet, tossing him a casual salute. "If you're the one who talked us out of that mess, I owe you a dozen Reactor Cores."

"Not me." Ula turned helplessly to Shigar for an explanation.

"I cut a deal," the Padawan said to all of them, although his eyes kept returning to Larin. "Tassaa Bareesh is letting us go."

"That's suspiciously generous of her," she said.

"Yes, well, there's a catch." Shigar pulled an unhappy face. "I'll tell you when we're on our way."

"You have a lift, too?" asked Ula, hope beginning to bloom.

"Better than that," Shigar said. "I have a ship and a captain."

"Anyone we know?" asked Jet hopefully.

The Twi'lek addressed Jet in clipped, officious terms. "The great Tassaa Bareesh has instructed her nephew to release your vessel, but your contract with our employer remains in force. You will provide passage for the Jedi and his companions to destinations of their choosing. You will not cut and run the moment you leave our airspace. You will return with the information gathered and provide said information in full. Any fiduciary losses incurred during this expedition will be your responsibility."

"What about the profits?"

"They will be distributed the normal way."

Jet grimaced. Ula guessed that "the normal way" meant all for Tassaa Bareesh and none for anyone else.

"It's not much of a deal," Jet said, "and, well, call me a stickler for details if you like, but I don't remember there ever being a contract between us."

The Twi'lek smiled. "There is now."

"I guess that's the catch," said Larin.

"Well," said Jet, "at least we're alive and soon to be in motion. There's nothing that can't be solved, I've found, with the application of a little velocity."

He winked at Ula, who was still too shocked by the sudden turn of events to manage a natural expression.

"*Where* are we going, exactly?" he asked the assembled group.

"After Stryver," said Shigar. "And the longer we stand around here, the bigger the lead he'll have."

He bowed to Tassaa Bareesh's nephew, who grunted something in reply. The Weequay and Gamorreans dispersed, marching with heavy tread off to pursue more important tasks. When the spaceport doors opened to allow them admittance, Jet took the fore, whistling jauntily as he led them to his berth.

"Don't expect much," he said. "The *Auriga Fire* is a loyal old thing but has seen better days. Like you, eh, old buddy?" He clapped Clunker on the shoulder, prompting a rattling noise that disappeared down the inside of the droid's left leg. "It'll get you from A to B, but I can't speak to anything much else."

He stopped at the disembarkation ramp, where a series of carrybags had been lined up. "Hello," he said. "Who might these belong to?"

"I think they're mine," said Ula. His quarters had obviously been emptied while he had wallowed in self-pity in Encaasa Bareesh's office.

"So you're joining us, Envoy Vii?" Jet asked with a knowing gleam in his eye.

"Yes," he said. "If—ah, if that's not inconvenient."

"I can't guarantee that you'll get back to Coruscant anytime soon."

"That's okay. I would very much like to leave here, immediately."

"Right you are."

Jet keyed an elaborate code into his berth, then another into his ship's air lock. The hull was pitted and scarred with dozens of micrometeorite strikes. Ula fretted about the state of the ship's particle fields, but supposed that if Jet had survived this long, they couldn't be that bad.

The air lock slid open.

Jet waved him up the ingress ramp. "After you, then. Mind the step. Crew quarters to your right. Guess that's what you qualify as now. Someone's got to help me fly this thing straight."

Ula grabbed a carrybag as he went by. His sole remaining escort did the same. The ramp creaked and swayed. He wrinkled his nose at the stink emanating from the ship's interior. It smelled like stale Rodian. The *Auriga Fire* would undoubtedly be a far cry from the official transport he had enjoyed on the way to Hutta.

Still, he didn't care. Utter disaster had somehow been avoided, and for that he was grateful. He was alive, and so was Larin; he had clean clothes and transport; there was even a chance he might be able to return with information for his masters on Dromund Kaas. When he thought back to the despair he had been feeling just minutes ago, his present circumstances seemed positively optimistic.

"Stang!"

Jet's warning forgotten, Ula stubbed his toe on the top of the ramp.

THE *AURIGA FIRE* was by no means a luxury vessel. From above, the stocky freighter was almost perfectly triangular, with hyperdrives at the base; sensor arrays, shield generators, and comms at the upper point; and a cockpit slightly off-center in the middle, above the main holds. Its low, cramped corridors were arranged in a rough Y, with main hold, crew quarters for five, and a cramped engineering bay at the termini. The cockpit was one level up, accessed by a ladder. Additional holds filled every available piece of ship space, including some, Ula was sure, that weren't visible to the naked eye. Jet claimed to have had a crew of ten on the run that had encountered the *Cinzia*. Ula wondered how they had all fit in.

The ship was hardly understocked in terms of equipment. On the short journey back from the refresher, Ula spotted a tractor beam, a crude interdiction device, and power supplies for no less than four tri-laser cannons. Thick cables suggested that the shields were well supplied with power, too. Jet might talk down its capabilities, Ula decided, but the ship could undoubtedly hold its own.

There was just enough room for everyone in the cockpit. Shigar had the copilot's seat. Larin had clocked more flight hours, but until her hand was properly treated she was relegated to astrometrics. Clunker had patched himself in to the ship's flight-control systems and shut down his photoreceptors. That left Ula and Hetchkee to ride out the short hop to orbit in the passenger seats.

As the brown atmosphere faded away to stars, Ula instantly felt lighter, both physically and in spirit. Jet deftly guided the ship into a stable parking orbit and put it on autopilot. Then he swiveled in his seat and folded his hands behind his head.

"Now for the ten-trillion-credit question," he said. "Where to?"

Everyone looked at Shigar, who shifted awkwardly in his seat.

"Easier asked than answered, I'm afraid," he said. "Tassaa Bareesh thinks we're going after Stryver, so I guess that's what we have to do."

"Why don't we just run?" Ula asked.

"I can't," said Jet.

"Because of a made-up contract?"

"Because she'll hunt me down and nail me to her wall if I do. She's planted a homing beacon somewhere on this old bucket. I'm sure of it. That's what I'd do in her shoes."

"So we go looking for Stryver," said Larin. "He'll head for the hexes' home, for sure."

"If we had the navicomp," said Shigar, "we'd do the same."

"He has to crack the cipher first," said Jet. "We had a go or two at it on the way to Hutta, without any luck."

"Is there any other data we haven't been given? For instance, when you interdicted the *Cinzia,* could you tell from its trajectory where it originated?"

Jet shook his head. "We tried that, too. Project the ship's

route back, and you get empty space to the edge of the galaxy, and then a lot more empty space after that. Same with everything else we picked up. It all points nowhere."

"They were smart," said Larin. "And they really wanted to stay hidden. I wonder why."

They pondered that question for a moment, in silence. Ula had no insight to offer into the psychology of Lema Xandret. The hexes were remarkable and strange, but that alone didn't reveal anything about the people who had made them.

Or did it? On Panatha, Ula's great-great-grandfather had been fond of collecting ancient Palawan sayings. "What you do speaks louder than what you say" was one of them. Another was "What you make makes you."

Applying that philosophy to their present situation seemed impossible to Ula, until he remembered something Yeama had told him.

"The thing that built the hexes," he said. "The nest. It was made of a strange alloy. What was it?"

"Lutetium and promethium," said Jet.

"So they're rare metals. There can't be many worlds where both are found, right?"

Jet poured cold water on this spark of an idea. "There isn't a single surveyed world with those metals in abundance."

"What about Wild Space? There are lots of unsurveyed worlds in there."

"Sure, but it's a big place and they don't call it *wild* for nothing."

Ula sagged back into his seat. "How did you convince Tassaa Bareesh you had the slightest chance of finding this place?" he asked Shigar. "It seems hopeless to me."

Shigar looked embarrassed. "I reminded her that I'm a Jedi. I told her we have our ways."

Larin reached into one of her suit's compartments

and lifted out a strip of silvery metal. "This is how we're going to find the planet," she said triumphantly, offering it to Shigar. "This, and your mysterious ways."

Shigar's eyebrows went down in confusion, then down even farther in a frown. "No," he said, pushing the metal away from him. "It won't work."

"It has to," she insisted. "You told me about your psychometric ability—"

"My *unreliable* psychometric ability, Larin."

"—and that your Master thinks you can tame it. What better time to try than now?"

"No better time," he agreed, "but you can't make it work just by wanting it to."

"I trust you," she said with unaffected candor. "And you haven't let me down yet, not even once. I don't expect you to start now."

That stopped his protests. He reached out, took the shard of metal from her hand, and held it up to the light. It gleamed like a metallic diamond.

"Is that what I think it is?" asked Ula.

"It's a piece of the nest," she confirmed.

"And Shigar can use his mind to find out where it comes from?"

"I can try," said Shigar, sternly. "That's all. I can't promise anything."

"Well, it's a start. How long will it take?"

"I don't know. I'll talk to Master Satele, first. She might be able to guide me through this. Can you put a call through to Tython?"

"Faster than you can ask me to."

"I'll take it in the main hold," he said. "There's a holoprojector there."

Shigar got up from the copilot's seat. Jet fiddled with the instruments in front of him, opening up comm channels and shunting data through the ship.

Larin was sitting thoughtfully, eyes staring blankly at the ladder down which Shigar had disappeared. A tiny worry line creased the bridge of her nose.

Ula leaned in to whisper, "You don't really think he can do this, do you?"

Her green eyes focused on him. "There's only one thing I think," she said. "If he doesn't even try, that'd be worse than failing."

Ula could only nod in the face of her unswerving integrity, and wish that he possessed half of it.

"Now," she said, "I have to get this glove off and look at my hand. In the absence of a field medic, I need one of you two to help me out. Private Hetchkee? Envoy Vii?"

"I'll do it," said Ula quickly. "You stay here and back up Jet, in case he needs it," he told Hetchkee.

"Medkit's in the aft air lock," Jet called out. "Let me know when you have a destination and I'll get this crate moving."

"Will do."

Larin headed for the ladder and Ula followed her, frantically dredging up everything he'd learned about medicine from a brief training session on Dromund Kaas, years ago.

CHAPTER 23

SHIGAR PACED THE *Auriga Fire*'s cramped hold as best he could while waiting for Jet to patch him through to Tython. He wasn't doing a very good job of it. He could only manage three long strides from one side to the other, and he had banged his head on a protruding instrument panel twice already. The pointlessness of the exercise was just becoming apparent to him when the old-model holoprojector flickered and emitted a soft whisper of static.

He pulled from the opposite wall a retractable chair designed for someone much smaller than him and sat down, feeling all knees and elbows.

A blueish image of the Grand Master formed. It flickered and jumped but held firm enough to follow.

"Shigar," Satele Shan said, raising her hand in greeting. "I'm pleased to hear from you. Are you on Hutta?"

He briefly outlined his current position: in a smuggler's vessel over the Hutts' homeworld, still wearing what remained of his impromptu disguise. "I find myself in an intractable position, and I need your counsel, Master."

She smiled, slightly but not unkindly. "You have agreed to things you do not feel you can accomplish, or which you do not want to accomplish. Perhaps both."

Her powers of perception startled him. "You can sense this from so far away?" Truly she was the most powerful Jedi in the galaxy!

She shook her head and smiled with charming self-deprecation. "No, Shigar. I just remember what it's like to be in the field. Responsibility, decisions, consequences—they feel very different when assumed in isolation. Do they not, my Padawan?"

He lowered his head. "Yes, Master."

"Tell me," she said, "and I will offer what counsel I can."

Shigar started at the beginning, with his and Larin's arrival on Hutta. He skipped the mundane details of his infiltration of the palace and described his first encounter with the unique technology offered for sale by Tassaa Bareesh, the silver roots spreading out from the vault into the underground tunnels, and Larin's account of the droid-nest that Jet Nebula had pulled from the wreckage of the *Cinzia*. He described his three-way fight with Dao Stryver and the young Sith, then the emergence of the hexes and their near-escape.

"You fought a Sith?" Master Satele asked him, sounding impressed.

"I believe she was an apprentice like myself," he admitted, "else I wouldn't have survived."

"Regardless. A Sith and a Mandalorian at once, and you *did* survive. Few Padawans could boast of such a thing, Shigar. The fact that you are not boasting of it I take to be a sign of good character."

"Master, I do not believe I survived by skill, or even luck." In the retelling, he noticed several things that hadn't occurred to him at the time. "Stryver would have defeated both myself and the Sith apprentice, given time. The interruption of the hexes changed everything. He no longer fought us. He stood back to watch us fight this new enemy. I believe he was holding back."

She leaned back into her seat, cupping her chin with one hand. Shigar recognized the background; she was in her private study, an austere, minimalist space with few ornaments, but constructed from the finest possible orowood.

"I see" was all she said. "Go on."

He described the hexes in more detail, beginning with the sixfold symmetry of their basic appearance, their identical lack of personality or individuality, and their deadly unwillingness to stand down, then moving on to the glimpses of their internal structure that he had received while killing one of them.

"The technology is quite outside my experience," he said, remembering honeycomb matrices and strange oily fluids leaking from the body. "The hexes are no more resourceful than any normal droid—certainly no more so than the training droids on Tython—but they display an adaptability I've never seen before. An injured one merged with another to form a single eight-legged version. Later, one activated a camouflage system that the others didn't seem to possess, and the weapons of a third became more powerful. It almost seems like . . ."

"Like what, Shigar?"

"I don't want to say *evolving,* Master, but I do think they're capable of adaptive redesign."

"In the heat of combat?"

"Yes. Particularly so, I suspect."

"That makes them very remarkable droids indeed," she said. "Who could have built such things?"

"Envoy Vii was interrogated by Dao Stryver, Master. The Mandalorian let slip that Lema Xandret was a droid maker."

"Do you think these are her creations, Shigar?"

"I have too little information to say for certain, but what we do have is suggestive."

She nodded. "Indeed. Dao Stryver was hunting both a particular droid maker and a ship containing the means to build remarkable droids. Lema Xandret is most likely the architect of these things. But what is their purpose? If they are weapons, whom are they meant for?"

"It's possible, Master, that they aren't weapons at all.

Not aimed weapons, anyway. They may simply have been fighting to get home."

"To do what?"

Shigar had no speculation to offer on that point. He vividly remembered the droids' screeching rage at being obstructed in their quest to escape. Such emotional programming was not normal for combat droids—or any droids at all, in his experience.

"There's something else," he said. "When Stryver confronted the Sith apprentice, he said something about her mother. I don't know exactly what he meant, but it got a reaction from her. Whoever her mother is, she's connected somehow."

He let that fact sit where it was. As it stood, the Sith's involvement was unexplained. While tempted to draw conclusions from suggestive facts, he thought it best to wait until they had more information. The wrong conclusion could be deadly, if they based their actions upon it.

Master Satele, it seemed, agreed.

"So," she said, "the thing in the *Cinzia* wasn't an ancient artifact that we or the Sith might find useful. It was something strange and new. Where does that leave us?"

"The Mandalorian has the navicomp," he said. "He'll be decoding the information it contains as we speak."

"And then what?"

"His motives are unknown," Shigar said, casting his mind back to the things Ula and Larin had said on the way to orbit. "I believe that the Mandalorians have been involved in this from the beginning. Stryver may have wanted the navicomp, in part, to destroy evidence that the *Cinzia*'s 'diplomatic mission' was with Mandalore—but that makes less sense the more I think about it. Mandalorians aren't unified, and they don't parley with anyone. Fight or conquer, that's their philosophy."

"They allied themselves with the Empire against us," Master Satele reminded him.

"Yes, but that's the *Empire,* not some isolated colony in the middle of nowhere."

She nodded. "What are your plans now, Shigar? Are you returning Envoy Vii and your friend to Coruscant?"

Shigar knew that look on his Master's face. She already knew the answer to her question. She had either worked it out or seen it in a vision. There was also a slight emphasis on the word *friend* that encouraged him to cast his answer in the frankest terms possible.

"Larin thinks I can use psychometry to find this world." He held up the sliver of silvery alloy that she'd recovered from the nest. It glittered in a way that wasn't beautiful, but was certainly eye catching. "I think she places too much faith in my abilities. I would rather bring it to Tython for someone reliable to read it there."

"That would waste time, Shigar, and time may be of the essence."

"Do you know this, Master, or do you just suggest it?"

"It doesn't matter. I do know that Larin's faith in you is not unwarranted. Perhaps you should have faith in her, too. Does she strike you as a fantasist?"

"Anything but." Larin was as solid as a rock. "She sees what she sees and she says what she says."

"Well, then. Maybe the one who doesn't see is you, Shigar."

"Perhaps, Master. But if I fail—"

"Metaphorically speaking," she said with a smile, "*if* is the smallest word in the Galactic Standard lexicon, yet it stands between us and our greatest dreams. Let it be a bridge, Shigar. It's time you crossed it. I will be waiting for you on the other side."

He took a deep breath. "Yes, Master."

"Meanwhile, I am hopeful that Supreme Commander Stantorrs will provide us with substantive backup. Where the Mandalorians are concerned, he's unlikely to take any chances. But it will undoubtedly be a military mission, not Jedi. I'll suggest rendezvousing at Honoghr. Send coordinates to me there, once you have them, and we'll get on our way."

Shigar's mind reeled at the logistical efforts unfolding in response to his actions. "Yes, Master."

"The Force is with you, Shigar."

The line crackled and died.

Shigar slumped momentarily into the seat, and then went to find somewhere quiet to meditate.

LARIN HADN'T INTENDED to eavesdrop on Shigar's conversation with his Master, but the *Auriga Fire* was too small to allow anyone actual privacy. Where she and Ula sat facing each other was less than five meters away from Shigar, and the metal-lined corridors carried every sound. Ula spoke softly so as not to disturb him, and it was easy for Larin to phase the envoy out.

She found it much harder, though, to ignore the mess the Sith wretch had made of her hand.

Just getting the glove off had been difficult. No painkillers existed sufficient to shield her entirely from the sensation of blended flesh and plastoid tearing apart. The Sith's lightsaber had melted both into a horrific seal, one that had stopped her from losing too much blood but would have to be removed before the wound could properly heal. The medkit's initial scan revealed a mess of truncated bones and blood vessels beneath. It could only deal with them once the wound was cleared.

That job fell to Ula, who wielded a sonic scalpel with more surety than she had expected. Ula talked her through the procedure, in an attempt to reassure both of them, most likely. She gritted her teeth, unable to look away, and at the same time tried to focus her mind on something else.

"What are your plans now, Shigar? Are you returning Envoy Vii and your friend to Coruscant?"

That had to be Shigar's Master, the legendary Satele Shan. Larin wished she could see her image. She spoke with such surety and confidence, and Shigar responded to both in ways he probably wasn't even aware of, simultaneously trusting and rebelling. It was hard to imagine him in a junior role to anyone.

"Maybe the one who doesn't see is you, Shigar."

"There," said Ula, gingerly lifting the glove from her brutalized flesh. It came off in three pieces. He had resealed the major blood vessels with a laser cauterizer and applied a bone stabilizer compound. "I think that's good enough to put in the medkit now. I'll dig around through the ship's cupboards later and see if I can find a prosthetic to tide you over until we get home."

She didn't want to look at the ruins of her hand, but she had to. The cut ran neatly across all her metacarpals, leaving her without even a single finger stump. The pain was hazy and indistinct now, but very present. Her nerves were obviously still working. That was a good thing, she reminded herself, if she was ever to have a full prosthetic attached.

The medkit swallowed what was left of her hand up to the wrist, and hummed patiently to itself.

"The Force is with you, Shigar."

Larin heard him sigh, then get up to move elsewhere in the ship. His footsteps thudded heavily, as though he were bearing a heavy weight. Doors opened and closed, sometimes prompted by a thump or two. Finally he stopped. A door closed and sealed. Apart from the combined hum of life-support and a dozen other machines, the ship was silent.

"I said, I have several carrybags full of brand-new clothes. If you or anyone else wanted to change . . . ?"

She focused on Ula's face. "What? Oh, yes. Sorry. That's a good idea. Could you help me get my armor off? I won't be able to reach the seals down my right side until the medkit has finished."

"Of course. I'd be happy to."

Together they wrestled her out of her arm and chest plates. The back defeated her entirely, so she showed him how to pop the waist seals and wriggle the shell free. Even through her body glove she felt the coolness of the air. She literally hadn't taken the armor off for days. On Coruscant, in the dangerous old districts, she had become used to sleeping in it most nights.

The state of the armor dismayed her. It had been well used even before she bought it, but the last few days had tested it beyond reasonable expectations. It was dented, slashed, melted, pierced, and blackened. More than once she found patches of blood she didn't even remember shedding.

"I can manage the rest," she said. "There must be a 'fresher in here somewhere."

"I saw a small one near the starboard hold. Are you sure you'll be okay on your own?"

"Most definitely. A girl's gotta keep some secrets."

He flushed a bright red, and she instantly regretted the joke.

"I'm sorry," she said, taking his hand. "You've been a great help, Envoy Vii. The painkillers are making me feel a bit woozy. I might lie down after I've cleaned myself up."

"Yes, yes, you should rest. And please call me Ula."

"Thank you, Ula."

His hand was warm in hers. She surprised herself by not wanting to let him go. They sat without saying anything for a moment, and maybe the painkillers really were getting to her because she felt herself tearing up at this tiny instant of human contact. She had been on her own for so long.

Don't be an idiot, she told herself. *Being in the*

Blackstars was never like this. We fought and killed together. We didn't hold hands.

"All right," Ula said, sounding embarrassed again. "The luggage is in the crew quarters. I'll let you rummage through it. Call if you need anything, anything at all."

Larin nodded and wiped her nose.

Ula let her hand go.

When next she glanced up, he was gone.

CHAPTER 24

THE IMPERIAL SHUTTLE came out of hyperspace above the green and empty world of Kant, deep in Bothan space. Kant's two moons possessed a sparkling array of asteroid companions. Among them lurked the seventeen vessels of the half division granted to Darth Chratis by the Dark Council. The bulk cruiser at its head, an aging hollow-nosed Keizar-Volvec behemoth called *Paramount*, hung low and heavy dead ahead. Ax felt an anticipatory dread as the shuttle swooped in to dock. She had cleaned the wounds on her face and neck and changed into clean attire. Still, she felt unready for what was surely to come.

A full detail awaited her on the hangar deck. She ignored their salute.

"Where's the technician I asked for?"

"Specialist Pedisic is on her way, my lord."

"Not good enough. I asked for one to be here when I arrived. What about Darth Chratis? Is he on his way, too?"

"No, my lord. He wishes you to attend him immediately."

"Again, not good enough." She wrapped the Force around the man's throat and squeezed until he gasped. "Tell him that I have important work to oversee, and I will not be distracted."

"Yes . . . sir!" the red-faced soldier managed.

She let him go and he scurried off to obey her orders.

Behind her, the pilot and another grunt carried a sealed metal case down the ramp with exaggerated care. She had impressed upon them the importance of its contents. If anything happened to the remains of the hex, she was sunk along with the mission.

"I need somewhere secure to open this box," she told the next soldier in line. "Show me to the nearest quarantine bay."

"Yes, my lord." He snap-turned neatly on his heel and led her to a glass-windowed room set into one wall of the hangar deck. The box promptly followed.

The quarantine bay was small but well equipped. The box went onto the floor next to a gleaming metal table. A heavy-breathing droid tech finally arrived, and Ax sent everyone else packing.

"Inside that box is a droid," she told the technician. "And inside the droid is information of the greatest possible importance. It's your job to get it out."

"I understand, my lord."

"Good. Well, open it!"

Specialist Pedisic unsealed the clasps, stared for a moment at what lay within, then reached in to scoop out the remains. The dead hex had collapsed in on itself and was now reduced to the size of a small human child. Its legs curled protectively around its midriff. Dark brown fluid stained everything.

"I've never seen anything like this before," Pedisic told her, wiping her hands on a cloth she produced from inside her uniform.

"What you've seen or done before doesn't concern me," Ax said. "It's what happens now that matters. If I said this was a matter of life and death, I wouldn't be exaggerating. For you, it certainly is."

Pedisic swallowed. "Let me send for some more equipment, and I'll get started right away."

Ax nodded. "You have one hour."

She swept out of the quarantine bay, past the double guard stationed at the door, and went to find her Master.

THE BLOW CAME so fast she couldn't avoid it, even though she'd expected it from the moment she boarded the *Paramount*. She felt herself swept up and thrust with crushing force into the nearest bulkhead, and held there, unable to move.

"You were sent to Hutta to claim one thing."

The deadly hiss of her Master's voice slid like a red-hot needle into her right ear. She could feel him next to her, even though the room was in absolute darkness. His presence was like a foul-burning fire in the fabric of space itself.

"One thing only," he repeated, "yet you return without it, you stand by while the Emperor's official envoy is killed, and you *delay* before reporting to me. What am I to do with you, Eldon Ax? What punishment would be most fitting?"

"The envoy was a puppet," she managed in her own defense.

"They always are, but they remain the public face of the Emperor. To slight one of them is to slight him. Would you be party to such a thing? Should he be informed that you have allowed his authority to be disrespected?"

"No, Master. That was not my intent."

"Perhaps it was not. It is hard to be certain. Your confusion is exposed to me. You are weakened by attachment, by the existence of a *mother* . . . "

She flinched away from him as though physically struck. "You lie!" she cried, even though part of her worried that it might be the truth.

The lights burst on, blindingly bright. She fell to the floor, released, and blinked away bright afterimages. The room was square, black, and empty apart from her

Master's meditation sarcophagus mounted securely in the center. He was inside it, his withered face hidden safely behind the lid.

He had never been standing beside her at all.

"Allow me to explain, Master."

"If you cannot, I will crush your mind to dust."

She began with her attempt to infiltrate the vault and moved quickly on to her confrontation first with the Jedi Padawan, then with Dao Stryver. Darth Chratis was displeased at her inability to slay either of her enemies, and she felt his feverish will coiling about her again, but she plowed on without hesitation. Her fate rested on convincing him of the worth of the hexes.

"Droids," he breathed. "Lema Xandret was a droid maker."

"This surely confirms beyond all possible doubt that the *Cinzia* was connected to her. Doesn't it, Master?"

"Do you have any other evidence?"

She pushed aside a memory of the hexes' relentless screeching. "They consistently attacked me first, as though they possessed an embedded resentment of the Sith. Otherwise, they lashed out only when either attacked themselves or their way was impeded."

"Suggestive indeed. You say the Mandalorian had the measure of them, as though he had seen their kind before?"

"He held back until it was clear the hexes were going to escape."

"I find that very interesting, too."

"The Hutts clearly had no idea what they had found, Master. They might have sold it for the material value alone, had it not been activated."

"Do you think your presence triggered some kind of awakening?"

"No, Master. It was a matter of expediency. The seed-factory remained relatively quiescent until circumstances ruled that tactic unworkable. Then it moved to another tactic. If the auction had been held a week later, I believe the hexes would have escaped unchecked into the Hutta biosphere, and from there made their journey home."

"To report, I presume."

"Yes, Master."

"Can you recover their route from the remains you brought here?"

"I intend to, Master."

"If you do not, I will flay you alive in front of the Dark Council, before they in turn flay me."

"Yes, Master."

"Abase yourself before me," he told her, "and swear to me that the thought I see in your mind is not another reason I should kill you now."

She froze. All she had been thinking was that the hexes fought her as hard as they fought her enemies—harder, in fact, because she was a Sith. Surely, instead, they should have recognized her and held back. After all, Lema Xandret had created both of them. She had even named the ship after her daughter. They should be her allies, not her enemies.

Darth Chratis held her mind like an egg, ready to crack it with a thought.

She did exactly as he said, pressing herself facedown onto the cold metal floor to reaffirm her allegiance to him.

"I remain your trustworthy servant," she said. "I am yours to kill if you deem it fit."

She waited, hardly daring to breathe, and gradually the pressure eased.

"You shall live," her Master told her, "for now. Find me the location of that planet. If you fail me again, I will show no mercy. Do you understand me?"

"Yes, Master."

"Leave."

She went.

Only when she was sure she had reached a safe distance did she dare think, *You can expect no mercy from me, Master, the day our positions are reversed.*

CHAPTER 25

THE VERY SECOND the medkit bleeped to tell her its work was done, Larin slid her half hand free and headed for the refresher. She was tired and ached all over, but this couldn't wait. There was only so much she could ask of a self-cleaning body glove. A good rinse was exactly what it needed.

When she was done, she did as Ula had suggested, and looked through his suitcases for anything she might be able to wear. Much of it was formal wear and still vacuum-sealed in its original packaging. A lot of it was also made from more expensive natural fabric, and therefore not amenable to on-the-fly adjustments, but Ula wasn't significantly larger than she. Eventually she found dark blue pants and a matching jacket with a militaristic cut. The sleeves and legs came up to match her length, and the other measurements pulled in tight enough. With the black body glove underneath, she almost looked stylish—but for the bruises on her face and the missing fingers of her left hand.

Larin considered what she had told Ula she would do, and rejected it. She was tired, but knew she wouldn't be able to sleep. The first thing she'd noticed on leaving the refresher was that the ship wasn't moving. It was still in orbit about Hutta.

She explored the main level of the *Auriga Fire*. Hetchkee was sound asleep in the crew quarters, and like any good soldier hadn't been disturbed by her rummaging around. The soft male voices coming down the stairwell from the cockpit belonged to Jet and Ula. All the holds she poked her head into were empty, bar one.

Shigar sat cross-legged with hands folded across his lap and eyes closed. The silver scrap sat innocently on the floor in front of him. His face was expressionless, but she could feel the tension radiating from him like an audible twang. He looked like she had felt half an hour earlier: exhausted, dirty, and beaten half to death.

She went and got the medkit.

"Your arm," she told him when she returned. "How are you going to achieve anything if you bleed out here in the dark?"

Without moving a single other muscle, he opened his eyes.

"I can't do it anyway, Larin."

"You know, you'll never be able to prove that true," she said, holding the medkit at him like a challenge. "All you can prove is that you've stopped trying."

"But if you distract me—"

"That's not the same thing as giving up. That's called a regroup. I'm your reinforcements."

His mask of concentration finally broke into a faint smile. "I'd happily trade places with you."

"Me, too," she said, raising her injured hand.

He took the medkit from her without another word.

She explained the clothing situation while he tended his arm. He nodded vaguely. She slid down the wall and sat with her back against it. He didn't stop her. By the light spilling through the open door, he looked much older than she knew him to be.

"Everyone is waiting for me," he said as the medkit hummed away. "Not just you and Master Satele. Supreme Commander Stantorrs, hundreds of soldiers and starfighter pilots, the entire Republic—waiting for me to do something I've never been able to do. Not properly, anyway. It comes and goes. It's not reliable. I can tell you where your armor came from, but this thing . . . ?"

The piece of droid-nest glinted impassively back at him.

"What about my armor?" she said.

"Once, when I brushed against it, I got a flash of its former owner. She was a sniper from Tatooine. She got a medal for taking out a local Exchange boss."

"What happened to her?"

"She didn't die in the armor or anything, if that's what you're worried about."

Larin nodded, feeling a small amount of relief. "Maybe she was promoted out of the field and took the armor with her. That happens, sometimes."

"But she sold it," he said. "Would she have needed the money that badly?"

"Her kids might have. It's *old* armor, Shigar, last in action before the Treaty of Coruscant. Took me a lot of work to get it into the shape it was, let me tell you."

"You could've bought new armor anytime," he said, "but you didn't want to. It's a symbol standing in for all the things that need to be fixed."

"Is that what you think?"

"Just a guess."

His green eyes watched her unblinkingly. She felt sometimes that they looked right into her. Sometimes she liked that feeling. Sometimes she didn't.

"You're thinking too much," she told him.

"That's what I've been trained to do."

"I'm sure it isn't. I'm sure the Grand Master trained you to think just enough, and no more. But the lesson hasn't quite sunk in yet because people only learn it the hard way. And that's where you are right now. Absolutely stuck, in a hard place. Right?"

Still he didn't look away. "Maybe."

"Maybe nothing. You know you have to do something. You know what it is and you know why it has to be done. But you can't do it because you're too busy going over it and over it, making sure you're absolutely right. Most of you knows you are right, but there's a small part that wants to think it over one more time. The reasons, the method, the fallout. Whatever. Like you can plan everything in advance and then just sit back and watch it happen, so perfectly you don't even have to be there to do it. Things will just happen on their own. Maybe you don't need to do *anything* if you think about it hard enough. That's always worth hoping for."

"You're speaking from experience, I can tell."

"You bet," she said, but then she stopped. The words had dried up.

"It's okay," he said. "You don't have to tell me."

"No, I do. I need to tell someone, one day. It might as well be you, now." She felt her face growing warm, and she turned away, hoping he couldn't see. "I ratted on a superior officer."

"I presume you had a reason."

"The best. Sergeant Donbar was corrupt. But that didn't change anything. I went against the chain of command and reported him to his superiors. They slapped him down and discharged him, but the reason for it was hushed up. There were always going to be people who didn't believe me, thought I was doing it out of a grudge, but because of the secrecy I couldn't defend myself. No one wants Special Forces to look bad, and he was about as bad as it gets. He was discharged, and eventually I quit. It got way too uncomfortable."

"Do you regret it?"

"Sometimes," she said, thinking of the Zabrak on Coruscant, "but it had to be done. If I tried to capture the weeks of agonizing I went through leading up to me actually doing it, I'd bore you to death."

The skin around his eyes tightened. "And now you think I should just get over myself and do what I have to do."

"You don't agree?"

"Not at all. Finding a planet that could be anywhere in Wild Space is a little different from putting in a report, don't you think?"

"Sure it's different. You don't stand to lose every friend you've ever had if you do the right thing. And you've actually been training for this most of your life. Remember, Shigar, that you didn't have to crawl up from nowhere to get where you are. You were handpicked from everyone on Kiffu to be a Jedi Knight. Whatever happens today, you'll go back to the life you know. So you can do it at your own pace, or you can do it when you *need* to do it. I for one think there's only one right choice."

He looked away. "You came to tell me you think I've got it easy. That makes a huge difference. Thanks."

His sarcasm stung. Larin didn't know what she'd come to him for, really, except to break him out of his funk. She was surprised at how deep the feelings ran and the harshness with which she had spoken. It was hard to tell how much was for his benefit.

"All right, then," she said. "I'll leave you to it."

When she stood, her knees practically shook with fatigue.

"I will do it," he said. "I have to."

"Well, keep it down when you do. I'm going to catch up on some sleep."

She didn't wait for his snappy comeback, if he had one. Letting her legs work on autopilot, she went to a bunk in the crew quarters and was asleep before her head hit the pillow.

SHIGAR LISTENED TO her go. Already he regretted the way he had reacted to her combined advice and confession. Clearly, she had been building up to the latter part for some time, and he should have showed more compassion. But he was so bound up in his own issues, his own self-centered mess, that he hadn't been able to see the raw wound she had exposed to him. Not her hand, but the aching severance from everything she had once held dear.

How would he feel, he asked himself, if he had to turn his back on the Jedi Order? It was impossible to imagine Master Satele ever doing anything counter to the Code he lived by, but famous Jedi had fallen to the dark side before. What if he discovered that she was in fact working against the Council? And what if he knew that her word would be taken against his? Was his sense of justice strong enough to make the call anyway, as Larin's had been?

Once he would have been completely sure of himself. Now, after his dealings with Tassaa Bareesh, he wasn't so sure.

And still there was the matter of the mysterious world, waiting to be resolved.

The piece of droid-nest glinted impassively back at him.

Larin was right on one point: sitting around thinking about it would get him nowhere. All the time he had been isolated in the dark, he hadn't even touched the silver sliver. He had been trying and failing to get his mind into the right state, believing that there was no point even starting until he was completely ready.

Larin's faith in you is not unwarranted. Perhaps you should have faith in her, too.

Shigar remembered how he had felt when Master Satele had ordered him to go to Hutta. He had invited Larin along because he felt she needed him to prove something to herself. She was full of bluster but lacking a clear sense of purpose. Now he understood why that core of her life was missing, and it was *he* who needed to prove something. If he didn't, he would do much worse than let down his Master and the Republic. He would fail himself.

There's only one right choice.

He picked up the sliver of metal. It was cool and sharp-edged to the touch. If he put it in his right fist and squeezed, it would surely draw blood.

He engulfed it in his fist and squeezed.

The bottom dropped out of the hold and he was suddenly falling.

His first thought was to grab hold of something and hang on, both mentally and physically. This was utterly unlike any psychometric information he had ever received before. But *what* he was reading this time was unlike anything he'd tried touching before, so fighting the vision could be self-defeating. Perhaps being plunged in the deep end was exactly what he needed. He braced himself against the rush of vertigo and tried to take from the experience what he could.

Falling. At first there seemed to be nothing more to it than that. Then he noticed details highly reminiscent of the strange blue geometry of hyperspace. Was that what he was glimpsing? The nest's last journey, or its first?

There was a blinding flash of light, and he stopped with a jerk. All was dark again. Voices came and went, too indistinct to make out words. They were raised, though, as if in an argument. He could make out no faces, no locations, no coordinates. Just a feeling: that the thing the sliver had belonged to was determined to survive.

The *Cinzia,* he thought. He *was* spooling back through the droid factory's history, in reverse. It clearly possessed a rudimentary self-awareness, which shouldn't have come as a surprise since it had single-handedly organized the surreptitious creation of four advanced combat droids without being detected. Even if most of its internal algorithms were automated, it had taken a certain degree of cunning to know when to lay low and when to become active.

The flash was probably the explosion that had almost killed it.

Shigar wanted to get moving again. The next jump would be the one that would take him home, to where the droid factory had originated. But his eagerness only caused the vision to fray about the edges—and suddenly he was dumped back onto the hard floor of the hold with nothing to show for the experience.

He sat, breathing heavily and cursing his impatience.

When he opened his right hand, the sliver rested on his palm in a growing pool of blood.

What had he done this time, compared with all the other times before, that had worked?

He could guess the answer, and it was dismayingly simple. He hadn't done anything special. He'd just done it. The Force had moved through him in exactly the right way, and the knowledge he'd been looking for had come to him. It hadn't taken any particular degree of concentration, or any fancy mental footwork. He had done it because he could do it. There was a fair chance he hadn't always been able to do it; he was sure that all those years of training hadn't been for nothing. But at some point, as Larin had said, all the extra thinking he did on the subject had been wasted. It had, in fact, been counterproductive.

The next question was: could he do it again?

He didn't need to ask. He didn't *want* to ask it. The time for questions was over.

He transferred the sliver to his left hand and squeezed again.

A second vision of hyperspace enfolded him. Falling faster this time. The blue tunnel was twisted, warped. He felt dizzy. Mysterious forces tugged at him, shook him violently at times. He felt like he was running down a steep mountain and that at any moment he might trip and tumble headlong all the way to the bottom. As the droid factory's journey unspooled backward in time, it took him into a deep, dark place.

Shigar didn't question the vision. He let it unfold at its own pace. The shuddering grew worse as he neared the *Cinzia*'s origin, until he felt that he might be torn apart.

When it ceased, all was quiet. He felt a sense of homecoming, even though that was surely illusory. The factory was a machine, and it had been leaving its homeworld, not arriving there. But the feeling was persuasive. He felt that he belonged here, and that here—wherever *here* was—was important and precious. Unique. Shigar understood that feeling, even though he'd never felt it for Kiffu, his birthplace. Shigar had been a citizen of the galaxy for too long to feel close ties anywhere.

Again he thought of Larin and her changed circumstances. She, too, had taken great strides across the Republic and beyond. But now she was stuck on Coruscant—or had been until his arrival. She had never expressed any unhappiness about her relative confinement, but he could only imagine how it must feel.

The droid factory felt as though it belonged. Wherever it came from, that was where it had wanted to be. And Larin had killed it.

Perhaps, he thought, that had been a mercy.

More voices, this time with blurry faces. Human men and women; Shigar didn't recognize any of them. He made out some words, though, including the hexes' furious catch-cry. It was being chanted by a group of people, including a woman of middle years, with short ash-blond hair and intelligent eyes. Her hand was raised above her head. She was shaking her fist at the sky—but it wasn't a sky at all. It was a roof. She was in a large space with a tubular tank at its center, filled with red.

Shigar didn't fight the vision. He just told it: *I want to be inside her head.*

And he was. He was enfolded by a turbulent flow of thoughts and sensory impressions. He tumbled, slightly in awe of how easy it had been. Nothing like this had ever happened before. Perhaps there was something special about her, this Lema Xandret.

For it was indeed her. He was buffeted by her rage. He found strength in her determination to live unfettered. He grew weary at the understanding that all things must eventually be compromised, or die. He felt satisfaction at all her achievements. He wept at the mingled love and loss of a child.

Shigar looked through her eyes at the world she had adopted for her own, and felt pride tinged with worry, and an intense desire for revenge.

We do not recognize your authority!

And there it was, at last. Everything he had been looking for: the dense, metallic world, rich with change and vigor, where no one would have looked for it in a million years.

His eyes snapped open. He didn't feel the pain of the cuts to his palms. He had forgotten the various aches and pains of his body, earned the hard way on Hutta. He felt only a degree of gratitude that he had never experienced before, blended with a powerful sense of achievement.

Climbing to his feet, he hurried to the crew quarters. Larin was already fast asleep. He thought about waking her to tell her the news but reined in the impulse. She deserved her rest. He could thank her later.

Ula and Jet were in the cockpit. He clambered up the ladder and burst into their conversation.

"I know where it is!"

"The world?" asked Ula, looking up in surprise.

"Yes. I found it!"

"Good for you, mate," said Jet. "Got some coordinates for me?"

"Not exactly," Shigar said, "but I can describe it to you. I think it'll be fairly easy to pin down."

"Well, great. I'm very tired of the view here. Take a seat and we'll get started."

Shigar felt his sense of triumph ebb slightly at the thought of what lay ahead of them.

"What?" asked Ula, staring at his face. "Is there a problem?"

"You could say that."

Their faces fell in unison as he told them.

Finding the planet was one thing.

Getting there would be another entirely.

CHAPTER 26

SPECIALIST PEDISIC LOOKED up as Ax walked into the quarantine bay. The space had been transformed. Large pieces of equipment hovered over the dissection table, connected by thick cables to the bulk cruiser's main processor arrays. The remains of the hex had been splayed out like a delicate tapestry, revealing intricate details of its structure and function. The cell walls that made it robust as well as lightweight were threaded with shining metal, suggesting that they performed key functions as well as providing internal support. She saw several fist-sized globes like round, silver eggs nestling against more familiar components. The legs had been removed entirely from complex-looking joints and stacked like metal antlers in a transparisteel jar.

"I have much to report, sir," the specialist said. She had rolled her sleeves up, and her arms were smeared with brown-black goo up to her elbows.

"Then do so." Ax stood with her hands on her hips at one end of the table. She had been generous. The specialist had had more than an hour. If Darth Chratis had not been so *conversational* in his discipline, Ax would have come back much sooner.

"Well, the first thing I can tell you is that this thing, whatever it is, isn't finished." Pedisic selected a slender-tipped tool from the many surrounding her work space and pointed as she talked. "See here: its neuro-web was interrupted before the completion of a full suite of reflex analogues. And here: there's a full array of senses about to come online down this dorsal region, but it's totally unconnected to the central computer. The reporting system has only grown to here and has yet to join the two."

"You mean it was released too early, before it was ready?"

"There's evidence to suggest that it was continuing to develop after it left the factory that built it. I suggest this thing would have finished itself, given time."

Ax remembered how ferociously the thing had fought. And it hadn't even been complete! "What would the final form have been like?"

"It's impossible to say. The main data bank doesn't contain a single template. Instead there are many, with lots of transitional forms. And there's a biological component, too, that I find very puzzling. This brown stuff must perform some function, otherwise it wouldn't be present in such quantities. Perhaps it acts as a randomizing agent, encouraging it to adapt more fluidly. It's hard to analyze, though, because it's been so severely cooked."

She looked at Ax reproachfully, as though blaming her for the condition of the sample. In this case, Ax was completely innocent. Either the Jedi or the Mandalorian had done that job for her.

And either way, it was irrelevant.

"So you've accessed the brain, then."

"Yes. Just this minute."

"How smart was it? Could it fly a ship, for instance?"

"Not likely, my lord, but if it needed to, it could change itself so it could. Like birds grow new parts of their brains in spring to learn new songs. It's just a matter of—"

Ax waved her silent. "Is the data encoded?"

"Naturally, but the cipher is based on an Imperial system that went out of use fifteen years ago."

When Lema Xandret fled the Empire, Ax remembered.

"I'll crack it soon. Don't worry, my lord. The fact that the thing was incomplete actually made getting in easier. All I have to do is map the architecture and find my way around . . ."

Ax didn't pay attention to the specifics. And she hadn't been aware that she'd looked worried. If this specialist couldn't do the job, she'd just get another.

"All I want to know is where this thing came from," she said. "And I want to know now."

Specialist Pedisic nodded. "Yes, my lord. With your permission, I'll resume my examination."

Ax indicated with a flick of one index finger that the specialist should return to work.

While Ax waited, she paced the crowded space, reading raw data and coming to her own conclusions. Nothing she saw contradicted the specialist's opinions, and there was much more to be absorbed than could have been crammed into that short conversation. The globes contained the hex's primary processors, where sensory data converged, was exchanged, and provoked various environmental responses. The weapons on each hand were little different in principle from standard blaster technology, but remarkably miniaturized and integrated into a limb capable of gripping and supporting weight as well. This hex had no camouflage system to analyze, and unfortunately the electromirror defense was too badly damaged to reverse-engineer. Whole sections of its body had been fried to ash.

"I've cracked the code, my lord," said the specialist.

Ax hurried to peer over her shoulder. Scrolling through a holopad was a list of symbols—the blocks from which the hex's mind and all its actions were built. None of the commands, language rules, and algorithms, however, looked remotely familiar to Ax.

"These controlled the hex? The droid, I mean."

"Yes."

"Could we use them to control others?"

"I fear not. These particular commands are generated within the device itself—a unique and purely internal system for coordinating its many parts. Each droid would have a different system, so what we've gained is merely the language for *this* droid, which is now dead."

"All right, but you *have* translated it, in this case?"

"Yes."

"So find me what I'm looking for. Time is short." *I have a Mandalorian to beat,* she said silently to herself, *and if I lose, you are going to pay dearly.*

The specialist bent low over the section of the hex she had exposed, remotely operating manipulators capable of tinier measurements than any human could make. Data scrolled dizzyingly in all directions through the holopad, too fast for Ax to follow. Her head soon ached from concentrating too hard on something she didn't really understand.

"You have one minute," she told the specialist.

"My lord, I've found it," Pedisic said. "Name, hyperspace coordinates—"

"Give them to me." A sudden upwelling of excitement filled her. "Now!"

Where are you, Mother?

Specialist Pedisic rattled off a long string of numbers. Ax closed her eyes, visualizing roughly where the location fit into the galactic disk.

It didn't. It was well above the Mid Rim, in the middle of nowhere.

Ax opened her eyes. "Are you sure that's what's in its head?"

"Positive, sir. Although it doesn't make sense, does it? There's nothing out there. Nothing at all."

Well, Ax told herself, that wasn't entirely true. There were cold dwarfs and orphaned gas giants and all manner of strange stellar beasts. And it *was* an undiscovered world, after all, fit for traitorous droid makers on the run from the Sith. It wasn't unreasonable that people desperate to keep their location a secret might have traveled parsecs out of their way to obscure any chance of pursuit.

But what had led Lema Xandret to that isolated haven in the first place? What had encouraged her to look in that direction? The odds of her taking a ship on a long jump to nowhere and just happening to arrive at a habitable world were minute.

"Run the coordinates through Imperial records," she told the specialist. "I'm guessing we'll find something in there."

The request went to the ship's data banks. Ax tapped her finger on the dissection table as she waited for the response. It took longer than expected, and she had time enough to observe just how much the baked organic residue looked like dried blood . . .

With a chime, the holopad produced a single line of information.

"Now, that really *is* impossible," said the specialist.

"Try again."

The specialist repeated the procedure from scratch, extracting the embedded data and feeding it into the records.

The same result came back.

"It must be a bluff," the specialist said. "A false location to throw us off the scent."

"I don't think so," said Ax. "Everything about it looks wrong, but that tells me we must be right. I told you we'd find something, didn't I?"

"But it's a *black hole,*" said the specialist.

"I know. I can read it with my own eyes."

Ax felt as though that distant, dead star had reached out and clutched her with its irresistible gravity. She was absolutely certain that this was where she would find Lema Xandret, builder of droids who spoke with her own voice.

"I think you'd better give me the name, now," she said. "We'll be leaving as soon as the course is plotted."

PART FOUR

SEBADDON

CHAPTER 27

IT WAS AN unassuming name, Ula thought as the *Auriga Fire* shook around him, for a colony that shouldn't exist.

Sebaddon.

"You know we're insane, don't you?" Jet said over the sound of the ship's straining hyperdrives. "If the black hole's mass shadow doesn't tear us to pieces, its gravity will suck us in when we arrive."

"We plotted the course to account for either possibility," said Shigar. "We'll be okay. Probably."

"I'll try not to think about it," said Ula through ground teeth.

"I'm just trying not to throw up," said Larin.

Ula twisted in his seat to look back at her. She winked.

"How much longer?" Shigar asked.

His calm confidence was infuriating. Ula didn't know how Jet put up with it.

"Somewhere between a minute and never. Most likely the latter."

The ship creaked from nose to tail as though something had grabbed it at either end and *twisted.* Ula clutched the arms of his chair and closed his eyes. This wasn't what he had signed up for. Being an informer was supposed to be sitting in the shadows, stealing information, and plotting the odd assassination. It wasn't fighting killer droids, being tortured by Mandalorians, or diving headlong into a black hole. That's what Cipher Agents did.

A strong hand gripped his elbow. His eyes flickered open.

"Don't worry," said Larin. "We'll make it."

He nodded and forced his hands to release their grip on the chair. Let her think he was reassured, when in fact he was the exact opposite. Shigar's psychometric revelation had raised her faith in him to new heights, although there was a new tension between them now, as though their relationship had fundamentally shifted. That, Ula thought, might be the most galling thing about his situation.

Her hand slipped away. Her *good* hand. The one cut in half by the Sith was encased in a mechanical glove, a paddle-like mitten that enabled her to grip, little more. That was the full extent of the *Auriga Fire*'s prosthetic provisions.

The ship lurched again. Clunker came forward, swaying and rocking, and ran a cable from his midsection into the main console.

"What's he doing?" Ula asked.

"Syncing his mind to the ship's computer," said Jet past his droid's battered casing.

"You're letting him fly the ship?"

"He's got a good head on his shoulders, and his reaction time's much faster than mine."

As if to disprove Jet's assertion, the *Auriga Fire* tilted alarmingly to starboard, then whipped back to port. Ula was thrown about in his seat harness, but somehow Clunker managed to stay both upright and plugged in.

A moment later the ship's flight grew calm. The vibrations eased; the complaints from both hyperdrive and hull receded into the background. The knot of tension in Ula's stomach began to unwind.

"Okay," said Jet, punching buttons. "It's coming up now. Hold on!"

Ula stiffened again as the warped textures of hyperspace receded. Normally, a speed-stretched vista of stars would take its place, but out here, on the very fringes of the galaxy, they were pointing out into the relative black. Only the faint light of distant stellar islands existed to be warped by the ship's motion.

With a gut-roiling wrench, the *Auriga Fire* returned to realspace, and the shaking resumed.

Jet shut down the hyperdrives and put the repulsors on full. Ula was pressed into his seat as the ship came about. Sensors swept the sky ahead, revealing vistas unseen by anyone apart from Lema Xandret and her companions in the history of the galaxy.

It was much lighter than Ula had expected. That was his first impression. As the ship hove about and the black hole came into view, he saw not a dark absence of light but two bright yellow jets squirting from either pole of the singularity. That was what remained of the hole's last meal—a dead star, perhaps, or a lonely gas giant that had been unfortunate enough to cross paths with this bottomless monster. As though someone had crammed too much food into their mouth at once, some of the meal squirted back into space, blazing away like celestial torches against the backdrop of the galaxy.

The second thing Ula noticed was the galaxy itself. The ship and its passengers were far enough away from the galaxy's inhabited disk that they could see it from the outside. A beautiful spiral with a fat central bulge, it occupied almost half of the sky. As it swung into view, Ula forgot his anxieties for a moment and experienced nothing but breathless awe. Every nebula, cluster, and gulf was revealed to him with more clarity and beauty than any map could show. It was hard to believe that something so sublime could be the locus of so much war and grief.

"There's the planet," said Jet, playing his instruments like a maestro.

"Sebaddon? Where?" Shigar peered out at the spectacular vista.

"There." Jet indicated a display. Ula could see nothing more than a dot. "It's farther out than I expected. We'll loop around the hole and catch it on the upswing."

"Is that safe?" Ula asked.

"Relatively. As long as we don't come too close."

Ula didn't want to ask: *Relative to what?*

Shigar was watching the display. "No sign of any other ships," he said. "There's a small moon."

"How could it have a moon?" asked Hetchkee from the seat behind Ula.

"How could it be here at all?" added Larin.

"A black hole will kill you if you come too close," said Shigar, "but not if you're at a safe distance. Things can easily orbit it. Sebaddon, any random piece of junk it's snapped up over the years, us."

The way the ship was rattling didn't make Ula feel remotely safe. "What about heat?" he asked. "Those jets are hot, but not *that* hot."

"As the planet orbits, the hole's gravity will stretch and squeeze it, stopping its core from solidifying. I bet we'll see volcanoes when we get closer. That must be what's bringing all the rare metals to the surface—and carbon dioxide, too, which would also help keep the atmosphere warm."

The jets were getting visibly larger ahead. Clunker remained plugged in. Sebaddon was still invisible to the naked eye, and Ula gave up looking for it.

An alarm sounded. "Ships," said Jet, "behind us, exactly where we came out."

"Who do they belong to?" asked Larin.

"Wait until we've gone around. Then I'll be able to tell you."

The display dissolved into static as they fell deeper into the black hole's frighteningly intense magnetic field. A smell of ozone filled the cockpit. Anything containing iron began to vibrate at an annoyingly high pitch.

There was no sense of weight because they were free-falling around the hole, using its gravitational pull to launch them out to where the planet was orbiting. Still Ula felt as though he was being simultaneously stretched and squeezed, just like Shigar had described when talking about the planet. Tidal effects, they were called. His lungs struggled to pull in enough air, and purple spots danced in front of his eyes.

Then they were past and the pressure began to ease. He sagged back into the chair, sweating heavily and thanking the Emperor he was still alive.

"Right," said Jet, "that's the hard part over. Thanks, Clunker. Sebaddon coming up ahead. We'll make orbital insertion in about a minute. As for those ships . . ." He scanned the revived sensor displays. "I count fifteen, with Republic transponder codes. Stantorrs must have moved Coruscant itself to get them here this fast."

Shigar nodded. It was clear he, too, was impressed. "No sign of Stryver?"

"That's what the scopes say."

"What about the Empire?" asked Ula.

"The only ships here are those fifteen and us," said Jet.

"How would the Sith know where to come, anyway?" asked Larin. "They didn't have the navicomp."

"They might have thought of something else, like we did," said Ula, trying to keep his hopes up even though he phrased it as a warning. "Best not to underestimate them."

"Indeed," Larin said. "There it is," she added, pointing through the forward ports.

Ula craned to see.

Sebaddon was a small world, scarred by tectonic activity, just as Shigar had predicted. Its surface ranged from gray basalt to red-glowing mantle exposed to the atmosphere by constant plate motion. The atmosphere was dense enough to breathe and showed signs of both clouds and precipitation. There were no oceans, just the occasional shining surfaces on the cooler parts of the planet that might have been lakes.

"If that's water," Larin said, "the surface could actually be habitable."

Near one of the "lakes" was a cluster of bright radiation sources, indicating a city of some kind. Elsewhere on the unfolding globe were other bright points, possibly mines or smaller settlements.

"Someone's been busy," said Jet. "How long have they been here?"

"We don't know," said Shigar.

"I'd guess twenty years, assuming only a small group to start with. The infrastructure is patchy, and there are some places they haven't spread out to yet."

Jet pointed at the viewscreen as he talked. There were no ships in orbit or satellites. The tiny moon was completely untouched.

"Do you want me to hail them?" he asked.

"No," Shigar told him. "Wait for Master Shan to arrive. She should be the one to make first contact."

"What about Ula?" asked Larin. "He's the Republic envoy."

"No offense," said Shigar, turning to speak directly to Ula, "someone superior to both of us should handle this. I hope you understand."

"Completely," he said, with manufactured grace. He would have preferred to bungle a Republic approach to the valuable world in the hope that his enemy's overtures would be repulsed. But there was no way to argue the point without making people suspicious. He would just have to bide his time and hope another opportunity arose.

The *Auriga Fire* slipped neatly into a long polar orbit around Sebaddon, and the ship's engines fell blessedly quiet. Clunker disconnected himself and returned to his place in the corner. It had been hours of racket and mayhem ever since they'd commenced the last jump, and Ula was profoundly glad it was over.

Jet clearly shared his sentiments. The smuggler stood up and tapped at the shielding above the instrument panels. "Come on," he muttered. "I know it's here somewhere . . ."

A hidden panel popped open, and he slipped a hand inside. "Aha! Those fragging Hutts didn't find *everything*, thank goodness."

The hand reappeared in view, holding a slender bottle of golden liquid. Jet cracked the seal and knocked back a swig. "Anyone else for a toast? To making it alive, despite crazy passengers and unreliable directions?"

Jet's behavior went largely ignored. For the moment, all eyes were on Master Satele's approaching flotilla. Like Jet, she had chosen to come around the black hole rather than try to power outward against its considerable pull. The vast forces acting on the ships were much more apparent from the outside. Ula was shocked by the speeds they reached at their closest points to the black hole. One of them failed to make the correct insertion and drifted just a fraction off its course. Instantly the hole snatched at it, tumbling it end-over-end into the gaping maw. It disappeared with a scream of X-rays.

One by one, the remaining fourteen ships came out the other side, shaken but intact.

"See if you can raise them yet," said Shigar. "Code word *hawk-bat*."

"Will do." Jet capped the bottle and put it away before

turning to the comm. "Long-range subspace is scrambled by the singularity, so you can't call home, but we should be able to open short-range transmissions with them in a moment or two."

"Weird to think that this could all be over in a few minutes," said Larin as Jet attempted to hail the approaching ships. "I mean, Stryver has either lost interest or fallen into the hole. The Empire has no clue where we've gone. Once Master Shan gets in touch with Lema Xandret, our job is done."

"You've forgotten the Hutts," said Ula. "If they have put a homing device on the ship, they'll soon track us down."

"Only if they're looking for the signal in the right direction. And who'd think to look up here? It's the perfect hiding place."

Jet had a point, but Ula didn't want to admit it. Once Sebaddon was annexed by the Republic, there was nothing he could do but report the planet's position when he returned to Coruscant, long after the issue of its ownership had been resolved. His mission was on the brink of utter failure, and there didn't seem to be much he could do about it.

"That Mandalorian seemed pretty canny to me," chimed in Hetchkee. "I can't see him falling into a black hole, unless he was pushed."

"I'm of the same mind," said Shigar. "It would be unwise to assume we've seen the last of him."

"Got her," said Jet, falling back into his seat in satisfaction. "Go ahead, Grand Master."

"Very good work, Shigar," crackled the voice of Satele Shan from the subspace communicator.

"Thank you, Master." The Padawan was clearly buoyed by the praise.

"The Supreme Commander would like you to return Envoy Vii to Coruscant as soon as possible."

"With your permission," said Shigar, "we'd like to join the companies you brought with you and observe the negotiations."

"Hang on a minute, mate—" said Jet, but Shigar cut him off.

"We've been chasing Lema Xandret for so long. It seems a shame to come all this way and just turn back."

Ula didn't know what he thought about that prospect. On the one hand, he expected nothing more interesting than very familiar diplomatic wrangling; on the other hand, he was in no hurry to report his failure to either of his masters.

"I expected that," Master Satele replied with the hint of a smile in her voice. "Colonel Gurin has command of the fleet. I'll suggest you fall in with Second Company and take the place of the ship we lost. Expect a tactical feed shortly."

"Thank you again, Master," Shigar said, surrendering control of the comm to an unhappy Jet Nebula. Already instructions and telemetry were flowing into the *Auriga Fire* from the approaching ships. When Jet patched his ship's computer into the feed, it would become part of a much larger tactical entity, no longer a free agent.

"Cheer up," said Shigar to Jet with a grin. "You've worked for the Republic before, haven't you?"

"Sure, but only for their money. Not for glory or the fun of it, like you seem to."

"It won't be for long. I just want to see this."

"You're not fooling anyone, Shigar. I know you don't want to make good on your deal with Tassaa Bareesh."

Shigar pulled down the corners of his mouth but said nothing to deny the charge.

The cruiser Master Satele occupied hove past them, a golden lozenge that looked deceptively smaller than it actually was, with a command nacelle protruding like an insect's sting from the rear and a hull studded with turbolaser and ion cannon blisters. By craning his neck, Ula could make out the telemetry streaming into the *Auriga Fire*. The cruiser was called the *Corellia*. He recognized its name from Supreme Command Stantorrs's reports.

Jet surrendered his ship to Republic command. Soon they were just one of eight vessels obeying instructions from Colonel Gurin. The assembly of ships moved smoothly into a lower orbit, juggling course and attitude changes with confident ease. Cheerfully business-like intership chatter filled the comm, both biological and droid. Clunker's usual blank posture became more attentive. Ula, too, listened closely for valuable intel. In such tense times, military protocols changed almost daily.

"I'm registering activity down below," said Jet. "Xandret and her people know we're here."

"Why aren't they saying anything, then?" asked Larin.

"Perhaps they're shy."

"What kind of activity?" asked Shigar.

"Heat dumps, mainly, perhaps reactors firing up. A couple look like industrial sites, but their signatures are off the scale."

"Are you passing the data on to Colonel Gurin?"

"He's seeing exactly what we're seeing, unless he's admiring the view elsewhere."

The galaxy formed a beautiful pinwheel backdrop as Satele Shan made her first broadcast to the people of Sebaddon.

"My name is Grand Master Satele Shan," she said, broadcasting on all frequencies, since most commonly used bands were clogged by radiation from the black hole. "I come not in the name of the Republic, but on behalf of the upholders of peace and justice across the galaxy."

"What's that all about?" asked Hetchkee.

"It's Jedi double talk," said Larin. "She doesn't want the Sebaddonites to think they're about to be invaded."

"Even though she's riding at the head of a fleet of Republic warships?"

"Even so."

Shigar raised a hand for silence. No one had replied, so Master Satele was trying again.

"We have reason to believe that a diplomatic mission sent from Sebaddon was intercepted before it could reach its destination. We are not responsible for its destruction but I wish to convey to you our sincerest regrets and to share with you the data we have collected regarding this unfortunate incident."

"More activity," said Jet. "Those hot spots are getting really hot."

"Are you sure they're not volcanoes?" asked Larin.

He didn't reply, and neither did the people of Sebaddon to Satele Shan's last message.

"They could be volcanoes," said Ula, unwilling to dismiss any suggestion Larin made, even one intended as a joke. "It would make sense to tap into geothermal power on a world like this. If they've found a way to store and release that power, that could be what we're seeing here."

"Or they could be launch sites," said Jet.

"If they're sending up a welcoming party, why wouldn't they say so?"

"It might not be the sort of welcoming party you're thinking of."

"I have come to speak with Lema Xandret," the Grand Master tried a third time. "I have reason to believe that she might be your leader."

At last something broke the silence from the planet. A woman's voice came over the airwaves, crackling faintly with interference.

"We have no leader."

"Very well," said Master Satele, "but am I speaking to Lema now?"

"We ask only to be left alone."

"You have nothing to fear from us. I swear it. We have come to talk, and to offer you protection if you need it. You are under no obligation to offer anything in return."

"We do not recognize your authority."

Ula's skin crawled. "That's what the hexes said. She sounds just like them."

Shigar was nodding. "This must be Xandret. The hexes share her voice and her philosophies because she was the one who made them."

"We have no wish to impose any kind of authority upon you," Master Satele was saying.

"We ask only to be left alone," Xandret repeated.

"Those hot spots are about ready to erupt," said Jet in ominous tones.

"Give me the comm," Shigar said. "Master, I don't think talking is going to work. She's as stubborn as her droids. I suggest finding another approach."

The Grand Master was already talking: "Perhaps I could speak with you face-to-face. That might help us reach an understanding. Just me and my Padawan, in a place of your choosing. The last thing I want is for you or your leaders to feel threatened or intimidated—"

"We have no leader!" Xandret shouted. "We do not recognize your authority!"

"Here it comes," said Jet, calling up in the viewscreen several bright flashes from the surface of the world. "They look like missiles to anyone else?"

Ula peered closely at the image. His knowledge of military hardware was patchy, but the rapidly rising dots did have a lethal air. For a start, they moved quickly, accelerating many times faster than most crewed ships would risk in atmosphere. There were eight of them, long and sleek. They spiraled like fireworks as they rose, presenting a much more difficult target to the ships above.

The *Auriga Fire* lurched underneath him, responding to telemetry from the *Corellia.* As one, all fifteen ships changed course in response to the rising threat.

"There's your answer," said Larin. "Someone is definitely taking this seriously."

"Fine," said Jet, "but I'm not slaving my ship to anyone while it's under fire."

"Wait," said Shigar, but it was too late. Jet had already broken the short-lived connection between his ship and those of the Republic. With a flash of its repulsors, the *Auriga Fire* peeled away from Second Company and accelerated to a higher orbit.

Behind them, the ships of the Republic adopted battle formation, with the *Corellia* in the center and support vessels in a crisp tetrahedron around it. While fighters launched from hangar decks, its cannons trained on the approaching targets. The Grand Master said nothing, and the usual interfleet chatter ceased.

"Fall in line, *Auriga Fire*" came a terse request from the *Corellia.* "Fall in line!"

Jet ignored it, but kept the tactical feed open.

"This doesn't make any sense," said Ula, thinking aloud. "If Xandret wants to stay isolated so badly, why would she want to talk to the Mandalorians? I'd have thought that's *exactly* the wrong thing to do."

"Maybe the *Cinzia* didn't represent everyone here," Larin said. "Maybe the people who blew themselves up were a dissident group."

"And why attack rather than talk?" he asked, moving on to his next point of puzzlement. "Firing without provocation is madness."

"Without a doubt," said Shigar. "They've practically signed their own death warrant."

The missiles roared out of the upper atmosphere and hit the first wave of defensive fire. A dense net of turbolaser pulses and ion torpedoes converged on the eight missiles. The nose of each missile activated a defensive shield not dissimilar to the ones seen on a much smaller scale on Hutta. Mirror-bright, they reflected laser pulses perfectly, and even deflected a large number of torpedoes. The space between the *Corellia* and the planet below was suddenly full of explosions.

Out of that stew of hot gases only six missiles emerged. The debris of the two that had been hit tumbled on, following their final momentum. Tiny white dots gleamed in the light of the black hole's jets.

The six missiles hit another wave of defensive fire. The shields flashed again, blinking on and off in rapid succession—to conserve power, Ula assumed. The missiles weren't large. They couldn't defend themselves forever against this kind of assault.

But they didn't have to. Four of the original eight were now close enough to the capital ships to be an imminent threat. Fighters engaged, strafing the missiles from all directions at once. The shields couldn't cover every possible approach. Three missiles faltered, their drive systems crippled and their sides spewing clouds of debris. The last thundered on, aimed squarely at the *Corellia*.

The look on Shigar's face was painful to see. His Master was aboard that ship, and a missile of that size was bound to do considerable damage, perhaps even destroy the *Corellia* outright. Ula wondered if she was hurrying for an escape pod at that very moment, hoping to outrun her fate.

The missile survived the final wave of defensive fire and struck the *Corellia* just forward of its stardrive.

Ula winced automatically, expecting a giant explosion.

None came. The missile hit the golden hull with enough

force to tear a hole right through it, but instead simply vanished inside. A blast of air and other gases roared out of the hole. No fire. The missile didn't blow up.

Fleet comms rose up again, betraying a slightly frantic note. Colonel Gurin was on the air, reassuring everyone that the cruiser was intact. There were no more launches visible from the ground. The attack from Sebaddon appeared to have completely fizzled.

The clouds of debris from the seven fallen missiles, still rising under their own momentum, began to arrive. Some of it was scraps of torn hulls and engines. Much consisted of the same white dots Ula had glimpsed earlier. They sparkled like snowflakes in sunlight, drifting around the Republic ships in undirected streams.

"Can we get a closer look at that stuff?" he asked. "If the missiles weren't packed with explosives, maybe they weren't missiles at all."

Jet complied, focusing the ship's sensors on a nearby patch. The white dots resolved into blobs swimming like amoebas against the black sky.

"I'll see if I can increase the resolution," he said.

The view crystallized. The blobs became hexagonal objects waving six slender legs.

Ula felt a wave of alarm. *Hexes.* Thousands upon thousands of hexes.

"Get us away from them," said Shigar. "Put me through to Colonel Gurin."

The view shifted to show one of the Republic attack vessels. The hexes were thicker there. Where the hexes encountered one another, they linked arms and bodies to form larger objects—long strings, nets, or clumpy balls. The cruiser drifted among them, blissfully unaware, even as the drifting hexes found purchase on its hull.

"Get those ships out of there!" Shigar shouted into the subspace communicator. "They're in terrible danger!"

The reply was crackling and intermittent. "—interference—please repeat—" Behind his voice was the shrieking of alarms.

Ula peered past Shigar to where the *Corellia* hung against the globe of the planet. Red fire now licked at the rent left by the missile. On Hutta, four hexes had almost beaten a Jedi, a Sith, and a Mandalorian. Over Sebaddon, a missile's entire payload of hexes had been released into the body of a cruiser. He could only imagine what kind of damage such droids were causing in their hundreds among ordinary troops.

"Forget the *Corellia,*" said Jet. "We have to warn the others." He switched the comm to general broadcast. "This is the *Auriga Fire.* You are under attack. Use your fighters and gun emplacements to clear your hull. Then break orbit and head for clear space. The missiles contain the hexes we saw on Hutta. They'll rip you apart if you don't get clear of them."

"Tell them to ignore all orders from the *Corellia,*" said Ula. "If the network is compromised, the hexes could sow misinformation or worse."

Jet took up the advice and passed it on to the other ships. Only then did Ula kick himself for helping the Republic.

But he couldn't sit by and watch thousands of people die. The Republic had won the race. There was no advantage to be gained by assisting a slaughter.

A blast of powerful static drowned out all communications for a second. Then a new voice spoke from the *Corellia.*

"We do not recognize your authority!"

"That's the hexes speaking," said Larin. "They've taken control."

"The *Corellia*'s launching escape pods," said Shigar, pointing. "We have to get in closer. The pods will be able to dodge the hexes better than the big ships, but they need somewhere to rendezvous. We can give them that until someone else arrives."

"All right," said Jet, tight-lipped. "I want you and Larin on the tri-lasers, keeping our path clear. If just one of those things gets in here, we're all dead."

Shigar rose from his seat and vanished with Larin back into the ship.

"Ula, up here," said Jet, waving at the empty copilot's seat. "Hetchkee, you'll be on tractor control. Clunker, stop the signals from *Corellia* messing with our systems." The droid came forward to jack himself into the ship's computer again.

As Ula changed seats, he noticed a bright flashing light on the instrument panel in front of Jet. "Is that important?"

"Maybe, but it's one thing we don't have time to worry about right now." Jet punched buttons in fast sequence across the instrument panel. "We have more company."

Ula adjusted his viewscreen so it pointed back at the black hole. By the light of the jets, he made out a string of ships emerging from hyperspace. A large cruiser and numerous smaller vessels, strung out in two precise lines. He recognized their configuration immediately, and a surge of surprise swept through him.

Imperial ships.

But how? Stryver had the navicomp. They must have tracked him down and taken it from him. That would explain why there was no sign of the Mandalorian in the system. Adrenaline made his heart pound harder and faster. Yes, it made sense.

More than how they had gotten here, though, their very presence meant that there was still hope for an Imperial victory. With the Republic forces in such disarray, it would be easy to swoop in and overwhelm them.

Only with difficulty did he suppress a triumphant grin. Sebaddon would become the Empire's prize after all, and his mission would not have failed.

Then he remembered where he was, and all thoughts of victory fell away. The *Auriga Fire* was helping the Republic. If the Empire beat the Republic, he would be dead.

Aghast, he stared at the screen as the Imperial engines fired up their drives and powered in to attack.

CHAPTER 28

AX GRIPPED THE metal rail separating the senior command post from the rest of the bridge. Her knuckles were white. She had never before experienced such turbulence in hyperspace. Pilots sometimes bragged of navigating the singularity-rich Maw and told stories of ships lost there in bizarre circumstances. She had always thought them likely to be exaggerated. Now, however, battling the influence of just one black hole, she wondered if she had been a bit hasty in her judgment. It hadn't seriously occurred to her that she might be snuffed out of the universe by something as simple as a navigational accident. If this last jump from Circarpous V hadn't been calculated to the greatest degree of precision possible . . .

With an earsplitting groan, the *Paramount* burst back into realspace. A new kind of force immediately gripped the bulk cruiser, sending its crew rushing about to compensate for it. Ax let go of the rail and stood straight, lest anyone think her weak.

"We have arrived at the coordinates, Darth Chratis." The colonel was as thin as a medical droid, and his expression betrayed as much emotion. "All vessels are accounted for."

"Very good, Kalisch. Show me where we are."

Images danced around them, projected on massive viewscreens and holoprojectors around the bridge. The jets of the black hole were the first thing Ax noticed, stabbing like shining blades away from an invisible central point. They looked like narrowed eyes staring back at the galaxy in hatred.

From the outside, the galaxy's potential was completely revealed to her. With so many systems under her control, what couldn't she achieve?

"We have located a planet," said the colonel, relaying a report delivered by one of his many underlings. "We believe it to be the one called Sebaddon."

Ax quelled a sudden rush of excitement. She could betray nothing in front of her Master: relief, ambition, hope . . .

The screens shifted. A world torn and twisted by gravitational forces appeared before them, blurred with distance.

"My lord," said the colonel, "the most energy-efficient route is around the black hole." A map appeared in one of the viewscreens showing a dotted line looping past the singularity then rising to meet the planet at apogee. "On your command, I will issue the orders to the fleet captains."

"Normally I prefer the direct approach," Darth Chratis said, peering through slitted eyelids at the views before him. "What is this I see here?" One long finger picked out a particular view. "Energy spikes? Drive signatures?"

The colonel cast a cold, questioning stare at his bridge staff.

"I-it appears to be a space battle, my lord," ventured one of them, standing timorously in the spotlight.

"Identify those ships," barked the colonel. "I want to know who sent them."

"Yes, sir." The girl who had spoken sat down and began hammering furiously at her workstation.

Ax wondered who could be fighting out here. Stryver had the navicomp, and she had the only whole Hex remnant. Therefore it couldn't possibly be the Republic.

Could the Mandalore have formed an army so quickly? What could have roused him to unify his people against this strange outpost rather than a more credible enemy?

"Republic ships, sir," called someone from the bridge staff, proving her wrong. "Definitely Republic, and they're taking a hammering, sir. No other visible combatants, but there may have been launches from the ground."

Darth Chratis grinned, and Ax grinned with him. The Republic had made its move and was being rebuffed. How much easier, then, to swoop in as the savior and "liberate" the planet, right into the Emperor's arms!

"Take us in, Colonel Kalisch," Darth Chratis said. "Launch all fighters and prepare for battle."

"At this distance, our fighters would not be able to break free of the black hole's gravitational pull," Kalisch said, smoothly countermanding the order. "The moment it is safe, my lord, I will launch them."

"Very well," hissed the Sith Lord. "That will have to do." He wasn't used to anything as lowly as physics standing between him and his wishes.

"Full power, all engines," Kalisch ordered the fleet. "Lock courses and prepare to engage!"

The Imperial fleet came about, straining to reverse the considerable momentum it had already gained just by being in the black hole's powerful gravitational field. The *Paramount*'s engines roared and rumbled, casting a bright blue light across those ships coming up in its wake. The lighter cruisers fared better than the massive bulk cruiser and its heavier support vessels. They caught up and began to draw ahead.

It soon became abundantly clear that Kalisch's original advice had been sound. Instead of picking up velocity as they whipped around the singularity's event horizon, propelled by freely available gravity, they would struggle to gain every drop of delta-vee, wrung out of the engines at great expense. Their progress was painfully slow. Ax could feel her Master's impatience growing—redoubled because he knew he could say nothing, threaten no one. This was his decision and his responsibility alone. The crew worked around him in perfect efficiency and with maximum effort. All knew that Darth Chratis would vent his frustration on the first person to fail him in the slightest possible way.

Ax watched the long-range telemetry closely, eager to learn anything she could about the planet's forces. What she saw puzzled her deeply. There were no ships apart from those belonging to the Republic. Furthermore, there was no obvious assault being conducted from the ground. It looked like the Republic fleet was fighting nothing at all.

Even stranger, the Republic ships appeared to be attacking one another. Half the fleet appeared to be retreating, while the other half either did nothing or actively impeded the rest. As she watched, one small cruiser suddenly switched its drives to full, propelling it wildly into another ship, disintegrating both. It was as though something had infected half the fleet, driving it mad.

Darth Chratis studied the same data with a deeply suspicious expression. Ax wondered if he thought it was a trap. But to what end? The Republic couldn't possibly benefit from the destruction of its own ships.

"Would you like me to hail either party?" the colonel asked.

"No," said Ax.

Darth Chratis and Kalisch both turned to her in surprise.

"Master, I advise against explicitly indentifying us as servants of the Emperor," she said. "Remember that we are the enemy in Lema Xandret's eyes."

"Perhaps the traitorous harridan will change her mind," said Darth Chratis, "now that these weak-willed fools have found her."

With a blinding flash, the Republic's capital ship exploded, casting debris in all directions. Ax shielded her eyes against the glare.

"They're certainly not putting up much of a fight," she said. Half the Republic ships had been destroyed or crippled. The rest were regrouping and recalling their fighters.

"Regardless, the situation is clear. Sebaddon is no longer a secret. Xandret must choose to bow to the Emperor's will or face the consequences."

"She'll never agree to her own execution."

Darth Chratis studied her with cold eyes. "Naturally I will say nothing of the fate in store for her. Cease your questioning of my orders. Colonel Kalisch, announce our presence to the citizens of Sebaddon and advise them that we will be taking possession of their world once we have cleared the skies of this Republic rabble."

"Yes, my lord."

Ax went back to studying the viewscreens. The firing pattern of the Republic ships looked wrong to her, although she couldn't quite put a finger on what disturbed her about it. Still no launches from the ground, although infrared showed numerous sites of activity. Cities and factories, Ax assumed, that would be bombed for certain if Xandret resisted. Ax's instincts told her that victory wasn't going to come as easily as an announcement of the Empire's intent to annex the world, but at the same time she couldn't see how a small, ground-based civilization could hope to prevail against the high ground of space. Even if they did have a mysterious weapon that drove ships and their crews crazy . . .

The Republic forces must have been taken by surprise. So she was forced to assume. Colonel Kalisch would be sure not to make the same mistakes they had.

No response came from the ground to the *Paramount*'s hail. Apart from garbled transmissions on Republic frequencies, the bands were empty.

"They ignore us," said Darth Chratis, "at their peril."

"Launching fighters in two minutes, my lord," said Kalisch.

Ax was already heading for the exit from the bridge. "Ready my interceptor," she called behind her. "I'm going to take a closer look."

It took her a minute to descend from the bridge to the hangar deck, but it felt like forever. Her Mk. VII advanced interceptor had been shipped from Dromund Kaas with the rest of Darth Chratis's matériel and kept fully fueled in case a fast launch was required. The ground crew had it warming up and ready for her by the time she got there. Its familiar jutting vanes reassured her in a way that no amount of deceptive diplomacy could. Forgoing a full flight suit, she slipped a helmet over her dreadlocks, climbed aboard, and activated the internal navicomp. It showed her the projected course for the many wings about to launch around her. She switched that off and mapped out her own trajectory.

The hangar crews retreated as fighters began to stream out of the cruiser. The launches were clean and well timed, despite their pilots' eagerness to engage. Ax slipped into their formation with ease, a sleek black predator surrounded by willing but lesser packmates. She listened to the comms as she monitored the fleet's disposition, but didn't respond.

Wave after wave of angular black ISF interceptors streamed away from the *Paramount* and its ancillary vessels. They were easily a match for the XA-8 and PT-7 starfighters the Republic had launched. Ship-mounted cannons selected targets and prepared to fire on the Republic craft. The range was slightly long, but the still-stately pace of the capital ships ensured a solid base to fire from. A lucky shot or two wasn't impossible.

Ahead, the vast field of wreckage left by the destruction of the main Republic cruiser was spreading at speed. Only as she neared it did Ax realize what had troubled her about the Republic ships' behavior.

The surviving ships were firing into the cloud, not at their own renegade vessels.

She peeled away from the wing she had been shadowing and headed directly for the cloud.

"Your primary targets are the damaged vessels" came the orders from the *Paramount*. "Enemy fighters secondary. We will engage the rest. Fire at will."

The sky lit up as a smaller Republic ship exploded.

Against that cruel light were silhouetted thousands of floating objects, suspended in space. Some were spinning circles; others were edge-on lines. All were instantly recognizable as hexes, the droids Ax had fought on Hutta, their regular hexagonal bodies identical and faceless apart from the utter blackness of their sensory pods. As she flew among them now, they reached for her with spider-like legs, firing bolts of plasma from their hand weapons to propel them forward.

In that instant, she understood.

"*Paramount*, recall the fighters immediately. Get them away from that debris field. It's full of hexes!"

She fired as she flew, destroying one hex with every pulse from her fighter's ion cannon. For every one she killed, however, three more appeared in her scopes.

"They're only droids" came back the reply from the *Paramount*. "What harm can they do against starfighters?"

"Put me through to Darth Chratis," she snapped. Someone's head would roll for this. "Master, the Republic ships have been infected with hexes. That's why they're self-destructing and turning on one another. I don't know how the infection occurred, but the debris field is full of hexes. Our targeting priority should be them first, then the fleeing ships."

"You want us to abandon a golden opportunity to

rout the Republic in order to play target practice against a handful of machines?" Darth Chratis's reply was full of contempt. "Colonel Kalisch's orders stand."

Ax heard one of the bridge crew call out in the background: "Launches!" She looked at her telemetry and saw what the *Paramount* had detected.

Four missiles were rising from the surface of Sebaddon. Full of hexes, she bet, not conventional explosives. Plus, all of the infected Republic ships still capable of controlled flight were abandoning their chase of the others and coming around to ram the Imperials.

The colonel's imperious broadcast to the citizens of Sebaddon hadn't been ignored at all.

"Move the fleet," she told her Master. "You'll be caught between them if you continue on that course."

The *Paramount* neither responded nor changed course. A wave of anti-missile fire was streaking out to intercept the ascending threats. She could only hope it would be enough.

Around her, hexes swarmed and clutched at the Imperial fighters. Some had linked arms to form wide nets and webs across the sky. Any ship that strayed too close was bound up and crushed. Other hex groups formed whips capable of slinging individual hexes to incredible speeds. Ax herself missed two such wriggling projectiles by only small margins. Other pilots weren't so lucky.

"Target the larger concentrations," she advised those fighting around her. "Ignore the infected ships. If they blow, we'll only have more hexes on our hands."

She received no official acknowledgment of the orders, but they were obeyed. Squadrons disrupted by the unusual and hostile nature of the debris field re-formed to strafe the densest concentrations of hexes they could find. Ax joined them, taking grim satisfaction every time her cannon blew such an agglomeration to pieces.

Part of her mind paid attention to the wider battlefield. The missiles had performed a startling maneuver in mid-burn by breaking up into four smaller pieces, each capable of independent flight. Now numbering sixteen, they slipped through the first wave of defensive fire. Six mini missiles were taken out in the next wave, and five more in the third. That left five to hit the fleet unharmed.

Ax winced as they struck. There were no explosions, as she had predicted. The *Paramount* was untouched, fortunately, but four of the larger support vessels were likely to turn, if the hexes gained control. There might be only a couple of dozen in each mini missile, but that could be enough, particularly if they infiltrated the ships' control systems.

In retaliation, the *Paramount* launched a series of ground strikes against the origin of the missiles. Ax had expected this, too. Instead of saving the munitions for fending off the hexes they already had, they were potentially being wasted on the people who had sent them. Punishment could wait, in her opinion. Better to be alive and angry than dead.

She turned her attention back to the fighters. The debris field was much clearer than it had been, with only a random scattering of individual hexes left. The infected Republic ships had come around and were accelerating headlong for the Imperial fleet, doing what she had feared they would do once the second fleet was identified. To the people on Sebaddon, to Lema Xandret, the Empire was enemy number one; everyone else had to wait their turn.

"Target the drives," she ordered the fighters. "Only the drives. We don't want to break them up, whatever you do. We have to avoid creating another debris field for the fleet to wander into."

"How do we destroy them, then?" asked one of the pilots.

"We let gravity do it for us," she said. "Once they can't maneuver, either the planet or the hole will drag them in."

"They're not the orders I'm receiving from Colonel Kalisch," protested a squad leader.

"I know that." The *Paramount* was still worried that the approaching ships were intending merely to ram them. "I'm the only authority you need to worry about, out here. The first pilot who punctures the hull on one of these ships will get a torpedo up their afterburner. Understood?"

"Understood. All right, you have your orders, people. Let's get to it."

The fighters peeled off to pursue their new objectives.

Meanwhile, the first infected Imperial ship was beginning to behave erratically.

"Master, I urge you again to move the *Paramount* to a safe distance." Where reason had already failed, she attempted flattery. "Were the unthinkable to occur, we would be left without your leadership."

"Perhaps that would be prudent," Darth Chratis agreed.

Ax barely heard him. In the background, filling the bridge of the *Paramount,* a familiar voice was shrieking.

She switched channels to the one Colonel Kalisch had used to broadcast his message to the ground.

"We do not recognize your authority!"

For an instant, Ax thought that her mother was broadcasting to the Imperial ships. Then she realized—with something that might have been a twinge of disappointment—that the voice had the slightly wooden quality of a droid. Why a droid and not Xandret herself?

While the fighters attacked the infected ships and the *Paramount* slowly ascended out of danger, Ax considered the pros and cons of broadcasting a message herself. It might give her mother cause to hesitate before launching more hexes at the Imperial fleet. But what could she possibly say to this woman she hardly remembered, if she was alive at all? *I'm a Sith now. I have no family.* That certainly wasn't going to help.

The retaliatory strikes launched by the *Paramount* detonated on the surface of the world far below. What had already been a bright hot spot suddenly became a whole lot brighter, and Ax wondered if the question of her mother's survival was now completely moot.

Two more missiles launched from a different hot spot entirely.

Then the first of the infected Imperial ships exploded, spreading hexes all through the fleet. With the survival of her own kind now at stake, she forced herself to concentrate on what really mattered.

CHAPTER 29

THE *AURIGA FIRE*'S tri-laser cannon emplacements were to port and starboard, just forward of its hyperdrives. They angled out slightly so they could cover every inch of the ship and were accessed by two tight tunnels that smelled of grease.

Larin had taken the port turret and eased herself into the cracked leather seat with easy familiarity. The prosthetic glove on her left hand was just sufficient to wrap around the cannon's hand grip, while her right hand handled the delicate movements required to target and fire. The cannon itself operated smoothly, swinging freely on its gimbals as though fresh out of the factory.

It wasn't the first time she had noticed the mismatch between the *Auriga Fire*'s appearance and its capabilities. Another concerned its compact tractor beam facility, recessed behind a hatch in the ship's broad belly. It was a wildly nonstandard feature for a ship of this size. She was curious to know how often it came in handy in the pursuit of Jet's normal job, but didn't really think Jet would admit to anything. For the moment, the flash and pound of the cannons was all that concerned her.

A quick depression of the trigger and a web of wriggling hexes vanished in a ball of gases.

"This is as easy as shooting stump-lizards on Kiffex," she called to Shigar over her head-mounted comlink.

"Watch that trio coming in from above" was all he said.

Larin swung the tri-laser and blasted them into atoms.

"Don't worry about the Grand Master," she told him. "We'll find her."

He had been subdued ever since the *Corellia* had detonated, shooting hexes with lethal speed and accuracy. Two thirds of the cruiser's escape pods were now accounted for, but Master Satele wasn't in any of them. Shigar had tried broadcasting over all channels, but the electromagnetic spectrum was a mess. What wasn't jammed by the black hole, Imperials, or panicked chatter was full of the hexes screeching. It was all the new Republic commander could do to coordinate the larger ships into safely picking up the escape pods without picking up hexes by accident as well.

"Dead ahead," said Jet from the cockpit. An escape pod had collided with two hexes that were in the process of cutting through the pod's thin hull. The *Auriga Fire* swooped in to help.

"One each, Hetchkee," Larin said as the tractor beam wrenched invisibly at the hexagonal droids. "Favoritism is strongly frowned upon back here."

She wondered if the former security guard knew she was joking. One hex tumbled away to port, for Shigar to shoot, while the other, after a protracted struggle, wriggled into Larin's sights. Then it was up to Ula to give the pod's panicked occupants coordinates for the rendezvous point.

"Stay in the channel we've cleared," he told them. "Don't take any shortcuts."

"It was horrible," babbled a young midshipman on the other end of the line. "There were suddenly so many of them, and they moved so *fast*—"

"You're safe now. Just stay in the channel and do what Captain Pipalidi says."

"Yes, yes—and thank you. Another few seconds, we'd have been holed for sure."

The pod fired up its retro-rockets and headed off in the right direction. Larin hoped its occupants would be okay now. Several had been rescued and then fallen afoul of the hexes again, through either bad luck or poor judgment. One had stopped to rescue another pod in distress, only to be overwhelmed by hexes hiding inside. The *Auriga Fire* had been too far away to help, but the screams had carried.

Captain Pipalidi, the Anx in charge of the *Commenor* and by default what remained of the fleet, had a difficult job ahead of her, distributing the traumatized survivors through the remaining eight ships at her disposal. Larin didn't envy her that job at all, with long-range comms scrambled and nothing larger than a light assault cruiser to fill the place of the *Corellia*. But at least the lesson had been learned: the hexes might not look like much individually, but they were tough, and in large numbers were to be taken very seriously indeed.

"There's another pod at the other side of the web ahead," said Jet. "Do you think you can get us through?"

Larin peered through the scope. The web was one of the densest they'd seen so far, with hundreds of the hexes linked in a multilimbed structure vaguely reminiscent of one individual hex, spinning slowly against the backdrop of the planet below. The limbs whipped and snapped, flinging hexes at far-off targets and scooping up replacements from the debris cloud around it. The pod Jet had spotted was drifting behind the main body, its retros damaged. The interior light flashed rapidly on and off, spelling out a call for help in Mon Calamari blink code.

"Easily," said Larin, knowing nothing would make Shigar happier than killing more hexes. Except, of course, finding the Grand Master.

"See those concentrations near the center?" Shigar said. "That's the best place to hit. Take them out and the structure will tear itself apart."

"Affirmative." Larin flexed real and prosthetic hands around the cannon grips, ready for action.

"Launches," said Ula as the ship roared forward.

Larin glanced at telemetry just long enough to take a quick snapshot of the wider battlefield. It was dominated by several overlapping debris fields in low orbit over Sebaddon, the largest centered on where the *Corellia* had broken apart. The "safe" segment of the Republic fleet and several dozen escape pods were now well clear of danger, regrouping near the planet's rocky moon. The Imperial fleet was in the process of splitting in two, as uninfected ships copied the Republic's tactic of retreat. Two squadrons of Imperial fighters were disabling the engines of several vessels, so they couldn't spread their infection by ramming or detonating nearby. Larin approved of the tactic. She might have suggested it herself had not the infected Republic ships seemed so intent on targeting the Empire.

Republic fighters swarmed around the uninfected section of the fleet, keeping the hexes at bay. Defying gravity and distance, some actually managed to reach that far. If just one was carrying a nest, the infection could take root all over again.

Her mind latched on to that thought—and for an instant she was back on Hutta, staring at the droid factory, and the Sith blade was flashing like a crimson lightning bolt past her eyes all over again. *Her fingers fell with the comlink to the metal floor and a scream of pain boiled in her throat.*

She blinked and was back in the present. The scream remained.

Launches, Ula had said. She focused on that instead.

Five missiles were rising through the atmosphere of Sebaddon, launched separately in groups of two and three. The first pairing was aimed at the Imperial forces. The others—she was relieved to see—were aimed nowhere near the *Auriga Fire* or the rest of the Republic fleet. They appeared in fact to be aimed nowhere at all.

The possible motives of Lema Xandret and her followers fell from Larin's mind as the *Auriga Fire* came within range of the giant hex agglomeration. She did as Shigar had suggested, putting bolt after bolt into the nearest internal cluster. That had a satisfactory effect, at first. The hexes' combined mirror-shield defense was soon overwhelmed, and the cluster began to look decidedly threadbare, like a crater-riddled moon on the verge of collapse. But then, once again, the hexes demonstrated their ability to adapt in the face of a threat.

The cluster rearranged itself into a stubby tube, with one flat end pointing at the *Auriga Fire*. Larin fired at the tube as a matter of course, and the mirror shields flashed into life, catching the laser bolt and channeling it along the tube's center. The bolt ricocheted backward and forward, joining others she fired after it, until the whole tube began to glow. She took her remaining thumb off the trigger just as the tube released all the energy it contained in a single, powerful pulse, aimed back at the *Auriga Fire*.

Even through the ship's unusually powerful shields, the impact was deafening. Larin fell back into her seat with one arm covering her eyes. A split instant later a second bolt struck the ship, this one created by Shigar's attempts to destroy the target. The *Auriga Fire* went into a wild tumble, then righted itself with a jerk.

"—fire! Cease fire!" Jet was yelling.

"All right, we get it." Larin adjusted her earpiece. "What are we supposed to do now? Pull faces at it until it goes away?"

"I don't know," he said, "but we can't take another hit like that. Our shields are down to forty percent."

"Angle the shields forward," said Shigar. "Set a course for the closest of those tube things. When I tell you to, put the sublights on full."

"That's madness!" said Ula.

"No, I see where he's headed." Jet brought the ship around to face the tube Larin had fired into. Bright discharges still sparked from hex to hex, running in waves up and down the length of the tube. "It wants energy? Energy I'll happily give it."

The *Auriga Fire* leapt forward as though to ram. The hexes fired ineffectually at the forward screens, and the agglomeration's arms curled in to embrace their attacker. Larin's hands lay restlessly on the cannon controls as the tube grew rapidly larger ahead of her. This, she told herself, was one situation where firing would definitely make things worse.

Instead, she was part of the bullet and the trigger at the same time.

The *Auriga Fire* reached the tube's open end. It was just wide enough for the ship to fit inside, a fact for which Larin was completely grateful: the tri-laser blisters marked the ship's widest point. The moment it and its passengers were completely encapsulated, Shigar shouted "Now!" and Jet switched the sublights to full.

There followed a horrible moment when the ship strained to move forward, but all the force it produced was sucked up by the weave of tightly bound hexes surrounding it. Larin could see the effect it had on them at horribly close quarters. The hexes writhed and shook, and slowly began to glow. Metal limbs flared like magnesium burning in pure oxygen. Black sensory pods popped and hexagonal bodies stretched. She couldn't hear anything, but she imagined the hexes screaming.

Turning a laser bolt back onto its owner was one thing. Absorbing all the energy required to accelerate a starship was quite another.

The *Auriga Fire* burst out the other side, trailing a tail of bright blue. The hex-tube shook and bulged as it tried to contain the energy it had absorbed. A ball as bright as a sun formed in its heart, and Larin feared it might actually shoot out at them, destroying them instantly.

But then the hex-tube buckled, as the ball didn't so much explode as discharge throughout the entire agglomeration. Thousands of hexes burst apart in an instant, spraying the surrounding vacuum with exotic shrapnel.

"Yee-ha!" yelled Larin, then added more soberly, "Let's never do that again."

The beleaguered escape pod and its occupants found themselves unexpectedly out of danger. It was a simple matter now to snatch it up in the tractor beam and haul it to safety outside the debris field, where other ships could look after it.

As the *Auriga Fire* turned about to look for another harried pod, Shigar said, "Wait."

"What is it?" she asked, hearing a note of urgency in his voice.

"It's her. Master Satele is calling me."

"I'm not picking up any transmissions," Jet told him.

"She's not calling me that way." Larin held her breath, not wanting to distract him as he concentrated on whatever he was receiving through the Force. "See that chunk of the *Corellia* over there, Jet? Head in that direction."

"Will do."

The *Auriga Fire* accelerated for a relatively large piece of the destroyed cruiser. The twisted, oval fragment was approximately fifty meters down its long axis, and featured a gold finish down one side, revealing that it had once been part of the hull. It tumbled freely through the hexes, and appeared to be the focus of a concerted scavenging effort leaching metal from one end.

Larin readied herself for the order to fire. When Master Satele's pod came into view, getting her safely and quickly clear would be the priority.

Then: "I don't see any pods," Ula said. "Are you sure this is the right spot?"

It wasn't the first time the former envoy had expressed doubts about Shigar's abilities. Larin wondered if he was part of the axis in the Republic government that mistrusted the Jedi and their methods.

"I'm sure," said Shigar. "She's not in a pod. She must be in a pressurized compartment in that chunk."

"I can ready a docking ring," said Jet, "if you can pinpoint her location."

"We won't have time," said Ula. "There are hexes all over that thing."

Shigar said, "You have vac suits, don't you? I'll jump the gap."

"I'm coming with you," said Larin.

"No," he said. "I'll need you on the cannon, making sure no more come aboard. Drop me off, back away, then come get us when we're out. I'll take a spare suit for her."

"And if her compartment doesn't have an air lock?"

"Then I'll think of something else."

She heard him crawling up his access tunnel, back into the ship, and turned to look at him. "Are you sure this is the right thing to do?" she called at him along the tunnel, unable to hide the intense worry she felt. The wreckage was crawling with hexes. One slip, and neither he nor his Master would come back.

"Positive," he said. "She's the most important person in the galaxy. It's my duty to save her."

Then he was gone, leaving Larin feeling slightly wounded by his words. On Hutta, he hadn't come to save her. If his deal with Tassaa Bareesh had gone awry, she would have ended up rancor food for certain. But for Master Satele, he swept in with lightsaber swinging, risking life and limb and not even letting Larin help.

She wondered if he thought she might slow him down.

Don't think like that, she told herself. *We're still partners, and this obviously isn't going to be over as quickly as we'd thought. Chances are we'll find plenty more opportunities to fight back-to-back.*

She swung the cannon around and picked off a hex standing high on the back of the wreckage. That was one less he would have to worry about.

THE *AURIGA FIRE*'S vac suits were simple models, with no armor, inbuilt weapons, or maneuvering jets, and barely fifty minutes of air in their backpacks. Shigar guessed they were normally used for quick repairs outside the ship, where they could be tethered to the main life support. Shigar stripped out of the new clothes he had improvised from Ula's official wardrobe—brown robe, black pants, and sand-colored top, the closest he could approximate to Jedi colors—then picked the cleanest suit from the rack and slipped it quickly over his unprotected limbs. Ideally he would have worn a body glove, like Larin's, but there wasn't time for such niceties. He would use biofeedback to regulate his body temperature.

He fixed his lightsaber to a clip on the suit's right hip, where it would be accessible in an instant, and slung a spare suit over the crook of his left arm.

"Aft air lock primed and ready," said Jet over the suit's intercom.

"Okay." Shigar tested the seals one last time. The air tasted stale, but that was the least of his problems. "Get in as close to the wreckage as you can."

His breathing sounded loud in his ears as the air lock's inner door opened and he stepped inside. As the air lock cycled, he took the opportunity to center himself. He knew what to expect. He had faced the hexes before. His priority, however, was to find Master Satele and get her out as quickly as possible. There wasn't time to fight or take any unnecessary risks. That would only get the both of them killed.

"Can you hear me, Master Satele?" he asked over the suit comm, using a band thick with the static of distant stars. Military forces normally avoided that channel, making it perfect for short-range transmissions that needed to go untraced.

"Perfectly well," Master Satele responded, faintly but clearly.

"How's your air?"

"Running low, but not critical yet."

The outer door opened with a puff of fog and Shigar kicked himself out onto the hull. For a moment the sheer weirdness of his position struck him hard. He was standing practically naked on the hull of a smuggler's ship, surrounded by killer droids and wrecked ships, with the galaxy's brilliant spiral to one side and the jets of a black hole to the other.

He couldn't tell if what he felt was joy or terror.

The twisted wreckage drew nearer. Larin's cannon flashed, and a hex went tumbling. Using the tractor beam, Hetchkee pulled another hex out of what had once been a window in the *Corellia*'s hull. That created a clear spot.

Shigar braced himself to jump.

"Here's as close as we can get," said Jet. "Don't miss."

With one explosive kick of his muscles, Shigar cleared the gap. For a moment the sky turned about him—the planet came into view from behind the *Auriga Fire,* blistered with magma domes—and then he hit the wreckage solidly, with arms outstretched to find the slightest grip.

He stuck fast, and paused to catch his breath. A hex, alerted to his arrival by the subtle shift in the wreckage's angular momentum, peered with black eyes out of a nearby hole. Its forelegs came out to point at him. Shigar reached for his lightsaber, but Hetchkee was quicker. The hex swept up and away from him, into empty space, where it was blown to atoms by Larin.

"Thanks," he said.

"Pleasure" came Larin's reply. "Are you going to lie there all day while we do all the work?"

He was already moving, tugging himself lightly from handhold to handhold in the perfect free fall of open space.

"You are close," said Master Satele over the comm. "I can sense you. There's a shattered access port ahead. Go in that way."

He obeyed without hesitation, keeping a sharp eye out for more hexes. When he was inside, there would be no rescue from Larin and Hetchkee.

The wreckage appeared to have been part of the *Corellia*'s forward command center and had been occupied at the time of the disaster. Shigar squeezed past several bodies as he wound his way deep into the twisted structure. The path was tight and occasionally dangerous, with sharp edges and spikes to negotiate. There was very little light.

"Come to the next intersection and stop there for a moment," she told him. "I have to tell you something."

The sound of movement came from ahead, through the bulkheads he touched, and Shigar slowed down to a bare creep, every sense attuned to the slightest change. The intersection must once have been broad enough for a landspeeder but was now barely large enough to admit a person, particularly one as tall as him. There was definitely something moving down the right-hand bend.

"What I must tell you is this," Master Satele said. "Ever since we heard the droids, I've been wondering just how much of herself Lema Xandret put into her creations. The answer is around that corner, Shigar. Can you see it yet?"

He edged around the corner to see what lay ahead of him. There were nine motionless hexes clustered around a pressurized door, as though waiting for it to open.

"I'm behind that door," she said, "and soon you will be, too."

"How, Master?" He couldn't conceive of a way to defeat nine hexes at once, when just two had been more than a match for him on Hutta. There was barely enough room to slide by them, let alone fight.

"You told me that the droid factory contained a biological component," she said. "It seemed reasonable to wonder if the hexes might also."

"There's a fluid inside them," he said, remembering what he had seen on Hutta. "It looks like blood. But they're definitely droids. They're not cyborgs."

"Not in the usual sense. They're something else. But the fact that they are at least partly alive is the only reason I'm still here."

"You're influencing them?"

"As much as I can, which isn't very much. They only attack when either obstructed or threatened. I'm doing neither, so they're letting me be. They won't go away, but at least they're not being aggressive. I think I can hold them back while you come to the door."

Shigar swallowed. "You want me to walk right through them?"

"It's the only way."

"And then what?"

"Then you open the door and let me out."

"I have a suit for you—"

"I won't have the chance to put it on. There's no air lock. I'll keep a bubble of air around me using a Force shield. That'll give me a couple of minutes. You'll have to move much faster than that, though. I won't be able to hold the hexes and the shield at the same time."

Shigar clenched his fists. It seemed impossible. But she was relying on him. No one else could help her.

"I'm on my way, Master."

He nudged himself around the corner and came into full view of the hexes. Despite his faith in Satele Shan's mental powers, he fully expected to be shot down at once. Instead the hexes just looked at him with their black sensory pods, and rearranged themselves slightly, so they could watch both the door and him at the same time.

Feeling like he was in some kind of surreal nightmare, Shigar pushed himself into the tangle of fat bodies and angular limbs, taking the utmost care not to touch anything. He didn't want a chance bump to wake them from their uncharacteristic complacency. He even breathed quietly, despite the perfect insulation of the vacuum around him. The intensity of the hexes' gaze made him squirm inside.

Finally he was at the door. A red light warned of pressure on the far side. He keyed an override into the pad and the light turned green. The door would open at his command now, expelling the air in an instant.

"Are you ready, Master?"

"Yes."

He pushed the button. The gale tried to blow him away but he was firmly braced against the opposite wall. The hexes flailed in surprise, suddenly released from Master Satele's calming influence and blinded by the frozen air coating their sensory pods. Shigar was partly blind, too—he could see only blurrily through the mist stuck to his visor—but he had the advantage of not *having* to see. His Master's presence was like a beacon to him.

He lunged into the tiny chamber and hit the switch to seal the door behind him. The hexes scrabbled to get in. It wouldn't be long before they cut their way through. He had maybe seconds to find another way out.

Master Satele floated in a ball in the center of the room, her Force shield shimmering around her, a milky luminescence maintained barely a finger-span from her body. Shigar was struck by how small she looked. In his mind, she always seemed of gigantic stature, not just dominating the Jedi High Council but influencing the course of the Republic as well. Now, though, she seemed tiny.

A grating noise came from the door. The hexes were already cutting through. Master Satele had left her lightsaber floating beside her, outside the Force shield. He took it in his left hand, reached for his own with his right, and activated them both simultaneously. Their greens were not quite identical, and by their combined light odd shadows danced across the walls.

The room was barely three meters cubed. Apart from the door, there were no other entrances. That didn't matter. Shigar could make his own. Raising both lightsabers, he stabbed into the wall at a point above his head, then spread both blades out in a circle before meeting at the level of his knees. A red-edged section of the wall fell free, and he kicked it into the space on the far side. Using telekinesis to gather up Master Satele, he propelled himself through the gap.

It was another room, requiring another makeshift door. He moved quickly, with confident strokes. Behind him, the hexes were wriggling through widening rents in the door and wall. In a second they would be upon him.

A hallway, this time. He swept Master Satele ahead of him and hurriedly took his bearings. He had come this way on the journey in. At the far end of the corridor, he could see the distant spiral of the galaxy.

A fat-bodied hex crawled into view, blocking his path.

"Get ready," he called over his comlink. "I'll be coming out fast."

"Good," said Larin. "It's getting a little tight out here, too."

Shigar didn't waste energy replying. Master Satele's shield was undoubtedly strong enough to deflect anything the hex could throw at them, so he kept her ahead of him. His job was simply to move both of them—fast.

The Force rushed through him. Ever since his earliest

discovery of his powers, he had loved the thrill of speed. It had helped him win races before his removal from Kiffu. It had helped him survive challenges at the academy. Remembering that wild feeling of acceleration, he dug deep into himself and kicked off against the wall behind him.

The corridor blurred. Master Satele preceded him like a cannonball, blowing the hex backward, out of the wreckage and into space. For an instant, all was turning sky and scrabbling legs—then an invisible force wrenched the hex away, and he was swept upward into the waiting air lock of the *Auriga Fire*.

"Got them, Hetchkee?" came Larin's voice over the comlink.

"Safe and sound."

Several quick blasts from the tri-laser put the hex out of commission and sent four others that had emerged after Shigar scurrying for cover. He gripped the sides of the air lock as the ship accelerated away, spinning agilely through the limbs of an approaching agglomeration, with Larin's covering fire clearing a brightly lit path.

Then the door was shut and warm air rushed in. Shigar hadn't noticed how cold his fingers had become. He rubbed them quickly together, then righted Master Satele on the floor.

"We're out of danger now, Master."

The Force shield shimmered and dissolved.

Grand Master Satele Shan unfolded to a sitting position and opened her eyes. "Thank you, Shigar." She stood and smoothed down her robes. "I owe you my life."

Shigar bowed his head and returned her lightsaber. "I did only what I must, Master."

Her right hand gripped his shoulder. "That's all we ever do, Shigar, in times of war."

The inner door opened.

"You'd better get up here," said Jet over the ship's internal comm. "Fast."

Shigar led his Master through the cramped corridors of the ship to the elevated cockpit. Ula and Jet were at the controls, with Clunker standing to one side, as motionless as a statue. Hetchkee was elsewhere—filling the empty tri-laser spot, Shigar assumed, now that the need for the tractor had passed. Ula glanced at them as they entered, then stood up and bowed.

"Grand Master," he said with a nervous expression on his face, "I am relieved to see you again."

"Have we met?"

"I am Envoy Vii—on the staff of the Supreme Commander—"

"Forget the introductions," said Jet. "We can have a tea party later. There's another ship on the scope."

"Imperial?" asked Master Satele, leaning over Ula's chair.

"I don't think so." Jet brought up a wide view of the space around Sebaddon. "Just when I thought we were getting a handle on this mess . . ."

The viewscreen showed the remaining Republic fleet at a much higher orbit than it had been before, well out of range of the hexes. Infected ships were lancing out in wildly different directions, thanks to crippled drives or gravitational pull from either Sebaddon or the black hole. The Imperial fleet, reduced to seven ships—including its bulk cruiser—was also ascending to higher ground. A quick glance at the projected orbits showed that they were likely to cross paths in a few hours—but that was something to worry about later.

"What's all this?" asked Shigar, brushing his hand through a layer of fuzz surrounding the planet's equator.

"That's where the last three missiles broke up," said Ula, "and two more launched since. They weren't aimed at anything. I think Xandret is laying down a defensive halo of hexes to protect the planet."

"As well she might," said Master Satele. "Show me the latest arrival."

Jet's finger stabbed at a bright dot hovering near the planet's tiny satellite. "It appeared a minute ago."

"From the same coordinates as everyone else?"

"No. It launched from a crater on the moon. I think it's been hidden there the whole time."

She nodded. "I'd like to broadcast a message."

Jet gave her the comm.

"It's about time you showed yourself," she said. "I'd very much like to talk to you, Dao Stryver."

"And I you, Grand Master" came the immediate reply. "It pleases me that you survived this unflattering rout."

"Can one take pleasure from the survival of one's enemy?" she asked the Mandalorian.

"One can indeed," he said. "I will explain in due course."

"I very much hope so."

"Meet me at the moon in half an hour. Send one ship. No escort. You have my word that you and your party will not be harmed."

Stryver clicked off.

"I don't trust him," Shigar said.

"We have no choice," she said. "Plot the course, Captain Nebula. Take us by the *Commenor.* I need to speak to Captain Pipalidi now, in case we don't get another chance."

" 'We'?" asked Jet.

"This mission has already lost seven vessels of war. I will not risk another."

"Doesn't anyone care what *I'm* prepared to risk?"

"Look at this," said Ula, drawing everyone's attention back to the viewscreen. "The Imperials are launching a shuttle."

"We can't let it reach the jump coordinates," said Shigar. "If they're sending for reinforcements—"

"I don't think that's where they're headed," Satele said. " 'One ship, no escort,' " she quoted.

"And Stryver did say we wouldn't be harmed *by him,*" added Jet. "Are you certain you want to do this?"

"Forget the flyby of the *Commenor,*" she told him. "Get us moving now. I'll talk with Captain Pipalidi on the way."

"Yes, ma'am," said Jet, casting Master Satele a sardonic salute. "We might as well run to our doom as walk."

CHAPTER 30

ULA WATCHED WITH mounting dread as the rendezvous point loomed. He was in the worst position imaginable, unable to act against the Republic's wishes because Satele Shan would immediately overrule him, and unable to reveal his identity to his real masters without blowing his cover. For a wild moment he considered throwing himself on the mercy of the Mandalorians, but sanity, fortunately, prevailed. Stryver had no mercy. The best Ula could have hoped for in his care was slavery.

At least he was alive, he told himself, and had a chance of staying that way if he stepped through this minefield with utmost care.

The *Auriga Fire*'s blunt nose was angling ahead of the Imperial shuttle on its approach to Sebaddon's solitary satellite. The moon was blocky and misshapen, more like a brick than a sphere, with a cornucopia of craters and fathomless fissures marring its ugly face. No wonder Stryver had stayed hidden for so long. It didn't appear to have been mined or booby-trapped, which was a major omission for a colonial administration so keen to remain undisturbed. Ula wondered if they'd simply never thought of it, or if they'd erroneously—but not unreasonably—assumed that they would never be discovered so far from the galactic disk.

The *First Blood*, Stryver's scout, anchored itself to the surface of the moon as the two ships approached. It was shaped like a crescent moon, with forward-pointing wings that bristled with weapons and a matte-black, nonreflective skin. There were no markings of any kind, just two glowing circles on either side indicating ready air locks. Jet prepared a docking ring and tube to cross the distance, and jockeyed to approach the starboard air lock. The Imperial pilot noted his intentions and moved to dock on the opposite side. Along with Larin and Hetchkee, Ula watched the shuttle closely for any signs of treachery. The way the Imperials had illegally destroyed the Republic shuttle on Hutta was still painful to him. He expected better.

"Who's going in?" asked Larin over the internal comm.

"Shigar and I," said Master Satele, "and Envoy Vii."

Ula swallowed. "I fear I can be of little use," he started to say, but was cut off by Larin.

"You'll need a bodyguard," she said. "Just for appearances."

"All right."

"And take Clunker, too," said Jet. "I'll watch through his eyes."

"Can you and Hetchkee pilot the ship on your own, if you have to?"

"In a pinch," said the smuggler. "With the right incentive, I could fly a battle cruiser on my own."

"Very well, then. Maintain the umbilical seal, but close the ship once we have disembarked. Leave on my signal, whether we're aboard or not."

"Don't worry about that," the smuggler told her. "I'll dust off if you so much as twitch funny."

Ula sought distraction in telemetry as the ship settled lightly on the low-gravity moon. Sebaddon hadn't launched any missiles since the last round. The main hot spot had been made considerably hotter by retaliatory fire, and activity was growing in other regions as well. It looked to him as though the occupants of the planet were regrouping in order to fight back, but it was hard to tell from such a distance. Every spy drone launched by the Republic fleet had been intercepted by the orbital halo of hexes and destroyed.

Maybe, he told himself, he could slip a message of some kind to his opposite number in the Imperial party. That was a small and unlikely hope to cling to.

With a series of clanks and thumps, the ship's belly grapnels took a firm grip on the dusty soil outside. The whine of repulsorlifts faded away. Jet took his hands off the controls and leaned back into the seat. For all his bluster, he looked exhausted, or at least hung over. His prematurely gray hair stood up on one side, and his eyes were heavily bagged.

"I'll mind the farm until you get back," he told them. "Don't do anything I wouldn't do."

Ula stood, hoping against hope that the Grand Master would change her mind. No such good fortune. She was already heading down the cockpit ladder, trailing Shigar like a pet. Ula waved Clunker ahead of him.

"Good luck," Jet told him.

"You didn't say that to the others."

"I figure they don't need it."

"Thanks for the vote of confidence."

Jet grinned. "You'll be okay. Just remember: you've got an unbeatable advantage."

"What's that?"

"The ability to see both sides at once."

Ula didn't know what to say to that, or to the many other hints Jet had dropped indicating that he knew what Ula was. Ula had never had the courage to ask outright—not even during the long hours when he and the smuggler had sat waiting for Shigar to make good on his psychometric promise. Whether it was true or not that Jet had guessed, Ula would rather it was never said aloud. His life relied on pretense. Once it was gone, he didn't know what that would leave him.

So he just nodded and headed down the stairs to meet the others at the air lock, wondering how anyone in his position could be considered advantaged. He felt like he was being pulled in a dozen directions. If he wasn't careful, one sharp tug might tear him to pieces.

AX WALKED THE short distance along the umbilical with measured fury. She burned to be back in her interceptor rather than wasting her time with Mandalorians and envoys again. It was as bad as being back on Hutta, only this time she had no clear advantage to hope for. All she could think of was the work she should have been doing at that moment—protecting the fleet from hexes, at least, or maybe even preparing an attack force to wipe Stryver from the sky. She didn't like coming to him when called, like some kind of menial.

"You will speak to the meddling Mandalorian on my behalf," her Master had told her.

"But Master—"

"Do I need to explain to you again what your duty is? It is to serve the Emperor, through me, his instrument. When you defy me, you defy him."

And that was the problem, of course. She *had* defied him, by ignoring his orders during the hexes' attack on Hutta. Now she was being punished for it, while he waited comfortably half frozen in the secret room in his shuttle. Whether her defiance had served the fleet or not was irrelevant. She could only forget all about doing anything constructive—let alone to the betterment of the Empire—until Darth Chratis changed his mind.

"I'm here," she said when she reached the *First Blood*'s external air lock. Her right hand fiddled with the hilt of her lightsaber. "Don't keep me waiting, Stryver."

The door hissed open. A token escort followed her into the ship—three soldiers in formal black-and-grays. She didn't look behind her to make sure they were keeping up. As a deliberate act of defiance aimed at both Stryver and her Master, she hadn't changed out of her combat uniform. It stank of oil and smoke and combat, exactly like Stryver's ship. Her hair swayed heavily down her back, like thick rope.

The *First Blood* had a low profile, head-on, but was surprisingly spacious inside. Its walls were ribbed rather than sealed with flat panels; sometimes there were no gaps at all delineating corridor from hold. Wiring and components were occasionally exposed—all, she supposed, in an effort to keep weight down. She also assumed that anything secret was kept well out of sight, so she didn't trouble herself with memorizing what she saw. She just walked, following the sound of voices leading to the center of the vessel.

". . . understand why you need all of us at once. Can't you tell us now?"

Ax knew that voice. She had heard it on Hutta. It belonged to a near-human who had fought on the Republic side, although clearly not a trooper herself. What was she doing here?

"I don't like repeating myself," said another familiar voice: the deep, vocoder-inflected tones of Dao Stryver.

Ax walked around a thick pillar of cables acting as conduit and support, and found herself in the main cabin. It was a circular room with glowing white floor and ceiling, and a central holoprojector. Stryver stood to Ax's left, helmet just clearing the relatively high ceiling. To his left were a motley group of people, including several more individuals Ax recognized: the Republic envoy, a droid she had seen hanging around Tassaa Bareesh's security air lock, and the Jedi Padawan. Next to him stood a woman she hadn't met before, but instantly recognized.

Ax stopped on entering the room, a wary hiss unconsciously escaping from between her teeth. The air was thick with the enemy's self-righteousness, concentrated mainly around the slight woman with the gray streak wearing the robes of a Jedi Knight. No mere Jedi Knight, she. The Grand Master of the High Council herself! Darth Chratis would grind his crystalline teeth in frustration at missing such a close encounter with the Emperor's most hated foe. To slay her would bring Ax considerable fame and fortune among those favored by the Dark Council.

Ax forced her hand to leave her hilt alone. For all her ambition, Ax knew that she could not single-handedly beat both Master and Padawan. She would have to strike with words instead of her blade.

"The Jedi Order must be weak indeed," she said, "for the Grand Master and a youngling to jump on a Mandalorian's whim."

The Padawan, Shigar, stiffened at her description of him as a child. "Not so weak," he said, "that I didn't save your life at least once on Hutta."

"You are mistaken," she said, feeling heat rise up her neck.

"Am I? I'll try harder not to be, next time."

"Enough," said the Grand Master, and the Padawan obeyed her instantly. "We're all here now, Stryver. Get on with it."

"I do not take your orders, Grand Master," said the Mandalorian. "Nonetheless, you have a point. I have brought you here to show you something."

The holoprojector between them flickered into life. Ax recognized the globe of Sebaddon, with its tiny, gem-like lakes scattered among irregular, continent-sized bulges of heat. Magma seams glowed orange, forming a tracery that on other worlds might have been rivers. Several blue circles at the intersections of such traceries indicated settlements or industrial centers. Ax recognized the one

Darth Chratis had bombed when the *Paramount* was attacked, and many others. Some that she remembered weren't visible at all.

"This is how Sebaddon looked when I arrived six hours before you," Stryver said. "This is how it looked when you arrived."

There was a clear difference: many of the missing hot spots were now present; the brightest were brighter still.

"This is how it looks now."

Ax didn't need to study what she already knew. "Your point?"

"They work fast," said the Padawan. "That's what Jet said when we arrived. He thought the colony was about twenty years old."

"It can't be more than fifteen," said Ax, remembering how long it had been since Lema Xandret defected.

"It's actually much less than that," Stryver said, resting his giant, gloved hands on the edge of the holoprojector and leaning over the image. "Study this sequence of images carefully and you'll see that the colony expanded five percent since I arrived. If you project that rate of growth backward in time, that gives a founding date of about three weeks ago."

"Impossible," she said.

"That's around when the *Cinzia* was intercepted," said Ula.

"So what? It's still impossible."

"Is it?" Stryver said. "Lema Xandret chose this colony partly because of its wealth of resources. With an army of willing workers and a means of making new ones, why couldn't she do whatever else she wanted?"

"If the colony could grow so quickly, why is it still so small?"

"That's a good question, Eldon Ax. You should know your mother better than anyone else here. What do you think?"

Instead of blushing, Ax felt her face grow cold and taut. "Start talking sense, man, or I'm leaving."

Both of Stryver's index fingers tapped heavily, just once, and for the first time Ax noted that he had only four fingers on each hand.

Not exactly a man, then, she thought. *But who cares about that?*

"I've been watching all of you," he said, "while you blunder about getting yourselves killed. That's the advantage of being first on the field of battle. Instead of testing Sebaddon's defenses myself, I sat back and watched you do it. It has been an interesting experiment, one that confirmed my previous observations. The inhabitants of Sebaddon are unwilling even to talk about opening their borders to outsiders—particularly the Empire—and they are capable of defending themselves when pushed."

"We were taken by surprise," said Ax. "That won't happen, next time."

"If you wait too long, surprise won't be the only thing you have to worry about."

"What do you mean?" asked Satele Shan.

"How long will it take you to call for reinforcements? You can't call, so it's a two-way trip to send a messenger. Then a fleet has to be assembled. The larger the fleet, the more time you'll need. And with each hour, Sebaddon is converting more of its precious metals to machines of war. More than thirty ships failed today. How long until fifty ships isn't enough? A hundred? A thousand?"

Ax sneered. "No single planet could withstand the might of the Imperial war machine."

"I might agree, if the Imperial war machine was available. But it's currently stretched across all the galaxy, thin and vulnerable, and the same can be said for the Republic's. Furthermore, we all know that neither would come if we called. They would think your concerns exaggerated. They are more interested in fighting each other than this single, isolated threat."

"*Is* it a threat?" asked Shigar. "Xandret won't talk to us, but at least she's stopped firing now we've moved away. Why don't we give her what she wants and leave her alone?"

"Do you really think that's possible, now?" said the female near-human.

"Why not?" Shigar looked at his Master for support, but she wasn't giving it to him.

"You are naïve," said Ax. "This world is too valuable. The Emperor will have it, or no one will."

"And your mother must be made an example of," said Stryver, "otherwise the power of the Sith will be eroded."

"Stop calling her my mother. Lema Xandret is a criminal and a fugitive. There is no possibility that she will escape justice."

"Would you strike her down yourself, if you could?"

"I would, and I will. She means nothing to me."

"Good. I believed once that I might reason with her. I believed that I could broker an agreement that would keep her and her creations in check. Now I fear that it is too late for any kind of negotiation. No reasoning or agreement is possible."

"Has she gone mad?" asked the trooper to Shigar's right. "If so, there are other options. We could take her out and talk to someone else, for instance."

"This plan suffers from one small but fatal flaw."

"That is?" asked the Republic envoy.

"Lema Xandret is already dead. She has been for some time."

An icy splinter snapped in Ax's heart at those words, leaving her unable to tell if she felt triumph or grief, or both.

* * *

"I THINK IT'S time you told us everything you know," said Master Satele.

"I agree," said Larin. "Since when do Mandalorians negotiate with *anyone*?"

Ula remembered Jet telling him, *They don't believe they* have *any equals.*

"You were the person Xandret's emissaries were hoping to meet," Ula said. "You came looking for them when they didn't show up."

The giant, domed helmet inclined in his direction. "Correct."

"Was Xandret herself supposed to be aboard the *Cinzia*?" asked Shigar. "Is that why you think she's dead?"

"No. She sent another. I believe she was here when she died."

"So you don't know for sure?" asked the Sith. Her face had a white, pinched look under her bloodred dreadlocks.

"I am certain of it."

"Did you kill her? Did you see her body?"

"No."

"So how can you be certain?"

Stryver tapped his helmet with one gloved finger. Ula couldn't see the Mandalorian's face, but was positive he was smiling.

"She means nothing to me," the young Sith said firmly, as though reassuring herself of the truth of it. "I just want to be certain."

"Be certain of this, Eldon Ax: when those droids your mother created leave this world, they will consume the entire galaxy in less than a generation."

Ula blinked. The claim was preposterous, but if Stryver truly believed it, that did explain another puzzling piece of the story.

"So that's why you were willing to talk to her," Ula said. "Lema Xandret was a threat or a possible ally—just like the Empire."

"A force to be reckoned with, potentially," said Master Satele. "A force we clearly underestimated. But you wouldn't have taken her word on it. You must have received some kind of proof."

"A demonstration factory," said Stryver. "In two days, it manufactured seventeen droids and two duplicates of itself using nothing but the materials around it. The duplicate factories went immediately to work, making another four factories and even more droids. Their rate of reproduction was limited only by the energy available to them; later we discovered how they send out roots to tap into the local supply, ensuring they never run out. Curious, we put the droids in the pit and they prevailed against all but the current champion. Then the droids and factories self-destructed, leaving insufficient remains for us to probe the secrets of their manufacture or function. The message was clear. The Mandalore sent me to pursue the conversation."

"Why did he send just you?" asked Larin. "You're not much use to us on your own."

"I can confirm several hypotheses that you might already be forming. This will save you time so you can begin to act." Stryver raised his right hand and began ticking off points. "One. Lema Xandret and her fellow refugees arrived on Sebaddon determined to cast off the hierarchy they had left behind. Fifteen years later, hiding was no longer sufficient: Xandret wanted revenge on the people who had stolen her daughter. So she sought out Mandalore to help her. She approached him because my culture eschews the Force. That, after all, was where all this started, with militarized religious cults turning children into monsters."

Ula didn't dare look at the young Sith's face. He didn't

know exactly how the Sith trained their acolytes, but this sounded plausible. He wondered if his Jedi "masters" had a similar system.

"Two." Stryver's count continued. "During her self-imposed exile, Xandret and her fellow artisans advanced robotics in directions no one has ever seen before. Finding inspiration and materials in human biology itself, they sought to make droids that would neither age nor grow inflexible and hidebound, so their small colony could last forever. The technical challenges were immense, of course, but they made some progress in unexpected directions. The droids you've seen are advanced prototypes called fast breeders. Given enough metal and raw energy, they grow from seeds into fully formed combat versions in a matter of days. The nest on Hutta could have produced dozens of such killers if left undisturbed, and the same is true of the nests on Sebaddon. The hot spots you've been observing from above, the ones that look like cities, are in fact droid-building factories. They are churning out fast breeders by the thousand now that the planet's defenses have been tripped. And not just fast breeders: new factories as well. That is where the true threat lies. This was the weapon she intended to use against the Empire.

"Three. If left unchecked, Xandret's breeder technology will inevitably outgrow its homeworld and spill out into the galaxy. The math of geometric progression is undeniable: one world this year, two worlds the next; then four, then eight; within a decade it's two hundred and fifty worlds, then another decade later it's a quarter of a million. One human generation is all they would need to take over the entire galaxy—along with Sith, Jedi, and Mandalorians alike.

"Four. Negotiation is no longer an option. Xandret put all her prejudices into her droids. You've heard their voices. You know what drives them. The only solution is to crush Sebaddon completely. We must be ruthless, decisive, and thorough, in order to ensure that Lema Xandret's legacy is completely eradicated. Just one nest would be enough to allow all this to start over again."

Stryver had run out of fingers on his right hand.

"Are you finished?" asked the Sith.

"I will be if this threat isn't neutralized."

Stryver's fists descended to take his weight, knuckle-first, on the side of the holoprojector.

The sphere of Sebaddon turned unstoppably between them. Glowing red lights appeared and spread like a plague in fast motion. Soon the whole planet was red, and streams of tiny, malignant dots began to leap off the surface and escape into unseen spaces.

"You said 'we.'" Satele Shan's voice made Ula jump. "*We* must be ruthless. I presume that was deliberate."

"It was. Everything I have seen, on Hutta and Sebaddon, confirms my worst fears. Sebaddon is responding to the threat you all represent by ramping up production. It must be stopped before the contagion spreads. Since neither Empire nor Republic can single-handedly destroy this menace with the resources available right now, you must work together to see it done."

"With you in charge, I suppose," said Larin.

"The end justifies the means."

"I will never take orders from a Mandalorian," said the Sith in mocking tones. "And I will never fight alongside a Jedi. You are insane even to suggest it."

"There must be an alternative," Master Satele said. "Another attempt at negotiation, perhaps—"

"The planetary defense system is automated," Stryver said. "The only voices coming from the planet originate with the fast breeders. That's how I know that Lema Xandret is dead. Everyone down there is dead. It's just the droids now, and you can't negotiate with them."

"Well, we can't trust one another," said Shigar. "That's some choice you've given us."

"Could I make it any other way, I would. Believe me."

Jedi and Sith glowered at one another over the hologram, and suddenly Ula knew exactly what he had to do. Once again, Jet had been absolutely right. Ula *could* see both sides at once, and save himself into the bargain.

"Are you the leader of the Imperial fleet?" he asked the young Sith. He already knew the answer. The Emperor would never trust such wealth to someone so young, no matter how powerful she might be. But he had to ask, for appearance's sake.

"No," she admitted.

"Whoever that person is, then, I want to speak to them, face-to-face," he said. "I believe I can bring the Empire to the table."

"You? My Master would gut a worm like you just to watch you die."

Ula's stomach roiled. Her *Master.* He had hoped for a non-Sith commander, but would have to settle for what he got. "Take me to your command vessel and let me try. If I fail, by the sound of things, I might as well be dead."

"Your death is closer than you think. He's in the shuttle."

"Well, then. All the better. It'll be over quickly."

"Envoy Vii," said Satele Shan, "be very careful. You must be absolutely sure of yourself."

"I am." He straightened and puffed out his chest. "If the Empire agrees to Stryver's suggestion, will you?"

The Grand Master showed no sign of uncertainty. "Of course. We're not at war, after all, and the threat is severe."

"Good." Ula turned back to the Sith girl. She was tight-lipped with rage, as though she couldn't believe his audacity. "This isn't a trick. I'll go with you now, if you'll take me. Please."

"Just you," she finally said. "No one else."

"That's out of the question," said Larin.

"No," he said, although his heart warmed at her concern. "I'm happy to go on my own. If I can't convince them with words, what difference would a rifle or two make?"

She reluctantly backed down. "Just be careful. We want you back in one piece."

"Not several?" said the Sith. She was grinning now, perhaps anticipating the sport her Master would have with him. "I refuse to guarantee anything."

Ula wondered if he looked as faint as he felt. What if she killed him the moment they were on the other side of the air lock, before he had a chance to speak? That would be the most awful irony of all.

"I'm ready," he said in as strong a voice as he could muster. "Let's not keep your Master waiting."

"Indeed," she said. "Let's not."

"If we don't hear from you within thirty minutes," Stryver said, "we'll assume you are dead."

Ula walked around the holoprojector and let the Imperial guards take him by the shoulders and frog-march him to the door. There was no turning back now. The eyes of his erstwhile allies in the Republic followed him as he was led off to betray them all.

THE MOMENT THE air lock closed behind them, the puny envoy started to struggle. Ax strode on, her mind full of ways to lessen the inevitable consequences of her failure. She didn't know what Darth Chratis had expected, but he was sure to turn this unexpected result against her. That she was finding it hard to think wasn't helping.

"Listen to me," the envoy called after her. "You have to listen to me!"

She didn't slow down. She barely even heard him. *Lema Xandret is dead,* Stryver had said. *Everyone down there is dead.* She didn't know why that pronouncement had made a difference, but it seemed to. Her family, her mother—what had happened to her father? She had never asked. Maybe he was dead, too, had died years ago, when she was a child. Maybe he was a Sith Lord who wouldn't lower himself to be associated with a common woman. Maybe, she thought, just maybe . . . ?

Impossible. She mocked herself for even thinking it. Darth Chratis was no kind of father to her, and never would be. She needed no father, just like she needed no family. If Stryver was right and the fugitives *were* all dead, that just made her life easier. She wouldn't have to expend the energy finding and killing them, in the Emperor's name.

"Please, I'm trying to tell you that I'm not who you think I am! We're on the same side and have been all the time!"

The squawking of the envoy finally penetrated her consciousness. On the brink of entering the shuttle, she stopped and reached out one half-gripped hand.

He swept out of the guards' hands and smashed into the air lock wall.

"Don't even think of lying to me," she said.

"I'm not." The envoy was as pale as marble and his voice little more than a whisper, but he didn't flinch as she approached. "I'm an Imperial agent."

She activated her lightsaber and held it across his throat.

"You don't look like a Cipher Agent. You're not even fully human."

Her contempt was ferocious. "All right. Not an agent per se, but an informer at least. And I am loyal regardless what species I am. Utterly loyal. I swear it."

Ax didn't move. She knew that many highly ranked Republic officers sometimes preferred nonhuman staff in the belief that this would protect them from surveillance. If this envoy *had* been turned, he would be highly prized by the Minister of Information.

"I tried to board your shuttle on Hutta," he pressed on, beginning to stammer now, "but the guards t-turned me away."

That much was true, and it made her hesitate. Ax couldn't believe she was listening to him—and more, actually considering his story. But his brazenness and bravery in the face of certain death were persuasive. She had to admire his guts, even if she would see them sizzling if she found out that he was trying to trick her. It wasn't impossible that he was a double agent placed by Satele Shan to lead her and her Master astray . . .

Ax smiled with her teeth. Darth Chratis would know. If the envoy was telling the truth, it would be a boon for her. If not, her Master would have someone else upon which to act out his displeasure.

"What species are you?" she asked him.

"E-Epicanthix."

"Never heard of it."

"We come from Panatha in the Pacanth Reach—"

"I don't care. If you ever want to see your home again—if you ever want to see *anything* again—then you'll tell my Master everything you just told me, and convince him that it's true."

"Who is your Master?"

"Darth Chratis. Does that name mean anything to you?"

If anything, the envoy went even paler.

"Good. Then you appreciate the gravity of your situation."

She deactivated her lightsaber and let him drop. The guards picked him up and dragged him after her, into the shuttle where her Master waited.

Darth Chratis awaited her in the shuttle's spacious but inhospitable passenger cabin, wearing a bulky armored suit. Only his face was visible, pinched and puckered into a permanent scowl. He leaned heavily on his lightsaber staff.

When he saw the envoy, his brow came down even farther.

"Explain."

Ax did so, starting at Dao Stryver's dire predictions and moving quickly on to the possibility of cooperation. The prisoner remained silent throughout, struck dumb by Darth Chratis's forbidding mien. That was a good thing; had he interrupted at any point, he might have been killed out of hand.

"And Satele Shan has been taken in by this Mandalorian's machinations?" Her Master's eyebrows, as thin as old scars, rose up toward his time-worn scalp.

"It appears so," she said. "She sent her envoy to negotiate on her behalf."

Now Darth Chratis's stare descended fully upon him, and the envoy quailed. "Speak."

"My name is Ula Vii," he stammered. "I report directly to Watcher Three in the operations division of the Ministry of Intelligence. I am your servant, my lord—a loyal agent of the Empire."

"A spy? How unfortunate for the Grand Master." Darth Chratis's face broke into a broad, cracked smile. "Tell me, spy, how you propose to betray her."

"Republic and Empire share the same initial objectives," the envoy said, pulling free from the two guards. He had clearly been thinking hard while waiting his turn to speak. "The smashing of Sebaddon's orbital defense system comes ahead of any invasion or mass bombardment—the purpose of which would be the neutralization of the planet's central authority, since it must have one, human or artificial—and together, I agree that we can probably achieve that. But once we have the planet toothless and brainless, the need for an alliance will be gone. I suggest we turn on the Jedi and Dao Stryver then—break the so-called alliance and take what's rightfully ours. Sebaddon will be the Emperor's at last. I'll supply misinformation at every opportunity, ensuring that the Grand Master does not ever find the chance to do the same to you."

"What do you ask for in return?"

The envoy looked surprised by the question. "Me? Nothing, my lord. I'm simply doing my duty."

"There must be something important to you, beyond your duty. Ask, and it shall be yours."

"Well, there is one that I would ask you to spare, after your inevitable victory."

"Tell me who."

"She is no one, lower even than a trooper. Her name is Larin Moxla."

"Do you know this woman, Ax?" Darth Chratis asked.

"I believe I do, Master."

"Good."

Darth Chratis's smile disappeared. The envoy was wrenched roughly forward and raised into the air. He struggled against the invisible hold on him, but there was no resisting it. Ax had experienced the power of her Master's Force grip. She knew how tight it could be.

"Listen to me, spy."

The envoy frantically nodded, too frightened to speak aloud.

"I cannot read you. Your mind is shielded from me, by either some unnatural contrivance or a natural talent. I suspect the latter. The Minister of Intelligence seeks out your kind in order to keep his secrets from both his masters and our enemy. So when I look into you, I see no loyalty to the Emperor. I sense only tangled allegiances, with no clear outcomes. Given a choice, I would never trust you.

"Yet you and your kind are a loathsome necessity in times like these. I must find a way to curb your natural instinct for treachery. To that end . . ." Here Envoy Vii jerked violently forward, so he was staring straight into the eyes of Darth Chratis. "To that end, be sure that if you betray me I will hunt down the fancy of your nonhuman heart and put her through such torments that you will be grateful when I kill her. And then it will be your turn. Is that clear?"

"Yes, my lord. Abundantly so."

The envoy dropped with a thud to the floor.

"Very good," said Darth Chratis. "Ax, get him out of my sight. You will return him to Satele Shan with the agreement he promised her, and you will accompany him as my official mouthpiece."

"But Master—"

"Be silent! I could hardly let him go alone. They would never believe that I trusted them unless I took such precautions. You will watch the Grand Master, and you will watch this one, too. At the slightest sign of treachery, you will notify me and my wrath will descend upon both of them."

She bowed her head, thinking: *Another dead-end task. And probably a suicide mission, too.* "I will do as you instruct."

"I sense your impatience, Ax. Remember that our rewards will be bountiful when victory is complete. When the Grand Master is dead and this world ours, then your apprenticeship will be over. Not before. Go now, and do my bidding."

"Yes, Master," she said, bowing deeply, sure that he sensed the burn of excitement in her mind. To be free of him at last, to be a true Sith—that was all she had ever wanted! And she deserved it. She knew that well. Not for nothing had she slaved this last decade and more, to the detriment of all else.

Lema Xandret is dead.

Ax suppressed even the barest hint of regret as she turned and left the shuttle, dragging the quivering informer behind her.

PART FIVE

FATAL ALLIANCE

CHAPTER 31

"DID YOU HAVE to bring her back with you?" Larin whispered to Ula as she escorted the passengers of the *Auriga Fire* to the *Commenor*'s conference room. "I don't trust her."

The envoy adjusted his collar as though he was feeling too hot. "No choice, I'm afraid. Darth Chratis was insistent."

"Well, he didn't offer to put one of us on *his* command deck."

"I suppose he wouldn't offer, given the choice, and I'm afraid I didn't think to ask. I thought the Sith would be valuable as a hostage, that's all."

"I suppose she will." Noticing Ula's discomfort, she forced a smile. "Hey, look, I'm not saying you didn't do your best. I'm just glad you got us this far. No one else could've done it." She patted him on the shoulder with her prosthetic half hand.

"Thanks," he said, looking embarrassed. "I'm glad you think so."

She couldn't help a smile. His social awkwardness was both touching and puzzling. How had anyone so clumsy ever risen so high in the Republic administration, let alone survived an audience with a Dark Lord of the Sith? Perhaps Darth Chratis had taken pity on him.

That seemed rather unlikely.

The Sith apprentice, Eldon Ax, walked steadily between

Master Satele and Shigar, surrounded by an entourage of business-like soldiers, all holding rifles at the ready. Her wild-haired head was held high, and she took each step as though fighting the urge to spin and fight. She was like a wild animal, held barely in check.

"I don't trust her," Larin repeated, "and I'm good at reading people."

Beside her, Ula cleared his throat but said nothing.

THE MEETING WAS uncomfortable from the beginning. Captain Pipalidi's crest was a deep purple, and her Basic difficult to understand, as was often the case with Anx, whose voices tended to be so deeply pitched that they bordered on the subsonic. Shigar swore he felt his rib cage rattle on a couple of occasions.

The captain first ordered all nonessential personnel out of the room. Larin was one of those, and Shigar caught the hurt glance she shot him. There was nothing he could do about it, though. He had no power here.

"Colonel Gurin had no opportunity to confirm his succession plans to me," said Master Satele, "but I know he had the highest regard for you, Captain Pipalidi. He would be glad to know that the fleet is in reliable hands."

"May it remain so," the captain growled, with a sharp look at Eldon Ax. The implication was obvious, and twofold. Many in the military harbored hard feelings for the Jedi after the events leading up to the Treaty of Coruscant, when the Order had been deliberately trapped between the Empire and the Mandalorians. The closing of that trap had left the Republic divided over the role Jedi Knights should play in future conflicts. Some even went so far as to mistrust the Order entirely, preferring to leave them out. The fact that Master Satele had brought a Sith to the negotiating table only confirmed those mistrustful feelings.

"My enemy is your enemy," said Ax. "That makes you useful to me. And vice versa."

Captain Pipalidi's crest turned bright orange. "We do not need you, you murderous witch-child—"

"Enough," said Master Satele, raising both hands. "This won't get us anywhere. The fact is that we *do* need her, Captain Pipalidi, and the Imperials as well, so we must negotiate accordingly. Have your analysts confirmed Dao Stryver's calculations?"

"Yes." The captain raised herself up to her full height, making her the tallest person in the room by more than a meter. "I have sent a long-range probe droid to convey a message to the Supreme Commander, but I do not anticipate a response of any kind within a day."

"The chance of Stantorrs sending a fleet on the basis of one message is remote," Master Satele said. "And by the time it came, Sebaddon would be boiling over."

"Yes." That single syllable conveyed a weight of import. For all her dislike of the situation, at least the captain understood its significance.

"I don't understand why Stryver didn't tell us this earlier," said Shigar. "As it stands we have just fifteen ships, now. If we'd combined both our fleets on arrival, it would've been over thirty. If he'd warned us—"

"Would you have believed him?" asked Ula.

"No," said Ax unexpectedly. "I tried to tell my Master about the hexes but he didn't listen."

Shigar didn't add *Me, too,* but he could have. "So Stryver let us take a hammering just to make a point? If we'd been beaten, that would've done no one any good."

"I'm sure he has his reasons," said Master Satele. "The same reason, possibly, that he's the only one of his kind here. If the Mandalore feels so strongly about this, why wouldn't he send more to back us up?"

"Perhaps he wants us to do his dirty work for him."

"Or he doesn't think his people are up to it," the young Sith said.

Shigar met her quick gaze. If they shared one thing, it seemed, it was a mistrust of the Mandalorians.

"Fifteen ships," mused Captain Pipalidi, "including one bulk cruiser . . ."

Ax said, "We have three thousand front-line troops, divided across the remains of three regiments—repulsorlift, heavy weapons, and armored—with two hundred TRA-Nine battle droids. We have shuttles sufficient to land them and support them, but we lost much of our munitions when the ships carrying them were destroyed by the hexes."

"Are those figures accurate?" asked the captain suspiciously.

"I have been ordered to withhold nothing. It is to our benefit, at the moment, not to do so."

"In that spirit, I will offer the same. Three thousand five hundred troops, two full regiments. Repulsorlift and armor. Our wings were in the air when their capital ships were destroyed, so most of the fighters themselves survived. Hangar decks are crowded, though, and refueling options limited."

"We have the same problem," said Ax. "Colonel Kalisch sent raiding parties to salvage what they could from the infected vessels, but none returned. One came back infected. We destroyed it."

"We noticed. Our intelligence staff is working double shifts, watching everything around the planet. Not helped, of course, by the fact that we were short-staffed to begin with."

The captain's tension visibly eased as she and Ax exchanged details of losses and setbacks. Shigar had heard how battle lines could be blurred on a war's bloody front. This was the first time he had seen it in action. Perhaps Stryver's unlikely plan had some merit after all.

Ula broke into the rapid exchange of intelligence.

"Every minute we stand around chatting," he said, "Xandret's droids build more of themselves, more factories, more who knows what? If we're going to stop them, we have to start making solid plans, and fast."

"Agreed," said Master Satele. "Our number one priority is stopping the droids from getting more than a toehold in orbit. While their factories are confined to the surface of the planet, it will be possible to defeat them."

"A whole planet with just fifteen ships?" asked one of the captain's senior officers. "And just one bulk cruiser?" The hard-skinned major shook his head. "No matter how you divide it up, it's impossible."

"Only if we tell ourselves it is," said Shigar. "Stryver's data clearly showed how the hexes radiated outward from a central point—the main hot spot your ships bombarded," he added with a nod to Ax. "I think it's safe to assume that this was where Xandret and the others founded the colony's capital. Destroying it didn't take out the hexes' coordinating intelligence, but must have hurt it enough to move elsewhere. If we look for the place that's growing the fastest, that'll be the place to hit."

"We have identified two such locations," said Captain Pipalidi. A hologram flickered to life between them. "Here and here," she said, indicating one spot at the equator and another at the south pole. "Perhaps the hexes have decided not to put all their eggs in one basket, this time."

Shigar studied the image. The site on the equator was in the middle of a vast sea of lava, dotted with islands of solid stone. The polar site was much more stable. Straight lines radiated from it in all directions, leading to other spots elsewhere.

"That's a factory," he said, pointing at the pole. "Perhaps the *master* factory, where everything else originates. And that's the brain," he said, transferring his finger to the equator.

"How can you possibly know that?" asked Ax.

"Because factories need physical means to get things in and out. Resources, power, finished droids. That's what these are." He followed one line from point to point. "Roads or railways of some kind. Or power cables."

"And brains don't need anything of the sort," she said, nodding. "It can just sit there, isolated in the middle of that mess, sending orders out by radio."

"I think you're right, Shigar." Master Satele moved around the globe, rubbing her chin. "Teams striking both at once, plus targeted bombardment at the secondary locations, should be enough to slow the hexes' growth."

"Enough to stop it, perhaps," said Captain Pipalidi, "until reinforcements arrive."

There was an uncomfortable silence. Shigar knew as well as anyone that, once the threat of the planet was reduced to zero, the alliance would break. This moment of solidarity was both fragile and temporary. No one had forgotten that the Sith and the Jedi, the Empire and the Republic, were anything other than mortal enemies.

"Let's worry about reinforcements when they get here," Ula said. "Captain Pipalidi, would you be willing to sketch out a basic plan now, to pass on to Darth Chratis and Colonel Kalisch for their opinion? I suggest dividing resources evenly over all tactical objectives, to ensure that both parties feel that they are included but not exploited, plus double the usual number of commanding officers to each platoon. Discipline must be maintained. We don't want the troops shooting one another at a critical moment."

"Naturally not," said the captain with a bluish cast to her crest. Shigar didn't know what that meant. Irony, perhaps.

Shigar caught another glance from the young Sith's direction—bored, this time, and again he sympathized. Their duel in the Hutts' security air lock felt a lifetime ago. His lightsaber hand itched, but he kept it carefully limp at his side.

THE DOOR TO the conference room hissed open. Larin was taken by surprise. She had long ago given up trying to read the lips of the people inside. On seeing a major, she automatically stood to attention.

"Private Hetchkee, a moment," said the sturdy Rellarin. "You, too, Moxla."

Larin followed Hetchkee and the major into the conference room. The air seemed much denser than normal, as was always the case during long planning sessions. A current projection of the planet hung in the center of the room, dashed and dotted with notations in yellow and green. People huddled around it, making suggestions. The Sith girl was one of them.

Both Shigar and Ula looked up as Larin entered, but it was the captain who spoke.

"We're sending strike teams to two locations," she said in a voice so deep it hurt Larin's breastbone. One long finger stabbed at the globe. "Here, and here. We need people familiar with the hexes to guide each team. Both your names have been mentioned for the assault on the master factory. Private Hetchkee, your detail was with the envoy, under the authority of Supreme Commander Stantorrs. I don't outrank him, of course, but I can promote you above the rank required for an escort. No one would dream of wasting a lieutenant on such a detail, and we're short of officers. Will you accept this assignment?"

"Yes, sir." Hetchkee snap-saluted, looking like he was equal parts delighted and terrified. This was not only the fastest leap up the chain of command imaginable, but it could also be the briefest.

"And what about you, Moxla?"

"Forgive me, sir, but I have a history—"

"So I'm told. I don't care what happened back then.

You're the closest thing we have to Special Forces now, so I'd be insane not to use you. All that matters is that you'll follow orders—and be followed in turn, by anyone who has any doubts. Do you think you can manage that?"

Her face was burning. In the service again! She didn't know whether to kill Shigar or kiss him.

"Yes, sir. I do. I will."

"Good. Major Cha, take them to the quartermaster and have them kitted out. I want them briefed and ready for action within the hour."

"Yes, sir."

The Rellarin saluted and guided them toward the door. Larin felt as though she were walking through a weightless vacuum—not floating, exactly, but cut loose from everything. One touch, and she could tumble out of control.

The major chuckled once the door was shut behind them. "You should see your faces," he said. "Well, I can't really see *yours*, Hetchkee, but I can imagine."

"Are we really going to attack the planet, sir?"

"You bet you are. Are you up to it?"

"I'll do my best, sir."

"That's all we can ask of you. What we *expect* is a different story."

In no time at all they reached the *Commenor*'s expansive technical storeroom. Larin gazed hungrily at row after row of clean armor shells, up-to-date weapons, and apparently endless cases of ammunition. She knew this wasn't a big ship, so the stores weren't as extensive as she imagined, but it was so much more than she had seen in a long time. She almost wept.

"Here we are. Sergeant, these two new lieutenants find themselves sorely underprovisioned. Make sure they're equipped with everything they need, and do it on the double."

"Yes, Major Cha."

The swarthy sergeant took charge of Larin and led her into paradise.

"WHAT ABOUT THE Mandalorian?" Ax asked when the stunned troopers were gone. "What role does he play in all this?"

She hadn't forgotten her vow. *I will kill you, Dao Stryver, or die trying.*

"Apart from supplying any other intel he might have," said the captain, "I expect him to join the fighters sweeping hexes from orbit."

"It might be difficult keeping him out of play," said one of her officers. "Mandalorians love nothing better than a good fight."

"He's done a very good job of staying out of this one," said the Padawan with a shrug. "Maybe he'll be content with that."

Ax kept her feelings to herself. She would be hundreds of kilometers away from them, then, intent on destroying the droids' coordinating intelligence. But she would advise her Master to keep an eye on Stryver's scout, in the hope that it strayed too close to an Imperial ship. In the chaos of combat, missiles often went astray. She wanted him dead, even if she couldn't deliver the killing blow herself.

"One of our signals officers believes the hexes identify us by our transponders," said another alien on the captain's staff. "We could feather our drives, confuse them."

"Better yet," said the Padawan, "we could avoid drives entirely."

"What do you mean?"

"Shuttle to low orbit, free-fall straight down from there, then chute onto the targets."

Ax was impressed. She *liked* that plan, despite herself. "It could work. We'll show up on radar, of course, but they won't know what we are. Toss out a bit of junk with us, and they might even mistake us for debris."

The captain was nodding. "Excellent. The only thing left to decide is who has overall authority."

There was another awkward silence.

Ax had known this moment was coming. "Darth Chratis or Colonel Kalisch. We have the bulk cruiser."

"But we have more ships," said Captain Pipalidi.

"Master Shan should make the call," said the Padawan, with perfect predictability. "Her foresight is legendary."

"Does she know how this is going to end?" Ax asked him.

"I do not," the Grand Master said. "But I do know that we'll never agree on this point. I suggest we give someone else the authority to oversee this engagement. Not the details, but the key strategic moments. Someone we have already trusted to act as a go-between in difficult circumstances."

All eyes turned to Envoy Vii.

"I, ah, would be honored, of course," he said, "but—"

"Darth Chratis will accept this proposal," said Ax, enjoying the way the traitor squirmed.

"So will I," said the captain.

"On one condition," Ax added. "We must be sure that Envoy Vii is acting independently, not under any kind of distress or influence. As we cannot guarantee that he will do so here, in a Republic vessel, we require that he be stationed elsewhere, and remain in constant contact with all parties."

"Not with you," said the captain. "Or Dao Stryver."

"Nebula's ship," said Shigar.

The Grand Master nodded. "The *Auriga Fire.*"

Envoy Vii's larynx bobbed once, twice, then he visibly got himself together.

"I will accept this responsibility," he said, "on the assumption that my instructions will be followed to the letter.

There's no point having me in this role if you won't listen to me. All of you."

He was looking at the captain, who nodded. Clearly a civilian authority was better than either a Sith or a Jedi. "I will play my part," she said.

"Darth Chratis will, too," Ax said. "I'm sure Envoy Vii will do the right thing by all of us."

He glanced at her, and she saw the terror in his eyes. He understood very well indeed what she had meant.

WHILE THE SITH apprentice relayed the orders to her Master, Ula took a moment to review the plan in his mind. Primary and secondary objectives were now defined. There would be three teams. The first would clear Sebaddon's orbit so that landing parties could get through. The second, led by Grand Master Shan, would attempt to destroy the droids' coordinating intelligence—their version of him, he now realized. No doubt the hexes would be seeking to take him out in return. The third team would be lead by Major Cha, with Larin and Hetchkee backing him up. They would drop into the master factory and prevent the droids from creating a new CI.

Ula's job was to oversee it all and somehow to stay alive.

The Jedi Padawan came in close.

"I don't know what you told them," Shigar whispered, "but you've got the Imperials jumping exactly in time."

Ula looked up from the holographic globe. "It was nothing special," he said, hiding many layers of truth behind a simple lie. "They're not monsters. They can be made to see reason."

Shigar's doubt on that point was impervious. "However you did it, keep it up and you'll be Supreme Chancellor one day."

Not if I'm caught. Ula was well aware of how agents were punished by both sides. But part of him was flattered by the Padawan's confidence in him. He remembered how Shigar had saved him from the collapsing wall on Hutta, and how Larin had volunteered to accompany him to what must have seemed like certain doom, when meeting with Darth Chratis. These acts had been offered freely, without promise of reward. He didn't understand where they came from, unless they genuinely thought him worth saving.

Him, he wondered, or his false face?

Either way, he felt somewhat buoyed by their regard.

"The Mandalorian agrees," said the Rellarin major, looking up from a separate holoprojector. "Intel and surveillance, engaging only as instructed."

"Darth Chratis concurs on all points but one," added the Sith apprentice on returning to the huddle. "He will fight with Master Shan during the assault on the CI. And I will fight, too."

The Grand Master nodded slowly. "Very well. My Padawan will be part of the strike force, so that is only fair."

"Excellent," said Ula, playing the part of mediator with something like aplomb, he hoped. "We are agreed. All that remains is to begin."

"No time like the present, I say," Captain Pipalidi rumbled.

"My sentiments exactly," said Ula. "I will retire to the *Auriga Fire* and set up my command post there. On notification that all is in place elsewhere, I will give the order. Nothing is to commence until then. Understood?"

They understood well enough, and he was under no illusions, either. It was all an act, a hasty bandaging of cracks that would inevitably tear the alliance asunder. But while they were prepared to play, so was he.

Captain Pipalidi clicked her fingers and an escort fell in behind him. They marched him through the ship to where the *Auriga Fire* remained safely docked, then left him there.

The smuggler looked up when he entered the cockpit. "How'd it go?"

"Could have been worse," Ula said, falling into the copilot's seat. "They put me in charge."

"Well, good for you. That's the seat to be in if you want to skim a little profit."

"I'm not interested in doing that."

"So what *are* you interested in?"

That was the question, Ula supposed. Was it to give the Sith what they wanted and thereby perpetuate their deadly regime? Was it to provide resources for the Minister of Logistics, in order to further his dream of a more balanced Imperial society? Or was it something else?

He'd always thought of Coruscant as cursed. Only now did he realize just how easy he'd had it there. Out here, the issues were the same, but the blasters aimed at his temple were much, much closer.

CHAPTER 32

LARIN LOOKED OUT a transparisteel portal and wondered if she was dreaming.

The *Commenor* was stationed in close orbit around Sebaddon's lumpy moon, in lockstep with the other Republic ships. The Imperial vessels had occupied a different orbit, but they were steadily falling into line. Once the fleets merged, the first attack run would begin. She would be heading down to the surface with the other soldiers to fight the enemy where it lived. Until then, there was nothing to do but stare at the view.

As Larin watched, an almost surreal conjunction occurred before her eyes. The moon, Sebaddon, and the dramatic spiral of the galaxy formed a straight line, with the jets of the black hole aligned at right angles, creating a stellar X. It reminded her of the Cross of Glory, the highest military award given by the Republic. She didn't believe in omens—or any kind of future-telling at all, really, despite talk of Master Satele's abilities in that regard—but she decided to take it as a good sign. Everything was lined up. Everything was perfect.

When the conjunction broke apart, she turned away from the viewport and tested her new armor. The suit was clean, fully charged, and equipped with everything she had ever wanted. All the pockets were full, all the seals checked. Her joints moved smoothly, without impediment, and provided assist when requested without jarring or losing control. Her helmet was a little snug, but the quartermaster had assured her they all were, these days. The newer designs were better equipped to prevent head trauma in even the most extreme situations. She would take a little claustrophobia in return for knowing her skull was safe.

In the mirror, she was unrecognizable, and that wasn't just because of the lieutenant insignia on her shoulders.

"You have fingers," said a voice from the entrance to the ready room.

She turned, saw Shigar standing there, freshly kitted out in the Jedi version of uniform and armor: browns and blacks, mainly, with loose folds of cloth hiding compact armor plating.

"That *is* Larin, isn't it?" he added with a sudden frown.

"Yes," she said, snapping out of her daze. She tugged the helmet off with her left hand—which, as Shigar pointed out, now had individual digits. The new prosthetic wasn't permanent; it was just a step up from the crude paddle Ula had found on the *Auriga Fire*. But it could hold the stock of a rifle while her right hand pulled the trigger. It could type digits into a keypad. It could point.

"It'll do," she said, feigning nonchalance.

He came deeper into the room, so they were standing an arm's length apart. "We're breaking orbit in ten minutes. I wanted to say good luck."

Her stomach roiled. She had plans to go over, equipment to check, troops to address—and the jump itself, waiting at the end of all that. She hadn't dived from orbit since basic training. Only crazy people did it by choice. So many things could go wrong.

She was acutely aware that this could be the last time they ever saw each other.

"Who needs luck?" she said. "You've got the Force on your side, and I have lots of blasters."

He smiled. "Does nothing faze you?"

"Not officially. Just plasma spiders. Oh, and the smell of Reythan crackers, for some reason."

His smile broadened. "Good for you. Frankly, I'm terrified."

Her stomach rolled as though it were in free fall.

"Actually," she said, "this kind of thing makes me a little nervous."

She leaned closer to him, moving quickly, so she wouldn't change her mind, and kissed him on the lips.

He pulled away with a shocked look on his face.

"Larin, oh—oh, I'm sorry—I don't—"

"No," she said, face burning.

I don't think of you that way, he'd clearly been about to say. They were words she didn't want to hear.

"Don't apologize. *I'm* sorry."

"It was my mistake. I thought—"

She stopped. They were talking on top of each other, and his face was as red as hers. She was suddenly afraid to move, to do or say anything lest it be utterly misconstrued. Where had the natural banter between them gone? What had happened to the connection she'd been sure was there?

If she was sure of one thing now, it was that prolonging the awkwardness guaranteed nothing but more of the same.

"I guess this is good-bye," she said, "for now. Good luck to you, too, Shigar."

"Thank you," he said, and although she couldn't look at him, she knew he was looking hard at her. "Thank you, Larin of Clan Moxla."

Then he was gone, leaving nothing but his smell behind.

She pressed her face into her hands. "Flack. Flack flack flack!"

"What's wrong?" asked an entirely new voice from the doorway.

It was Hetchkee. She blinked up at him and tried to focus on something other than what an idiot she felt like.

"Nothing. Just getting myself in the mood."

"Our platoons are assembled," he said. "What am I going to tell them?"

He was as scared as she was. "Nothing but the truth," she told him, "that you'll kick them in the cargo hold if they make us look bad."

She scooped up her helmet and followed him to the briefing rooms. Hetchkee's was first in line. With a deep breath of his unique atmospheric mix, he plunged inside. Larin's was third along, and she had barely enough time to compose herself before getting there. She was a lieutenant in charge of a vital mission, she reminded herself. She had survived two encounters with the droids of Sebaddon before this, and now she had also survived the most embarrassing romantic encounter of her life. She was Special Forces–trained. What could a bunch of low-life grunts possibly do to throw her?

"Well, well," said a voice from the troops assembled in the room. "If it isn't Toxic Moxla, the snitch from Kiffu."

There, in the front row, was the Zabrak who had challenged her on Coruscant.

Perfect, she thought. *Just fragging perfect.*

AX LOOKED UP as the Padawan entered the staging area. There wasn't literally a cloud over his head, but there might as well have been. His face was shadowed, overcast, on the brink of some kind of internal storm.

She moved out of the corner she'd found for herself, far away from the Republic throng waiting for the shuttle to launch, and crossed to him.

"You're angry," she said.

"Only at myself."

He tried to shrug her off, but she wasn't letting him go so easily.

"That's the first time I've seen you this way. It's an improvement."

He gave her a scathing look. "What are you talking about?"

"Anger is a good thing," she said. "It frees you, makes you stronger."

"That's a lie. Anger is a path to the dark side."

"You say that as though it's a bad thing." She drew him closer to her. "You know, you fight pretty well. Imagine how much more powerful you could be if you could shrug off the repressive ways of your masters and—"

"Don't." He wrenched his arm free. "Your mother was angry, too, and look where that got her."

She recoiled.

"What did you plan to do to her when you found her?"

She let the truth of that show on her face.

"Anger and hate bleed *everything* dry."

He stalked off.

Ax didn't smile until she was sure he wasn't looking. His disgust made him beautiful, and that was reward enough for her.

SHIGAR PUT AS much distance as he could between himself and the Sith girl. She was pretty, but her face hid a foul heart. Best, he told himself, to stay well away.

His revulsion was inevitably entangled with feelings of regret for Larin. How could he have handled that encounter so badly? He should have been less astonished, gentler. Was this what Master Satele had meant about being kind?

His Master came up to him and put a hand on his

shoulder. He felt instantly calmer, as though she had sucked the tension out of him.

"We'll be descending in the same shuttles," she said. "Imperials and us alike. You will meet far worse."

"I know, Master. She just took me by surprise."

"That is ever their aim. When I was a Padawan—"

A clang of metal on metal cut her off. The external air lock hissed open. A squadron of Imperial soldiers marched in, matching the Republic contingent one for one. This was clearly the squad that would be joining them on the drop onto the island containing the hexes' coordinating intelligence. They were human, hard-faced and heavily armed. Their discipline was impeccable. Not a cheek twitched out of place; not a lip curled.

Behind them came a dark presence that turned Shigar's blood to water. A tortured amalgam of flesh and metal, he stood a head taller than anyone else and radiated a deep, bone-piercing chill. He had once been a man, but the dark side had twisted every last drop of humanity from him, leaving a husk that looked barely alive. Only his eyes contained any genuine vitality. From them radiated boundless reserves of loathing. He breathed in hurried gasps as though the air smelled foul—or as though each intake might be his last. A long, thin staff tapped in time with the heavy tread of his boots.

"I am here," Darth Chratis announced. "This operation can now commence."

"Envoy Vii is awaiting only our personal assignments," said Satele Shan, standing up to him as though he were any ordinary being. "When we give them to him, he will issue the order."

"Refer to him as 'envoy' no longer." The Sith Lord looked down his twisted nose at her. "I will obey no servant of the Republic."

"*Director* Vii, then, of Independent Operation Sebaddon." She folded her hands patiently behind her back. "I will take my Padawan on the first of two assaults from the—"

"No. You will take my apprentice, and I will take yours. That is the only way to ensure impartiality."

The words hung like icicles. Shigar wanted to beg his Master to deny Darth Chratis this condition. *Don't give in to him,* he yearned to say. *Don't send me anywhere with that . . . creature. He'll kill me as soon as your back is turned!*

Master Satele only smiled. "Of course, Darth Chratis. I'm happy to accommodate your wish. Do you wish to divide the rest of our personnel any particular way?"

"They do not concern me." He waved a hand in easy dismissal.

"Very well. I will assign them randomly. Is that all?"

His gaze narrowed. Her question made him sound like he was being pedantic, and he clearly didn't like that. "The arrangements are sufficient."

Master Satele typed rapidly into a datapad. Imperial and Republic comms had been hastily married into one contiguous network, allowing orders to be transmitted from the *Auriga Fire* via various command vessels. Almost immediately a series of chimes and spoken commands divided the two cohorts into two intermixed groups. Half would stay behind and launch from the *Commenor.* The rest would return with Darth Chratis to the Imperial shuttle.

Shigar was in the latter group, and he watched with his heart in his mouth as the troopers he would soon be leaving behind fell into their new arrangement, spaced neatly if awkwardly across the staging area. In a very short time, he would be cast adrift in the world of the Imperials, in the clawed fist of Darth Chratis.

Master Satele came up beside him. Once again, she correctly divined the source of his disquiet, but this time there was no calming hand.

"I agreed to Darth Chratis's request," she said, "because I cannot afford to trust him. I'm relying on you to make sure he sticks to the arrangement."

"I'm no match for a Sith Lord," Shigar said, aghast.

"Oh, he won't kill you," she said. "I'm sure he has something worse in mind."

He understood, then. She was testing him—and if he failed, they might never meet as Jedi again.

"I won't let you down, Master."

"The Force will be with you."

They embraced and went their separate ways.

CHAPTER 33

"SHUTTLES AWAY," SAID Jet.

Ula fell back into the copilot's seat, watching the telemetry confirming Jet's simple statement. The combined Imperial–Republic fleet had obeyed his order to deploy. Their mad plan might actually work.

In the next hour, four thousand people would converge on Sebaddon singly, there to recombine as attack squads to take out primary and secondary objectives. The Jedi and the Sith would lead the attack on the equator while ordinary soldiers, including Larin, would attack the master factory at the pole. Another two thousand would remain in orbit, keeping the skies clear of hexes and providing occasional bombardment of the ground below. The rest would provide vital support from several distributed HQs, two of which were on the *Commenor* and the *Paramount*.

All reporting to him.

And to Jet and Clunker.

The smuggler had refused all offers of security details, comm officers, and gunners, on the grounds that he didn't want a potentially fractious crew. Choosing one side over another would be politically fraught.

"Don't we at least need someone to help defend us?" Ula had asked him, slightly aghast at how vulnerable that would leave them.

"Not at all. Clunker can operate the tri-lasers by remote from the bridge."

"So what was all that on Hutta about needing a crew? Why have you ever needed a crew at all?"

Jet had smiled. "For the company."

Ula now wondered if it was for an entirely different reason: for a *cover.* He had noted how silent Jet was most of the time. When he wasn't playacting the role of a dissolute smuggler, he was watching and listening to everything going on around him. And now, somehow, he had inveigled himself into the center of everything. He was privy to every order that came through the *Auriga Fire*. Every piece of information on which Ula based those orders was filtered through Jet's sensors. If Jet pulled the plug, the combined fleet would be left leaderless.

Ula reassured himself that this wasn't Jet's style, that if he were ever to try to change the course of the battle, he would do so in a much subtler fashion. Still, Ula would be on the ball for anything at all, and had armed himself with a new hold-out blaster, just in case.

"Deploy fighters," he ordered the fleet. "Commence bombardment of primary targets."

Instantly the dots in the main display began to shift. Four squadrons of mixed Mk. VI Imperial interceptors and Republic XA-8 starfighters would strafe the orbital shell of hexes with laser cannons and proton torpedoes, creating holes in four crucial locations. Two of those locations would allow the all-important troop transports access to lower orbit, there to discharge the free-jumpers, Larin among them. It was vital they weren't interfered with en route. The other two orbital holes would provide critical windows for the bombardment from *Paramount,* mainly by B-28s with Imperial pilots. In the first engagement, 20 percent of the missiles launched at the planet had been disabled during descent by interfering hexes. Every shot fired now had to count.

The interceptors and starfighters hit the shell of hexes. Space lit up with explosions, sparkling almost delicately in the distance. The *Auriga Fire* maintained a respectful distance from both main attack forces and the combined Republic–Imperial fleets, stationed at a point equidistant between the planet and its moon, but it wasn't the only ship ranging freely across the battlefield.

"We're receiving a hail from the *First Blood*," said Jet.

"Put him on."

"I'm noting an increase in subspace communications," said Dao Stryver in miniature. His face was one of several at the bottom of the *Auriga Fire*'s main holodisplay. The crescent of his ship swept across the battlefield in a silver streak. "Since the black hole warps all attempts to communicate outside the system, I suggest that these are all short-range messages, originating on Sebaddon."

"The hexes," said Ula. "Could this be how they communicate with one another?"

"It's a strong possibility that this is the voice of the coordinating intelligence. We've detected no other meaningful signals by radio or microwave."

"Can you locate the source?"

"I'm working on it. With two more ears listening, I'll be able to triangulate."

"Consider it done," Ula said, making a mental note to requisition the resources from Colonel Kalisch and Captain Pipalidi.

"Launches," announced Jet.

"Us or them?"

"Them."

Two locations on the globe of Sebaddon had been highlighted. Six missiles were rising on ion engines, their payloads most likely intended to patch the holes the interceptors and starfighters had made in the orbital defense.

"Get those transports through," Ula broadcast to the fleet's commanders. "Those holes might not last long."

Confirmation came from both sides. A dozen medium-sized vessels broke ranks, accelerating at the maximum capacity of their drives. Imperial Vokoff-Strood VT-22 light troop transports raced Celestial Industries NR2 light transports, each carrying hundreds of men and women, humans and aliens, Jedi and Sith, and combat droids, all intent on doing what they could to crush the hex threat.

Already he regretted pressing Larin onto Captain Pipalidi's staff. It had been worth it for the look of surprise and delight on her face, but what if something were to happen to her? Was that a cost he was willing to bear?

"Don't forget what Stryver wanted," said Jet.

"I haven't," he said, although it had entirely slipped his mind. "Put me through to Colonel Kalisch."

The Imperials claimed a lack of resources, and so did Captain Pipalidi when he got through to her. It could well be true, Ula thought, but it was still frustrating.

"Not even one ship?" he pleaded. "It doesn't have to be battle-worthy. We can be the third ourselves, if necessary."

"All right," she said. "You can have my personal transport. Its arms and shields were stripped, so don't put it in harm's way."

"You have my word. Thank you, Captain."

"Transports through," said Jet.

Ula kicked himself for not paying attention to the bigger picture. The descending troop transports had powered through the temporary gaps in the orbital shell. Most were unaffected, but one was releasing its jumpers prematurely, fighting a swarm of hexes released from a close-passing missile. All were accompanied by interceptors and starfighters, which would remain under the shell once it closed, to do what damage they could from underneath.

"Launch second bombardment," Ula ordered. Anything to keep the hexes busy while the free-jumpers fell.

"Confirmed," said Jet. "No, wait. Kalisch wants to attack a different target. Some of the missiles came from a location that wasn't on our grid. He's requesting permission to take it out."

Ula ground his teeth. On the one hand, it was good that Kalisch had asked permission first. On the other, there wasn't any doubt in Ula's mind that he would do what he wanted regardless what Ula said. The *Paramount* was the ship most at risk from ground launches. As the largest in the combined fleet, it was only natural that the hexes would target it first.

"Tell him to stick to the plan," Ula said, "and next time I ask for resources, he'd better comply. He can hit that target in the next round."

Jet grinned as he relayed the order. Kalisch's response was curt, but he did obey.

"Where are my ears?" asked Stryver.

"Uh, on their way," said Ula, hastily noting that Pipalidi's shuttle had left the *Commenor* and was awaiting instructions. Jet sent the pilot permission to obey Stryver's orders, within reason, and synchronized its comm with the *First Blood*'s.

"We're your third ship," Ula told the Mandalorian. "You can use our location as a fixed receiver."

"Don't forget to share your data," said Jet. "If Clunker can work out their code, we might gain ourselves a better tactic than just blowing things up."

"You think you could slice into their command systems?" Ula asked.

"I'm not promising anything."

Something else for them to keep an eye on, thought Ula. As if there weren't enough things already.

One of the ground-launched missiles hadn't exploded in low orbit or targeted the *Paramount*. It was headed for the moon, and coming very close to the *Auriga Fire*.

"That's either aimed at us," he said, "or it's the first escaping factory."

"First of all, let's get out of its way," said Jet, activating the ship's ion drives. "Second, Kalisch seems to have it covered already."

Ula noted only then the dozen Blackhawks pursuing the missile with weapons locked. He was glad that someone else was on the ball.

As the *Auriga Fire* moved out of the path of the approaching missile, he noted that all the free-jumpers had left their transports and begun their descent. Behind them came the infected ship. Its drives were locked on full, powering nose-first into the atmosphere. That was official fleet policy now: when infected beyond all hope, crew members were to aim their vessel at the nearest target and ditch. Already its skin glowed bright red, and fragments of hull metal were peeling away, providing both cover and hazards for the free-fallers.

Voices called for him over the comm. A hundred data streams awaited his attention. He couldn't sit staring at the holo forever.

Good luck, Larin, he thought, trying not to feel like he was saying good-bye forever. *I hope this is what you wanted.*

CHAPTER 34

THE VT-22 TRANSPORT rattled and shook so much that Larin could barely hear the countdown. Was that one minute or ten to go? She checked the inside of her helmet, which displayed different views of the planet below, their path toward it, and the many, many hexes in their way. Two minutes—that was the answer. She resisted the urge to quadruple-check her airfoil and jet-chute before the hull opened up beneath her and dropped her into the void. Better to use that time to breathe deeply and calmly, and to remember who she had once been.

"Nahrung—keep an eye on those orbital sweeps," she said to her sergeant over the platoon's private channel. "If you see anything that looks like a central complex, flag it." New intel was pouring in every second from the transport and its escorts as they approached the surface of the world. "Ozz—watch the weather. It's your job to make sure we don't land in the middle of a volcano." Ozz was an Imperial, short on words but willing to follow her orders, so far. "Mond—your squad's the first down. Come in hot, take no prisoners. I want you to put your best shots first. Jopp, for instance. Let's see if he's as good at firing a rifle as he is his mouth."

"Yes, sir," said Sergeant Mond. The Zabrak, Ses Jopp, muttered something too quiet to catch. He had been nothing but insubordinate ever since he had crossed her path again. Reinforcing the chain of command was the best way to deal with people like him.

"When we're down, first priority is to take out the factory. Target supply lines, power lines, conveyor belts, heavy lifters—whatever looks essential. Don't stop to count kills. There'll be plenty of hexes for everyone. And remember—they redesign *fast,* so don't take anything for granted, even if it's not moving. We don't know exactly what they're building down there. Treat everything with caution until you've blown it sky-high."

"Twenty seconds" came the announcement from the transport's bridge.

The bay doors opened, letting in the light of the black hole. It happened in near-silence, since there was no atmosphere outside. Only mechanical vibrations came through her suit and the harness holding it in place, adding a low whine to the general hubbub.

"Ten seconds."

The transport rotated to bring its bay doors directly in line with the planet below. Hundreds of troops held their collective breath at the sight. Sebaddon looked forbidding enough in holoprojectors. Rivers of lava, near-molten mountain ranges, and patchy mirror-flat lakes—now known to be sheets of gleaming metal, frozen solid—were clearly visible through the hazy atmosphere.

"Five seconds."

One last burn put the transport on the correct trajectory. Their destination was the pole, on a completely different path from those heading for the equator. Shigar was among the latter cohort, and even in that moment, with the voice counting down individual seconds, she had time to think of him, and to feel a sudden flash of shame and hurt.

"One."

"Go."

Suddenly she was weightless and the transport was rising above her, repulsorlifts flashing, receding rapidly as she fell. All around her were troopers adopting the same position as she was, face forward, arms and legs swept back into straight lines. There was no drag as yet, and there wouldn't be for some minutes, but atmosphere was unpredictable. She'd heard of limbs and even heads pulled right off by simple telemetry errors. The deceleration when it came would be crushing.

"Good launch, people" came Major Cha, just one suited being among so many. Clumps of TRA-9 battle droids hung motionless among them, as silent as stone. "Now find your squadmates and tighten up your formation. Maintain comm silence at all times. Going to intel blackout . . . now."

Larin's helmet views suddenly simplified as the company's network went largely dormant. In order to present the illusion that the falling objects were innocent debris, there would be no internal chatter and no data feeds from the ships above. It would stay like that until the ground was just seconds away. Until then, barring emergencies, it was just her and the data collected so far.

She felt strangely isolated, descending among so many people without exchanging a single word. Other falling troopers, identified by bold black markings on their helmets and chute-packs, clustered into groups of ten or twelve, and those groups in turn fell into their own formations. She stayed where she was, and let her squadrons fall in around her. A rough color-coding system had been improvised to ensure the mixed troops didn't get their command lines tangled. Like the rest of the lieutenants—brevet or otherwise—Larin's helmet was green; the three sergeants' were blue. Major Cha was orange, hanging on his own in the center of the formation.

From far across the other side, she saw another green-helmeted figure give her a thumbs-up. She returned the gesture, knowing it was Hetchkee.

One of her sergeants approached, attitude jets puffing to bring him into physical contact with her. It was Nahrung. They touched faceplates.

"Map grid twenty-five-J," his muffled voice said. "That's my best guess."

She called up the last sweep received before the blackout. The grid reference showed an artificial X, a giant complex of some kind, with numerous smaller tributaries running off in all directions. The black-hole jets cast long shadows across the polar landscape, shadows that might have come from smokestacks—or weapons emplacements.

"That'll do," she said. "Good work."

Something bright and fast flashed by them: a missile, followed by three more in quick succession. Bombardment from the ships behind them, softening what lay ahead. Nahrung drifted away, and she resumed the ready position. Her display was blinking: nearly time to hit atmosphere.

Conscious of everyone watching her, she nudged herself closer to Mond's squad. Jopp was at point. She came in alongside him then moved a fraction ahead, hoping to send a message to him: that, while she might have put him on the firing line, she wasn't afraid to be there with him.

Yellow and white mushrooms blossomed on the ground below.

The first fingers of atmosphere touched her, whistling faintly, rocking her almost gently from side to side.

Then she slammed forward, feeling as though she had hit a brick wall. She roared in defiance at the air screaming past her, adding her own noise to the deafening racket. Her first experience of Sebaddon shook and hammered her, rattling every bone in its socket. Her brain rattled and vision blurred. Time became meaningless. There was no point counting the seconds when each overwhelmed her, and nothing changed.

It had to end, and it did, finally. The shaking and shrieking eased. Her suit's external temperature readings dropped out of the red. The view was no longer vacuum-perfect, since they were in atmosphere now. The neat formation around her gradually re-formed.

Instead of counting the seconds since launch, she was studying an altimeter countdown. The surface of the planet was only kilometers away. They had drifted off-course, probably due to a stronger-than-expected high-altitude wind, but it wasn't a disaster. Giant mushroom clouds gave her a visual fix on their target. Her suit's internal guidance system confirmed it.

Clicking twice over her suit radio, she warned the platoon to get ready.

They steadied, angling at a forty-five-degree angle.

When she clicked once more, their airfoils unfurled neatly, like birds in a flock opening their wings at the same time. The wings didn't open all the way just yet; a full spread would have been torn to shreds, even at such rarefied pressures. As their altitude and speed dropped, they would slowly unfurl to their full extent. One hundred meters from the ground, their jet-chutes would kick in, allowing them to control their landings to the second. They were still moving very quickly. An unassisted landing would result in certain death.

Jopp gusted closer to her, caught by turbulence. The master factory was directly below them, barely five hundred meters away. Intel would be kicking in any second now. Larin checked her suit's targeting systems and unlocked the rifle she'd handpicked from the quartermaster's weapons store. The hexes wouldn't be sitting idly as the assault teams grew near. They would be working busily on *something*, she was sure, but there was no way to tell yet what that might be. She would just have to be ready for anything.

Her HUD cleared and refreshed with data broadcast from above. The target appeared in perfect clarity, revealed underneath the smoke by radar.

"You know the drill, people," said Major Cha. "Keep low and tight until you reach your objectives, then disperse. If comms are jammed, follow the flares. If you can't see the flares, move so you can. This isn't a free-for-all. Anything with blood in it is not a viable target."

"You heard the man," Larin said. "Jet-chutes in thirty seconds. Watch those washes. Don't singe the head of anyone coming in before you."

She took a quick scan of the rest of the battlefield.

The *Paramount* was still intact, although under siege from several directions at once. Some of the orbital hexes had linked bodies to form an energy weapon like the one Jet had taken out earlier. Missiles from below had repaired the holes in the orbital defenses, and there seemed to be some kind of fuss out near the moon. One of the Imperial VT-22s had been infected and was on its way down. Its fiery wake was visible by satellite, carving a black streak across the globe's upper atmosphere and due to impact near the suspected CI location.

Quickly, not really wanting to know, she checked the manifest of the falling ship. Her heart sank. Shigar had been on that transport. Now it really pained her to think about what had happened in the ready room. If that had been the last time they saw each other, how could she live with herself?

A beeping in her ears told her it was time for her jet-chute to kick in. She pushed the superfluous intel—and feelings—to one side in order to concentrate on the maneuver to come. The jet was little more than a modified thruster retrofitted to suit standard-issue Republic armor. Riding it down would be like taming a wild horse.

"Burn!"

On her command, the platoon lit up the sky. Spears of downward-pointing flame stabbed at the surface of Sebaddon. The silver airfoils reflected the light, transforming the troopers into fiery angels that were visible from below. Intel confirmed that at least some of the tall stacks were weapons emplacements. Perhaps they were swinging to track her and her troopers even now. She braced herself for the first shots even as she tried to keep her bucking jet under control.

She wasn't the only one having trouble. The comms were full of whoops and warning cries as troopers struggled to maintain position. Two near-collisions between Imperial and Republic troopers prompted an exchange of harsh words, which Sergeant Ozz put a sharp stop to. The last thing they needed now was an internecine fight to break out.

Then the emplacements started firing, and all was chaos. Bolts of blue energy flashed past them, searing the air. Two of her troopers died in the first exchange, tumbling out of control in balls of flame. Larin returned fire, even while struggling to fly the jet. She doubted any of her shots hit home.

Bombardment from above came almost immediately, called in by Major Cha. One emplacement exploded, adding another ball of smoke to what already lay close over the master factory.

A savage grin split Larin's face. She had forgotten how beautiful aerial combat could be.

A blast at close range wiped the smile away. She'd been hit! Her jet guttered, sending her careening across the sky. Her airfoil whipped in streamers behind her.

Cursing her poor luck, she struggled to control her descent and succeeded only in putting herself into a spin. Her flailing hands reached for the nearest soldier, desperate for something solid to hang on to. The soldier hesitated, and in that fleeting moment, she remembered who he was. *Ses Jopp.*

Mouthing off out of misplaced loyalty was one thing. Letting a fellow soldier drop to their death was another. She knew he would change his mind—and he did within an instant. His right hand reached for her, timing his grab to match the moment when her arm was nearest to him. Too late.

Larin's jet-chute failed, and she dropped like a stone out of the sky.

CHAPTER 35

EVEN BEFORE THE alarms started ringing, Shigar knew something was wrong. The transport containing him and Darth Chratis lurched as though hit, and the major in charge of the drop broke off in the middle of issuing a general announcement. Shigar wasn't patched directly in to the Imperial network, so he couldn't tell what was happening to the ship in real time. Instead, he was receiving data from the Republic troopers, relayed via neutral command node. The delay between the systems was very nearly fatal.

"Something's not right," he told the troopers packaged up next to him in rows, ready to drop. His instincts were warning him to move. Punching the overrides on his harness, he was on his feet as the first of the hexes burst through the outer hull into the troop deployment bay.

Shigar was ready for it. He Force-pushed the droid backward, sending it tumbling into space. There were more behind it, scrabbling for claw-holds on the torn metal. He leapt at them with lightsaber swinging, severing legs and stabbing at sense organs before the hexes could activate their electromirror shields. If he could stop them from getting in, he and the other passengers might have a chance.

The bay wall ripped open at another point, too distant for him to take on both at once. Fortunately, the troopers behind him were ready and brought their own weapons into play. Imperial and Republic blasterfire converged on the invading hexes, knocking several back into the void. Still more came after them, climbing over one another in a horrible swarm. The hexes were returning fire now, those at the back shooting past those in front, and Shigar felt the defense of the bay beginning to turn in the hexes' favor.

"Get these troopers out of here!" he told the major between cutting two hexes each in two.

On the other side of the bay, he saw the orange helmet nod. Orders went out to open the bay doors early and launch the troopers on their way to Sebaddon. Acknowledgment came from two of the other three bays, and the doors below Shigar opened smoothly, jettisoning their precious cargo, the major with them. Several hexes went, too, which would no doubt make the journey more interesting for all.

Shigar stayed behind, clinging to a stanchion with one hand and kicking another hex back where it came from. It wriggled and spun in free fall, six legs waving frantically.

How long, he wondered, until it redesigned its innards to match the ones in orbit and "grew" a retrothruster or two?

He wasn't sticking around to find out. The fourth and final bay hadn't sent any kind of acknowledgment. If they were in trouble, he had to help them.

The ship rocked underfoot as he passed through the air lock and hurried through its empty corridors. Nearing the fourth bay, he heard blasterfire, explosions, and a persistent crackling over his comm. The hexes were jamming both Imperial and Republic frequencies. That was a disturbing development.

An interior bulkhead breached, sending hexes spilling over themselves into the hallway. He braced himself to meet them head-on, using a Force shield to deflect their laser pulses while stabbing with his lightsaber. They hadn't expected him to be there; that much was certain. They were firing at someone attacking them from inside the bay, and it took them a moment to bring their own shields to bear. Shigar whipped the legs off three, not stopping to impale the fallen bodies. Immobility was good enough.

A black figure leapt through the rent in the wall, wielding a red lightsaber. Lightning flashed from his open hand, sending hexes twitching and smoking in every direction. Caught between Shigar and Darth Chratis, the hexes stood no chance. In moments, Jedi Padawan and Sith Lord stood alone in a field of red-dripping droid debris.

The jamming let up, allowing them to speak.

"The rest have launched," said Shigar. "We have to get these bay doors open."

"Do not think to give me instructions, Padawan. You have survived this far by luck alone." Darth Chratis stalked up the hallway. "The mechanism is damaged. Lieutenant Adamek will either repair it in our absence or widen the existing hole. Failing that, she will exit the ship via the other open bays. That is not our concern. Your priority, and mine, is to stop this ship being turned by the hexes into a weapon."

"To the bridge, then?" said Shigar, swallowing his annoyance at being spoken to like a child.

"To the bridge."

They encountered three swarms of hexes on the way. Traveling in groups of six, the droids appeared to be scouring the ships section by section, destroying all evidence of Imperial insignia. The appearance of Darth Chratis and his red blade drove them into an immediate frenzy. On two occasions, Shigar was ignored completely, allowing him to flank the hexes and attack from behind.

The element of surprise was working for him for a change, turning an impossible situation into one that was merely difficult.

The Sith Lord swept through hexes with little apparent effort, leaving them for Shigar to finish off. The Sith Lord's lightsaber had an unusually long reach, emerging as it did from a collapsible staff of some kind. Darth Chratis also had another weapon that Shigar did not. His lightning was much more powerful than Eldon Ax's efforts and had an effect similar to the electrified nets Stryver had fired at the hexes on Hutta, sending them into paroxysms that left them vulnerable to conventional attack.

"The Grand Master has taught you poorly," Darth Chratis said, observing Shigar's efforts to subdue the last of the hexes. "She allows philosophy of mind to interfere with outcomes in combat. That is how the Sith will triumph over you and your kind, in the end. You will hold yourselves back from achieving your true potential."

Shigar blinked sweat out of his eyes. Satele Shan regarded Force lightning as a pathway to the dark side, and had counseled Shigar many times against its use. Now, though, he could see how Darth Chratis might have a point.

He wasn't so naïve, however, that he couldn't see where the Sith Lord was going with this.

"Save your breath, Darth Chratis. Nothing will tempt me to join you."

The Sith's smile was horribly humorless, even through the glass of his faceplate.

The bridge was two levels up, sealed behind thick blast doors that even the hexes were having trouble penetrating. Comms were down again, so there was no way to signal the crew within. Darth Chratis tried overriding the locks, but they had been fused into solid lumps of metal by the hexes' attempts to get in.

"Together," said Shigar, thinking of the huge masses he had seen Jedi Masters move using nothing but the power of their minds and the Force.

"On my command," agreed the Sith Lord.

Operating in tandem, they were able to twist the blast doors aside as though they were made of tinfoil. Shigar considered their cooperation a small moral victory until he broke off the effort and shivered. Something of Darth Chratis had clung to him during the effort. A coldness, and a foulness. His fists clenched as he stepped over the buckled metal and onto the bridge. He wanted to strike out at something, but there were no hexes around. Just Imperials, who were temporarily reprieved.

The frightened-looking commander of the transport saluted as Darth Chratis closed on him.

"Tell me the drives are locked" was all the Sith said.

"I-I cannot, my lord. The engine room is not responding. I ordered a maintenance team—"

"They will already be dead. Stay here. We will effect the repairs ourselves."

Darth Chratis was already leaving.

"Perhaps you should evacuate," said Shigar to the commander before following. "There's nothing you can do here."

"Leave my post?" The Imperial looked affronted at the suggestion. "Never!"

Shigar wanted to argue. The blast doors were down, and the hexes would be back before long. Staying meant certain death for the commander and his bridge crew.

Instead he shrugged. Who was he to fight the stubbornness of the Imperial officer? That wasn't a Jedi's job.

"It's your decision, I guess."

Putting them from his mind, he hurried after Darth Chratis.

"You waste time," said the Sith when Shigar caught up.

"You waste lives."

"Humans are replaceable. Seconds are not."

Shigar didn't have a good answer to that, so he concentrated on what they were doing. Darth Chratis was leading him along the transport's spine, past endless rows of viewports. Outside, the galaxy turned around them, completing a circuit once every few seconds. The transport was spinning, although thanks to the artificial gravity within there was no way of telling. Several hexes were visible, either swimming helplessly through space or crawling along the outer hull. The sphere of Sebaddon came and went, and Shigar couldn't tell if it was growing nearer or not.

A mass of hexes was waiting for them at the far end, at the entrance to the engineering section. Force lightning spread through them in waves, breaking the mass into manageable parts. Shigar leapt into their midst, deflecting laser pulses back at their owners and dismembering anything that came within reach. When he misjudged a sweep and caught a flesh wound on his side, the pain only heightened his concentration. He moved as though in a dream, with the Force guiding his every step.

Almost with regret he reached the far side. There, Darth Chratis was examining the ion drive controls. They had been partially dismantled by one of the hexes, presumably with the intent to take control and send the transport angling upward to infect the rest of the fleet.

Darth Chratis worked quickly, rewiring the controls into an approximation of their former state. The deck shook as downward acceleration resumed.

"You've done it?" Shigar asked him.

"I have."

Darth Chratis raised a hand, and a section of the wall peeled in, exposing the space outside. Not space anymore, Shigar realized, hearing a rising howl around them. They were entering atmosphere.

"After you, my boy," said the Sith.

Reluctant though Shigar was to turn his back on one of the Jedi's ancient enemies, he knew that for now he was safe. His Master had been utterly correct. That bloodred blade was the last thing he had to fear.

Four running steps took Shigar to the hole. The fifth would take him all the way from the burning ship to the planet's surface.

He leapt, vowing, *I will never be your apprentice, Darth Chratis.*

A silken sinister voice came back to him in reply.

Make no rash promises. After all, I may soon be in need of a new one.

Shigar closed his mind against any further intrusions, and concentrated solely on falling.

CHAPTER 36

AX TOUCHED DOWN neatly on both feet. The ground was secure: no hidden traps or pitfalls. She punched the button on her harness, and the jet-chute shut down and her airfoil fell away. Sebaddon's gravity was a little less than standard, leaving her feeling slightly light-headed, but only for a moment. Apart from the yellow jets from the black hole, the sky was red, reflecting the glow of the surrounding lava. Keeping her eyes peeled for hexes, she took two steps forward and looked around for the others who had dropped from orbit with her. Master Satele was one of them. She didn't like knowing there was a Jedi loose she couldn't account for.

The squad she'd been nominally part of had aimed for one of the most complex sections of the CI center. From the air, the island as a whole resembled a giant hedge maze, with long, winding buildings connected by thick cables and pipes. She had landed in what could have been an angular, steep-walled street, except that there were no doors, windows, or pedwalks. The purpose of the buildings was unknown, but it was clear that the site was still under construction. One squad had targeted the machines responsible for expanding the structure, while the rest intended to strike at its heart—or what appeared to be its heart from orbit, at least. There were three possible locations, and she was in one of them.

Above her, troopers rained from the sky like seedpods,

dropping into their own droid-made little canyons. None appeared to be landing near her. She tried her suit's comlink, but both Darth Chratis and Master Satele were either off the air or being jammed. The former's stricken transport shone in the sky like a bright star, haloed with black smoke. It appeared to be coming right for her.

She quickly decided that her landing spot was jinxed, lacking even hexes to kill. So, picking a direction at random, she loped along the canyon, taking what cover she could in blurry-edged shadows. She kept her unlit lightsaber in her hand. Discretion was the better part of valor, particularly on a planet of hexes programmed to kill Sith warriors on sight.

If only, she thought as she had many times, there was some way to tap into that core programming and turn it to her advantage. It was entirely possible that Lema Xandret had put a little more of herself in them than just her thoughts and prejudices. The biological component of every hex had to mean *something*, after all. If she could appeal to that something, make it listen to reason—*her* reason . . .

Around a bend came a Republic trooper, swinging his gun back and forth and running lightly on his feet. Ax stepped back into the shadows. Better to run on her own, she decided, until she was sure what lay ahead of her. She didn't want anyone getting in the way at a critical moment.

As the trooper went by, she noticed a strange thing. The air was literally shimmering before her eyes. At first she thought it was something to do with her—her sight being interfered with, perhaps. But then she realized that the distortions came from the air itself. It was *hot*.

Kneeling down and touching the ground, she could feel the heat even through her gloves. All around the CI complex was lava, so that made sense, she supposed.

Something dropped soundlessly behind her.

She was up with lightsaber lit in an instant.

"Impressive reflexes," said Master Satele, to all appearances unconcerned by the possibility that Ax might have cut her in half. She hadn't even activated her own lightsaber. "Your peripheral vision could use some work, though. I've been on your tail ever since you landed."

"Well, that's a productive way to spend your time." Ax lowered her weapon to her side. "It didn't occur to you to do something about the mission, I suppose?"

"I'm the first to admit that I've got a lot on my mind." The Jedi smiled. "But not that much. Take off your helmet and tell me what you hear."

"But—" *It's hot,* she was about to say. Then she noticed that Master Satele was sweating inside her own helmet. Clearly she had done exactly as she asked Ax to do—and if she survived, so could Ax.

"All right," she said, triggering her neck seals. The helmet hissed, and she tugged it off.

The air seared her skin and the inside of her nose. It stank of chemicals, and fire, and ozone. In the distance she could hear voices shouting familiar phrases over and over again.

"We do not recognize your authority!"

"We ask only to be left alone!"

"Hexes," Ax said. "They're here somewhere."

"Not that," said Master Satele with a quick shake of her head. "Deeper. Behind everything."

Ax listened again. Then she heard it: a low-frequency growling at the very edge of her hearing, almost impossible to catch.

"Is it the ship?" she asked, indicating the transport still falling from the sky. It was larger now, and still coming right for them.

"I don't think so. Sounds to me more like drilling."

"What's the CI doing mining at a time like this?"

"Material for more hexes, perhaps."

"This isn't a factory."

"No, but there must be nests here somewhere."

"So let's find them," Ax said, not hiding her impatience. "Isn't that what we're supposed to be doing?"

High above, an orange flare blossomed into life, painting strange shadows across both their faces.

"That's what I was waiting for," Master Satele said. "The troopers have found a way in. Let's go help them."

Satele Shan moved from a standing start with surprising speed. Ax was taken by surprise, and had to hustle to keep up. They followed the base of the artificial ravine to the next intersection, and then leapt to the top in order to travel in a straight line, leaping from wall to wall over the empty spaces below. The maze seemed to stretch forever. Ax was reminded of circuit diagrams or logic flow charts, but this strange landscape lacked any overall order or purpose that she could discern. It was more like the random etchings of a wood-boring insect than anything a sentient might design.

Explosions puffed brightly in the distance, reflected from wispy clouds above. The sound of each retort arrived split seconds later. Master Satele changed direction slightly to head straight for the combat zone. Troopers still dropped from the sky, firing at cannon emplacements mounted over the maze. A pall of smoke hung over everything, denser in some places than others. Ax could smell the hexes' "blood" faintly on the air. It gave her the jitters. She was missing out on the fun.

Glancing over her shoulder, she saw a dozen hexes following them, leaping on their six legs from wall to wall. She laughed. She wouldn't be missing out for much longer!

Master Satele unexpectedly dropped down into a ravine, and Ax followed. There she stopped dead. The Jedi was standing on the ground with one finger to her lips. She counted down three fingers with her other hand,

and then leapt straight up into the air with lightsaber flashing. The first of the pursuing hexes fell in two equal pieces. The rest shrieked and rushed in to fight.

The battle was fast-paced and glorious. On seeing Ax, they immediately fell upon her, but she had the measure of them now. Her Force shield repelled all but the most concentrated fire, and she had more than a mere Padawan and a disinterested Mandalorian to back her up.

The Grand Master possessed prodigious Force powers. A gesture crushed hexes into balls or blew them apart from the inside. A look stilled them in mid-lunge while Ax rushed in to finish them off. In a matter of moments, the dozen were dealt with and Ax was looking around for more.

"This way," said Master Satele, guiding her to where the flare had come from.

"Shouldn't we be worried about that?" she asked, pointing at the transport. It was huge in the sky now—or seemed so—and blazed like a false sun.

"Worry all you want," said Master Satele. "Unless there's something you can do about it, I don't see what good it will do."

Ax had no good answer to that, so she followed with something approaching obedience. The Grand Master had impressed with more than her telekinetic and telepathic skills. Her speed and decisiveness in combat were unbelievable—but she never once made a sound. Her face was calm, almost serene, as she slashed and hacked through the hexes. There was a tranquillity about her, almost a blissfulness, that spoke of an intimacy with violence Ax had not expected.

To the Sith, violence was an art form. To Master Satele, it seemed like life itself.

That didn't marry at all well with what Ax knew about the Jedi. Weren't they emotionless, self-righteous hypocrites who fought only when it suited their interests?

Didn't they disdain passion and preach powerlessness to all who would listen and obey?

For the first time, Ax saw that there could be strength in serenity, and steel beneath stillness.

Something exploded in the next ravine across. Before the debris ceased falling, Master Satele had them in the middle of a firefight between a squad of entrenched troopers and no fewer than thirty hexes. The explosion didn't seem to have had much effect on the hexes' operation as a whole. If anything, they fought more determinedly than ever. The assault teams had to find another way to attack the installation if they were to have any effect on the CI at all.

The platoon's lieutenant, an Imperial, acknowledged their presence with a grateful wave.

"The major's over there," she said, pointing, when the skirmish was over. "We're picking up vibrations consistent with geothermal drilling."

"Of course," Master Satele said. "*That's* what they're up to. If the CI can tap into the planet's deeper layers, it'll have all the power it needs."

"To do what?" asked Ax.

"That we don't know," said the lieutenant. "We've found a shaft two avenues away, but it's heavily defended. We can't get close enough to lay charges."

"We'll take care of that," said Ax.

"No need," said Master Satele. "Tell your troops to fall back. I want the area evacuated as quickly as possible."

"What?" Ax couldn't believe what she was hearing. "You're giving up?"

"Not at all. Just letting something else do our work for us."

She pointed at the sky, at the stricken transport bearing rapidly down on them.

"Yes, sir." The lieutenant began calling orders through her comlink, and backed them up with another round of flares, just in case the message wasn't received. Immediately the troopers began pulling back, firing at the hexes coming in their wake.

"What happens if it doesn't land in exactly the right spot?" Ax asked Master Satele as they leapt across the maze.

"I don't think it needs to," the Jedi replied. "If the CI is drilling for geothermal energy, those shafts will be tapping right into the magma layers. Unplug the shafts, and what will we get?"

"A volcano," she said. "*Lots* of volcanoes."

"Exactly. We could take out the hexes' brain with one hit. Best we not be standing too close when it happens, eh?"

Again, Ax was struck by Master Shan's calm. How could she be so sanguine when the island they were standing on might be about to erupt into flows of molten lava? Surely she felt *some* apprehension about what might happen?

Ax flipped down the visor of her helmet so she could track exactly where the transport was going to hit. It wasn't as close to her as it seemed: the island was two kilometers across, and the impact point was on the northernmost edge. Still, she ran southward with Master Satele as fast as she could, keen to put space between herself and the inevitable explosion.

While leaping from one artificial canyon wall to the next, another similarity between the maze and computer chips came to her. The walls were barely a meter or two across; they therefore couldn't possibly contain rooms or corridors, or indeed anything of any substance. She hadn't wondered what function they performed in and of themselves. Now, though, jumping through waves of hot, rippling air, it occurred to her that the walls looked like the thin ridges engineers added to some computer components to increase the surface area exposed to air.

The greater the area, the greater the cooling effect. Heat sinks, they were called.

What if the island wasn't the hexes' coordinating brain itself, but a massive heat sink for the brain?

That would mean the assault teams were attacking the wrong thing entirely.

She had just enough time to wonder if the falling transport would be any different when it came down in the distance, lighting up the sky with a bright blue flash. The sound came a second later—both the sonic boom of its passage through the atmosphere and the titanic concussion of its impact and detonation. The ground bucked beneath her feet, and she misjudged her landing on the wall of the next ravine. Wobbling for balance, she felt herself gripped by the left arm and pulled down.

Master Satele steadied her on the floor of the ravine as a rush of superheated gases roared overhead. The ground bucked and buckled beneath them. Ax looked down and saw cracks spreading around her feet. That wasn't a good sign.

A growing thunder drowned out the sudden return of comms—not that she could have made anything out from the mass of warnings and contradictory orders. A rush of air swept by them. Master Satele cocked her head and pulled Ax along the ravine, away from the source of the wind.

In its wake came a flood of red-hot lava.

"Jump!" Ax cried, wrenching the Grand Master up out of the ravine.

The wall crumbled beneath their combined weight, and they jumped again. The maze was collapsing around them, followed by a tide of red that spread from the crash site. The edge of the flood moved with astonishing speed, consuming troopers and hexes in broad, bubbling swaths. The volcanoes Ax had imagined were nothing compared with this silent, swift seep. The section of the maze she had explored was already subsumed.

All too suddenly the tsunami-like flood was upon them. Two thick crimson tongues closed in front of Ax and Master Satele, cutting off their best route to safe ground.

Master Satele turned, pulling Ax after her. It was clear that she could have run faster on her own, but she didn't abandon Ax to her fate. Ax didn't question why. She just accepted the gesture, even as it became clear that it would doom both of them.

The path of stable ground they occupied was shrinking fast.

"One more jump might do it," said Master Satele. "Are you ready?"

Ax wasn't, but there was no way she'd admit it. The boiling red gap between them and safety was too large already, and it was growing by the second.

"Ready," she said.

They ran and leapt together. For a moment, they were high above the drowning maze, held aloft by the Force and momentum, and nothing could touch them. Ax wished she could stay there forever, in that peaceful place where contradictory forces canceled out and all was still.

But gravity conquered all. The ground came closer too quickly, and she screamed as bright red lava rose up to engulf them.

CHAPTER 37

AN HOUR INTO the battle, Ula realized that betraying the Republic was going to be much harder than he had imagined, even from his privileged position high above the battlefield. The problem lay in the sheer amount of data pouring from the battlefield into the *Auriga Fire*. It was impossible to keep track of it all, let alone to decide which isolated part could be best manipulated in order to benefit his masters. He could barely keep up with the torrent as it was.

Missiles full of hexes had restored the orbital defenses, and provided new weapons with which to pound the combined fleets, making it difficult to lend ground support to the teams below. The CI target was burning, and the pole was hidden under smoke. Comms were erratic at best. Ula had no way of knowing what was going on down there, and the situation on the moon was little different. The hexes had been strafed repeatedly, but without sending in troopers to tackle them face-to-face, it was impossible to tell if the infection had been contained. Every time the alliance made progress, Lema Xandret's tenacious creations bounced back in a new and surprising way.

"I have locks on three subspace targets," reported Stryver. "They're relays, scattered across the globe."

That was good news. "Send the coordinates to Kalisch and Pipalidi. Tell them to take all three out."

"We should keep one intact," said Jet. "How are we going to infiltrate their comms if they don't have any comms left?"

"How close are we to cracking their cipher?"

"I don't know. Clunker has worked out the transmission protocols, allowing us to pretend we're the CI, but we're no closer to figuring out the actual language it's using."

"Then I can't afford to take the chance. We know they'll build new relays anyway. This way we gain a momentary advantage. We need every one of those we can get."

Jet killed the ship's comm for a moment. "Here's something else to worry about. What if Stryver's staying out of the fight purely to get those ciphers? With them, he could turn the hexes on us."

Ula hadn't thought that far ahead. "You're right, and we can't have that. When Clunker cracks the code, let's keep it to ourselves."

"That would make *us* unstoppable. You don't strike me as the ruling-the-galaxy sort, but I'm not sure about your masters."

Ula had absolutely no desire to rule anything. There would be no hiding in the shadows at all while seated on a throne. And he wasn't going to say anything about his masters, true or false. "What about you?"

The question was a loaded one, and Ula had his hand on the hold-out blaster while he asked it.

Jet laughed. "What, give up my carefree life? I don't think so, mate. Too much red tape by half."

A new red light joined the many flashing on the instrument panel. An alarm joined it.

"Multiple launches," Jet said, all laughter forgotten, "from the planet and the moon, too, this time." He stopped and peered closer at the viewscreens. "Something's headed our way. The CI must've noticed us sitting here, keeping entirely too low a profile. Time to move."

Ula notified the leaders of the combined fleet that he was now a target and would be changing orbit. The *Commenor* acknowledged immediately but didn't offer any kind of tactical support. The *Paramount* said nothing at all, just sent a squadron of interceptors.

"Negative, negative," said Jet to the squadron leader. "Return to the fight. We'll be okay, and we'll holler if that changes."

"The colonel's orders were very specific" came back the reply. "We're not to let you out of our sights."

The phrase had threatening connotations that Ula was certain were intentional.

"Kalisch, get those ships off our tail," said Jet to the *Paramount*. "I've got more important things to worry about than your trigger-happy hotshots."

"Put me through to the director" came the reply.

No name, thought Ula. Just a title. "Colonel," he said, "this is Director Vii. Your resources are needed elsewhere. We have to punch through that defensive shell to gain access to the polar regions—"

"Darth Chratis explained your situation," Kalisch said over him. "I really must insist."

Ula closed his eyes. This was an open line. If he bowed to the colonel's wishes, it would be tantamount to acknowledging that he favored—or could at least be influenced by—the Imperials. The time was not yet right to do that.

"Negative, Colonel. I have advised you to send your fighters elsewhere. Recall them or I will be forced to interpret your intentions as hostile and request assistance from Captain Pipalidi."

Again, the *Paramount* said nothing, but the ships did at least change course.

Ula mopped his brow. Not only was he failing to betray the Republic, but he was now being forced to defy an officer in the Imperial navy.

"Why are we doing this, again?"

"Beats me," said Jet. "Officially I'm still hoping to turn a profit, but that's looking less and less likely every minute."

"Is that really all you're interested in?" Ula asked, suddenly irritated by the smuggler's pretense.

"Can't it be?" Jet shot back.

"I think you're doing yourself a disservice. If people knew what you and your ship could really do—"

"No one would ever let me dock anywhere. If they think I'm a hopeless bum, that gives me an edge. It keeps me safe. Like Tassaa Bareesh. If she'd known that I could've taken my ship back anytime, she wouldn't have let me hang around to see what happened. And if I hadn't hung around, I wouldn't be here. Granted, here is not looking so comfortable at the moment, but that could change. Life is surprising. I think we'll pull something out of the hat."

"It just seems dishonest."

Jet said, "You should talk."

Ula bristled. "What do you mean?"

"Come on, mate. I know what you are. I've known from the second I saw you. Why do you think I asked you for a drink?"

Ula drew the hold-out blaster and pointed it at Jet. "Tell me what you think I am."

"I think you're a braver man than you're letting on," Jet said without flinching. "To your superiors you're just a pawn. To your enemies you're worse than evil. You're caught between wanting to do your job and trying to keep your job hidden. It drives you crazy, but you can't confide in anyone. You have to keep it all locked away, and no one ever appreciates how hard that is. We're expected to just keep on going, blokes like us, because if we trip, there's no safety net."

Ula bristled. "I'm nothing like you."

"We're more alike than you think. I've been a pawn, and recently, too. Why do you think I was working as a privateer? It wasn't for the good times, let me tell you."

"You're unprincipled, amoral."

"I'm glad you think so. That means the cover's working."

"You're not making any sense! Why are you telling me this? Do you want me to shoot you or not?"

"I want us to work together exactly as we have been."

"How can we possibly do that now?"

"You're speaking like one of *them*," said Jet, gesturing at the holoprojector. "You're not human, but you look human to me. What does it matter who we really are? It's what we do that matters."

"But what am I *supposed* to do?"

"You can put the blaster down, for a start, before I ask Clunker to take it from you."

Ula stared at him for a long, tortured moment. They had a battle to coordinate, and what *had* really changed? Jet could have revealed Ula's secret at any time—just as Ula could have revealed Jet's, making them even. Nothing was causing the confrontation between them except his own uncertainty and doubt. If Jet thought him brave, perhaps it was time to be.

"All right," he said, lowering the blaster. Clunker, who had approached somehow without Ula noticing, stepped away.

"Thank you," said Jet with a loose grin. "You know what the weird thing is? I can't tell who you're working for. I mean, I know how it's *supposed* to be playing out, but on a practical level you've got me beat. As far as I can see, you're just trying to do the right thing."

A series of alarms began to sound.

"Uh-oh." The smuggler's carefree mood evaporated. "This is what happens when you don't pay attention."

Ula hurriedly scanned the telemetry. More launches.

More agglomerations forming to target the combined fleets. Still no good news from the ground, and no word at all on Larin or her platoon. A mixed squadron of Republic and Imperial fighters had suffered an internal disagreement, leading to an exchange of fire, and a Turbodyne 1220 drop ship had collided with a Republic NR2 during an assault run. Fierce recriminations were being exchanged by the two sides, and neither Captain Pipalidi nor Colonel Kalisch responded to his hails.

"Now what?" asked Ula.

"Well, if we're not going to run," said Jet, "I suggest we turn the full capacity of our scheming minds to finding a way to survive—

"Wait a minute. Where's Stryver?"

"I can't see him. He could be around the back side of the moon, or—"

An urgent beeping joined the already strident alarm calls. The map of Sebaddon turned red at the south pole. Ula stared in amazement as the defensive shell of hexes began to part, creating an opening.

"They're letting us in?"

"Don't bet on it," said Jet.

Through the opening in the orbital defenses flew the familiar silver quarter-moon of Stryver's ship, rising up in a perfectly vertical line.

"What's he doing there?"

"Running, I think."

Close on Stryver's wake came a monster bursting from the heart of the planet.

CHAPTER 38

LARIN IGNORED THE shrieking of alarms and the flashing red lights filling her suit's helmet. The unlucky shot appeared not to have damaged the fuel line to her jet-chute, but its gyros were completely destroyed. If her airfoil had been intact, that would at least have had a stabilizing effect, but it was nothing but tatters now. Kicking and skidding wildly across the sky, she was completely out of control.

She refused to give in. There had to be a way to bring the jet-chute down safely, and her with it.

First thing first: to get manual control of the jet. It was behind her, but by letting out the restraints she could wriggle around so it was thrusting from her chest. The noise was deafening. She darkened her visor so the flashes wouldn't blind her.

At least she still had her instruments. It was hard to get a sensible altimeter reading, so she didn't know exactly how much time she had, but the temperature outside was clear: well below the line. Any exposed flesh would freeze solid in just moments. All the better to work quickly, then.

Tugging off her left glove, she used the artificial digits of her prosthetic to pull at the thruster casing. It fell away behind her—up or down, she couldn't tell. The horizon was turning wildly around her. Just glancing at it made her feel giddy.

She concentrated on the wiring inside the jet-chute casing instead. Steam hissed into the thin, cold air. Luckily, her fingers weren't affected by heat, either. The jet-chute was an uncomplicated machine, designed to be rugged rather than versatile. There would be all sorts of safeties and overrides, but she didn't need them. She just wanted the switch that turned the thrust on and off.

A sharp tug on a particular component had the latter effect. Suddenly everything was still and she was weightless. The world below still turned, but at least it wasn't changing direction three times every second. Now that she had to look at it, she could see how much closer it had come. Perilously so.

That wasn't what mattered. At the moment, she had to correct her spin. She counted furiously under her breath, judging the correct burn by instinct more than conscious calculation. She shoved her artificial fingers into the hot innards and switched the thrust back on, just for a second.

She jerked across the sky, slewing madly. Too much, too long. She had to be more precise. Counting again, she tried a second time, with more success. She was still tumbling afterward, but not so badly that the thickening air couldn't get a stabilizing grip on her. She spread her limbs in a star shape until she was falling steadily face-forward.

The complex at the planet's south pole was coming up at her with frightening speed. She activated the jet-chute and kept it on full, fighting it at every moment to keep it pointing straight down. It was like trying to balance on a pin: the slightest wobble threatened to tip her over and put her back where she started. She gritted her teeth and held on.

Slowly, steadily, her downward plunge began to ease.

She had time to examine where she was landing. It was a broad, flat plain, crisscrossed with deep cracks that looked too straight to be natural. *A door* was her first thought, leading to something underground. Around it stood a number of cannon emplacements, all aiming for targets elsewhere, fortunately. It was hard enough just coming down straight, let alone dodging. She wanted to look behind her, to see where the others were, but the merest attempt to do so threatened to upset her delicate balance.

Slower and slower she fell, until she was traveling barely more than running speed. The ground was just dozens of meters away. She began to feel relief. Against all odds, she was going to make it!

With a guttering cough, the jet-chute ran out of fuel.

"No!" she yelled.

But words weren't enough. She was falling again, and rapidly gaining speed. Just seconds lay between her and being squashed like a bug against the hard face of Sebaddon. Nothing could save her now.

Strong limbs wrapped around her chest. With a gasp, she felt herself squeezed tight and pulled backward. She couldn't see what had happened, but she recognized the gloves gripping together in front of her. They were standard Republic issue. The jet-chute belonging to the owner of those gloves strained and whined, slowing them so they landed with a tumble, not a splat.

Larin couldn't believe her luck. Clambering to her feet, she helped her savior free of his jet-chute and airfoil harness. His faceplate cleared and she recognized Hetchkee.

"Couldn't let you go like that," he said matter-of-factly. "Equipment failure is inexcusable."

"Thank you," she said, meaning both syllables with all her heart. "What happened to Jopp?"

"Called me for help. Didn't you hear him?"

Larin hadn't, but she didn't press it. She had been a little busy at the time. The important thing was that she had survived. As long as Jopp stayed out of her way, they need never talk again—about how his hesitance had almost cost her her life.

"Right," she said, slipping her glove back onto her frost- and heat-blackened hand. "We've got some regrouping to do and hexes to kill. Any idea where our squads came down?"

They ran together for the rendezvous point, jumping over two of the deep cracks along the way. They were definitely machined into a ferrocrete-like surface, with some kind of black sealant at the base. If they weren't the edges of a massive door, then they could have been canals. But for what? Any water lying around would be frozen solid. They could conceivably have been roads for hexes, only none were in sight.

The rendezvous point was a mess of weapons fire. Republic and Imperial troopers had dug in and were either setting charges or laying covering fire, hoping to take out the cannons in range. Major Cha barked orders over the patchy comms as bombardment rained down from above. Imperial combat droids lumbered in perfectly straight lines across the battlefield, spitting fire at distant targets. Larin hadn't grasped how large the master factory site truly was. Standing on top of it, she couldn't see the edges.

"Moxla! Take a squad and put tower number five out of business. I'll send someone after you once you're laid in."

"Yes, sir." There was no easy way to tell one squad from another, so she picked a sergeant at random and assigned him to the mission. He was an Imperial, but that didn't matter. On the ground, under enemy fire, troopers were all the same.

Several supply sleds had come down nearby, and she helped herself to all the launchers and charges she could carry. With the sergeant and his squad in tow, she loped across the flat dome, carefully watching the orientation of the cannon emplacement. At some point, they would be noticed.

She crossed another crack and dropped down inside. It was just deep enough for her to crouch out of sight. She followed the crack until they were as close as they needed to be, and there she ordered the squad to stop.

"Get those launchers unloaded and ready to fire. Sergeant, I want three of your best shots to go on ahead to provide distracting fire, another three to go back and do the same. Spread out, and space your rounds. Keep that emplacement busy."

"Yes, sir."

The launchers were lightweight and easy to assemble. They were ready in moments. As a broad field of fire converged on the tower, more potent punches attacked it at regular intervals, shrouding its uppermost reaches with thick, black smoke.

Still it fired, though.

"You and you," Larin said, pointing at two troopers at random, "with me."

She grabbed a belt of explosive charges and leapt out of the trench. The troopers followed, running hard for the base of the tower. The emplacement was already busy tracking multiple targets. Hopefully three more would escape unnoticed.

Halfway, they were targeted. The trooper on her right went down, blasted up his middle by pulses of purple fire. Larin and her sole companion dodged left, and the next wave went wide. Then it was targeting the grenade launchers again, and they reached the base unharmed.

It was ten meters across and as solid as a mountain.

She gave half the charges to the trooper. "One every two meters, set to blow on my command."

He nodded and set off, moving around the base in the direction opposite hers. When they met up, they retreated as far as they dared and dropped flat. The emplacement didn't seem to notice them. It was firing upward, at something she couldn't see.

She pushed the remote detonation switch, and debris exploded over their heads. The top of the tower leaned, began to fall.

Then a much brighter flash came from behind her, and the ferrocrete ground bucked. Larin glanced back and saw a large mushroom cloud rising from the rendezvous point. It had been hit by heavier munitions than she'd seen in play from the hexes before. Either Xandret's droids had evolved again, or they'd knocked something from above off-course. Maybe, she thought, that was what the emplacement had been firing at right before she'd destroyed it: bombardment, deflected just enough to hit the invading forces.

It was going to take ages for the dust to settle, but at least the comms had cleared. She got up and put out a call for all officers to report in.

Hetchkee spoke up from the other side of the dome, and one Imperial lieutenant. No others. No Major Cha.

A silver shape flashed through the clouds above, glinting in the sun. "Is that you, Stryver?" she called. "Tell me what you see up there."

"One of the major subspace sources is right under your feet," the Mandalorian replied. "Why put it so far from the CI?"

She didn't know the answer to that question, and the comm dissolved into static again before she could ask him anything else.

She signaled her trooper to follow her back to the trench. The rest of the squad had re-formed and were packing up the launchers, preparatory to moving elsewhere. Larin didn't know what her next objective should be. Keep taking out towers? Try to find the others? Without Major Cha, it was going to be difficult to coordinate everyone who remained.

As she hastily considered her options, the black surface at the bottom of the trench shifted. She looked down at her feet and saw a ripple pass through the rubbery black material. It shifted again, and a deep subterranean groan surrounded her.

"Move," she told the squad. "If this whole thing is a door, then—"

The world fell out from under her before she could finish the sentence. She lunged and barely caught the nearest edge of the trench. The black surface had dissolved as though its molecular structure had suddenly changed from a solid to a liquid. Two troopers fell into blackness, firing at nothing. Their shots ceased after less than a second.

Larin hauled herself out of the suddenly bottomless trench. Another groan shook the air. The opposite walls lurched apart. Ten meters, twenty meters. She was standing with half the squad on the edge of an ever-widening trench. On the other side, the rest of her troopers receded into the distance.

The dome was unfolding, sliding finger-like segments of roof into deep recesses at its edge and releasing a vast upwelling of warmer air. Tendrils of fog sprang into being, mixing with the smoke and creating strange shapes all around her. She looked down, and saw something huge and indistinct stirring. Whatever it was, the hexes must have been building it nonstop, using all the prodigious resources of the metal- and energy-rich world.

"What is that thing?" one of her troopers asked, loud enough to be heard without a comm.

"I don't know," she said, "but those look like repulsors—there, around its edge."

"It's a ship, shaped like that? Where are its engines?"

A crazy thought occurred to her. "Maybe there aren't any."

The troopers looked at her like she was talking gibberish.

The segment of dome they were standing on was nearing the edge of the roof.

"We can't stay here much longer," she told what was left of the squad. "I advise you to get ready to jump."

"Down onto *that*?" asked one, pointing at the object rising toward them.

"I think it's a skyhook," she said, bracing herself, "so we won't be going down for long."

CHAPTER 39

SHIGAR STEPPED OUT of his jet-chute harness and stared in horror at the bubbling, bright red lake where his intended landing site had been. He had watched the furious, equator-bound descent of the transport while riding down in its wake. Its impact had sent a shock wave through the complex maze, which buckled and then subsided into the fluid beneath. Everyone on that maze had been swallowed. There were only a few late arrivals left, standing around the edge of the crater like him, staring down into the death of all their hopes.

Master Satele had been in the maze, somewhere, with Eldon Ax. Shigar had tried calling his Master via both the suit and the Force, but received no response to either. All he could see moving were hexes, bobbing and swimming through the red tide, apparently unharmed. Three surviving cannon emplacements fired at anyone in range, to little effect.

Darth Chratis had descended with him and landed not far away.

"Not only must I seek a new apprentice," said the Sith Lord, red lightsaber standing out at his side like a standard, "but it appears that you are in need of a new Master."

Shigar's grief and frustration found a target. "You made this happen," he said, turning away from the awful view to confront the ancient enemy of the Jedi Order.

"Not I, boy."

"The Emperor, then, with all his dreams of murder and domination, slaughtering his way across the galaxy."

"I don't see the Emperor here, do you?"

"You're mocking me."

"Because you deserved to be mocked, boy. You are naïve and sheltered, thanks to the nonsense your Masters have fed you. The true face of the universe frightens you, and you fall back on that nonsense to explain your fear. Only a child closes its eyes when frightened. Look around you and grow up."

Shigar felt his hackles rising, even though he knew Darth Chratis was trying to get exactly this reaction from him. "You can't deny that the Sith stole Cinzia Xandret from her mother. That's what led us here."

"Lema Xandret was brilliant and mad. She is the one to blame, Shigar. Or Stryver, for not letting the matter rest. Or you."

"Me? What did I do?"

"It was you who brought the matter to your Master's attention."

"Stand back." Shigar activated his lightsaber. Darth Chratis was getting entirely too close. The red of his blade matched the lava and the sky above. It looked to Shigar like the whole world was turning to blood.

Darth Chratis stopped five paces away, a contemptuously amused expression on his withered face.

"Blame the Emperor for all your troubles, if you must," he said. "Blame the Empire as a whole. Given the chance, would you explain to all of them how they have been so very wrong? Would you address the Sith, and the ministers, and the troopers, and the spies? I fear they wouldn't listen to you, not even the people you might imagine to be on your side: the oppressed, the disenfranchised, the dissidents. There are fewer of them than you imagine, you know. And to the rest *you* are the enemy—you and your Jedi and your Senate. They curse your name just as you curse ours, for the loved ones they've lost at your hands, for the goods stolen by your privateers, for the many hardships they've endured. You'll never win them over with your words, with your nonsense, so you'll be forced to kill them all. How does that sound to you, Padawan? Do you fancy yourself the greatest mass murderer in the history of the galaxy? If not, perhaps you should, for that is the path you are heading down. You and the Emperor—no different at all."

"You lie." Shigar backed away, even though Darth Chratis had made no physical move. The weight of his words was threat enough.

"That empty litany will not protect you now, boy. Not from yourself."

"We fight you because you are evil. Because you are slaves to the dark side."

"All those billions and billions? Would that the Sith were so plentiful."

"You have seduced them, twisted their thoughts. They obey you because they fear you."

"Is the Republic so different?"

"We have laws, safeguards against abuses of power—"

"We have laws, too, albeit different ones, and the Emperor is the ultimate safeguard. There can be no miscarriage of justice under his rule, for his word is law. Where is your precious justice on Coruscant? How has the Republic benefited from your leaders' inept fumbling?"

Something blossomed in Shigar's mind like a flower: a flower of certainty, growing strong and sure in the darkness of the hour. He felt as though years of history had condensed to this moment: the reappearance of the Empire and the Mandalorians; the sacking of Coruscant and the fragile treaty that restored it to a greatly diminished

Republic; the Annexation of Kiffu and the subjugation of his people.

It boiled down to him and Darth Chratis

"You are the source of every bad thing that's happened to the galaxy," he said. "That's why we have to fight you. War is inevitable, just like people say it is. There can be no lasting peace with the likes of you."

"You are more like us than you care to admit," Darth Chratis snarled. "I am offering to save your life, boy. Join me as my apprentice, and I will open your eyes for good. There can be no peace because *peace* is the lie. Strength comes only from conflict, and for there to be conflict there must be an enemy. That is the truth that lies behind your Masters' teachings. Acknowledge it, embrace it, and you will understand why you can never serve them."

Shigar steadied his lightsaber in a tight, two-handed grip.

Darth Chratis's deep-set eyes glittered. The tip of his lightsaber didn't move a millimeter.

Shigar watched it closely, waiting for the first blow to fall.

The Sith Lord laughed, a dreadful cackling sound all at odds with their circumstances.

"Do you think I intend to kill you now, boy? You forget: we have a truce. Unless you plan to attack me, and I am forced to defend myself—"

"I ought to attack you. Any kind of alliance with the Sith is flawed at its heart. Master Shan should never have agreed to it."

"It was her suggestion, remember—and see how it has trapped you? Obey me and the truce holds. Attack me and the truce is broken." Darth Chratis chuckled. "Which is it to be?"

Shigar wavered on the verge of acting. He could feel the need for it simmering in every muscle, every nerve.

The Force was ready. It filled his veins like lava, burning hot.

He thought of Larin saying, *You're thinking too much.*

His lightsaber moved as though of its own accord, sweeping forward into Darth Chratis's reach with an almost delighted hum. Their blades clashed together once, twice, three times, and the Sith edged back a step.

"Yes, excellent—"

Shigar didn't let him talk, pressing him with another combination of moves, staying light on his feet for the inevitable responses, feeling with every instinct, every breath, what must be done. They danced together along the lip of the crater, in full view of the surviving members of the attack force. No signals went up; no word to disband the alliance; comms were down, so the joint assault of Sebaddon went on.

Darth Chratis rallied with a series of bold, vicious strikes that cost Shigar the ground he had made, and more. He struck back only with his blade, knowing that he would lose if the duel descended into a free-for-all of telekinesis and other Force powers. That was inevitable. His only hope lay in Darth Chratis making an early mistake, giving Shigar an edge. Even then, it was going to be hard. Sith didn't die easily.

Neither do Jedi, he told himself, even as sweat trickled into his eyes and he tossed his helmet away, the better to fight unhindered.

"You are growing weary," said the Sith Lord. "Your resolve is weakening. I can feel it. You know that you will never beat me this way. Your only hope is to reach into your heart for the anger that we both know is there."

"Anger will never rule me."

"Think of the Grand Master. Think of your homeworld and all who died there. Tell yourself that I killed them, and seek the strength that knowledge brings."

"You had nothing to do with Kiffu."

"Didn't I?"

Shigar fought on, matching Darth Chratis blow for blow. The red blade took three centimeters off his braid. He scored a line across the Sith's right shoulder.

"You cannot fight without the dark side."

Shigar silenced his thoughts and feelings. He was only the blade. He was only the Force.

"You cannot *win* without the dark side."

Darth Chratis sent a wave of lightning across the gap between them. Shigar tried to catch it with his lightsaber. The shock coursed up the blade, into the hilt, and from there into his right arm. It burned like acid, much more powerful and insidious than the blast Eldon Ax had hit him with on Hutta. It didn't just hurt. It ate at his resolve, telling him to fight fire with fire, to use the Sith Lord's own weapons against him in defiance of his own Master's advice. If he didn't, he would surely die.

Shigar fell to his knees, the beginnings of a scream whistling through his clenched teeth.

Why didn't she warn you? The whisper of doubt in his mind had a voice now. *Your Master is famous for seeing the future, so why didn't she tell you this lay ahead of you?*

Because there was nothing she could do about it. That's why. Her teachings are weaker than those of the Sith, and she knows it. She knows that the Jedi will lose the war that's inevitably coming. She knows the Emperor will win. By keeping this secret from you, she has killed you.

She lied to you, just as the High Council has lied to you. They don't care about justice. They are corrupt and weak.

All you have to do is turn your back on them, and you will live.

Darth Chratis's lightning passed through Shigar's body and down to his left hand. There it concentrated into a ball, blindingly bright. Waiting to be set free.

Strike me, said the voice, *and rise up again, stronger than ever before.*

"Die," said Shigar in a voice that didn't sound like his own. "Die!"

When he raised his hand, Darth Chratis wasn't even looking at him. The Sith Lord's attention had been captured by a shadow that had fallen across them. The thing that had cast it was enormous and bulbous, like a fist as big as a city rising slowly out of the lake. Lava dripped from it like water.

Such was his shock that the Sith lightning concentrated in Shigar's left hand fizzled out. The rest went with it, along with the pain. Shigar understood then, with piercing clarity, that he had been the source of all of it, ever since Darth Chratis's initial lightning strike. The voice whispering in his mind—and the doubts it had expressed—had been none other than his own.

His lightsaber lay in blackened pieces at his feet. His suit stank of smoke.

He stood up. The thing from the lake towered over them, no longer rising, just looming, blocking out the sky. The noise it made was deep and resonant, like the song of a deep-sea mammal. It sounded like a summons, offered in the language of worlds.

A small silver dot moved across the sky: Stryver's scout. Beyond that hung the brilliant constellations of the combined fleets. Flashes of light danced among them, indicating that they were returning fire. Shigar couldn't tell if they were firing at the hexes or one another.

He looked down at his hands. His gloves were burned right through, but his fingers and palms were undamaged.

This is the path laid down for you, said Master Satele into his mind. They were the same words she had used on Coruscant.

Shigar almost wept with commingled triumph and despair. She was alive, but where did that leave him? Was he tainted by the dark side even though he hadn't *actually* struck out at Darth Chratis? Had Master Satele truly known all along that it would come to this, and never warned him?

Again he thought of Larin, telling him that he was lucky for being lifted out of obscurity to train for the Jedi Order. He had even believed her, and found strength in the knowledge that his Master and the High Council would endure. *Whatever happens today, you'll go back to the life you know.*

Not anymore.

The galaxy is painted in black and white, he realized, feeling the truth and certainty of it deep in every bone. *But from far enough away, it all looks gray.*

CHAPTER 40

THICK RED CURRENTS pulled Ax irresistibly downward, tumbling her like a red blood cell in a heart attack. Master Satele gripped her wrist so tightly she feared her bones might break, and she gripped the Jedi back just as hard. She could see nothing but her heads-up display and hear nothing but alarms. The precise specifications of the Republic armored environment suit were unknown to her, but she imagined its cooling systems screaming as they tried to radiate the excess heat, only to be overwhelmed and fail.

She waited, but that didn't happen. They were tumbling just as violently as before, but she wasn't getting any hotter.

Instead, a strange feeling came over her, a feeling that was neither entirely physical nor entirely psychic. For all the battering and pummeling going on, she wasn't in any immediate danger of being crushed or burned. The fluid just looked like lava. She wasn't being drowned. Tasted, perhaps? Or embraced . . . ?

A powerful urge to swim overcame her, but not to reach the surface. There was something in the lake with them, something that wanted her to come closer. She began to kick and struggle against the current. Master Satele was a deadweight until she divined Ax's intention and joined in the effort. They wriggled through the thick, red mass, body length by painful body length, occasionally striking solid objects being swept along with the flow. Some clutched at her, but Ax couldn't tell if they were people or hexes, or an entirely new manifestation of the Sebaddon phenomenon. Instead of stopping, she swam on, following the only compass she had: her gut.

Her questing fingers found something hard and stable submerged in the lava-like liquid. It was smooth and slightly curved, like the side of a submarine. She and Master Shan explored it, looking for a way in. They found extrusions that might have been antennas, cannons, and sublight drives.

A ship. That was where she was supposed to go. Something inside had brought her here.

Satele Shan pulled her closer, touched faceplates. The red liquid parted just enough for Ax to glimpse the Grand Master's private universe. Her face was drawn but composed.

"Air lock," she said. "This way."

"Do you think it'll work in this stuff?"

"There's only one way to find out."

They pulled apart, and Master Satele guided her hand to the panel she had found. The controls were instantly recognizable. Ax had seen them on thousands of ships. Thousands of *Imperial* ships.

She pushed the top button: OPEN. A sudden current swept them closer as the empty chamber sucked in fluid. When the door was completely open, they swam inside and fumbled for the interior controls.

The door slid silently shut, leaving the unceasing turbulence of the fluid outside behind them. Ax floated in silence for a moment, grateful for the respite, the chance to think. Where were they? What was she doing? What had brought her here? She should be swimming for the surface, not exploring sunken artifacts while the rest of the mission fought around her.

"Are you going to open the inner door?" asked Master Satele, pressing close again.

Of course she was. She'd come too far to turn back. Her instincts tugged her on, despite her misgivings.

When she touched the CYCLE button, pumps in the walls strained to drain the fluid away. Weight returned, along with light and air. They finally let each other go. Ax wiped her faceplate clear, and she saw Master Satele doing the same. In the midst of such strangeness, she looked as small as Ax herself. She was glad she wasn't alone.

The inner door opened, revealing a stock-standard ship's corridor, scuffed and dusty with age. Ax stepped out of the puddle left in the air lock and put her dripping feet gratefully on a dry surface. She checked her HUD. The air was fine. Cracking the seal on her helmet, she swung the faceplate open.

All she smelled was blood.

Master Satele stepped up beside her with her faceplate open, too. "Any idea whose ship this is?"

Ax kept her thoughts to herself for the moment. She walked along the corridor to the first intersection, mentally plotting the layout. If this was a light cruiser, she decided, the command deck would be to the right, holds to the left, crew quarters down the first ladder, and engineering ahead. She chose to go right, and was rewarded with success. The command deck was small, but felt spacious for being so empty. No instrument panels glowed. No holoprojectors projected. The only signs of life were the lights shining down from above.

"Generator's clearly functional," said Master Satele, "but the control systems have been disconnected. If you're thinking of getting off Sebaddon in this thing, you can forget about it."

The floor shook beneath them, and Ax was reminded that, although the fluid that had engulfed them hadn't been lava, they were still standing on top of a giant geothermal drilling site, on a world whose skin was about as stable as a water balloon's.

The ship rattled and creaked around them. The echoing of its many complaints sounded like a voice, gradually fading into silence.

"Comms are blocked by the hull," Master Satele went on. "That wouldn't have been part of the ship's original design."

"They never intended to go anywhere," Ax said, "or to talk to anyone. I bet this is Lema Xandret's ship."

Master Satele looked around. "No artwork, no personalized touches, no signs of home. How can you tell?"

"There's a freight air lock aft," Ax said, avoiding the question. They headed back the way they had come. "Let's see what's through there."

On the way they passed row after row of empty rooms, confirming Ax's feeling that the ship had been abandoned. Xandret and the other fugitives had stripped everything useful or personal and moved it elsewhere. Maybe the ship reminded them too much of what they had left behind; maybe they had built more comfortable quarters elsewhere. Perhaps they had kept it as a memento mori, as a symbol of their isolation and abandonment, and never intended to use it again. When they had returned to the galaxy, they had used a different ship entirely, one they had built themselves.

Nowhere in Imperial records, Ax realized, was the name of this ship recorded. Unless she found a survivor, or some kind of record, she might never learn it. That hole in her mother's history bothered her as they walked and climbed through the ship. She knew it meant nothing, really, and that sticking on this point was a kind of self-defense against the much wider holes that might soon be filled in. But she couldn't help wondering what it had been like to live with the rock-solid reminder of your betrayal constantly at hand. Maddening, probably.

The aft freight air lock was twice as large as the one they had come through on the port side. It was open, a tubular umbilical leading to spaces unknown. The tube swayed and rocked uncertainly under the influence of the fluid around it.

Ax pressed forward, telling herself there was nothing to fear. She agreed with Stryver. *Lema Xandret is already dead. She has been for some time.* There was no life in here. The colony had survived long enough to build the hexes, but then it had failed. Either the hexes had killed them, recognizing that the humans had outlived their usefulness, or they had killed themselves. All the evidence Ax expected to find of them was their bodies.

She wasn't prepared, therefore, for the intimately decorated quarters they had left behind: the pictures, journals, clothes, mobiles, meals, and more that lay scattered throughout the winding corridors of the colony, perfectly preserved in the cool, dry air, as though they had been put aside only an hour ago. There had been children living here. There were memorials to the dead, and to those left behind. Likenesses of the colonists stared out at her from every angle. She recognized her mother's face in some of the pictures. Lema Xandret had grown older here. Her face was lined, and her hair had turned gray. Her stare was sharp.

"You were right," said Master Satele with something like admiration in her voice. Concern, too, if Ax's ears didn't deceive her.

She hurried on in determined silence. The empty colony was testimony to many things: hopes and fears, bravery and cowardice, the everyday and the profound. Ax wasn't interested in any of that. She hadn't come to

Sebaddon in search of a museum. She had come because the Dark Council ordered her to, because fate demanded it, and because of Dao Stryver. Maudlin sentimentality was irrelevant to her.

Still, Ax's pace increased until she was almost running from room to room, seeking something she couldn't put a name to. Master Satele followed, moving lightly and silently in her wake. The corridors wound deeper and deeper, connecting to larger spaces and more business-like structures, including air and water purifiers and power plants. The pressure steadily increased around them. In several places they saw slow leaks, dripping red into growing puddles.

They came at last to a large, square room that looked more like a warehouse than a laboratory, although clearly it had once been the latter. Droid parts lay scattered in various states of repair alongside tools of all shapes and sizes and arcane instruments of measurement. Holoprojectors displayed rotating designs, revealing several hex variants that Ax hadn't seen before: versions with ten legs or more, multiple bodies, specialist limbs, and agglomerated into larger machines capable of space travel or mass destruction. Some of them changed as she walked toward them, indicating that the evolutionary algorithms responsible for them were still running. Thick cables ran everywhere through a centimeters-deep layer of red. Some of them led to a tubular glass tank, five times larger than a bacta tank, which stood in one corner of the room. It was full of opaque red fluid, apparently identical to the stuff outside.

Master Satele approached the tank, but Ax hung back. She sensed that this was what had drawn her here, but now that she was standing in front of it, she was nervous. Did she really want to know what her mother's fate had been?

"It's warm," said Master Satele. She had taken off a glove and pressed it against the glass. "Body temperature, or thereabouts."

"That red stuff," said Ax. "It's in all the hexes. It looks like lava, but it's not. It's the biological component the Hutts detected."

"Is it blood?"

"I don't know." She shuddered. "I hope not."

The Grand Master was still standing with her hand touching the glass. She watched Ax closely. "This is what I tap into when I subdue the hexes. It's alive, but at the same time not alive. It's incomplete, like a body without a mind."

"Could the CI be its mind?"

"It could be, but we've seen no sign of the CI so far. If it's in this section of the planet, it's keeping a very low profile."

The fluid in the tank stirred, and Master Satele pulled sharply away.

"There's something else in there," she said. "I felt it."

Ax hugged herself without realizing. She wanted to run but couldn't move. Her feet were frozen to the floor. Her eyes couldn't look away.

Inside the tank, something white swept against the glass. It vanished almost instantly, back into the red murk, but then returned a moment later, pressing hard.

Ax gasped. It was a human hand. Another appeared beside it, with fingers splayed out wide. The red fluid stirred as the body the hands were attached to steadied itself in the fluid.

Something whirred in the laboratory. A cam turned to stare at Master Satele, then tracked to take in Ax.

"I recognize you."

The voice came from all around them. Female, breathless, surprised.

"I know you."

A face loomed closer to the glass wall of the tank, coming slowly into view.

"I am you."

Ax felt her insides turn to water. The face was her own.

CHAPTER 41

ULA WATCHED THE repulsor platform rising from the planet's south pole with something approaching awe. The skyhook was huge and well defended, and the hexes had built it in almost no time at all. If Stryver still needed to convince anyone of the reality of his geometric growth theory, the proof was right there in front of him.

"What's a skyhook doing at the pole?" Jet asked. "It'd be useless, floating there."

"Why?"

"Because the best place to get to higher orbits is at the equator, and that's what they'll be wanting to do. Isn't it?"

Ula just shrugged. Skyhooks had many uses, not just as a staging point to orbit, as they were usually employed, hanging motionlessly over points on a planet's surface. They could provide defense or act as displays of wealth. Who knew what the hexes wanted? He was still learning what they could do.

"Target that thing," he ordered the combined fleet, just to be sure. "Bring it down!"

The *Paramount* sent a halfhearted salvo in the skyhook's direction, but it was clear Kalisch was keeping significant firepower in reserve. The *Commenor* sent nothing at all.

"Didn't you hear me, Captain Pipalidi? We need to stop that thing from reaching the upper atmosphere."

"And I need to ensure the security of what ships we have left," said the leader of the Republic contingent. "If the *Paramount* turns its weapons on us while we're looking elsewhere, we'll be defenseless."

"If the hexes escape, we all lose."

"On Kalisch's head be it."

He punched the instrument panel in frustration.

Jet looked at him in reproach. "Hey, take it easy."

"It's just so—so pointless! What's the point of fighting each other? All they have to do is cooperate a little longer and we stand a chance."

"They're too alike. That's the problem. You see that in primitive cultures when schisms divide religions into similar but not identical sects. They hate each other more than the enemy."

"What are you talking about? The Empire isn't a primitive culture."

"No, but the principle still holds. Similar hierarchies, with a dominant high priest caste; similar beliefs but different practices; competing over the same territory—"

"Stop it," said Ula. "You're not helping."

"Just trying to point out why it was never going to work."

"So we shouldn't even have tried?"

"Everything's worth trying once. And I have been known to be wrong on occasions. Unfortunately, this isn't turning out to be one of them."

"So how do we turn it around? What can we do to stop the hexes from getting out?"

"There's always Plan B."

"Which is?"

"I was hoping you might have one."

Stryver was heading north, away from the south pole. Ula projected the Mandalorian's progress across a map of the planet's surface and found the likely CI location at the end of it. That portion of the map was a mess of activity. Ula used satellite and fighter data to zoom in closer.

Something was rising up from a lake of lava, filling the crater where the landing site had been.

"Another skyhook?" he said, pointing at the image.

"It's in the right spot," said Jet, "but I don't think so. The design isn't right, and it doesn't appear to have the repulsorlift capacity it would need to get off the ground."

A circular hatch irised open on the top of the thing, like an enormous iris. Another space opened up among the hexes directly above.

Ula waited, but nothing emerged from the hatch.

"This doesn't make any sense," he said.

"There's Stryver again," Jet said, pointing at a solitary blip circling the new arrival.

"I guess he's chasing those subspace foci," Ula said. "That one must be a biggie."

"Like the skyhook's." Jet pointed at the south of the planet. "Which is moving, by the way."

He was right. The skyhook had drifted away from the pole and was accelerating ponderously northward.

Ula thought fast. If the skyhook kept accelerating at that rate and stayed on that heading . . .

"They're two halves of one thing," he cried. "The skyhook was at the pole because that's where the master factory built it. Now it's coming to pick up the CI and take it offworld. I bet the drives are being built on the moon, as we speak. They're getting ready to break free. We have to stop them!"

"I think you're right," said Jet, "and I agree that this is serious. Try Kalisch and Pipalidi one more time. Maybe they'll change their minds."

Ula knew it was pointless. The fleet was breaking up. Shots were being fired by fighters passing perilously close to the opposite side's capital vessels. It was clear that lines were being drawn and beads taken. All it would take was one mistake for open warfare to erupt.

"If there was only some way to *make* them do what's needed," he said.

"I knew you had the makings of an emperor."

"How can you joke at a time like this?"

"Who's joking?" Jet turned in his seat and said to Clunker, "Time for Plan B."

The droid inclined its battered head. A series of new screens flickered in and out of the main holoprojector as the droid sent a series of commands through the *Auriga Fire*'s main computers.

"Don't tell me," said Ula. "You cracked the hex code but have been sitting on it, waiting for the rest of us to figure it out for ourselves."

"Believe me, I wouldn't have waited. Also, there's nothing to be gained in doing that. Once the code is cracked, the hexes are dead, and I'm out of pocket."

"So what are you going to do?"

"Something noble and probably quite stupid. In return, I need you to do something for me."

"Just ask."

"I need you to pretend it never happened."

Ula stared at him.

"Watch the screens," Jet said.

The combined fleet was breaking up, but not down faction lines. The *Paramount* was leading one mixed contingent down to a lower orbit, there to target the CI with greater precision. The *Commenor* was heading for the moon with a smaller retinue and two squadrons of fighters. All internecine squabbling had abruptly ceased.

Comms weren't down, but they were suspiciously quiet. No one was giving orders to coordinate the fleet's movements. It was just happening.

"You're doing this," Ula said, appalled.

"Clunker is. He's got a *very* good head on his shoulders."

"You used me to infiltrate the Imperial and Republic networks. You cracked their codes. Now you've taken over!"

"The end justifies the means, right?"

"That's what Stryver said. I'm not sure I agree."

"Being alive is always better than being dead. That's my golden rule."

"But what comes afterward?"

"The fleets change their codes. Business goes back to usual."

"If you let them go."

"Why wouldn't I? I'm not power-mad like you. There might be money to be had in empire building, but never at the top. You only end up on the wrong end of a coup, or an invasion, or a sniper's rifle. Your Emperor will learn that eventually, the hard way."

Ula was trapped. He *had* betrayed the Republic, after all, but he had betrayed the Empire along with it. And now he was utterly powerless. All he could do was sit back and watch—and wonder if he *would* intervene if the opportunity arose. Jet was, after all, doing the job that he had failed to do. Who was he to get in the way?

Maybe Jet, too, was defying his baser instincts and trying to do the right thing.

A voice crackled from the planet on a Republic frequency. Ula recognized it instantly.

"—higher now so the jamming might not be as effective. This is Lieutenant Moxla calling Director Vii. I've hitched a lift on the back of the skyhook and I'm placing transponders on the vulnerable points. Strike them as hard as you can. Please respond. Let me know I'm getting through. We're higher now so the jamming might not be as effective. This is Lieutenant Moxla calling Director—"

"It's a recording." Jet reduced the volume. "I see the

transponders. If she's done her job properly, we can hit the skyhook with everything the *Paramount* has and take it out of commission before it reaches the equator."

"What about Larin?"

"Maybe she's already ditched."

"We can't know, can we?"

"No. So what do you want to do?"

"Are you really giving me the choice?"

"Not really. Just seeing if you could come up with a decent argument."

Tiny points of light flared in the holoprojector as the *Paramount* sent every missile it had on the way.

CHAPTER 42

LARIN RAN LIGHTLY over the uppermost dome of the skyhook, keeping low to avoid the occasional potshot. The structure was made entirely out of linked hex bodies. Some of them retained a modicum of individuality and raised a limb to fire as she went by. She couldn't watch everywhere at once, but she had managed to avoid any serious injuries thus far.

That would change the moment her message was received, or the fleet opened fire regardless. There was no way off the skyhook now that it was in flight. If it went down, so would she and all her squadmates. Not all of them had jumped aboard with her, but those who had knew what they were getting into. There were perhaps two dozen troopers like her scattered across the moving skyhook, all operating independently.

Comms came and went; she had set her transceiver to broadcast at the earliest opportunity and let it spool on without her hearing. Each transponder she placed pointed to an air vent or sensor array, or anything else that might suffer from an accurately placed hit. She hadn't wasted time on trying to sneak inside the skyhook. There would have been little benefit in getting herself killed that way.

It was ironic, she thought. Telemetry told her that the skyhook was bringing her closer to where Shigar should have landed, but she probably wouldn't make it, and neither had he, most likely. His transport had gone down in flames. She might share the same fate as he had and never know it.

Blue light flashed to her right. A trooper had been pinned by three widely spaced hexes, all firing simultaneously. He returned fire, crouching low to present a smaller target, but he couldn't fire at all of them, and he had nowhere to retreat to. As she watched, taking the measure of his predicament, a shot clipped the neck seal of his helmet, triggering a jet of precious air. He went down, thrashing about to reach the leak, but his shoulder joints wouldn't flex that far.

She came in low and fast, shooting the nearest hex first, before getting a bead on the others. They shifted their sights to her, but she was practiced at fighting hexes now. She aimed for the sensor pods first because they were easiest to hit. Without eyes, how could they shoot back?

Two other hexes joined in before she reached the fallen trooper. She scooped him up with one hand under his left underarm and kept moving, firing as she went. Using gravity and her own momentum, she took him down the dome as if they were running down the side of a hill.

When they were out of range, she skidded them to a halt. The edge was in sight. Beyond that point, there was nothing but Sebaddon, far below.

He was still thrashing about. She reached for the repair kit in her thigh pocket and urged him to stay still. He obeyed. As she applied the fast-acting sealant to his damaged neck joint, they recognized each other.

The trooper looking up at her was Ses Jopp.

His voice traveled clearly through the material of their suits.

"You're the last person I expected to see."

She didn't want to say that the feeling was mutual. "I couldn't just leave you there."

"And I'm grateful, believe me. Thank you, Lieutenant."

She couldn't tell if he was sincere or not, but it was something.

"There," she said, smoothing down the last of the sealant. "You'll live to fight another day."

His eyes tracked to her right, over her shoulder.

"Probably not," he said. "Look."

She turned and stared up at the sky. Clearly visible were the white streaks of Imperial artillery coming their way. It looked as if the crew of the *Paramount* were giving it all they had—precisely as they ought to, she thought.

Rather than craning awkwardly up at the approaching missiles, she turned and sat down next to Jopp.

"Best seats in the house, eh?" she said.

He laughed. "Yeah. People would kill for 'em."

She thought of her former colleagues in the Blackstars, of the bravado and the bonding and the sense of belonging that she had missed so deeply.

"Grunts like us never learn. Fireworks are only pretty from a distance."

Jopp nodded soberly. "Makes a pleasant change to have an officer down here with us."

He turned to look at her.

"Guess you're not so bad after all, Toxic Moxla."

She smiled. That was as close to an apology as she was likely to get, but in the service it amounted to a vow of loyalty that would endure until they died. It was a shame, she thought, that that wasn't going to be very long.

CHAPTER 43

EXHAUST TRAILS DREW complex hieroglyphs across the sky. No less than fifteen missiles were converging on the object that had risen out of the lake. The blast radius was going to be so huge, there was no point running.

Shigar braced himself for the explosion. There was a small chance that he could shield himself from the worst of it, but what happened afterward was the great unknown. There might be no island left at all. He couldn't float about forever on a sea of lava.

On the brink of death, he caught a glimpse of how his life would have played out, had he lived. He knew, intellectually and viscerally, that he had earned the rank of Jedi Knight. Master Nobil couldn't deny him that now. He had fought and made deals with enemies. He had wrestled with the dark side. He had conquered his one remaining weakness. And, most important, he was willing to fight.

You are a product of your time, he heard his former Master saying. *You must confront the times ahead with great care. The Sith are the enemy, but we must not become like them in order to beat them. We must remain true to all that we stand for.*

He couldn't tell if her voice was in the present, or an echo of the future that would never be. Similarly, he couldn't tell if she was reproaching him or offering him encouragement.

I cannot stand by while politicians play their games, he said in reply. *It was an act of thievery that led us here—an act conducted on behalf of the Republic. Even in this corner of the universe, privateers and false treaties have endangered billions of lives. When the whole galaxy is at stake, who can stand idle?*

Not you, Shigar Konshi. Not you.

I don't understand. Are you telling me that I'm wrong, or that I'm right?

Perhaps both. The answer is beyond my sight.

He snapped back to reality.

A powerful roaring filled the air. The lines in the sky converged on a point. The hieroglyph was complete.

Darth Chratis vanished behind a shimmering Force shield.

Shigar stood unprotected, at one with the other troopers staring up at their deaths. He wasn't afraid to die.

There was a bright flash, then another, then so many they became one simultaneous assault.

Shigar shielded his eyes with his hand.

That he still *had* a hand and eyes surprised him.

He squinted through his fingers.

The massive structure had generated a broad electromirror shield, and was deflecting the full force of the blasts back out into space.

Relief flooded him, then dismay. He was still alive, but the plan had failed. What now?

Darth Chratis emerged from his shield as superhot clouds radiated above them. He looked as surprised as Shigar felt.

"Unacceptable," he said.

A second series of flashes came from the south, where something else was undergoing bombardment from above. They turned to see another work of mega-engineering from the hexes drifting across the sky, trailing explosive streamers in its wake. An identical electromirror shield protected it, too.

A skyhook, Shigar realized. The other half of the thing looming over him, undamaged by everything the Empire and the Republic could throw at it.

He almost laughed. "It was all for nothing," he said to Darth Chratis. "You, me, Larin—everything."

"Do you find this amusing, boy?"

He didn't, but the moment had a hysterical edge all the same. He could agonize all he wanted about the choices he had made and would make, about the Jedi Order's role in the Emperor's plans, and about the Republic's feet of clay when it came to taking decisive action—but if nothing stopped the hexes, there wouldn't be a war at all. The future of the galaxy ended here.

You win, Lema Xandret, he thought, *wherever you are.*

CHAPTER 44

CINZIA XANDRET STARED out of her tank at the girl she might have been.

"Don't look at her," whispered her mother.

"Why not?"

"She's not real."

"She looks real enough."

"But she's not you."

"She's me as I might have been."

"You are not her. You will never be her. She is a lie and she is evil. She is—"

"Shut up, Mother."

The whisper ceased. Cinzia's attention returned to the two people outside the tank, a mature woman with gray-streaked brown hair and her more youthful companion, both dressed in bloodstained armored suits, both strangers, at least to the complex. One she recognized. She had seen that face all her life. It was her own.

"Who are you?" The more senior woman of the two looked shocked and surprised. "Are you Cinzia?"

"I'm her clone," she said. There was nothing to be gained by hiding the truth, and there was no harm in just talking. "My mother took a tissue sample from me before I was taken away. She made me all over again. The same daughter, but better, purer."

"That explains why you look younger," the woman said. She glanced at her companion, who seemed incapable of speech. "My name is Satele Shan. What do you mean—purer?"

"The fluid I'm breathing suppresses my Force abilities. There's something in it—a metal, I think, or an extract from something that feeds on metal. It keeps me safe."

"Safe?" Now the other Cinzia spoke. "Dead, more like it."

The sneer on her own face—beautiful, she was pleased to see, with the addition of a couple more years—was simply horrid to behold.

"See?" her mother whispered. "She thinks you a monster. Call the droids, now. She must be stopped!"

"No," Cinzia said. "Let me talk to her first. I want to know what happened to her. I want to know why she's here."

"She's come to destroy everything. That's what they do. They take and they destroy. They will show you no kindness, just as they showed none to her."

"I told you to be quiet, Mother. Besides, I don't trust the droids anymore. You know why."

That did the trick. The eddying swirls of the fluid around her grew quieter.

"Have you lived here all your life?" the woman called Satele Shan asked.

"Yes. I can access all the complex's cams. Much of it's automated, you know. The droids are my eyes and ears."

"You control them?"

"If I want to," she said, although she was less sure of that now than she had been.

"So you're responsible for what's happening out there?" asked the other Cinzia.

"To be honest," she said, "I don't know what's going on out there. They do seem rather busy, though. They're designed to protect me, and the definition of *protect* is a bit vague. I guess at the moment that means not telling me stuff. Whatever they're up to, I'm sure they mean well."

"You should take a look, Cinzia," said Satele Shan. "The hexes are killing people."

"Are you sure?"

"Positive."

"They would only do that if they were attacked. Why did you attack them?"

"They are a threat to the entire galaxy."

"I don't believe you," she said. The thought was entirely too preposterous. "You're just trying to distract me. This is a momentous day. The two Cinzias finally meet! I've been waiting for this, well, ever since I was born. At last we are together! I want to hear everything about your life. I want to know if we like the same things, think the same thoughts—"

"I'm not you," said the older version of herself. "My name is Eldon Ax."

"Don't say that."

"I'll say whatever I like. You're a freak, a mistake. I should kill you now, just for existing."

The other Cinzia produced a glowing red sword and held it up between them.

"See?" hissed her mother. "She will do you great harm if you let her, perhaps even kill you!"

"Don't be cruel," said Cinzia to both her mother and her twin. "It doesn't have to be this way."

"She's right," said Satele Shan, putting a hand on the other Cinzia's arm. "Don't act rashly."

"Yes." The red blade came down. "We need what she knows—about the hexes, about Lema Xandret."

"How did your mother die?" asked Satele Shan.

"The droids killed her," Cinzia said, "and the others as well, but she's not really dead."

"Don't tell them," whispered the voice in her ear. "Don't tell them!"

"Why did the hexes kill her?"

"They didn't want to sign a treaty with anyone. When the ship left—"

"The ship named after you?"

"Yes—Mother built that before she made me, and she never came up with another name. The droids didn't want people coming here, ever. It wasn't safe for me." She almost shied away from the thought of what had happened next, but she forced herself not to. The disclosure was important, if she and herself were ever to become one. "The droids killed my mother to stop her sending any more ships. The others tried to stop them, so the droids killed them, too. It was all very stupid, really. Mother should have known how the droids would feel."

Satele Shan nodded slowly. "So she wasn't on the ship?"

"No, that was Kenev and Marg Sar."

"Why didn't she go with them, if she was their leader?"

"They had no leaders. They didn't want to live like they had before. They wanted a change."

"All right, but Kenev and Marg Sar never came back, did they? They killed themselves when the ship was intercepted by a privateer. They blew up the ship."

That was a shock. The fluid rippled all over her skin, and she hugged herself tightly. "They would've wanted to keep the cargo a secret," she said, thinking it through.

"The droid factory?"

"The plant. That's what we call them."

"Something interfered with the explosion," said Satele Shan. "The plant wasn't destroyed."

"It must've been one of the droids. They wouldn't want to die, even though they had to."

"That's what led us here, Cinzia. We came to find your mother, to ask her what she wanted to tell the outside world. That's all."

Cinzia waited for her mother to say something. For once, though, she was quiet.

"I don't think she wants to talk to you," Cinzia said.

"You said she was dead."

"She is, mostly. The droids took her body away, probably for recycling. But she's still here, talking to me."

"Don't tell them!"

"She doesn't want me to talk to you, either."

The two women outside the tank exchanged a concerned glance.

"I'm not mad," Cinzia said, feeling affronted.

"I don't see how you could be anything but."

"We just don't understand," said Satele Shan, shushing the other Cinzia.

"No, you don't. My mother protects me. That's why the hexes are the way they are. She put herself into them, too."

"We worked that out. Both her flesh and her philosophy. They are flexible and single-minded at the same time, combining the very best qualities of machines and organics in one creature. Your mother must have been quite brilliant to think of doing that."

"I still am," whispered Lema Xandret.

"She says she still is."

"Don't you see how the hexes could be a threat?" said Satele Shan, ignoring her comment. "They acknowledge no leader and they want to be left alone. They don't want to die and they want to protect you. How better to keep you safe than to destroy everyone else, including your mother?"

"It's logical," she admitted, remembering how they had disobeyed her, too. Cinzia had begged them to leave the original Lema Xandret alone, but there had been no turning them back, not once their creator had betrayed them. Cinzia's mother had programmed them too well.

"It's insane," muttered the other Cinzia.

"You have to understand them," she insisted. "If what

you say is true, then it does make sense. It'll be hard to talk them out of attacking your friends."

"Do you think you could?" asked Satele Shan.

"I could try. But you'd have to promise to leave and never come back."

"I don't think that would be possible."

"Why not?"

"Your world is too valuable. Too many people know it exists now."

"So? They don't have to come here. You have the whole galaxy. I just want one world. Is that too much to ask?"

"For some it is."

"Well, then. We're at an impasse."

"Yes. I'm afraid so."

Cinzia didn't like the way her other self was looking at her. There was such fury and hurt in those familiar features. She could never imagine looking that way, having that amazing *hair*.

"Why do the hexes protect you," the other Cinzia asked, "and not me?"

"Because they don't know you. You don't look exactly like me, or live like me, in here. You look like one of the people who took you away."

"I *am* one of the people who took me away."

"But you're me, too, even though you try to deny it. You don't have to be the way you are now."

"How else can I be? I don't remember anything else."

"Really?"

"Yes, really. And what's the point of trying? The droids will kill me anyway."

"Maybe if we gave them a taste of your genetic code. Maybe then they wouldn't kill you."

"So it'd just be me and you in a galaxy full of hexes. Is that what you want?"

She shook her head. "I just want everyone to go away. Everyone *else,* I mean. Not you. We've got so much to catch up on."

"I've got nothing to tell you."

"But you have! Where you live, what you do. I don't know anything about anywhere. All I know is Sebaddon, where I was cloned. You can tell me about where I was born."

"I don't remember any of that," said the other Cinzia. "All I know is the Empire."

"The what?"

Satele Shan stared at her in frank surprise. "You've never heard of the Empire?"

"No. Should I have?"

"What about the Sith? The Republic? The Mandalorians?"

Cinzia shook her head in irritation. "Stop showing off. You're making me feel stupid."

"I'm not showing off. I'm just amazed that you've been so isolated here. It doesn't seem fair to me that your mother did that to you."

"She's trying to turn you against me," whispered the voice. "Be careful of that one."

"Mother says I should be careful of you. Why is that?"

"Maybe she's afraid I'll take you from her. I promise I won't try to do that, Cinzia." Satele Shan's face was as expressionless as someone trying very hard not to have an expression. "Is your mother with you now? In the tank?"

"Yes."

"Is she another clone?"

"Not exactly."

The fluid swirled around her, agitated and wild. Cinzia was pulled away from the glass, into the center of the tank.

"I said, don't talk to them! Why don't you ever listen to me?"

"I always listen to you, Mother."

"But you never do as I say. I told you not to tell them about me!"

"They'd guess anyway. Why make it harder for them?"

"They won't understand, Cinzia. You have to tell the droids to take them away. They'll obey you this time. You know they will. When there's a clearly defined threat, they have to act against it."

"Just like they acted against you."

"Yes! Even me! The logic was impeccable. I was stupid to try to fight it."

Cinzia remembered the days leading up to that terrible moment all too well. There was no suppressing them entirely.

"I think you saw it coming, Mother. You were afraid of the droids. You gave me the overrides in the hope that they would listen to me, but I didn't use them." She remembered her passivity with painful keenness. Sometimes she felt bad for not intervening. "The droids are my protectors. You are my protector. I still have both. Was it wrong to do nothing?"

"I'm still here, Cinzia. That's right. We'll all protect you, together."

"But what if you were right, Mother? What if the droids have grown too powerful? That means you *agree* with Satele Shan and shouldn't argue against her. I should listen to her, too. Maybe I should use the overrides to stop the droids now, before it's too late."

"No, Cinzia, you mustn't!"

The fluid coiled around her tighter than ever. Even though she struggled, she couldn't get a grip on the glass.

"Mother, let me go!"

"No!"

"I can't stand by and let innocent people be hurt. You wouldn't have wanted that."

"I must keep you safe!"

"But I have to—you have to—"

Thick currents closed around her throat and filled her mouth, silencing the words. She choked and coughed, unable to fill her lungs.

"Cinzia!"

The cry came from outside the tank.

Help me, she tried to shout. *Save me!*

With a shattering of glass and a great rush, the tank exploded. Cinzia was tossed and flung on a wave of writhing liquid. Her mother was screaming. She was screaming, too. Something hard smacked against her flesh all down her back and legs. For the first time in her life, she felt her full weight. She couldn't move. She couldn't breathe. The pressure around her throat eased, only to be replaced with another.

"She can't get enough oxygen," someone said. The sound was all wrong. So was the light. "She's not used to breathing air."

"What do we do?" That was the other Cinzia. "We have to keep her alive."

Cinzia flapped weakly with one hand.

"Gene . . . sampler . . ." She pointed to the machine that would feed the other Cinzia's genetic pattern into the hexes' collective memory. "Promise . . . save . . ."

"We're doing everything we can for you," said Satele.

She shook her head. "Save . . . Mother . . ."

"She's in the blood, right?" said the other Cinzia. "I thought she was killing you. I thought you were drowning."

"Promise!"

"All right, all right. I promise."

Cinzia couldn't lift, but she could still grip. "Her daughter . . . her daughter . . ."

The other Cinzia came closer, dragged into focus by the last of her strength.

"Tell me . . . everything."

* * *

THE BODY OF the hairless, emaciated girl became still. Master Satele shook her head. Apart from the trickling and dripping of crimson fluid, the laboratory was silent.

Ax fell back onto her haunches and put her hands over her face. What had just happened? Had she been trying to kill the girl or save her? Not just any girl, of course: her own clone. Did that make it murder, suicide, or fratricide?

She suspected she would never know.

"I'm sorry," said Master Satele, touching her lightly on the shoulder. "The shock killed her. With the right equipment, we might have—"

Ax shrugged her off and stood too quickly. Her head swam. She imagined she heard a voice from the far depths of her memory, weeping and demanding her attention. She ignored it.

The gene sampler was exactly where Cinzia had indicated it would be. Ax crossed to it and stuck her hand into its diagnostic chute. The cold machine pricked her, drank her blood, hummed to itself, and then beeped inquiringly.

Ax felt a brief moment of panic. The machine wanted confirmation of something. A password? A command phrase? A code?

She remembered everything Cinzia had said in her final moments. She'd made Ax promise to save what was left of Lema Xandret. Was there anything else she'd emphasized? Anything at all?

" 'Her daughter,' " Ax said.

The machine beeped confirmation.

"What does that mean?" she asked the room in general. "Do the hexes now think I'm *her*? Am I immune to them? Will they obey my orders now?"

Master Satele had no answers, and neither did anyone else. The way the fluid from the tank tugged at her ankles told her nothing she wanted to know. It had nurtured and smothered Cinzia at the same time—just like Darth Chratis had Ax herself. Cinzia had broken free the only way open to her. Ax hoped to have more options.

There was just one way to find out how the hexes would react to her.

"Let's go get one and see what happens."

CHAPTER 45

LARIN WAS BEYOND surprise. After escaping the rain of artillery from the *Paramount* and riding the skyhook all the way to the equator, it was with only a mild sense of concern that she felt the structure beneath her begin to drop. What now?

Jopp echoed her confusion. "I thought this thing was taking off, and now it's coming in to land. I wish the hexes would make up their minds."

The skyhook lurched beneath them, and they gripped each other for support.

"This doesn't feel like landing," she said. "Something else—"

She didn't finish that thought. Every hex in the structure chose that moment to let go of its neighbor, causing the whole structure to slump and sag downward. She was suddenly riding an accelerating wave of individual hexes, not one solid structure. It was like surfing, but without a board, and a sea of molten lava instead of a beach at the other end.

"Hang on!" she cried as the wave of hexes carried them downward.

Jopp clung to her arm as long as he could, but the tide inevitably swept them apart. Larin crouched down and gripped the leading edge of a single hex with all the strength of her prosthetic left hand, hoping to ride out the wave without tumbling or being crushed. The hex didn't object. It seemed utterly passive. That surprised her, but she didn't complain. It was just another surprise on the heels of so many.

The torrent of hexes was sufficient to fill the crater that was all that remained of the former CI site. She flinched as a mass of red fluid rose up to meet her, but it wasn't lava at all. The bloody fluid came up to her knees, then stopped rising. She let go of the hex and found that she could stand.

Feeling like she was walking in a dream, she stepped from hex to hex toward the nearest crater wall. There was no sign of Jopp, but she did make out a figure watching her progress on the edge of the lake, waving encouragement. As she drew nearer, she recognized the forbidding black shape of Darth Chratis. It wasn't him waving. That was the tall, slender figure standing next to him.

Her heart tripped. It was Shigar.

She increased her pace. Dream or no dream, she was going to take advantage of this development while it lasted.

SHIGAR WATCHED THE green-helmeted figure crossing the seething mass of hexes in the lake. He couldn't be sure it was her, and he told himself not to get his hopes up. But his gut was certain. There was something about the way she moved, the slight stiffness of the figure's left hand as it waved cheerily back.

Darth Chratis stalked away, still trying to raise the *Paramount* on his comlink. Thus far there had been no answer from the fleet above, even though the comms were finally beginning to clear.

Shigar walked carefully down the bank as the wading figure approached. He held out his hand, and finally caught a glimpse of the face inside the helmet. It was indeed Larin, and she was beaming. With one powerful tug, he pulled her ashore.

She flipped up her visor, and he did the same.

"Fancy meeting you here," she said.

"Arc you crying?"

"What? No. I have allergies. And what if I am? It's been a long day."

He embraced her. "It sure has."

She returned the hug, but not for too long.

"What's with the hexes?" she asked as they pulled apart.

"I don't know," he said. "The thing in the lake disintegrated as the skyhook arrived. I didn't even know it was made of hexes until then. They looked confused. Now they're not doing anything at all."

He spoke too soon. The center of the lake boiled and bubbled. Hexes writhed as the leading edge of something large and gray emerged from the depths. Shigar put his left arm around Larin, ready to protect her behind a shield if this turned out to be a new kind of attack, but she pulled away.

"It's a ship," she said, hurrying back down to the lake's edge. "Look!"

He shaded his eyes. The object did look like a starship. An older model, of Imperial make, perhaps.

The ship rolled, presenting one broad flank to the sky. A hatch opened and two figures climbed out. A strange sound swept across the surface of the lake—a clicking of metal limbs moving through thick fluid. The hexes were stirring, forming a new agglomeration.

All they made was a bridge connecting the ship to the shore. The bridge was aimed directly for Darth Chratis. He looked up as two figures began to walk toward him.

Shigar and Larin loped to join him. A handful of other figures scattered along the crater rim did the same. Shigar picked up speed when he recognized Master Satele as one of the pair that had emerged from the ship. He felt a resurgence of optimism. First Larin, and now her. Perhaps disaster had been averted after all!

Accompanying Master Satele was the Sith apprentice, Eldon Ax. Her helmet was off, exposing wild red hair and dark-rimmed eyes. Shigar was close enough to hear what she said as she approached her Master.

"I release myself from your service, Darth Chratis."

"Nonsense," he said with a look of startled outrage. "You are my apprentice, and so you will remain until I judge you fit to be called a Sith."

"You will release me," she said, coming to a halt two paces from him, "or suffer the consequences."

He laughed. "What possible consequences can you threaten me with? Don't tell me this pathetic Jedi has turned you." He raised his lightsaber and adopted a ready pose. "I will kill both of you before you take a single step toward me."

Master Satele drew her blade in response and Shigar wished he hadn't lost his.

But Eldon Ax didn't move. "I have not been turned," she said. "I have simply realized how I have been used. My anger was constantly directed outward, at my mother and Dao Stryver, or inward at myself. The person I should have been most angry at was standing right beside me. My teacher. My Master. You."

Darth Chratis grinned like a skull. "Anger leads to hate," he said. "Hate leads to power. See how well I have taught you?"

"You have indeed taught me well. And so I release *myself* from your service, my lord, knowing that you never would."

A growing sound from behind her caught Darth Chratis's attention. The hexes were rising up in an enormous swell and flowing out of the lake. Dripping blood-like fluid, they came en masse for the huddle standing on the crater's edge. Larin took Shigar's arm and pulled him well out of the way. Master Satele joined them. Only Ax and her Master stood before the ghastly tide.

Lightning flashed. Darth Chratis's lightsaber stabbed and cut. But there were too many of them for one man—even a Sith Lord—to hold them back. Ax did nothing as the swell enveloped them both.

"What's going on?" asked Larin.

Over the noise of the hexes, Master Satele replied, "I think our young friend has discovered who she really wants to be."

"And who is that?" Shigar asked.

With a high-pitched whine, a shuttle swooped low overhead. Master Satele looked up as the craft came around to land. It displayed Republic insignia, and was closely tailed by an Imperial counterpart. They touched down on either side of the tentacle of hexes that had lunged out of the lake.

A junior officer of the Republic jogged from the craft that had landed near them and saluted Larin. Keeping one eye closely on the swarm of hexes that had engulfed Ax and Darth Chratis, the Adarian spoke breathlessly: "We picked up the fringes of an Imperial transmission calling for an emergency evac and followed it down. Is everyone all right?"

"For the moment," said Master Satele, guiding him away. "What's the situation in orbit?"

"It's hard to explain. Our comms went haywire for a while, and now all our data banks have been wiped."

"By who?"

"I don't know, sir. Captain Pipalidi will fill in you and Director Vii when I get you back to orbit."

"Ula made it, too?" asked Larin.

"We have him aboard right now," he said. "Found him drifting in a capsule, hollering for help, and picked him up on the way down. Won't explain how he got there, but he seems healthy enough."

"That's good," Larin said. "I'm glad he's okay."

Shigar glanced at the shuttle. Was that the envoy's face he could see, peering out a viewport? He couldn't tell.

"About the hexes," the young officer ventured, glancing back over his shoulder. "I mean, is it over?"

"I don't think so," said Master Satele. "Not quite."

ULA WATCHED FROM the safety of the shuttle. There was nothing stopping him from leaving his seat. He wasn't under guard, or even under suspicion. He could have walked out at any time, and thrown himself to the hexes if he'd wanted to.

Jet's betrayal of him still stung, though, so he stayed right where he was.

It had started to go wrong before the skyhook had collapsed. After the deflection of the *Paramount*'s missiles, Jet had considered throwing the *Paramount* itself down onto the target, in a desperate attempt to thwart the hexes' plans. Ula had argued against it, unable to bear such a waste of human life.

"A thousand or so to save trillions," Jet had said. "Isn't that a fair exchange?"

"We don't even know if it would work! And if it doesn't, we'll be even worse off than we are now."

"If you're worried about destroying an Imperial ship—"

"Do you really think I'd let that get in the way of doing the right thing?"

Only as he said the words did he realize that he meant it.

The issue had become entirely moot when the skyhook had gone down.

"Looks like someone's found a way to do what we can't," said Jet. "In which case, we're no longer needed.

Out of the seat, Director Vii. It's time for us to go our separate ways."

The announcement had taken Ula completely by surprise. "What are you talking about? I'm staying with you."

"No, you're not." Jet had produced a blaster and covered him while Clunker dragged him from the cockpit. The droid's strength was too great to resist. "We've got business elsewhere."

"Wait!" Ula had clung to the lip of the air lock. "Take me with you, please!"

Jet had shaken his head, but not without compassion. "You have to find your own place, mate, and I don't think it's going to be with me. Say hello to that lovely lady—and stop faking it, if you ever hope to have a chance with her."

The air lock had hissed shut, explosive bolts had fired, and Ula had been flung out into the void. Had the passing shuttle not found him, he might have fallen to the planet below—or even into the black hole—but Ula didn't suppose that Jet would have left something like that to chance.

Now he was within waving distance of Larin, and he didn't know what to do.

The mass of hexes that had overwhelmed Darth Chratis retreated into the lake, leaving just the young Sith behind. She turned to face the lake, raised her arms above her head, and spoke to them. The hexes responded, forming new agglomerations, turning their collective mind to new tasks. Some descended back into the lake; others swarmed toward several different places on the crater wall and combined their pulses into powerful cutting lasers. Vibrations reached him even through the walls and floor of the shuttle. He saw Larin and the others shift on their feet, as though the ground was kicking beneath them, too.

Master Satele approached the young Sith. They exchanged a few words, then parted. The Grand Master returned to Larin and Shigar and the officer who had run out to meet them. Together, they hurried into the shuttle.

"Recall the rest," she was saying as she mounted the ramp and entered the main passenger hold. "If they can't make it here in time, send another shuttle."

"What's happening?" Ula asked. "What's going on out there?"

Master Satele had already left for the cockpit.

"I don't know," said Larin, smiling at him. The engines whined. "But it looks like we're leaving."

Shigar acknowledged him with a nod, which Ula gravely returned. The Padawan looked no less battered than Larin and Master Satele. The ground war had obviously been just as grueling as that fought in the air.

The shuttle's repulsorlifts pressed Ula back into the seat. He took one last glimpse through the window and saw the crater walls collapsing around the bloody lake. Fiery lava from the molten sea outside crashed in, burning and destroying as it came. Clouds of smoke thickened and curled, hiding the young Sith from view.

"YOU'RE GOING TO destroy them," said Master Satele.

Ax didn't respond. It wasn't a question, but it demanded an answer, and she was careful to keep it to herself. The hexes were streaming downward to tear the flooded habitat to pieces. When they were done, they would break into the geothermal shafts and keep drilling until raw magma flooded in from below. What the real lava sea didn't burn, the heat of the core would melt and turn to slag.

"What about Lema Xandret?" Master Satele pressed. "There's not much of that amniotic fluid left, but it could be saved."

"Do you think it should be?" Ax asked, thinking of her

clone's life in the tank, cut off from the Force, so insulated from the universe around her that she didn't even know what the Empire was. Cinzia could have stopped the hexes at any time, but she hadn't. Lema Xandret's daughter reborn, and herself, mutated into a horrible echo of motherhood, were more responsible for the damage than the hexes themselves.

It was all about control, she realized now. Xandret had tried to control the cloned Cinzia, and had lost control of the hexes. Darth Chratis had tried to control Ax, but she had turned on him. Anger wasn't enough on its own.

She could still hear her mother screaming.

"It's not up to me to decide whether you should save her or not," Master Satele said, "but you did promise Cinzia."

Ax had promised many things, to herself, to Darth Chratis, to the Dark Council, and ultimately to the Emperor.

But that had been before. Before she had understood that she had choices.

You can expect no mercy from me, Master, the day our positions are reversed.

"I lied," she said.

The Grand Master nodded. Ax didn't know whether she understood or not. That she stopped talking was enough.

Ax stood and watched the hexes at work while the others fled. The smell of burning blood was sweet in her nostrils. The ash that gently rained on her felt soft and warm, like feathers. Slowly, the voice faded from her mind. She breathed deeply, feeling at peace. Only the constant bleating of the shuttle's pilot disturbed her tranquillity.

She stayed as long as she could. When the ground threatened to dissolve under her and the sky lit up with shooting stars—orbital hexes, falling to their doom—she turned to leave the home her mother had made, forever.

PART SIX

PREPARATIONS FOR WAR

CHAPTER 46

LARIN HAD NEVER met Supreme Commander Stantorrs before, and she barely felt that she had met him now, even after half an hour of debriefing in his office. There were so many aides hurrying about bearing messages and sudden crises needing an instant decision that she rarely had his attention for more than a few seconds at a stretch. Even when she did, she found him very hard to read. Instead of watching his dour Duros face, she concentrated on his long fingers. They tapped, curled, folded, and rested in ways that, she hoped, gave her an insight into what he was thinking.

"You say you were followed there?"

"Yes, sir," she said. "The Hutts placed a homing beacon in the *Auriga Fire*."

"You knew about that before you left Hutta. I seem to recall reading about that somewhere."

"That's correct, sir." This had all been in her report, and was no doubt in numerous other reports about the incident, but she let no sign of impatience slip through her guard. If he wanted to hear it from her face-to-face, so be it. He was the Supreme Commander, after all. "We thought the beacon left with Jet Nebula, but it later turned up in the capsule he used to expel Envoy Vii."

"This 'Jet Nebula.' Is he a real person?"

"Yes, sir. His parents had a strange sense of humor, he says."

"What, yes?" An aide had pressed a datapad in front of him. His left index finger stabbed at something on the screen. "That one, of course. Was Tassaa Bareesh herself present in her expedition to Sebaddon?"

"No, sir. She placed someone else in charge, a deputy called Sagrillo."

"He's the one who claimed ownership of the planet and declared the remaining joint forces trespassers."

"Yes, sir. At the time, he outgunned us. His mistress was taking no chances."

The tips of the Supreme Commander's fingers joined to form a triangle in front of him. "I can imagine his surprise when your reinforcements turned up."

Not just our reinforcements, she wanted to say, *but the Imperials' as well.* It had only been a matter of time before everyone else arrived. The universe's usual freakish sense of humor had ensured that they all came more or less simultaneously.

She remembered those stressful hours very well, even though she hadn't been on the bridge with the senior officers and the negotiators. She had been down in the crew hold, exchanging stories with Hetchkee and Jopp and the others who had survived the ground assault. They had stopped to watch through the viewports as ships flashed in and out of hyperspace around the black hole. There had been several clashes, leaving wreckage to spin helplessly into the impossibly steep gravity well, and several outlier ships had fallen afoul of the jets themselves. They had waited with minds and bodies poisoned by exhaustion for the call to arms, as it surely had to come. The Republic ships left over from the original mission were going to be pulled in eventually, and every available trooper would be desperately needed.

Then suddenly it had been all behind her. The *Commenor* had jumped to hyperspace, leaving fresh ships and their commanders to sort out the mess. And that was the last she had seen of Sebaddon and its hexes. Every scrap of data from the campaign had been erased—by some kind of exotic electromagnetic pulse, she had been told. All that remained were confused recollections and reports like the one she had filed on returning.

Very few of them mentioned Dao Stryver. During the confusion the Mandalorian had disappeared as though into the depths of the black hole itself, never to be seen since.

"Do you believe Captain Pipalidi acted responsibly in the ensuing confrontation?" Stantorrs asked her.

Larin chose her words with care. The matter of her reenlistment and promotion was still very much undecided, and she didn't want to jeopardize any chances that might remain.

"I think she did her best in a difficult situation, sir. No one could fault her for that."

"The service asks of us not our best, but *the* best possible. Is that what Captain Pipalidi offered?"

It was the same question in different words, and Stantorrs didn't strike Larin as a being who repeated himself very often.

"I believe so, sir. Every installation on the planet was in flames. All our troops had been evacuated. The mission had already cost the Republic more resources than it could afford, and sticking around would have squandered even more. Withdrawal was therefore the most sensible action to take."

The Supreme Commander's hands came to rest facedown on the desk in front of him.

"That's good to hear, Moxla, because I'm thinking of promoting Pipalidi to colonel over some pretty stiff opposition—the kind of people who think we owe everything to the Jedi, if you can imagine—and it's good to be backed up by the opinion of someone I can trust. I'm not wrong in thinking that I can trust you, am I, Moxla?"

He undoubtedly knew her history with the Blackstars, so there was no point prevaricating now. "Sir, you can always trust me to speak out if I think a superior officer isn't pulling her weight."

"That's what I thought. And that's exactly what I need. There's—what? Can't he wait?"

Another aide, this time whispering in the Supreme Commander's ear.

"All right." His hands rested impotently in his lap. "Well, I'll make this brief, Moxla. The SSOs you fought with on Sebaddon—a messy bunch, but showed a lot of guts. We're going to form a new Special Forces squad around them, and we want you to be part of it. We can't erase your record, but we can add a commendation or two, post factum, to spruce it up a little, and change some of the wording. You'll retain the rank you were given, brevetted of course, and have the first pick of the troops. What do you say to that?"

Surprise got the better of her tongue. "Uh, yes, sir."

"You don't sound particularly enthused, Lieutenant Moxla."

It didn't take her long to snap out of herself. Anything was better than sitting around in Coruscant's underbelly, waiting for the ax to fall. Either outright war with the Empire was going to break out any day, or the Republic's ability to maintain the peace on its own worlds would fail. This way, she would be right in the thick of it, where she could maybe do some good. She would be working—and if she was lucky, she might be able to bring some people she trusted absolutely along with her. Ses Jopp, for one. She snapped to attention and saluted with appropriate enthusiasm.

"You couldn't have picked anyone better," she said. "Give me a month, and your squad will be as polished as your desk."

"Don't get me started on that, Moxla," he said with a

sudden rap of his knuckles on the greel wood surface. "Nothing's as clean as it looks." Another aide approached, and the Supreme Commander waved her away. "Get to it, Moxla. You have my absolute confidence."

Larin saluted again and marched for the door. Aides parted before her, watching with eyes that gave away nothing.

"How did it go?" asked Ula, meeting her in the antechamber outside and matching her pace for pace along the corridor.

"Very well, considering," she said. "Did you have anything to do with that?"

"Unlikely," he said. "I've been shifted to a portfolio in data collection."

So he wasn't being modest this time. "I'm sorry, Ula."

"No, it's okay. I found my last job a little too . . . stimulating."

He smiled, and she found herself smiling along. Ula—still acting as envoy then—had looked out for her on returning to Coruscant, greasing the path to the Supreme Commander's attention by making sure officers senior to her didn't dismiss her out of hand, or take credit for her actions. Captain Pipalidi might have played a role in that, as well. That the captain was being promoted suggested she had Stantorrs's ear on many things to do with Sebaddon, and Larin had certainly helped the whole affair from becoming a complete rout.

"What are you doing now?" Ula asked her.

She didn't answer immediately, remembering how Ula had cleaned up her wounded hand on the *Auriga Fire*, and how pleased he'd been to see her when the shuttle had collected them from the burning world. She flexed her new fingers—a proper prosthetic at last, surgically grafted to her, indistinguishable from a real hand—and wondered who would look after him in his new role.

"I have to meet someone right now," she said, "and

then it looks like I'll be on the move for a while. But I'd like to catch up with you when I get back."

His smile grew wider. "I can wait."

"That's assuming you'll still be around, of course."

"The chances of me going anywhere are very slim, now."

"Great. We can drink Reactor Cores and talk about old times."

"I'm sure we'll have lots more to talk about by then."

"What, the birth and death statistics of Sector Four?"

"Just for starters."

At the exit to the building, they stopped and looked at each other. Was it her imagination, or did he look younger, lighter, than he had before? It was probably the smile, she decided. She wanted him to stay that way when she was around.

She reached out and took his left hand in hers. Her artificial fingers squeezed lightly. When she walked away, she knew he was watching her, all the way down the steps to the plaza below.

SHIGAR WAS WAITING for her at the Cenotaph of the Innocents, pacing back and forth in front of the first bank of asaari trees. The troubled cast to his brow perfectly matched the heavy gray skies above. He was back in Jedi browns, with a new lightsaber swinging at his hip, but he seemed a completely different person from the one she had met in the old districts not so very long ago. He moved stiffly, still favoring a wound in his side. His hair, cut shorter by Darth Chratis on Sebaddon, hung limply around his face. Watching him, Larin almost regretted coming.

He glanced up as she approached. The blue clan markings on his cheeks looked faded and worn.

"You're still in uniform. That's a good sign."

"Did you think they'd strip me naked and throw me onto the street?" She came to a halt in front of him.

"And now you're smiling. Things must have gone well."

"They did."

"I'm pleased, Larin."

"Well, likewise. Hello, by the way."

"Hello. Let's go over here."

He led her to a stand of trees planted as a memorial to the people who had died during the Empire's sacking of the Jedi Temple. One sapling for each victim had grown into a small forest, with grottoes and benches for people to pass a moment in contemplation. They sat side by side, close but not touching, and it seemed for a long while that Shigar wasn't going to say anything at all. The restless branches rustled above them, moving back and forth in ways that had nothing at all to do with the wind.

"I want to ask you something," he finally said.

"And I want to tell you something, so we're even. Do you want to go first?"

"Not particularly, but I will if you want me to."

"Fire away."

"Did I do the right thing, bringing you along with me?"

That surprised her. She had been afraid that he was about to reveal that he had changed his mind and wanted to revisit the possibility of romance between them. If he had said that, she would have been forced to find words to explain the way she had felt on that front, and she doubted any such words existed. She knew exactly where those feelings had come from, but she hadn't quite worked out what they were now. And then there was Ula, whom she definitely intended to look up when she got back.

"I guess," she said, "it depends on what you mean by 'right.' "

He grimaced. "That doesn't really help."

"Well, let me tell you what I was going to say, and maybe that will help. It's this: thank you."

"For what?"

"Just thanks."

"Why?"

She rolled her eyes. "You're going to make me explain it, aren't you?"

"If it's not too much trouble." He managed a twitch of his lips that might have been a smile.

"It's pretty simple, really. You came across me when things were the darkest they had ever been. I had no security, no family, no purpose—no life, really. You offered me all of those things. Relatively speaking, of course. I'd never come up against anything like the hexes before, and I'd always prided myself on keeping most of my limbs intact. But the essentials were there. We had the mission; we had roles to play. And I had you."

She raised a hand to stop him talking over her. "I know I didn't *have* you, in any possessive sense, but you represented more to me than just some guy I'd bumped into. You're Kiffar like me, and there aren't many of us out there now, so that made you family. And you had my back when things got tough, so that made you—made you like my squad, I guess. You were everything I'd been missing, without ever being able to say so."

"I'm flattered," he said.

"Don't be," she said. "It wasn't really anything to do with you. Any other handsome, well-armed Kiffar would have fit the bill." She smiled to take the sting off her words, and he smiled in return.

"I'm glad," he said. "That makes me feel like I did do the right thing."

"Well, think that now, but the day I'm in the Empire's sights and out of ammo, know that you'll be the first I blame. At least I'll have a proper squad with me then, so that's one box ticked."

She was surprised by a sudden upwelling of emotion. She really was grateful, but she didn't know how to convey it, except with a joke.

"Were you seriously thinking I wished I'd never come? Don't you remember how I used to smell?"

"It still gives me nightmares."

"Besides, I reckon you have a lot more to worry about now."

He sobered. "What do you mean?"

"Well, the fact you're wondering about what you did tells me you've entered a whole new world of uncertainty. Doing the right thing isn't so easy in the real world, is it?"

He studied the grass at their feet. "No."

"So you learn that lesson, which means you'll probably become a proper Jedi Knight now, but in the process you come to the shocking realization that nothing will ever be black and white again. It's all gray."

"Not all of it," he said. "There's still some black."

"But white is hard to find, right?" She put her prosthetic hand on his shoulder. "You're a warrior now. Eventually you only see in two colors: black and red. Best get used to that, if you're going to stay on the front line."

"Do I have a choice?"

"Sure you do. With the life you've had, you've always had a choice."

"Do you still think I've had it easy?"

"No, my friend. No." The flash of anger in his deep green eyes had come too quickly. She worried about that. But she knew she'd said enough. It wasn't her job to bang his head into shape. "Everyone knows Clan Konshi got a raw deal when it came to looks."

That put the anger back in its place, where it could simmer until it found another outlet. She pitied the next person who met him on the wrong end of his lightsaber.

"I should go," he said. "The Council must surely be finished deliberating by now."

"That's life in wartime," she said. "A whole lot of waiting around between bouts of being shot at."

"Don't forget to duck, Larin."

They stood and faced each other.

"Don't you forget to keep looking for the white," she said, putting her arms around him and giving him a quick squeeze. "It's out there somewhere. You just have to find it."

He nodded.

They left the Cenotaph of the Innocents by separate paths. She didn't look back.

CHAPTER 47

"HELLO, MOTHER. SORRY I've been out of touch for so long. Work has kept me very busy, but I'll tell you all about that another time. Call me on Coruscant when you have the chance."

Ula closed the line and settled back to wait. He didn't think it would be long. After the loss of Darth Chratis, the failure of the *Cinzia* to amount to anything, and the erasure of the fleet's data banks, he was sure someone would want to hear his side of the story.

What that would be he had given a great deal of thought.

His comlink bleeped, warning him the call was imminent. That was impressively fast—so fast, in fact, that it made him wonder. Ordinarily someone on Panatha would note the message, then relay the coded request up through the lines of command to Watcher Three, who would then issue orders that would filter back down the lines of command, resulting in that simple ping. Ordinarily, this process could take hours. Occasionally tens of minutes. Never seconds.

Ula looked around his apartment. It seemed smaller than he remembered, and now had a hostile cast to it as well. He would conduct a sweep later that evening in the hope of finding the bug he was now sure was there. Whether he would destroy the bug or not remained an open question.

The holoprojector flickered. He stood in front of it and blanked his face. One of the first things he had learned about espionage was that an apparent lack of emotion enhanced both the credibility of one's reports and the illusion of authority. That, he suspected, was why he had never seen Watcher Three's face in more than shadowy outline.

That outline appeared before him now, flickering and straining, as though coming from the other side of the universe. For all Ula knew, though, Watcher Three was on Coruscant as well, perhaps just up the road. Anything was possible. He knew of at least two other intelligence operatives who lived on his block, seeking a similar balance between easy access to the Senate and a ready escape route.

"Report," said Watcher Three.

Ula needed to go back as far as his arrival on Hutta in order to tell the story properly. He didn't lie once, but he told far less than the whole truth. As with all intelligence work, much was told by implication. He left Watcher Three to deduce that his rapid advancement from envoy to commander of the joint fleet had less to do with his own abilities than the need for a puppet in both positions. He also let Watcher Three decide that Darth Chratis was the person behind the second placement. Who better, after all, to place the blame on than someone who couldn't defend himself?

"The last report Stantorrs received that I saw before being transferred," Ula concluded, "suggested that Sebaddon's orbit had been disturbed, leading to its imminent destruction by the black hole. Some small amounts of rare metals have been scavenged by the Republic, but Imperial attacks have kept that to a minimum. No wreckage has been recovered from any of the sites established by Lema Xandret and her fellow fugitives."

Watcher Three didn't divulge whether or not that

accorded with reports made by Colonel Kalisch. He also didn't mention the mysterious takeover of Kalisch's ships or the matter of the data banks' erasure. A computer virus propagated by the infected ships was sufficient to explain away the latter, and the colonel's natural disinclination to admit that his ships had ever been out of his control fixed the former. Better to have a slightly botched mission on one's record than a complete failure of command.

That didn't surprise Ula at all. Jet Nebula had anticipated exactly this outcome. He had made the fleet do what it needed to do, knowing full well that his role in events would never be recorded. The only weak link in his wild plan had been Ula himself. Anyone less confident, less sure of himself, would have killed Ula out of hand, for fear of his secret getting out. But Jet had let him live. And now Ula would repay that favor the only way he could, by making sure that both sides believed the fake version of how things had played out over Sebaddon.

It wasn't a complete whitewash, of course. Troopers would be telling wild stories about Sebaddon for years, as troopers always did, when wild stories were demanded. No one would believe them, though. And there the matter would finally rest.

"What of the Mandalorian?" Watcher Three asked.

"Gone. He left long before reinforcements arrived. Once the hexes were on the run, he presumably had no interest in the outcome of the battle."

"Why invest so much in tracking the *Cinzia* to its source and then play no role in what happens? That doesn't make sense."

"He was just one Mandalorian who happened to be personally involved, remember. A raider operating on little more than his own initiative. Xandret might have hoped for some kind of alliance with the Mandalore, but it's clear he was no more than idly interested. Had he believed the hexes truly remarkable, he would've sent more than Stryver to deal with them."

"And they *weren't* remarkable?"

"I leave that for more qualified people than me to decide," Ula said, safe in the knowledge that Watcher Three would have a markedly vague intelligence on that score. Again, Colonel Kalisch wouldn't want to be remembered for being routed by a gaggle of droids. Better instead to paint his early losses as the result of a Republic ambush, and minimize all involvement by the hexes, as Captain Pipalidi had. None of the surviving records would contradict either story, thanks to Jet.

Sometimes the smuggler's brilliance overwhelmed Ula, along with his utter gall. Where was he now? Ula would've given his left hand to know.

"The minister is displeased by your demotion," Watcher Three said. "You are to make every effort to regain your former post."

Now, *that* was interesting. Not only was it a completely unreasonable demand, that Ula should have betrayed the Republic while at the same time keeping his position under the Supreme Commander, but the urgency with which they expected him to get back into Stantorrs's good books suggested that there were no other operatives in that department. Ula would bear that in mind in his future dealings with both sides.

"Yes, sir. I will keep you informed on my progress."

"Dismissed."

The holoprojector emptied.

Ula didn't move.

Before he had counted to ten, a new face appeared before him.

"Hello, Ula," said Shullis Khamarr, Minister of Logistics. "It's been a long time. I was becoming concerned."

Once, Ula would have been struck dumb by this unprompted overture. In their previous dealings, he had invariably been the supplicant. For her to call him out of the blue bespoke a considerable alteration of their dynamic.

"My apologies, Minister, on many accounts. The search for the world I told you about did not go well, and the resources I had hoped to provide the Empire went unrealized. I can only assure you that the enemy did not get the better of us."

"Well, that's something. I hope you are not too disappointed."

"No, Minister. My role here will be much reduced, but I am sure others will rise to take my place."

"There will be others, yes. None like you, though." She smiled. "I have always admired your passion and found our conversations to be thought provoking."

"Minister, on that matter, I fear—"

"Yes, Ula?"

"I fear I may have been mistaken in my former opinions."

Her smile slipped away. "How so?"

This was the one lie he allowed himself to tell. "During the course of my mission, I worked closely with Darth Chratis and his apprentice, and their actions persuaded me to reconsider the prejudices I held regarding them. I see now how foolish I was to dismiss them so readily. They are crucial to the war effort, and integral to the proper functioning of the Empire."

The guarded cast to her face eased. "I'll confess to being relieved, Ula. It was a dangerous heresy you had embraced. Well meant, naturally, but not one that can be tolerated at any level of governance."

"I see that now. You were very forgiving, Minister."

"Nonsense, Ula. We are friends, and friends forgive much."

He wondered if part of her was disappointed. There must have been some advantage—even if merely psychological—to having a private informant intent on maintaining her own advancement. If so, she hid it well.

I am tired of seducing you to my way of thinking, Shullis Khamarr, he said to himself, thinking of Larin and Shigar, who had both rescued him from terrible fates, and the calm stoicism of the Grand Master, Satele Shan. The survivors of Sebaddon would be changed forever by what had happened to them there, and he was no different. *I am persuaded that there is more to governance than just rules, laws, and discipline. A culture must have a heart, too. A strong heart that never falters.*

"Thank you, Minister," he said, and offered her a respectful bow.

She concluded their conversation with a hollow platitude, and signed off. Ula wondered if he would ever speak to her again. Probably not. Friendships of any kind were difficult to maintain in the intelligence business, all the more so when one had been demoted.

In the coming weeks he would consider the benefits of playing both sides against the other, attempting to juggle the interplay between them as Jet had. He didn't have access to an army of unstoppable hexes or a droid that could take over entire fleets, but he was coming to believe that maybe the end did justify the means, sometimes. If he could guide the Empire and the Republic away from war, or at least spare their citizens the worst of their excesses, then that could be a good thing—and a *real* thing, not fake like everything he had tried before. He would be on his own side, at last, as Larin had been when she had been discharged from Special Forces—on the side of the trillions of ordinary people trapped in a warring galaxy.

He stood in his tiny apartment and considered his next move. Search for that bug? Draft a coded message for the Ithorian he had spoken to in Strategic Information Systems? Sleep?

Ula didn't know just yet, which in itself was a pleasing thing.

The walls might be closing in around him, but his horizons were broader now than ever. Even Coruscant didn't seem as cursed as it once had. Larin was back in the Special Forces. Satisfaction fairly glowed from her face when she talked about the future. *We can drink Reactor Cores and talk about old times*. No mention of Shigar, or any of the other survivors of Sebaddon.

That, at least, gave him something to look forward to.

CHAPTER 48

AFTER HOURS OF waiting, Shigar's moment had come.

"We find you ready for the trials, Shigar Konshi," said Master Nobil. "You will be unsurprised, I think, to learn that mastering your psychometric powers was only the smallest part of your journey."

Shigar wasn't surprised, but at the same time he couldn't hide his relief. He bowed deeply before the holographic images of the High Council members, many of whom he had yet to meet in person: brooding Wens Aleusis, brilliant Giffis Fane, young Oric Traless, the newest member of the Council . . .

"Thank you, Masters," he said. "I'm sure I won't disappoint you."

"Tell me how you resolved your agreement with Tassaa Bareesh," Master Nobil said. "That was not mentioned in your debriefing session."

"I'm afraid it remains unresolved," he said. "The agreement was expedient at the time, but it was always likely to become a liability. She used a homing beacon to find the world herself, so I have no qualms about allowing the Republic there first. She can claim no disadvantage, since the world itself has fallen to no one."

"There's the damage to her palace on Hutta," said Master Fane, "and the very public loss of face. Suudaa Nem'ro must be rubbing his hands with glee."

"And there must be ramifications for dishonoring her, no doubt."

"Yes, Master Nobil. I believe there is a price on my head."

"We've all had one of those, at one time or another," said Master Traless with a wry smile. "Don't lose any sleep over it, but do keep an eye out."

"Thank you, Master. I will."

Shigar knew what they were trying to say. *Don't expect to play this game without breaking the rules. You've done it once, and you'll do it again. Get used to it.* It was Larin all over again.

The squabbling of Hutt crime lords didn't worry him in the slightest. He had much bigger concerns.

"May I address the Council freely?" he asked.

"I think you should," said Grand Master Shan, the first time she had spoken during the discussion. He had almost forgotten she was there, standing quietly in the corner of the audience chamber they had requisitioned. "There's been something on your mind ever since Sebaddon."

"It's true, Master. I'm not sure where to start."

"Start with what pains you the most."

He had never thought of his new understanding as painful, but he saw that it was true. It burned in his chest like fire.

"So many people have died," he said, "for nothing. Don't tell me that this is what it's like in wartime, because officially we're not at war. Xandret and her hexes weren't our enemy; Darth Chratis was in fact our ally for a while. Yet they are all dead. I see no sense to it."

"Go on," said Master Nobil.

He tried to explain himself clearly. "This whole affair is endemic to the current crisis. The Sith are on the rise. We are on the wane. The Mandalorians and the Hutts stand between us, creating confusion and jostling for advantage. Our options are limited. If we do nothing, millions of people die. If we fight back, we engage with them at their level."

"Tell us your solution, Shigar," said Master Traless.

"Attack now. The war is coming—we all know it—so why sit on our hands waiting for the Emperor to make his move? Preempt him before he has a chance to consolidate his power any further. Use the element of surprise while we have it. Don't expend lives for nothing."

"The owners of those lives might question the necessity of it," said Master Nobil. "There is much talk of how we caused the current misfortune by making enemies of the Sith in the first place. Starting a war now would not ease those misgivings."

"When we've won the war, people will see the necessity for it."

"And if we lose?" asked Master Fane.

"We must not," Shigar said. "We cannot. And we will not if we act quickly enough. With every day the Emperor grows stronger and we grow weaker. How many spies and traitors erode the fortresses we've built around ourselves? How many fruitless battles must we fight before everyone in the Republic deserts us? How many other Sebaddons are out there, waiting for us? The next one might be the one that finishes us."

"Our mission is to promote peace," said Master Nobil. "Have you forgotten that?"

"Never, Master. But there are degrees of war, just as there are degrees of peace. An early strike might spare the galaxy from total war."

"But at what cost? Remember, Shigar, when you used to argue for justice for the billions of ordinary people, caught between the two sides in this conflict? If we act now, their deaths will be laid at our door. Do you want that on your conscience, my young warmonger?"

"No, Master. That is, I don't—I just—" He looked down at his hands, so startlingly unburned after holding so much power on Sebaddon. If he could do it, why couldn't the Jedi Council? That was the one lesson Darth Chratis *had* taught him. "I just think it's worth considering."

"We have considered it," said Master Fane. "And we will continue to consider it until the proper solution presents itself."

"You're not the only one who feels this way," said Master Traless, leaning forward. "We have a thousand young Jedi just waiting—"

He might have said more, but a glance from Master Nobil stilled his tongue.

"Your passion is undiminished, young Shigar. You must take care that it never rules your head. Thank you for your opinions. Come to Tython and finish what you started. When you are fully installed as a Jedi Knight, then you may play your part more fully in the times to come."

But what is *my part?*

He let those words sit silently on his tongue as, one by one, the images of the Jedi High Councilors flickered and disappeared.

"We will go together," Grand Master Shan told him. "The trials are difficult. Many try and fail, so I advise you not to be complacent."

Her face was unreadable.

"I'm sorry if I've displeased you, Master," he said.

"You haven't displeased me at all, Shigar. I am simply tired. Like you, I wish a speedy resolution to these times."

"But not through war."

"Not if it can be avoided, no. I understand that you don't see it this way, though. You are a product of your time."

He started, recognizing her words from the vision he'd had on Sebaddon.

"I know what you're about to say," he said. "I've seen it. You're about to tell me that I must confront the times ahead with great care. But I've already said that, so now maybe you won't."

She smiled. "It's disconcerting when what you've seen doesn't quite turn out the way it's supposed to."

That was true. The conversation had already headed off in a different direction, thanks to his intervention. Next she was supposed to warn him that the Sith were the enemy and that he shouldn't become like them in order to beat them.

"So the future isn't always laid in stone?"

"No, and I am glad of that sometimes, Shigar." She put a hand on his shoulder and guided him toward the door. "You will learn to be, too, I think."

She *did* seem tired. He wished there was something he could do to make her feel better. But how could he, a lowly Padawan, understand or even begin to shoulder the heavy load she was under?

Again, a spark of predestination told him that he was brushing closely against something seen in the past.

Be kind, Shigar.

Had she meant herself all along? Had all his agonizing about Larin been for nothing?

Then another thought occurred to him.

Some roads are harder than yours have been.

Were the words *so far* left unspoken for him to consider now?

She was talking about him.

As they left the audience chamber, he decided that it was okay to feel torn. In fact, he should get used to it. There were serious challenges to come, whether the High Councilors succeeded with their diplomatic efforts or not.

In a universe that demanded black and white, he would settle for gray.

And when he passed his trials, he would talk to Master Traless in private. If a thousand Jedi Knights really felt as he did, there would bc hope when diplomacy failed.

CHAPTER 49

DARTH HOWL, DARK Lord of the Sith, was less imposing on second meeting than he had been the first time. He wore a black uniform lacking both insignias and trophies, and Ax interpreted that to mean he wasn't out to impress. That he had asked to meet her in private, on his personal hunting range on Dromund Kaas, she took as a mixed sign.

"Pick a rifle," he said, indicating an extensive collection lining the wall of his study. "Follow me onto the deck."

Ax selected an antique weapon with a stock made of bone. Its charge was full and its sights, perfectly aligned. She bet herself Darth Howl kept them all that way, and not just for show.

She was right. The "deck" was an extensive viewing platform overlooking dense, tropical terrain that had been cleared in patches, allowing an unobstructed line of sight to the undergrowth. The sun was at its zenith above the clouds. Conditions were as good as they would ever be on the Imperial capital.

Darth Howl rang a bell. Somewhere in the trees, a cage door rattled open. "I brought you here, Eldon Ax," he said as he raised his own rifle to scope the range, "so you could explain to me how you killed Darth Chratis."

She froze. How did he know? She had told no one, and she was sure none of the troopers on Sebaddon would have understood what had happened that day. The hexes had killed so many people. Darth Chratis had been just one of them.

Darth Howl's rifle emitted a sharp, high-pitched crack, making her jump. Something cried out in the trees below.

The Dark Lord glanced at her and offered her an eerie, sharp-toothed smile.

"Don't worry," he said. "As long as you're up here, you'll be fine."

She wondered how long that good fortune would last.

"What makes you think I killed him, my lord?"

"Whenever a former apprentice returns without her Master, the question asks itself. It's something of a tradition, although not one you'll hear spoken of much. First you survive the Academy; then you have to survive your Master. That's how I earned my reputation, and I presume that's how you plan to do it, too. The question is: how?"

The rifle cracked again.

"If you don't fire soon, young Ax, I'll be forced to assume you've lost your nerve."

Ax did as she was told, raising the rifle and holding it steady against the ball of her shoulder. She couldn't remember the last time she'd fired a blaster of any kind. Certainly not since building her first lightsaber.

She scanned the foliage through the scope. When a fluffy, dark-eyed head peered warily out from cover, she took a shot at it. The rifle produced an odd whining twang but launched an impressive bolt of bright green energy in the right direction. The terrified creature exploded into a ball of flaming fur.

"I used the hexes," she told Howl, appropriately satisfied, as she lined up for another shot.

"How did you get them to do your bidding?"

"It's, uh, hard to explain."

"I've not brought you here to make life easy for you."

Another shot from his rifle; another squawk below. "You've already told us about the remnant of Lema Xandret present in all the droids. What did you call it, again?"

"The amnioid."

"Yes. You mentioned in your report that you and the Jedi Grand Master were both able to influence the hexes, thanks to the amnioid. I didn't realize that you were able to do so to such an overwhelming degree."

"That wasn't how I did it."

Her second shot missed. He was beating her three kills to one.

"Be assured, young Ax, that I'll get it out of you one way or another."

There was no denying the threat now. She sought the same steely strength Satele Shan had demonstrated on Sebaddon.

"There was something I omitted from the report, my lord," she said. "The amnioid didn't exist solely to control the hexes. It was designed also—mainly, perhaps—to sustain a child in a Force-free bacta tank. She was Xandret's child. A clone."

"Of you?"

Ax wouldn't use the word *me*. She refused to. "Her name was Cinzia. She believed that I was her."

"You talked to her?"

"Yes."

"Then you killed her?"

"No, but I might have. The Grand Master released her when the amnioid tried to smother her. She died upon exposure to air."

They both fired. At the very same time a bolt of lightning shattered the gloomy sky into a thousand jagged pieces. The synchronicity was unintended but impressive.

"When the hexes weren't operating independently," she went on, "they obeyed Cinzia, not the amnioid. Because we possessed identical genetic codes, they also obeyed me. It was easy to make them turn on Darth Chratis."

"And of course that was necessary. You couldn't have killed him on your own."

"No." It burned her to admit it, but that was the truth, and this seemed like a moment when only the truth would suffice. Darth Howl's game was utterly unlike any Darth Chratis would have played. She was learning the rules as she went along.

"The omission of the clone from your report," he said, "was premeditated, deliberate, and dangerous. The Dark Council disapproves of anything that smacks of disloyalty—or of emotional attachment to anything other than the Council itself."

"I felt no kinship with the clone, my lord," she said.

"None at all?"

She struggled to find words for the emotions that still stirred her when she thought of the pathetic creature in the tank. "Lema Xandret refused to let her daughter go, so she created a new one, whom she imprisoned. She refused to be controlled, yet she herself was possessive and controlling. What imprisonment might she have fashioned for me had I not been rescued from her by Darth Chratis? Was that why my memories of her have been so easy to suppress? The only thing stirred up in the entire affair was a recollection of her screaming. I think, in short," she concluded, "that I had a lucky escape. And the clone, too, in the end."

"Did you order the hexes to commit suicide?"

"That I didn't do," she said, "but I probably could have ordered them not to."

He nodded. "It was the amnioid, then."

"This time, yes. Lema Xandret lost her daughter twice. There was nothing else to live for. Not even revenge."

"So instead of becoming their master, you let them die." Darth Howl lowered his rifle and fixed her with an obsidian stare. "Some might find it puzzling that you did not use the hexes to fulfill your vendetta against Dao Stryver, and then go on to conquer the galaxy."

"Yes." *I could have been Emperor!* "The thought did occur to me. But the Mandalorian had already escaped by then, and I remain loyal to the Dark Council."

"Some might say that your exposure to the Grand Master of the Jedi addled your thoughts. Some might use this as an argument to never trust you again."

"I don't care what people say."

"You only need to worry about what the Dark Council decides to do about you."

"I met with them yesterday. They—you said—"

"Many things are said, Ax, and many things are done. They are not always the same."

She knew it. "So are you going to have me killed?"

He laughed at her, and raised the rifle. Another shot; another scream of pain.

"That depends entirely on how you spin it," he said. "Were the fugitives punished?"

The fate of her mother and the clone left her in no doubt on that score. "Undoubtedly."

"Did the planet fall into the Republic's hands?"

"No."

"So you survived where your Master did not, and you returned with valuable intel. You are strong and determined, like your mother. You deserve nothing but admiration, and a close eye.

"If anyone does learn the secret about the hexes, the explanation is simple. Your loyalty to the Emperor is such that you would never attempt to unseat him. Note that I said 'Emperor,' not the Dark Council. It's a Sith's job to try to unseat us. That's why we have to keep a close eye on you. Fire the gun."

Ax closed one eye and stilled her hammering heart. Perhaps she would survive after all.

The creature in her sights did not survive, and neither did two more that came to investigate.

She wasn't going to tell Darth Howl that the only reason she had not spared the hexes was because trying to control them would have undoubtedly backfired. Riddled with the twisted spirit of her mother, the hexes would have turned on her eventually, and she would have ended up as trapped as her clone. Far from becoming Emperor, she would have been a bitter princess in a cage, shouting for help at an empty galaxy.

Better that it all disappear into a black hole, literally and metaphorically, and she get on with her life. *Her* life. However much of it she had left.

"Why did you invite me here?" she asked. "It wasn't to grill me on my report or to offer me advice."

"True. You are young and inexperienced, but you are observant, and you survived this crisis unscathed. Perhaps you are hiding your true feelings well, or you are more resilient than you look. Either way, you can be useful to me. I brought you here to offer you an alliance."

Ax didn't even see what lay down her sights. "What kind of alliance?"

"One considerably more to your advantage than the last one. Darth Chratis deserved what came to him. His methods were unreliable, his philosophies dangerous, and his ambition unchecked. It was therefore inevitable that he would fall. The only question was: how far would you fall with him?"

She didn't answer.

Darth Howl's teeth gleamed faintly in the night. "Darth Chratis failed you, just as my last apprentice failed me. It's time to look beyond failure and see the successes awaiting you and I. With my power and your potential, can you imagine what we might accomplish together? We might shake the Supreme Chancellor from his seat, and earn rewards beyond our wildest dreams!"

She wasn't thinking that far ahead. All she had in mind was how useful it would be to have a Master actually on the Dark Council, not just dreaming about it.

"What happened to your last apprentice?"

"She liked to keep pets," he said, taking aim and dispatching another hapless furball down below. "And now I keep her in the observation dome directly above our heads. She loves it when I entertain guests."

His smile was cold and vicious, and something about it thrilled Ax to her core. Darth Howl needed her, and she needed him. There was no shame in admitting it. There were bigger games to play now.

Dao Stryver could wait. When she needed to feel anger in its purest form, he would be there, ready to inspire her. It didn't matter where he was or what he was doing. The longer her vow remained unfulfilled, the greater her anger would become. *The end justifies the means,* as he himself had said.

"I would be honored, my lord."

"Good. And I will accept you as my student. You will put the messy business of your mother behind us and we'll both look forward to slaughtering the Jedi scum in their beds. And, most important . . ."

He winked like the chopping of a guillotine.

"Most important of all, my young apprentice, we will both watch our backs."

EPILOGUE: TATOOINE

THERE WAS NO shortage of cantinas on Tatooine, nor of cantina brawls. Akshae Shanka had come in second in yet another combat tournament, and emotions were running high. There had been riots around the arena, and several full-blown shoot-outs had rivaled those of the contest itself.

Dao Stryver wasn't there to fight, however.

From the shadowy depths of the Wing and Wanderer, the Mandalorian watched the arrival of the human who called himself "Jet Nebula" with a keen eye.

The smuggler had a sandy air, as most people did on the desiccated planet. His gray hair was as wild and his uniform as spaceworn as ever. The droid trailing him had earned a couple of extra dents in his travels since Seaddon. But they looked much as Stryver had expected. They were watchful in a way that older warriors learned to be.

"Jet Nebula" looked around the bar, saw the impassive Gektl sitting alone, and performed a subtle double take.

Then he held up two fingers to the bartender, who chattered confirmation, and he and the droid pressed through the dusty crowd.

"Fancy meeting you here."

"You recognize me?"

"Dao Stryver, in the flesh. You looked better with your helmet on."

Stryver showed teeth in a way that might have been mistaken for a smile. "In my culture, this expression is considered a challenge."

"Come on. I know you can take a joke." He pulled up a chair. "Besides, you're obviously waiting for me. I reckon I'm safe at least until you tell me what you want."

"I've come for the droid."

Nebula raised an eyebrow. "He's not for sale."

"I'm not offering you money."

Two tiny glasses clunked down between them. Stryver made no move to pay, and neither did he. He obviously had a tab.

"Good fortune in battle," Nebula toasted. "May all your eggspawn hatch as soldiers."

"You know about that, too?"

"I've got a good sense of smell. And I transported some life-paintings from Hoszh Iszhir once. You've a nice planet, there, if you breathe poisonous gas."

Stryver raised the other glass and tipped the fiery liquid down her throat.

"I was wrong to take you for granted," she said.

"It's not your fault. I go out of my way to give a certain impression."

"I am not apologizing. I am offering you a compliment. Few deceive me."

"We both have our masks. Do you keep your tail trimmed to fit into that armor or have you had it permanently removed?"

She shook her head, unwilling to be deflected. "I've been looking for you ever since the Sebaddon affair."

"I'm gratified it's taken you so long to find me."

"The word on the grapevine is that you have been shopping technical data to the black market. What kind of data?"

He shrugged. "Everything I had on the hexes, which wasn't much. Chemical analyses, video footage, a sample of their subspace code. I sold it as a job lot to a character called Shavak. Don't worry: there's nowhere near enough for him or anyone else to rebuild them."

She let him believe that this was her concern—if he did in fact believe it. He was a man of many masks. In Tassaa Bareesh's palace he had been careful not to play things too smart lest he be considered a threat, while at the same time he was reinforcing his value as the man who found the *Cinzia,* and who might find other bounties like it, in order to avoid being conveniently disappeared. While the Hutts had been watching the envoys, the smuggler in their midst had kept his eyes and ears carefully open.

In the same way, he had pulled the strings of the Republic's puppet envoy, making certain the Xandret affair ended to his advantage. He might be doing much the same thing right now.

"You know, I'd make an excellent Mandalorian," Nebula said, "were I that way inclined."

Stryver stiffened in her seat, resisting the urge to reach across the table and tear his puny head right off.

"Explain," she growled.

"We both have a sense of irony." He signaled at the bartender for another round of drinks. "And our goals are the same. I mean, seriously. You engineered the whole Sebaddon thing from the start, right? You gave Xandret coordinates for a meeting that would take her through privateer-infested space. You knew where the ship would end up once it was caught, and what the Hutts would probably do with it. Then you hopped around the Empire and the Republic, escalating the situation. You wanted people to think that you were chasing the *Cinzia* to stop it from falling into anyone else's hands, but in fact you were doing the exact opposite. That's why you didn't kill any of the players you came across. You wanted a fight over the hexes just as much as you wanted to erase your own involvement in it."

The drinks came. Stryver let hers sit untouched on the table as Nebula went on.

"You were testing the Empire's and the Republic's responses to the hexes. You wanted to see who has the edge, these days. Has the Republic recovered from the near-beating you gave them a decade ago? Has the Empire grown strong enough to be considered a serious contender in your next campaign? I'd say the results were tied, which suits me. What do *you* think? Who's Mandalore going to fight next, when he gets tired of working for everyone else? That's the question I bet every Jedi and Sith would like answered right now."

He skulled the contents of his glass without taking his eyes off her.

She was careful not to give him an answer. "Where does the irony come into it?"

"*We have no leader.* Do you remember that? I'm sure you do, and I'm sure it struck a chord. Your kind is of a fairly individualistic bent, as is mine. We sympathize with Lema Xandret's desire to follow her own path, even if we don't share her methodology. After all, we don't have the army of droids that allowed her political indulgences—an army that was probably more about building and terraforming originally than fighting anyone, until we showed up. And that's where the irony lies.

"The Emperor certainly didn't endorse Xandret's egalitarian aspirations, and I'm positive the Supreme Chancellor would have disapproved, too. Empires and Republics dislike those with the capacity to overturn their regimes. In that sense, our two squabbling friends are more alike than they prefer to think—and Xandret's political meme might have been even more dangerous than her hexes, had it escaped."

Stryver nodded, thinking of the stratified hierarchies, bureaucracies, and underclasses she had witnessed in both Empire and Republic, all foaming with discontent, not all of it brought about by the cold war that had existed for more than a decade now. It wasn't impossible to imagine either regime being overturned by rebellion from within.

Just as dangerous, however—and far more important—was the possibility that the two rival factions might one day unite against a common enemy, as they had against the hexes. Keeping the two at each other's throats was therefore vital, from a Mandalorian perspective.

"Are you nodding off," Jet asked, "or agreeing with me?"

Stryver focused her thoughts. "I am thinking that the most dangerous thing in the galaxy is an ambitious serf."

"As every exploitative regime discovers to its cost, when those who do the work decide they want to keep the profits for themselves."

"What would happen if droids ever came to the same decision?"

"It would mean the end of civilization as we know it. Luckily, the hexes weren't ambitious per se—just badly programmed."

"I'm not talking about the hexes. I'm talking about Clunker."

Nebula showed enough teeth to suggest that his smile might be a threat, too. "Don't you think we'd already be his slaves, if that's what he wanted?"

"You tell me what he wants. What motivates a machine that can take over Imperial and Republic ships at will, and then just run away?"

"Not power or glory, obviously. Or profit, otherwise I'd be a trillionaire. Sometimes he does what I ask him to, and sometimes he doesn't, so it's not about obeying me. To be honest, I've been trying to figure him out for years and may be no closer to the answer than I was when I started."

"You didn't make him like this?"

"Not a chance. He was a mistake, some kind of factory error, and he'd been scheduled for melting when I found him. His brain had a reset problem, apparently. Every few minutes, he'd shut down and lose his memory. A droid with no capacity for storing incriminating evidence appealed to me, so I nicked him and patched him up as best I could. These days, he can manage days at a time without flatlining, but it still happens. The only things he remembers are me and the ship, I guess because we were where his life really started."

Stryver peered up at the stationary droid. "So he won't remember Sebaddon and what happened there?"

"No. He's reset four times since then. I've come to think it's all connected—like his thoughts get too big for his brain to handle, so it shuts itself down periodically to stop him going crazy. After all, what could be worse than a droid with ambition, as you put it? You've seen what people do to them when they get ideas."

"And with good reason, when it came to the hexes."

"Clunker is no hex. He's just a damaged droid struggling to cope in a big, bad universe."

"Then perhaps the time has come to relieve him of his burden."

"I advise against trying."

"I advise against resisting, Jeke Kerron." Something hardened in his eyes. Stryver stood and reached for her carbonizer.

She was never entirely sure what happened next.

Clunker moved. That was expected. She had planned for that. But the attack didn't come from his direction. It came from four other angles simultaneously and she was flung back into her seat by convergent energy pulses. Her suit sparked and smoked; her limbs shook. For a potentially fatal moment, her vision grayed out into nothing.

Then she recovered, and the crowded cantina was exactly as it had been—except that the smuggler and his droid were gone.

"Better drink up," the bartender chittered, indicating the glass still sitting before her. "He asked us not to kick you out immediately, but there's a limit to my generosity."

"He asked—?" She snapped her mouth shut as her brain caught up. He had been coming here for days. That was how she had found him. She had thought him wasting money on fellow gamblers and lowlifes, when in actual fact he had been preparing a trap. For her.

The crowd studiously avoided her challenging stare.

Stryver laughed on the inside, profoundly pleased on two points.

One: she was still alive.

Two: it was good to have a worthy adversary.

Dao Stryver had come a long way from her pit fighting days, when a young Gektl's life was cheap and expected to last not even a single week. She had accrued considerable glory since then, and considered herself the living embodiment of the Mandalorian creed. War was fought by individuals, not by Emperors and politicians. Battles were decided by people whose names might never be recorded in history. But the point wasn't history, or even who won. Anyone who strove hard enough could become a hero. *That* was the point.

Her enemy understood. It was important to her that he did. She had traced his history backward from captain to first officer of a very different vessel, where the trail had ended. But the captain of that ship, Jeke Kerron, had had a reputation for being entirely too smart for his own good. He had made enemies among several cartels and ultimately disappeared. It was a simple leap to wonder if one had taken the place of the other.

They might never be on the same side again, Stryver thought, but at least from now on they would be playing the same game.

She downed the liquor and shouldered her way out of the Wing and Wanderer, into the dry glare of Tatooine. With her helmet back in place, she was just another Mandalorian, one among many on the gladiatorial world. She would search every spaceport in the city as a matter of course, even though she suspected the *Auriga Fire* would slip through her fingers once more. Then she would report to the Mandalore. If required to do so, she would hunt her enemy to the ends of the galaxy, and she would be ready for him when they met again. If not, she would go back to studying the Empire and the Republic, safe in the knowledge that there would soon be glory enough for everyone.

War was coming. The certainty of it warmed her warrior's soul.

She raised her eyes to stare at the sun and wished the man who called himself "Jet Nebula" good fortune in battle.

READ ON FOR AN EXCERPT FROM

STAR WARS:
FATE OF THE JEDI: VORTEX

BY TROY DENNING

PUBLISHED BY DEL REY BOOKS

BEYOND THE FORWARD VIEWPORT hung the gossamer veil of Ashteri's Cloud, a vast drift of ionized tuderium gas floating along one edge of the Kessel Sector. Speckled with the blue haloes of a thousand distant suns, its milky filaments were a sure sign that the *Rockhound* had finally escaped the sunless gloom of the Deep Maw. And, after the jaw-clenching horror of jumping blind through a labyrinth of uncharted hyperspace lanes and hungry black holes, even that pale light was a welcome relief to Jaina Solo.

Or, rather, it *would* have been, had the cloud been in the right place.

The *Rockhound* was bound for Coruscant, not Kessel, and *that* meant Ashteri's Cloud should have been forty degrees to port as they exited the Maw. It *should* have been a barely discernible smudge of light, shifted so far into the red it looked like a tiny flicker of flame, and Jaina could not quite grasp how they had gone astray.

She glanced over at the pilot's station—a mobile levchair surrounded by brass control panels and drop-down display screens—but found no answers in Lando Calrissian's furrowed brow. Dressed immaculately in a white shimmersilk tunic and lavender trousers, he was perched on the edge of his huge nerf-leather seat, with his chin propped on his knuckles and his gaze fixed on the alabaster radiance outside.

In the three decades Jaina had known Lando, it was one of the rare moments when his life of long-odds gambles and all-or-nothing stakes actually seemed to have taken a toll on his con-artist good looks. It was also a testament to the strain and fear of the past few days—and, perhaps, to the hectic pace. Lando was as impeccably groomed as always, but even he had not found time to touch up the dye that kept his mustache and curly hair their usual deep, rich black.

After a few moments, Lando finally sighed and leaned back into his chair. "Go ahead, say it."

"Say what?" Jaina asked, wondering exactly what Lando expected her to say. After all, *he* was the one who had made the bad jump. "It's not my fault?"

A glimmer of irritation shot through Lando's weary eyes, but then he seemed to realize Jaina was only trying to lighten the mood. He chuckled and flashed her one of his nova-bright grins. "You're as bad as your old man. Can't you see this is no time to joke?"

Jaina cocked a brow. "So you *didn't* decide to swing past Kessel to say hello to the wife and son?"

"Good idea," Lando said, shaking his head. "But . . . *no.*"

"Well, then . . ." Jaina activated the auxiliary pilot's station and waited as the long-range sensors spooled up. An old asteroid tug designed to be controlled by a single operator and a huge robotic crew, the *Rockhound* had no true copilot's station, and *that* meant the wait was going to be longer than Jaina would have liked. "What are we doing here?"

Lando's expression grew serious. "Good question." He turned toward the back of the *Rockhound*'s spacious flight deck, where the vessel's ancient bridge-droid stood in front of an equally ancient navigation computer. A Cybot Galactica model RN8, the droid had a transparent head-globe, currently filled with the floating twinkles of a central processing unit running at high speed. Also inside the globe were three sapphire-blue photoreceptors, spaced at even intervals to give her full-perimeter vision. Her bronze body casing was etched with constellations, comets, and other celestial artwork worthy of her nickname. "I *know* I told Ornate to set a course for Coruscant."

RN8's head-globe spun just enough to fix one of her photoreceptors on Lando's face. "Yes, you did." Her voice was silky, deep, and chiding. "And then you countermanded that order with one directing us to our current destination."

Lando scowled. "You need to do a better job maintaining your auditory systems," he said. "You're hearing things."

The twinkles inside RN8's head-globe dimmed as she redirected power to her diagnostic systems. Jaina turned her own attention back to the auxiliary display and saw that the long-range sensors had finally come on line. Unfortunately, they were no help. The only things that had changed inside its bronze frame were the color of the screen and the appearance of a single symbol denoting the *Rockhound*'s own location in the exact center.

RN8's silky voice sounded from the back of the flight deck. "My auditory sensors are in optimal condition, Captain—as are my data storage and retrieval systems." Her words began to roll across the deck in a *very* familiar male baritone. "Redi*rect* to *des*tina*tion* Ashteri's Cloud, arri*val* time seven*teen* hours fif*teen*, *Galac*tic *Stan*dard."

Lando's jaw dropped, and he sputtered, "Tha . . . that's not *me*!"

"Not quite," Jaina agreed. The emphasis was placed on the wrong syllable in several words; otherwise, the voice was identical. "But it's close enough to fool a droid."

Lando's eyes clouded with confusion. "Are you telling me what I *think* you're telling me?"

"Yes," Jaina said, glancing at her blank sensor display. "I don't quite know how, but someone impersonated you."

"Through the Force?"

Jaina shrugged and shot a meaningful glance toward a dark corner. While she knew of half a dozen Force powers that could have been used to defeat Ornate's voice-recognition software, not one of those techniques had a range measured in light-years. She carefully began to expand her Force-awareness, concentrating on the remote corners of the huge ship, and, thirty seconds later, was astonished to find nothing unusual. There were no lurking beings, no blank zones that might suggest an artificial void in the Force, not even any small vermin that might be a Force-wielder disguising his presence.

After a moment, she turned back to Lando. "They *must* be using the Force. There's no one aboard but us and the droids."

"I was afraid you'd say that." Lando paused for a moment, then asked, "Luke's friends?"

"I hate to jump to conclusions, but . . . who else?" Jaina replied. "First, Lost Tribe or not, they're *Sith*. Second, they already tried to double-cross us once."

"Which makes them as crazy as a rancor on the dancing deck," Lando said. "Abeloth was locked in a *black hole prison* for twenty-five thousand years. What kind of maniacs would think it was a good idea to bust her out?"

"They're *Sith*," Jaina reminded him. "All that matters to them is power, and Abeloth had power like a nova has light—until Luke killed her."

Lando frowned in thought. "And if they're crazy enough to think they could take Abeloth home with them, they're probably crazy enough to think they could take the guy who killed her."

"Exactly," Jaina said. "Until a few weeks ago, no one

even knew the Lost Tribe *existed.* That's changed, but they'll still want to keep what they can secret."

"So they'll try to take out Luke and Ben," Lando agreed. "And us, too. Contain the leak."

"That's my guess," Jaina said. "Sith like secrecy, and secrecy means stopping us *now.* Once we're out of the Maw, they'll expect us to access the HoloNet and report."

Lando looked up and exhaled in frustration. "I *told* Luke he couldn't trust anyone who puts *High Lord* before his name." He had been even more forceful than Jaina in trying to argue Luke out of a second bargain with the Lost Tribe—a bargain that had left the Skywalkers and three Sith behind to explore Abeloth's savage homeworld together. "Maybe we should go back."

Jaina thought for only an instant, then shook her head. "No, Luke knew the bargain wouldn't last when he agreed to it," she said. "Sarasu Taalon has already betrayed his word once."

Lando scowled. "That doesn't mean Luke and Ben are safe."

"No," Jaina agreed. "But it *does* mean he's risking their lives to increase *our* chances of reporting to the Jedi Council. *That*'s our mission."

"Technically, Luke doesn't get to *assign* missions right now," Lando pressed. "You wouldn't be violating orders if we—"

"Luke Skywalker is *still* the most powerful Jedi in the galaxy. I think we should assume he has a plan," Jaina said. A sudden tingle of danger-sense prompted her to hit the quick-release on her crash harness. "Besides, we need to start worrying about saving our *own* skins."

Lando began to look worried. "What are you saying?" he asked. "That you're sensing something?"

Jaina shook her head. "Not yet." She rose. "But I *will* be. Why do you suppose they sent us someplace easy to find?"

Lando scowled. "Oh . . ." He glanced up at a display, tapped some keys—no doubt trying to call up a tactical report—then slammed his fist against the edge of the brass console. "Are they *jamming* us?"

"That's difficult to know with the ship's sensor systems offline for degaussing," RN8 replied.

"*Offline?*" Lando shrieked. "Who authorized *that*?"

"*You* did, ninety-seven seconds ago," RN8 replied. "Would you like me to play it back?"

"No! Countermand it and bring all systems back up." Lando turned to Jaina and asked, "Any feel for how long we have until the shooting starts?"

Jaina closed her eyes and opened herself to the Force. A shiver of danger-sense raced down her spine, and then she felt a mass of belligerent presences approaching from the direction of the Maw. She turned to RN8.

"How long until the sensor systems reboot?"

"Approximately three minutes and fifty-seven seconds," the droid reported. "I'm afraid Captain Calrissian also ordered a complete data consolidation."

Jaina winced and turned back to Lando. "In that case, I'd say we have less than three minutes and fifty-two seconds. There's someone hostile coming up behind us." She started toward the hatchway at the back of the cavernous bridge, her boots ringing on the old durasteel deck. "Why don't you see if you can put a stop to those false orders?"

"Sure, I'll just tell my crew to stop listening to me." Lando's voice was sarcastic. "Being droids, they'll know what I mean."

"You might try activating their standard verification routines," Jaina suggested.

"I *might*, if droid crews this old *had* standard verification routines." Lando turned and scowled at Jaina as she continued across the deck. "And you're going *where*?"

"You know where," Jaina said.

"To your StealthX?" Lando replied. "The one with only three engines? The one that lost its targeting array?"

"Yeah, that one," Jaina confirmed. "We need a set of eyes out there—and someone to fly cover."

"No way," Lando said. "If I let you go out to fight Sith in that thing, your dad will be feeding pieces of me to Amelia's nexu for the next ten years."

Jaina stopped and turned toward him, propping one hand on her hip. "Lando, did you just say '*let*'? Did you really say '*no way*' to me?"

Lando rolled his eyes, unintimidated. "You know I didn't mean it like that. But have you gone spacesick? With only three engines, that starfighter is going to be about as maneuverable as an escape pod!"

"Maybe, but it still beats sitting around like a blind bantha in this thing. Thanks for worrying, though." She shot Lando a sour smile. "It's so sweet when you old guys do that."

"*Old?*" Lando cried. After a moment, he seemed to recognize the mocking tone in Jaina's voice, and his chin dropped. "I deserved that, didn't I?"

"You *think*?" Jaina laughed to show there were no hard feelings, then added, "And you know what Tendra would do to *me* if I came back without Chance's father. So let's *both* be careful."

"Okay, deal." Lando waved her toward the hatchway. "Go. Blow things up. Have fun."

"Thanks." Jaina's tone grew more serious, and she added, "And I mean for *everything*, Lando. You didn't have to be here, and I'm grateful for the risks you're taking to help us. It means a lot to me—and to the whole Order."

Lando's Force aura grew cold, and he looked away in sudden discomfort. "Jaina, is there something you're not telling me?"

"About this situation?" Jaina asked, frowning at his strange reaction. "I don't think so. Why?"

Lando exhaled in relief. "Jaina, my dear, perhaps no one has mentioned this to you before . . ." His voice grew more solemn. "But when a Jedi starts talking about how much you mean to her, the future begins to look *very* scary."

"Oh . . . sorry." Jaina's cheeks warmed with embarrassment. "I didn't mean anything like *that*. Really. I was just trying to—"

"It's okay." Lando's voice was still a little shaky. "And if you *did* mean something—"

"I *didn't*," Jaina interrupted.

"I know," Lando said, raising a hand to stop her. "But if things start to go bad out there, just get back to Coruscant and report. I can take care of myself. Understand?"

"Sure, Lando, I understand." Jaina started toward the hatchway, silently adding, *But no way am I leaving you behind.*

"Good—and try to stick close. We won't be hanging around long." A low whir sounded from Lando's chair as he turned it to face RN8. "Ornate, prepare an emergency jump to our last coordinates."

"I'm afraid that's impossible, Captain Calrissian," the droid replied. "You gave standing orders to empty the navicomputer's memory after each jump."

"*What?*" Lando's anger was edging toward panic now. "How many *other* orders—no, forget it. Just countermand my previous commands."

"*All* of them?"

"Yes!" Lando snapped. "No, wait . . ."

Jaina reached the hatchway and, not waiting to hear

the rest of Lando's order, raced down the rivet-studded corridor beyond. She still had no idea what the Sith were planning, but she *was* going to stop them—and not only because the Jedi Council needed to know everything she and Lando could tell them about the Lost Tribe of Sith. Over the years, Lando had been as loyal a friend to the Jedi Order as he had to her parents, time after time risking his life, fortune, and freedom to help them resolve whatever crisis happened to be threatening the peace of the galaxy at the moment. He always claimed he was just repaying a favor, or protecting an investment, or maintaining a good business environment, but Jaina new better. He was looking out for his friends, doing everything he could to help them survive—no matter what mess they had gotten themselves into.

Jaina reached the forward hangar bay. As the hatch opened in front of her, she was surprised to find a bank of floodlights already illuminating her battered StealthX. At first, she assumed Lando had ordered the hangar droid to ready the *Rockhound*'s fighter complement for launch.

Then she saw what was missing from her starfighter.

There were no weapon barrels extending from the wingtips. In fact—on the side facing her, at least—the cannons themselves were gone. She was so shocked that she found herself waiting for the rest of the hangar lights to activate, having forgotten for the moment that the *Rockhound* did not have automatic illumination. The whir of a pneumatic wrench sounded from the far side of the StealthX, and beneath the starfighter's belly, she noticed a cluster of telescoping droid legs straddling the actuator housing of a Taim & Bak KX12 laser cannon.

"What the . . . "

Jaina snapped the lightsaber off her belt, then crossed twenty meters of tarnished deck in three quick Force bounds and sprang onto the fuselage of her StealthX. She could hardly believe what she saw. At the far end of the wing stood a spider-shaped BY2B maintenance droid, her thick cargo pedipalps clamped around the starfighter's last laser cannon while her delicate tool arms released the mounting clips.

"ByTwoBee!" Jaina yelled. "What *are* you doing?"

The pneumatic wrench whined to a stop, and three of the droid's photoreceptors swiveled toward Jaina's face.

"I'm sorry, Jedi Solo. I thought you would know." Like all droids aboard the *Rockhound*, BY2B's voice was female and sultry. "I'm removing this laser cannon."

"I can see that," Jaina replied. "Why?"

"So I can take it to the maintenance shop," BY2B replied. "Captain Calrissian requested it. Since your starfighter is unflyable anyway, he thought it would be a good time to rebuild the weapon systems."

Jaina's heart sank, but she wasted no time trying to convince BY2B she had been fooled. "When Lando issued this order, did you actually *see* him?"

"Oh, I rarely *see* the captain. I'm not one of his favorites." BY2B swung her photoreceptors toward the hangar entrance, and a trio of red beams shot out to illuminate a grimy speaker hanging next to the hatchway. "The order came over the intercom."

"Of course it did." Jaina pointed her lightsaber at the nearly dismounted laser cannon. "Any chance you can reattach that and get it working in the next minute and a half?"

"No chance at all, Jedi Solo. Reattaching the power feeds alone would take ten times that long."

"How'd I know you were going to say that?" Jaina growled. She turned away and hopped down onto the deck. "All right—finish removing it and prep the craft for launch."

"I'm sorry, that's impossible," BY2B replied. "Even if we had the necessary parts, I'm not qualified to make repairs. The specifications for this craft weren't included in my last service update."

"I flew it *in* here, didn't I?" Jaina retorted. "Just tell me you haven't been mucking around with the torpedo launchers, too."

"This craft has *torpedo launchers*?" BY2B asked.